King
Bartholomew

Tales from the Isle of Man

By

K Scott Brown

Hedgewood Press

Dedicated to my brother Daniel Patrick who brought me to the island and saw through the mist

Inspired by the comprehensive body of legend, myth, and folklore associated with the history around *The Isle of Man*, this book is a work of fiction, not a retelling of that existing folklore. I approach this task cautiously and humbly, for the richness of this history is a thing of wonder and stands alone and proud. Manannan Mac Lir shrouded this tiny island in mist to protect it from invading armies, and though I may have penetrated this mist, I am not an army and I have not come to conquer. The chronological list of Kings is well documented and it is true that King Bartholomew never existed. He along with every other character in this book is fictional. I have taken many liberties with historical as well as geographical events and places, but I have done so out of genuine love and inspiration for the beauty and magical quality surrounding this tiny island in the Irish Sea between Ireland and The United Kingdom, and my intent is not to obscure the rich history that belongs to them. Once immersed in this mythology my imagination conjured these stories like words spoken from the mouth of the fabled *Salmon of Knowledge* tasted by Finn Mac Cool. Some of the discrepancies herein I may have committed out of ignorance, and I apologize in advance, but other discrepancies I have intentionally committed to render a desired consistency of style and purpose. My true intention was to offer a book steeped with the flavor of this wonderful folklore. Lastly, some of those that read this book may be far more informed about these traditions than I, and I only ask that you suspend your judgment of what I have done and take away from this something that was meant to be special, perhaps beautiful.

K. Scott Brown
Feb, 2012

Table of Contents

𝔓rologue

A solitary man dressed in a long grey cloak walked out onto the Crossag Bridge in the gloaming and looked down into the water. It was just before Samhain, marking the festival of the dead, and the air was crisp with the pungency of lifted earth. The harvest was in and this year's harvest had borne bitter fruit. The man brought his hands up to his face mournfully. His hair was streaked white and a silver band around his forehead kept it in place. He came to the bridge often to think and to be alone with his questions, but now he was come to the bridge for something different. His back was turned as he stood alone on the bridge and his body trembled gently, for he was sobbing. Anguish drives men to many things and in truth he wanted only to be alone with his overwhelming grief. Some grief can be shared that is true, and some grief must be borne alone, but perhaps some grief is too bitter to share, and then it can only be trusted to God

All men suffer greatly for their pride and that suffering can be great. But how much grief can one man be expected to bear? Men suffer grief for the things that have been, but men suffer far more grief for the things that have not been, and for the things that can never be. And so it is that a heart burdened with too much grief turns away and looks for new fields in which to sow new seeds of hope. New fields must be planted, for hope must needs heal the hearts of men, and without hope there is only death. And so bitter were the tears of a man yet so young and strong. Into the water his tears did fall and there was no one to comfort him in his hour of need. Finally he looked up from the water and turned his head to the sky. The first twinkling of starlight sparkled in his moist eyes.

"I promise by the grace of God," he lamented tearfully. "Teach me to endure the gift of life you have given me, only do not make me endure it alone. Make not my life to have been lived in vain, for I am brought down and I am humbled. I stand before you a humbled man and I give my life to your will . . . only do not allow me to forget for I seek no comfort in forgetfulness. Lord, take my body and use it . . . but never to forget."

Then the man took an object from his pocket and brought it to his lips and kissed it. It was a ring. And after taking one last look, he cast the object into the slowly moving water. Turning away at last, he walked slowly back to his home.

Once inside a young girl immediately came and helped him take off his coat. She hung it on a hook without a word, and then she asked if he would take his tea alone in his study as usual.

"Thank you," he said warmly, but he could offer no smile because his face was still tight with the passion of his grief. "And will you always be so kind to me?" he asked.

"You are my King," she answered respectfully. "I will gladly serve you until the day you die. "But that is a long way off I pray," she said quickly.

"You are a good girl, Iona," said the King. "Someday you will be married."

"No, never," she replied at once. "It is my pleasure to serve."

"We all serve in one way or another," said the King. "But you are young and you will not always feel this way."

The young servant lowered her eyes. "We shall see," she said.

The King looked closely at the girl. He was drawn to her but he did not know why. The poor child had lost her parents and she was alone. Now she served a lonely King who was also alone. Perhaps his heart was drawn to her grief.

"To serve the Lord is a noble gesture indeed," he said suddenly. "But to serve a King . . ."

"I can do both," the young girl said innocently, "for I am humbled."

The King winced noticeably but quickly regained his composure. The girl did not see it.

"You should marry a prince one day," the King said as he began to walk away because his eyes were beginning to water again. "But for your blood Iona, you would be a queen."

Later that night the King had a dream, an ominous dream. In his dream he was young again. In his dream he was carefree and untroubled by the terrible vicissitudes of fate. He stood alone on a white bridge. The bridge was radiant. Behind him was darkness out of which he had emerged. Before him were splendor and colors and green fields of light. Below was void, an impenetrable emptiness. The bridge was narrow but he had no fear of falling because he was righteous.

The King began walking toward the light until an angel appeared and blocked his way. In one hand the angel held a book, and in the other a pen. The angel raised his arm and ordered the King to stop.

"Why do you prevent me from passing into the light?" the King asked. "I see that you are one of the Seraphim. Are you Lucifer?"

"My name is Metetron," the angel said. "You do not belong here. You live in darkness. Go back from whence you came."

"You are wrong," the King said. "I come from the light."

"You come from the darkness," the angel insisted. "It is in your heart."

The King was defiant. "You do not know what is in my heart," he said to the angel.

"Holy, holy, holy . . . I know what is in your heart, just as I know what is in the heart of all men."

"Then pray, change my heart Metetron. Change my heart so that I can go into the light. I cannot go back into the darkness. I will not go back into the darkness."

Metetron answered without anger. "Then you will be cast into the void."

"I wish to go into the light," the King demanded. He stood firm for he was righteous in all ways.

"Then you must know the price that has been paid for you, for a terrible price has been paid so that you may pass."

"The Lord has paid the price for me," the King said firmly.

"Holy, holy, holy . . . the Lord did not build this bridge," Metetron said sadly. "The bridge that can bear you to green pasture is a bridge of innocence, for there is no glory in the sin of man."

"I will pay any price," said the King. "Tell me what must be done and I will make it so."

"Who among you is innocent?" said Metetron. "Look down at your feet."

The King looked down. Revulsion and anger rose up inside of him, and in horror his jaw fell open. "Ahh . . .! Ahhhh . . .! Ahhhhh . . .!" he screamed involuntarily because he could not articulate a single word. His screams were the screams of an animal. "Ahhhhh . . .!"

Suddenly Iona burst into the room and ran up to the bed as she tried to close her nightgown. She began shaking the King, shaking him violently to rouse him from his nightmare. He was in a terrible state and his face was ashen and wet with perspiration. She shook him until he stopped screaming.

The King's eyes opened and they were wild, like one still trying to comprehend the incomprehensible. He sat up but he was still shaken. "No, no, no, no," he muttered. Iona put her arms around him and held him tight even as he continued to lament. "No, no, no," he cried. "Oh my God."

Then Iona stroked his face and kissed him on the forehead. He was raving, and in his raving there was pain. She continued to hold him until his horror should pass.

"Oh my God," he said faintly. Then he looked into her face compassionately. "Oh, my God Iona, the bridge is a bridge of bones!"

The Magical Garden of King Sigmus

What may seem like magic to one man can seem like utter folly to another man. One man's tears may seem foolish, but to another man, those same tears would be defended with blood. In truth, one man sheds tears while another man sheds blood, and who would dare to call one folly? Yes, the magic of a thing created is never lost on the Creator.

It is not good for that a kingdom should be without a king or for that a man should abide without a woman in earthly endeavors, returning once again to dust out of which no tear has yet fallen or blade of grass yet grown. The people look to the steady hand of their sovereign king even as their king must look to heaven for guidance through dark and dangerous times, for that he be proper and just in his own judgment. And so it was that on the fifth day before Midsummer's Eve, during the fourth year of the rule of King Sigmus, he would take the hand of the beautiful mistress Kathryn Beauchamp and that they should become husband and wife before God and the good people of Man.

The good King Sigmus ruled like a shepherd, never harsh, never vengeful or petty but leading his flock by example and allowing them to wander into pastures of wild grass and varicolored clover. The pre-Christian paganism of the Celts was alive, as it had become infused with the very earth out of which it had been buried. Alongside him in everything he did was the lady Kathryn, comely and beautiful in her playfulness, and stately and elegant when it was required for her to be elegant. But Kathryn was not an elegant person by her very nature, and it was even more natural for her to thrust her own hands into the soil than it was to cause it to be done.

One day Sigmus kissed the hand of his beautiful new wife. Her hands were soft and delicate like the fronds of milkweed. Then he smiled to her and drank in her goodness of beauty and goodness of soul. The King was truly happy.

"Tell me something you desire," he spoke to her playfully. "Tell me something you desire that I may make it so."

Kathryn smiled and her eyes sparkled like two sparks of starlight behind a crystal sphere. "Build me a garden," she said. "I love the sound of songbirds and together we can sit and listen to their music and make our own music of love."

"A garden?" Sigmus replied merrily. "Is that all you want, my love?"

"A special garden," Kathryn said. "Let it be a place where we can go to escape. Let it be a place of wonder."

"A place of wonder?" Sigmus repeated brightly. "Now that is a tall order," he said. "I suppose there will be flowers in this garden," he teased. "And you are going to want plants too I suppose. Hum . . ."

"I want it to be a magical place," Kathryn said with passion. She took her husband's hand in her own and found that it was warm. "I want us to become lost in this garden," she said.

"Lost?" Sigmus answered with a smile, drawn in by the enchantment of his beautiful wife. "If we are to become lost in this garden, it will have to be a special garden indeed."

"And a gate too," Kathryn added cheerfully. "I want there to be a gate to pass through. And then when we go into our garden we can imagine that we are walking into another world."

Sigmus kissed her passionately and stroked her beautiful hair. "It will be my pleasure," he replied.

The King thought about Kathryn's garden and how to begin. He could send to England for a master gardener, but he wanted the garden to be special in a way that could never be designed by another man. He wanted to design the garden himself.

One morning he stood outside the east window of his castle and surveyed the plot of ground on which the garden would be built. It would cover approximately 10,000 square [1]cubits and be accessible through a set of casement doors which he would have installed. The

[1] *Cubit. Ancient unit of length. Equal to the distance from the elbow to the tip of the middle finger.*

King looked at the area and began to imagine how his garden would look. He had seen many formal gardens on trips to the Continent. Many of the gardens he had toured were constructed into geometrical arrangements and seemed to follow patterns of design that were similar or related to one another by strict adherence to these forms, as if a mere deviation of the form would be a sign of defiance and disrespect. Of course, regal gardens required regal forms of expression. Regal forms required a stated elegance and a subservience that it not overshadow the very object of which it is but a symbol. Sigmus wanted Kathryn's garden to be different. That morning King Sigmus decided that Kathryn's garden would be constructed as a maze.

Kathryn came into the room where Sigmus was looking over drawings. Facing the east, the small alcove was tucked away behind thick red curtains and featured a thick, rounded compass window with leaded glass. The sun was coming through the window and when Sigmus looked up he saw her awash in the morning spectral light. On the table before the King were drawings, in his own hand, of geometrical designs to be considered for the garden. He smiled, leaned back in his chair and stretched. Then he stood up and kissed her warmly.

"Are you very busy?" she asked politely because she could see that he was.

"I am never too busy for you," he said. "What do you want? Tell me, and I will make it so."

"I want to give you a son," she answered with a mischievous laugh.

"I have not even finished your garden yet," Sigmus scolded her playfully. Then he raised an eyebrow suggestively and said. "Are you talking about today?"

Kathryn went around the desk and sat on her husband's lap. She threw her arm around him. "Wouldn't it be wonderful?" she said. "Wouldn't it be wonderful to have children roaming through the castle and looking for Easter-Eggs? Just think," she continued with joy. "Just think about how it would be to have a son to hunt with and to tell stories to on stormy nights. Just think, Sigmus."

"Nothing could make me happier," said Sigmus. "Do you have a name picked out already?" he chided her.

"I want to name him Bartholomew," she answered at once.

"And why pray tell, do you want to name him Bartholomew?"

"Bartholomew was there when the Lord ascended into heaven and the angels came to escort him. He was there when the Lord came to him on the Sea of Galilee after the Resurrection, and the Lord prepared breakfast for him. And when he was martyred when they flayed him alive, he did not deny the Lord."

"All right," said the King thoughtfully. "If that is your wish, we will name him Bartholomew."

Soon King Sigmus began work on the actual garden. He had an image in his mind that was also represented on paper which he kept nearby so that he could consult his plans when the image in his head began to fade. He first decided that he would begin from the center and progressively work his way out until he had enclosed everything he wanted to enclose. At the center of the garden he would place a pair of stone benches where Kathryn could sit in the sun on warm days and tell stories to their children. In front of the benches he would build a grotto where a small fountain would drain into a delicate pool filled with water flowers. He outlined the center of the garden and then he sent for the stonemason that the garden be newly begun.

When he was satisfied that the center of the garden was perfect and that the newly laid flagstones were to his liking, he knew that he needed to enclose the center that the intimacy of this sacred place not be encroached upon from the outside. He would protect the sanctity of his private grotto with a wall of dense greenery, a circular hedge that would surround the grotto but for a small opening in the barrier. He sent for Fritz the gardener and they discussed the type and quality of the foliage to be used for the wall.

"I don't want just any plants to be used in my garden," said the King. "What I want are special plants, magical plants that will give my garden a magical quality not to be found anywhere else."

"Then we should build a wall made from yew," said Fritz the gardener. "Yew is everlasting and it is said that the *Tree of Life* that adorned the Garden of Eden was the noble yew."

"And this tree is magical?" Sigmus asked with growing interest. "I want this to be a place of power, Fritz."

"Yew is everlasting, my lord. It is impossible to say how old the oldest yew is. The oldest tree in the world, the *World Tree*, is a yew, and it is said that Pontius Pilate played in its boughs when this tree was already ancient. It regenerates itself and becomes reborn, just like the Savior," said Fritz. "Its branches grow downward into the earth, and from this burial the new roots are formed. Soon, the new roots grow into the structure and enclose the aging roots within itself. The yew represents the Resurrection, my lord."

"The garden . . . would survive me?" Sigmus asked thoughtfully.

"The garden will survive your descendants," Fritz interjected resolutely. "Your garden will survive in perpetuity."

King Sigmus gave the design of his maze to Fritz the gardener so that he could examine it and decide the best way to proceed. He trusted Fritz with carrying out his unique vision. Every day the King would go out to the garden to see how it was progressing. The lady Kathryn was not yet allowed to see it yet however. Sigmus wanted it to be further along before Kathryn could see it, and it was her anticipation that belonged to the King and inspired him anew.

One day Kathryn gave the King startling news that forced him to sit down. He was looking out the window at a cart coming up the road laden with new supplies for his garden. The fine team of horses snorted against the load as if they too knew how important it was to the King. Today the carved flagstones from Edinburgh would be arriving. Kathryn came into the room in her carefree, wispy way, swaying with her arms demurely placed behind her back.

"Do you want to know a secret?" she asked playfully.

The King turned to her and smiled. "Good morning," he answered. "And a better morning it will be when I hear your precious secret."

"You are going to be a father," she blurted out with joy. "I just found out for true."

King Sigmus embraced his wife and they were truly happy. They talked about how wonderful it would be to have children playing in the castle and how important it would be to have an heir.

"Our child needs be a son," said Sigmus. "For the legal heir must needs be a King and not a Queen."

"But I have already told you," quipped Kathryn. "I have already told you that our son is to be called Bartholomew."

"There is plenty of time to talk of heirs," said the King. "I pray only that the child be healthy and beautiful."

King Sigmus wandered through the grounds of his burgeoning garden looking for Fritz the gardener one afternoon shortly after learning that he was to be a father. The news had so struck him that he was wont to make a change in his garden to commemorate the news. He found Fritz pruning the hedge with a pair of small shears.

"I would like you to add a row of [2]primrose to the grotto," he said. "I am going to be a new father, and I have heard that primrose is the flower of birth and becoming."

"I see, I see," Fritz said with a smile. "Your firstborn will be like an early rose, is that it?"

"Yes, that is it," Sigmus replied casually.

The garden was beginning to take shape. Sigmus stood and inspected the continuing execution of his design. Much of the hedge was planted, but there was much that needed to be filled in as the outline of the maze was geometrical, it would need to be aligned carefully. Fritz had already planted hundreds of trees as the outline was looking formidable and difficult. It would take several years for the hedge to grow together and fuse, but even at such an early stage Sigmus was impressed.

"It is an outstanding design," said Fritz from behind. "Is it your intention to trap people, or to amuse them?"

---

[2] *Primrose. Latin, prima rose. First rose, so called because of its early flowering.*

The King turned and spoke. "No, of course not Fritz, you do not understand. This is not intended to be an escape from the world," Sigmus commented enthusiastically. "This is intended to be an escape into the world . . . into another world. I can see that it is beginning to take shape already."

Months passed in which the King was busy with the task of running his realm, or as was most often the case, of gently guiding the forces of change. Disputes over fishing waters was an ongoing issue made more difficult due to the fact that fish did not always stay in one place and must needs be chased across the dangerous and turgid waters. The King was often called to settle issues concerning property rights and the rights of hunters to cross private boundaries in pursuit of game. Above all, he wanted to protect the ancient and sacred places that they be not forgotten. Taxes from the revenues of mining and farming and fisheries also occupied his time although he had account experts in place to handle the vagaries and the myriad exemptions of rights claimed generations before his birth. If compromises could be achieved without resolving to specific statutes and the interpretations of specific phrases and local colloquialisms of the Manx tongue, then the King would go away happy, for the people loved him and he tried to be fair. And so time passed away as it always did on the isle, thoughtlessly and removed from any distinction that would ever connect it to any other part of the world. The people were quite content to be left alone, and any interference from outside forces was met with laconic, puzzled stares and curses, for the people of Man were not known for being erudite or learned.

It was a cold day on the Isle of Man when Queen Kathryn suffered her first miscarriage. Cold clouds scudded across the sky like lamentations of gloom heralding great discontent from the Continent. The day was made even grayer by her having to go through the ordeal alone, as King Sigmus was away in Peel, at the castle meeting with local [3]deemsters on a matter of great importance to their close, parochial way of life.

Terrible tragedies of birth were common in the isles, and there was not a woman on Man that was not personally touched by such a tragedy. Death was a way of life, a marker and a great sigh of grief, but even premature death only brought greater expectations for new life. It was

---

[3] *Deemsters. Local judges. Not a permanent body, but a jury called upon when needed.*

accepted that life was hard and some few tiny flames would inexplicitly go out before they could be kindled. The people did not imagine that the Lord would have so prematurely called such an innocent child home. Instead, the people merely accepted that there were some things better left unknown.

When King Sigmus learned of the news he fell to his knees and wept bitterly. He stayed by the side of his wife those long, agonizing days, and he tried to comfort her. But in the end he knew that grief was a very personal thing and did not manifest the same for different people even though their grief be shared. He knew that even the closeness of love was not close enough to share, what to a single heart, was unique. He spent much time staring through the great windows as if he were waiting for something to comfort him. No, even the sun was ashamed to shine on his tiny island those bitter days. But soon it came time for him to do something that he dreaded but could be put off no longer. He knelt down beside Kathryn in her bed and took her hand in his.

"We will have to give the child a proper burial," he spoke though his grief was tremendous. "The child was a boy my dear, just as you predicted. We must give Bartholomew a proper burial."

Suddenly the Lady Kathryn's face changed through an inner emotion that Sigmus could not fathom. The sudden shift in her emotion shocked the King and he hesitated for a moment to absorb the change. The muscles in his throat tightened, for now it was the Lady Kathryn that was comforting him!

"We will place a marker for him," she said softly. "But a headstone is unnecessary, for that was not Bartholomew. The poor child we shall bury together was never intended for this life."

"Kathryn!" a tearful Sigmus muttered through tightening lips. His ashen face was contorted and twitched involuntarily. "Please Kathryn," he cried. "Please do not do this to yourself. I promise you there will be another child . . . God willing."

"God willing," she repeated.

Slowly, but inextricably things did return to normal on the Isle of Man. There is a season for all things. There are seasons of great joy and there are fallow seasons when one must needs take a rest and allow the earth to return to normal. Such seasons cause one to learn to respect the earth for what it must do, and it is a foolish man that asks for what can never be done. And then there are seasons when one must needs plant a different crop. The King spent much time in his garden those two long years. He learned to work with tools and he learned to sweat. Fritz the gardener became something of a mentor to the King, for Sigmus spent much time cultivating his garden and he almost forgot that it was intended to be homage to Kathryn though she had yet never stepped into it.

Sigmus had planted at the entrance of the garden two great [4]hawthorn trees; one guarding each side of the enclosing hedge and planted to form an imposing gateway. At night, the loyal sentinels would continue to serve him and his house. The magic that he hoped to enclose in his garden he did not want to escape, for the thorns of the hawthorn tree are sharp and able to catch more than just tiny stitches of clothing.

Before leaving, Sigmus gave Fritz one final instruction. They were standing together between the sentinels. Sigmus put his hand on Fritz's shoulder, a gesture of great importance.

"I want you to do something important now, Fritz. Do you know the plant, [5]woundwort?"

"Are you referring to mint, Sigmus?" Fritz replied. "Do you mean hedge-needle?"

"Yes, Fritz," he said, "Hedge-needle indeed, the mighty orchids of night. I want you to plant it along the four corners of the garden. It must be planted in the shade, do you understand?"

"Yes, of course, but for what purpose? The woundwort is used by wizards and witches, Sigmus. It has no purpose in a garden."

"This plant is from God," said Sigmus didactically though he was speaking to someone much more learned in plant lore than himself.

---

[4] *Hawthorn Tree. One of the Nine Sacred Woods of the British Isles. Used to guard sacred wells and places. An old legend says that the first Hawthorn Tree grew out of the staff of St. Joseph.*
[5] *Woundwort. Healing plant known and used on every continent for centuries for healing almost every ailment; something of a panacea.*

"This plant was sent from God. Can this have been given as a curse and not a gift?"

"The witches brew teas from the roots of the woundwort, Sigmus!"

Sigmus laughed. Then he patted his gardener on the shoulder and said. "I am not going to brew any tea from this plant, Fritz. I want it planted for another reason. You are my gardener and I have no intention of misleading you. Now go, my friend."

Then Sigmus reined his horse and rode to the edge of the island overlooking the Western Sea, a sea navigated by saints and marauders alike. And strangely, were it not but for the marauders, the saints would not have come he mused. Atop the precipice he stood hundreds of feet above the surging, swelling breakers. This was his favorite place to come to be by himself to think, and while his tiny garden was but an isolated respite from the rest of the world torn asunder by greed and fear, his tiny island was just such a respite to the good people of Man. He wanted to protect his tiny respite from harm, and if he could, like the [6] wizards of yore raise the creeping mists to hide his tiny island from invaders, he would well serve his people.

One day Kathryn came to him and told him the news that she was alive with another child. Sigmus was overwhelmed. They shared a light breakfast because Kathryn suffered child sickness in the morning. But her sickness could not obscure her joy.

"I have prayed for this," said Sigmus.

"As have I," Kathryn answered. "Now perhaps I can give you that son I promised."

Sigmus looked stunned. The blood drained from his face and his eyes began to sting. He had never spoken of his desire for a son after her terrible misfortune, but he now knew that she had not forgotten. He smiled warmly and she mistook the mist in his eyes for joy.

"Yes, it is another chance, Sigmus. The Lord has a plan for everything, and I could not be happier if an angel told me I was wrong."

---

[6] *Manannan. Referring to the wizard who raised a mist to obscure the island of which it is eponymously named.*

"An angel?" Sigmus repeated merrily. "That is just what I need, another angel."

Kathryn kissed her husband passionately and she touched his face with her warm hands. Sometimes she feared for her husband. She sometimes worried about losing him, so she would hold his face between her hands and stare into his eyes that they be fixed in her mind.

"I am proud to be your angel," she said.

Rushen Abbey is less than a mile from the King's castle in Ballasalla. The King rode his horse along the familiar path to the abbey. The trampled soil felt soft beneath his horse and the fragrant smell of damp earth was in his nostrils. Stopping on top of the rise overlooking the abbey he always stopped to take in the beauty that the abbey was built upon. Built by the Cistercian order of Brotherhood, the abbey was intended to be a place for contemplation and austere living and was founded by reformist Benedictines in 1098. Much of the time spent in the abbey was in quiet contemplation and prayer. Sacred books were copied and annotated with color and contextual notes. The monks kept a few sheep and tended vegetables to supplement their meals. The monks were also known for the fine ales they brewed and mostly exported to supplement their income.

Abbot William was a fine man. True, he was witty, but never overbearing or morose. He was quiet, but he was fair. Occasionally Sigmus would meet the Abbot for lunch and they would talk about matters of faith, for King Sigmus was also interested in trying to balance the ecclesiastical nature of Christianity with the desire to preserve, but not endorse, the ancient heritage of the paganism of the original ancestors of the Manx. The many Celtic rune-stones and archaic sites strewn about the island made it unlikely that the traditions would fade from memory, but memories not cultivated tend to be absorbed into other cultures and disappear but in name only, to be revived with greater significance at a later time. Sigmus thought that it was dangerous to seed over such an ancient belief. William however, was only too happy that the pagan-past had been absorbed into the Church, and he was adamant to the King that such things as paganism would wither on the vine if only left alone. The cross made irrelevant, the scratching on stones, reading of entrails of goats, and whispering into teakettles. The cross made everything irrelevant, but for the cross.

They shook hands warmly. William came out onto the terrace in the traditional white habit. He carried a tray with two glasses and in his other hand he carried a clay bottle of the abbey's outstanding ale. The two men raised their glass together and took a long drink.

"Excellent," said the King. "Ah, this is just what I needed after that arduous ride from my home."

William laughed. He and Sigmus were able to meet as friends and not let the vestments of their respective offices make them gloomy. "Yes, it is. But, unlike [7]St. Arnold, we must brew our ales and store them in barrels. It is a miracle we keep enough for our own needs."

Sigmus sniggered at the little joke. They were meeting as friends now, and there was no need to stand on ceremony.

"What brings you to the abbey today?" Abbot William asked.

"I want to ask you about magic," Sigmus said.

Abbot William set his glass down and wiped the corner of his mouth with a napkin. He narrowed his eyes, and the King could tell that he was not comfortable with the question.

"What would you like to know?" William replied.

"Has the Lord provided us with secrets, if only we can figure them out? What I mean William, is . . . are there mysteries yet to be known?"

The Abbot smiled slightly. The conversation was not going where he thought it may go, and he was relieved. He reached for his glass and said.

"Everything about our life is a mystery, Sigmus. The world is a mystery. Life and death are the ultimate mysteries. But, are you asking me if there are things that have been hidden for a reason, Sigmus?"

"But if they are," Sigmus eagerly replied. "If there truly are things that

---

[7] *St. Arnold. Arnold, Bishop of Metz. Patron saint for beer. Once performed a miracle upon his death, involving a single mug of beer that did not diminish.*

have been hidden for a reason, it can only mean that God wants us to discover what He has hidden, for He would no sooner hide a thing from Himself."

The Abbot raised an eyebrow. "What you say does not follow," he replied. "What could be the purpose of prayer if all could be discovered without divine intervention? Do not take upon yourself, the right to question God, my friend."

They finished their drink together and Sigmus said it was time for him to leave. The Abbot handed him an extra bottle of ale to put in his saddlebag. Then he looked up into the face of his friend.

"You asked me about magic," he spoke pointedly. "I say to you, dear Sigmus: The Isle on which we both must live is alive with magic. But do not confuse the magic of the Earth with the magic of the Cross. I pray that you not distract yourself with such secrets."

As the months passed, Sigmus grew progressively apprehensive about Kathryn's pregnancy. He continuously asked her how she felt and if she wouldn't like a blanket or a piece of cheese or some cold water to soak her feet in. He wanted to read passages from the *Lives of the Saints* of [8]Me taphrastes, but she would only balk at such suggestions and that she could read without his help. Kathryn would smile and shoo him away with a gesture. Then she would thank the Lord for his heart.

And then one day he came upon her prostrate body on the floor in a pool of blood. She had suffered another miscarriage! He carried her to her bed and gently lay her down. Kathryn's eyes were rolled back in her head and there were red streaks in them. Her skin was clammy and cold and the King started rubbing her arms frantically to work life back into them. It was then her handmaiden burst into the room carrying an armful of towels. Gretchen saw what had happened and started giving orders to the King, for it is a great misfortune that this thing should be so common in these blessed isles. She was confident in her work and needed to ask no questions. The King saw her deft hand and unshakable courage and he was humbled before her. Soon, the crisis was over, and it was at this time that the King fell to his knees again and sobbed.

---

[8] *Metaphrastes. St. Simeon Metaphrastes. 10th century monk who compiles a 10 volume book of the lives of saints from written and oral traditions. He arranged the lives in the order of the saints' feast days.*

Sadly, as is sometimes the case, the lady would recover before her husband.

Over two years had passed when Sigmus walked alone in his garden. He was grief stricken to the core and could not put behind him the unbearable sadness that he felt for his wife and for himself. He had not been intimate with Kathryn and he could not bring himself to give himself to her lest there be another tragedy. No, he could never put her through that again. Perhaps some of God's children were never intended to have children of their own, for who could understand the mind of God?

His garden seemed so frivolous and trivial to him now. The hedge, though it had now fused together and towered as high as a man, did nothing to hide his own doubts and fears. Where once he had imagined that his garden would be a place to escape into a new world, a better world, now it only kept him outside and he could not penetrate the permanence that was wrought in shrubbery. The maze acted like a lock to keep him out and though he could wander through the twisting path at will, he was not comfortable and his creation was slipping away from him.

Like a lost sojourner, Sigmus walked through the narrow pathway between the hedge like he were being ushered through the gates of the underworld, for the beauty of a maze is that it looks the same in all directions and one can become lost. The denseness of the foliage surprised him that it should become such a ponderous barrier so soon. He knew his way through the maze, though he was often lost in abstraction while he wandered and oftentimes would become disoriented. Winding in and out like a complex lock, the maze eventually came to an end at the center.

Sigmus could smell the strong scent of primrose before he reached the center where he sat down on the bench and closed his eyes. All around him was a dense wall of thick vegetation. Here he was alone. Here he was isolated from those that would seek to question him. He took a deep breath, and when he exhaled the sound of chirping birds and flying insects filled his mind like an exhalation from deep inside the earth, and as he exhaled and inhaled, a strange breathing took place inside his soul. The longer he listened, the more completely the ambiance filled him. But the calmer he became and the greater his relaxation, the greater became his grief and bitter sadness as if the calmness of his mind only allowed him to sense his grief on a deeper, more profound level or that the solitude allowed him to hear sounds that were outside his mortal range. No, the garden was too quiet, too serene, and were he to find a place to escape from the memory of his loss he should be ashamed. He decided that there is truly no magic in escape, and there is no solitude in denial of precious gifts lost.

He found Fritz the gardener and told him what he wanted. Fritz scratched his face in bewilderment.

"You want me to plant [9]goose-leek between the hedgerows?"

"Yes," Sigmus answered. "I want the very essence of my magic garden to be tinged with the scent of narcissus."

"I can do that, I suppose," Fritz said with growing ambivalence.

"And that is not all," Sigmus continued. "I want you to surround the primrose with a border of belladonna."

"Nightshade is poisonous!" Fritz exclaimed passionately. "You surely cannot surround such a beautiful arrangement of orchids with poison."

"That is what I want you to do," Sigmus said. And then he left the garden and went to the stable where he mounted his horse and rode away across the Crossag Bridge in the direction of Castletown.

Outside of Castletown is a small grove of [10]elderberry trees behind which a small, latch and wattle house has been built. The elderberry is older, far older than the dwelling, and is the reason the small cottage was built.

Sigmus reined his horse after giving her a handful of oats to munch on while he visited. An old man stood in the doorway holding a corn broom. He smiled when he recognized the King, for his eyes were

[9] *Goose-Leek, sometimes known as grave flooers, White Narcissus, or daffodil. Considered unlucky to have in the house until the goslings have hatched. These flowers hang their heads and bring melancholy and tears of unhappiness.*
[10] *Elder tree. Associated with visions and spirits. Used to make magic tea. Ancient Druids dispensed justice beneath this tree. Damaged branches re-grow and signify rebirth out of death.*

failing and his memory grew shorter every day. It was midday, and as usual the sky was gray and overcast. The old man wore a long cassock that hung loosely about his shoulders and reached down to his sandaled feet. He had thinning hair and a long, grey beard, and his face was etched deeply by the sweep of time and the power of the penetrating sun.

"You seem well, Ikshog," said the King.

"The moon travels slower and slower every night," Ikshog replied. "It is good to see you, my friend. What brings you here?"

King Sigmus smiled broadly. "You are older than the moon," he replied. "But the moon still passes over your house."

"Would you like to share some tea with me?" Ikshog asked.

"You are a wise man, Ikshog. And you are the oldest man I know of. I'm certain that you haven't changed since the first time I met you that rainy morning on the wharf. Do you remember?"

"Yes I do," Ikshog admitted. "You were coming off of a ship. You were arriving for your own coronation."

"And you said to me . . ."

"I said to you that The Isle of Man would perish before it went without a King, for a crown must needs have a jewel."

"Yes, yes you did," Sigmus replied as the memory made him smile. "But all things must pass and return to dust."

"I am not as sharp as I once was, my friend. Tell me what you mean."

Instead, Sigmus only asked another question. "Is a piece of a thing, that thing, Ikshog? Can death truly be conquered in this way? I must pass, that is certain, but a part of me is no more me . . . than is the call of a sparrow, a sparrow."

With a knowing smile, Ikshog replied: "You are correct, Sigmus. No, that son is not the man."

"But something must remain!" Sigmus added sharply. "And a part of me should die with the death of that thing."

"Surely you are not dying, Sigmus."

"New things can be created," said Sigmus confidently. "But tell me, Ikshog, where does the life come from?"

". . . the life of what, Sigmus?"

"When we create something . . . where does that thing come from?"

"Come with me," said Ikshog, walking into the house.

Inside the house was very dark. Candles burned and cast off flickering light but did little to illuminate the dark corners and shadows into which nothing could penetrate. More than anything, Sigmus could smell the pungent odor of herbs. A small fire burned in a fireplace. Herbs and sprigs of drying plants hung in bunches from the rafter, and glass jars filled with mixtures were stored on a shelf beneath. Kettles were hanging and steam escaped and poured vaporous clouds into the air. The closeness of the air and the thickness of the smoke made it difficult to breathe normally. Ikshog took the kettle off the fire and poured some of the contents into two small cups. Then he handed one to Sigmus while he brought his own cup to his lips and sipped.

"It is good," he announced. "Sip slowly, for this is a very powerful mixture."

Only after Sigmus had tasted his tea and raised a questioning eyebrow to him warily, did he continue his thought.

"I believe that this is the way that God intended our world to be. It is a good thing that we need to have others around us, Sigmus. The desire to create is born from the desire and need for love. It is what love is."

"And death," Ikshog. "Do we follow our loved one into death as well?"

Ikshog knew that the King was searching for something from him, but he could not understand what it was. The King perhaps only wanted to probe the wandering mind of a man older in years than he, hoping that he should find something to learn. Ikshog finished his tea and set down his cup slowly. Then he turned back to Sigmus.

"There is a plant that I have heard of, Sigmus. It is called [11]harkus bloodwort."

"I have not heard of the bloodwort," said the King.

"I am not surprised," Ikshog said. "The bloodwort is poisonous, Sigmus. The bloodwort is poisonous to itself. Yes, it is very dangerous."

Sigmus looked surprised. "Then how does this plant flourish?"

"By a very strange interaction, Sigmus," answered Ikshog, and he looked into the King's eyes. "This is a very special sympathetic interaction. The plant survives through a complex process of death."

Sigmus started to smile. "Are you having fun with me?" he asked.

"The flower of the bloodwort is white, but is colored with red threads of crimson struck through. The flowers send out a powerful signal to the special insect that must come. The flower allows the nectar to be extracted, but then it does not eat the insect, Sigmus. No, the flower instead releases its poison and poisons itself. It dies."

"Is that so special that it should die, Ikshog?"

"When the bloodwort dies, it is no longer poisonous," Ikshog said triumphantly. "It is then, that the plant may be eaten by the numerous creatures of the earth, and it is how its seed is passed."

Sigmus looked confused. He waited for Ikshog to explain what it all meant. Ikshog looked at the King and only waited. The pungent odor of the mixing, mingling herbs was beginning to overcome the King and he felt lightheaded. Finally he stood up and awkwardly stumbled out of the cottage. He walked out into the grove of trees that adorned the property and sat down. Ikshog came behind him and sat down next to the King.

"What does it mean?" Sigmus asked finally.

---

[11] *Harkus bloodwort. This is an invention and has no basis in reality, although the symbiotic relationship is in fact real.*

"If the bloodwort is eaten before it has been visited by insects, it remains poisonous. Man is like the bloodwort."

Sigmus waited for more, because he still did not understand what Ikshog was trying to tell him. Ikshog saw his confusion.

"The poison is not intended for harm, Sigmus. The poison is intended for life! Do not poison yourself until you have been visited by insects."

The King returned to his castle, but for days he was overcome with a melancholy that affected all those around him. Kathryn tried to talk to him but he avoided her and often would sit by himself in his library.

One night while the King and Kathryn dined together, the conversation turned to the garden. Kathryn waited for Sigmus to finish chewing before she asked.

"When am I finally going to get to see the garden you promised me, my dear? Or have you forgotten?"

That careless comment hurt Sigmus and he winced imperceptibly. In truth, it was Kathryn that was always on his mind, and that the garden should be perfect before she could see it was harder yet for him to bear. He tried to avoid the question, but the lady misinterpreted his ruse and was herself offended.

"The garden is not yet ready for you," Sigmus said. "You don't want to see it until it is ready, do you?"

"What if it takes forever?" Kathryn answered. "It does not have to be perfect for me, Sigmus. I'm sure that I would love whatever you did for me."

"You would hate it," snapped Sigmus. But then he felt guilty and tried to change his tone. "What I mean is that . . . it is almost ready Kathryn. Can't you wait just a little bit longer?"

Kathryn was appeased and she chided herself for making such a big issue out of it. "I can wait, if that is your wish," she said tenderly.

On a misty afternoon late in the year, just before [12]Feast of St. Michael,

King Sigmus rode his horse to a little village in the west, just south of Peel Harbor. This was the village of Glenmaye. The quaint village was in disarray over several sightings of what they could only refer to as a monster, a sea serpent of great magnitude it was said. Sigmus knew of the long history of supernaturalism associated with the heritage of the Manx, but he never expected to come face to face with an actual monster. The most likely explanation probably involved fear mixed with strong drink, for the Manxmen loved to talk about their fear if they could temper it in strong drink. Legends of fairies, shape-shifting animals, goblins, wandering wizards, and creeping mists were common. Sigmus had heard them all, or so he thought.

Later that night Sigmus was riding back home after leaving the village tavern where he had listened patiently to their stories and nodded his head in acquiescence when they looked to him for understanding. He let them speak and he only listened, for in truth, the Manxmen love to tell stories. The road back to his home is nothing more than an old cart path overgrown with weeds and narrowed even more by the thick bracken that grows along the path. The villagers begged Sigmus to spend the night and ride back to Ballasalla in the morning, but the King kindly refused.

"There is a waxing moon tonight and I feel like a brisk ride," he said to them. Then he nodded respectfully and rode away into the night.

At a slow trot there was enough light from the starry firmament to see well enough to safely ride home, and there were not many tall trees along the way to block the light. He sat atop his horse and thought to himself how strange it was to live in such a place so immersed in folklore, and he smiled because it was good. He had met with many important men from the Continent that would scoff at such tales though they would bolt their shutters at night. The life here was slow, and if now and then news of a buggane or a wandering wizard came to the people, it would do no harm to the battling, bartering kings of the Continent, for they should be so lucky.

The path steeply descended around a giant oak tree that refused to move. Sigmus walked his horse slowly and carefully as the darkness

---

[12] Feast of St. Michael. Saint Michael is one of the principal angels in the battle fought against the followers of Satan. Michaelmas, or Autumnal Equinox. September 21, and marks the last harvest before winter.

made the steep slope dangerous and frightening for the horse. Suddenly he pulled up on the reins. He had heard a noise that startled him. Waiting in silence he listened, but the sound did not come again. Sigmus involuntarily reached to his side and felt for the pommel of his sword and the gemstone that crowned it. If he was attacked, he would be able to handle himself against all but the best swordsman. He waited. The only sound he could hear was the murky nocturnal insects and the wind as it slipped through the trees. After a few moments he decided that what he heard was probably nothing unnatural, and that is when he heard it again. It was a low pitched warbling like the sound of distant thunder.

Sigmus did not recognize the sound. It was unlike any other sound he had ever heard. And then his horse began to quiver and move from side to side. She was spooked.

"Who's there?" Sigmus cried into the night. "Show yourself!"

The horse was now snorting and shivering nervously, prancing from side to side. He patted her flank.

"Easy now," he said. "Easy now, girl."

The King jumped down from his horse and tied the reins to a tree. Sigmus was a brave man, but now even he was becoming uncomfortable. A cloud passed over the moon. Then he heard the sound again, but this time it sounded closer. He reminded himself that legends of goblins and mowing devils was just so much folklore, the kind told in pubs and taverns late at night. But then he saw something through the darkness. It was a light . . . a glowing, feeble marsh-light of some kind. He watched the light intently. It was moving! He laughed aloud.

"Phantom? It's just marsh-light," he thought.

He watched the weird light. It was like a spectral apparition that shifted in and out of view like a vanishing fog. The strange phantasm was seventy or eighty yards away in a slight depression and hung above the ground like dense, eerie phosphorescence. Sigmus waited for the shape to form again. His fear was that he was looking at a phantom, a ghost, and his fear was steadily mounting. Like a child drawn to the flames of a burning shack he could not take his eyes off it, and like a curious child, his mind was prepared to accept anything.

Then the amorphous cloud began to rise. Higher and higher it floated above the ground. The cloud was dark, but it was tinged with light and there was movement inside. Then he saw shapes descending from the cloud. He rubbed his eyes. They were angels! The King covered his face at once. He had witnessed something holy, and now he was frightened and ashamed. Turning away awkwardly, he mounted his horse and trotted away without looking back. When he was at the Crossag Bridge he stopped, because he was not yet ready to return to his home so shaken he was by the apparition. He knew that when he crossed the bridge he would be home again and his encounter with angels would be left behind. But he did not want to cross the bridge yet and however long he stayed, it should remain real in his mind.

He sat on his horse atop the stone bridge and the longer he remained the calmer he became and peacefulness overcame him. He was in a state of grace. Of course, he would never speak about it.

The King stood on the bridge for a very long time until he was overcome by fatigue. He sat down and leaned his back against the cold stones and fell fast asleep. When he woke it was morning. During the night his horse had found her way home, so Sigmus walked the rest of the way to his castle. He was refreshed and in such a state of ecstasy that he fairly ran home. When he got home he ran up to his bedchamber and found Kathryn still asleep. He woke her with a gentle kiss on the head.

"Good morning, my love," he said with trembling emotion. "Wake up now and come with me. I want to show you your garden."

Kathryn blinked her sleepy eyes. "Where have you been?" she asked.

"Never mind that," he said. "Something wonderful has happened to me, Kathryn. I was dead, but now I am alive."

King Sigmus held the lady Kathryn in his arms and carried her past the sentinels, into the garden he had built for her. He set her down tenderly and took her by the hand and led her into the magic garden. Her soft hand was warm and the King's eyes twinkled in the morning light. Kathryn gasped and held her breath as the spell of the enchantment fell upon her.

"Oh, Sigmus!" she exclaimed with delight. "This is wonderful."

They walked together and Sigmus pointed out the various plants and told her what to be careful of. Everywhere the fragrance of flowers and flowering plants and rushes and grasses mixed into a powerful vapor that wafted through the rows and permeated the entire garden. Kathryn began to hum a melody, and the sound of her voice touched his very heart. The melody was like a children's lullaby and he would always remember it.

"This is a maze," she said with feigned coyness. "Are you trying to trap me, Sigmus?"

"Now you know," Sigmus replied joyfully. He was so happy and so relaxed at this moment that he wanted the moment to last forever.

"Then you will have to catch me," Kathryn said suddenly. And she broke free of Sigmus and ran ahead of him, disappearing around a corner in the hedge, laughing.

Sigmus smiled to himself, mischievously raising an eyebrow like in his younger days. And then he started after her. Kathryn was younger and faster than Sigmus, and though he knew the way through the maze and she did not, she had so many places to hide that it took him several minutes to find her. He found her hiding with her pretty backside tightly against the hedge in one of the dead-ends. Sigmus poked his head in, and the sound of the lady Kathryn's soft giggle gave her away.

"I've found you," Sigmus chided her. "Where are you going to run now?"

In response, the lady Kathryn threw her arms around the King and kissed him on the lips passionately. She was so close to him, and the touch of her warm, soft body went through him like a rushing wave. He felt his legs going numb and he held her close as the weariness and doubts were washed away by the ardor of his love. The King reached his arms around her waist and drew her to him. Her body felt so good in his arms that for a moment he lost himself and forgot where he was. Kathryn knew how to respond to her husband, touching his lip with her little finger. She brushed his loving face, and the couple lay down together in the crook of the maze that Sigmus built, and there they made love passionately without fear and without expectation. Sigmus lost himself in the expression of love and he could only see her and feel her and smile because of her happiness.

And it was in that moment that the magic garden truly came to life, for the power of love is the power of change. And just as a part of a thing is not that thing, sometimes that thing can lose its parts and become more than what it ever was. Truly, King Sigmus lost himself in that garden and gained the whole world.

The magic garden came to life with the infusion of love, and the garden from that day forth truly was wrought in magic. And so it is that sometimes magic can be hidden inside of a human heart. The garden of King Sigmus saw many miracles, the first of which was the birth of a fine baby boy early the very next year that was named Bartholomew.

The Stubborn Stone

King Sigmus strolled through his garden one afternoon and happened upon Iona who was pulling out a giant weed by the root. She held the weed firmly with both hands and pulled mightily, but the weed proved to be beyond her strength. She pulled and pulled until she was flush, and with a great sigh she resigned herself to failure. The King saw her kneeling on the ground and asked if she was alright. Iona wiped her brow and smiled. Her hands were dirty and now her face was dirty too. The King offered his hand to her and pulled her up. Then he wiped her forehead with his hand and laughed because the strength in her heart was greater than the strength in her hands.

The very young Prince Bartholomew spent the lonely, frozen nights of winter in his tower bedroom, dreaming. He would dream away the bitter nights and the bitter drafts of cold that crept in through the stone walls of his private chamber. Great winds often blew across the island during the long darkness of winter, and a young boy needed dreams to sustain him through such times. He would dream until he was awake, and then he would daydream until he fell back to sleep again. He was dreaming about having his own horse; yes, he wanted a horse just like the steed that his father rode proudly through the fields and glens of his kingdom. And who could ever blame such a young boy for having such noble dreams? In those days a boy needed a dream, as a dream needed a dreamer, just as a king needed a horse.

One morning after a long night of expectant dreams he asked his mother if he could ever expect such a dream to come true, because in truth, to a young boy a moment is like an hour and an hour is like a day. The Lady Kathryn looked up from her plate. She smiled tenderly before wiping her mouth on a napkin.

"A horse, you say?" she repeated joyfully, for she loved to listen to the dreams of her precious boy. "You have been dreaming about having a horse?"

"Just like daddy's horse," answered the boy.

"But daddy is a king, and you are only a prince," she teased. "Shouldn't you be dreaming about prince horses before king horses?"

"Prince horses are too small," said the boy with growing disappointment. "Prince horses are just for looking at and for petting, but I want to ride. I want to sit up high and I want everyone to see me and wave."

Queen Kathryn brought her beautiful hand to her young prince and tweaked him on the nose. "You are too young for a king horse," she said lovingly.

The boy did not smile, and the tweak on the nose only confirmed in his young mind that his mother thought he was just a boy. He looked down at his food, but he was in no mood for chewing. The Lady Kathryn tried to eat, but she could see the disappointment in her young boy's face and she could not bear to see him thus heartbroken. She brought her hand to his chin and tickled him.

"Someday you will have your own horse, and he will be a horse meant for a king, but these things take time, Bartholomew. We need to be patient sometimes, for the Lord never intended for that all things should happen at once."

The boy still did not raise his head. Kathryn sat back in her chair and waited.

"But if I had my horse now," the boy said without raising his head, "I could wait until I got bigger before I rode him."

Queen Kathryn smiled and her heart swelled. Yes, this was a special boy she could see. But she had to be strong, so she picked up her fork and continued with her breakfast.

The days passed and still the boy could not let go of his dream. Often he gazed out his window to the road leading away from the castle and he would watch for horses. When he saw one coming from far away he would try to guess the errand of the rider, and whether it be significant or folly. He would watch the steam snorting from the flaring nostrils of the thundering horse and he would wonder. Then he would imagine himself riding away from the castle on a mission of importance, a mission both secret and dangerous. Yes, a mission needed secrecy as a secret mission needed a horse.

One day King Sigmus came upon his son unexpectedly as he went about his business. The boy was sitting alone on a corner sofa near a window overlooking the garden. The King came into the room to pick up a parchment left on a table. The boy looked up briefly before putting his head down again. King Sigmus took hold of his parchment and started to leave the room. At the door he stopped.

"Are you feeling well, Bartholomew?" he asked politely.

"Can I ask you something?" the young Bartholomew asked carefully. He knew that to find his father in an agreeable mood was necessary to his goal and he needed to access the situation before beginning his argument for a horse.

King Sigmus suppressed a smile. He knew exactly what his young son was doing, for what parent does not know the needs and desires of his children as if they were his own? The King also had the advantage of having talked with the Lady Kathryn. So, he knew just what the young boy was contending for. He pretended ignorance.

"What is it, Bartholomew?"

Tentatively the boy asked, "Is it hard being a King?"

"Not if you have a horse," answered King Sigmus innocently. Now he would gauge his son's wit.

"That's just what I was thinking," Bartholomew answered. "And some day I am going to be King . . ."

King Sigmus waited for the final justification that would crown the boy's argument. He bobbed his head in anticipation as if his son needed to be coaxed into clinching his own argument. Finally Bartholomew said.

"I really need to start riding now. For how can I ever become a king if I do not have a horse?"

"I am not dead yet," said King Sigmus with a smile. "But, tell me Bartholomew, you do not think you are too young? What would your mother say about you wanting your own horse?"

The boy did not want to lie, so he said. "I'm sure that she already knows what I want."

"And does a prince always get everything he wants?"

"I'm willing to work for it," said Bartholomew. "I don't expect you to just give it to me."

King Sigmus raised an eyebrow. Bartholomew saw it and he knew that he had a chance of getting what he wanted.

"I'll do whatever you want," the boy said. "I don't have any money, so if you want me to do some work . . ."

King Sigmus thought for a moment. He raised his hand to his chin and pretended to be concentrating on an idea. Finally he spoke.

"Alright Bartholomew," he said. "I do have a little project that I need to have done. But I warn you, it will not be easy."

"Of course!" Bartholomew said energetically. "I don't want it to be easy."

"Come with me," the King said.

Then he led his young son out of the castle and onto the lawn on the west side of the castle near the boundary of the abbey. Near the stone wall that marked the boundary was an old stump from a fallen tree. The stump had been there for many years until it had become petrified. Nearly three feet in diameter, it had once been a prodigious tree, a sacred oak tree. Now it was just a stump, a vestige of what it once was. King Sigmus pointed to the stump.

"Do you think you can get that out?"

The boy looked at the stump with a combination of hope mixed with utter disbelief. The stump was monstrous. King Sigmus saw doubt in the eyes of his son.

"If you think it is too hard . . ."

"No, no." Bartholomew responded before he even had time to think about it. "If this is what you want."

"Now you don't need to get this done all in one day," Sigmus said casually. But even as he spoke a pang of remorse rose up in his mind and he wondered if he had done the right thing.

And so on a cold November morning young Bartholomew began his long battle with the stump. Dressed in a wool coat and heavy gaiters, a woolen cap and mittens, the boy went out to survey the job he was determined to do. The first thing he realized was that the ground was frozen and that to dig through the frozen earth was impossible. He stood all alone that cold, grey morning and his parents watched him through a window in the warmth of the castle. The boy threw down the assorted instruments he had brought along, including a heavy axe and maul, on the ground before the stump. Then he rubbed his hands together for warmth. He hesitated before striking the stump because he did not want to be disappointed and he feared that any attempt to destroy it would only bring utter failure, but if he waited at least his hope would not be destroyed.

That first day the boy did nothing more than to stare at the stump. When he grew tired he decided to sit down on the stump, for it made a perfect chair. From that point forward the boy would come to the stump and merely sit down and ponder until he was bored, then he would walk away until the next morning. This went on for a week until on the first day of the second week, after waking up from a significant dream, he had a plan and he began his campaign.

Bartholomew trudged out to the stump like always. Then he took something out of his pocket and rubbed it all over the stump, it was honey. Into the honey he sprinkled seeds before turning around and walking away. He sat on the stone wall partition that bordered the abbey and waited. Then he turned around and sat facing the monastery grounds and his legs dangled over the wall. The corner of the abbey was visible through the trees. No one was out, and all he could see were the few goats and wandering sheep that huddled together for warmth. It looked so peaceful and quiet. Inside they would be praying he thought, for what else was there to do in a monastery? The wind slipped through the trees and the sound made the boy sleepy. A dreamy, peacefulness came over him and he felt warm. He thought he heard his name in the wind, but it was only a bird. But then he saw a man out walking along the fence. The man was coming in his direction. Bartholomew could see that he was a monk because he wore a white habit beneath a heavy overcoat. The monk stopped in front of the boy. He smiled.

"You are Prince Bartholomew, are you not?" he said softly.

The boy nodded and waited for the man to speak again. He looked very calm and there was something very compelling about him that interested the boy.

"You come here every day," said the monk. "Are you looking for something?"

"Am I allowed to speak?" asked the boy innocently.

The monk laughed. "Yes, you are allowed to speak my boy. I am Abbot William. I know your father well. How is King Sigmus?"

"Very well," Bartholomew answered.

"You have a particular interest in that tree stump. Are you trying to destroy it?"

"How did you guess?" said the Prince. "I am trying to get it out, but I still haven't figured out how to do it."

"All things pass," said Abbot William. "There is a season for all things, and the Lord alone knows all the seasons. Perhaps that tree stump still has a purpose, and that is why it is stubborn. Who can guess the purpose of the Lord?"

"I don't know much about that," Bartholomew admitted.

Abbot William pointed to the stump. "Turn around and look for yourself."

Bartholomew turned around. Several black ravens were standing on the dead stump, pecking wildly. Bartholomew could hear the soft sound of chipping wood.

"You are very wise for your age," said Abbot William. Then he smiled warmly. "It will still take them forever to eat through that whole stump however, so I trust you have made other plans."

The next time Prince Bartholomew came out to the stump he had a new plan. With him he carried some tools from the stable. One of the tools was an old rusted plowshare. He also brought along a large hammer and a handful of nails and some rusty brackets once used on an old barn door. In his pockets he carried other things that he might need: pieces of twisted steel, bolts, washers, little bits of rope. He threw down the rusty junk and then sat down on the stump to think, for he was still not sure that his idea was sound. Once again he tried to reason his way through the idea. The earth turned, of that he was certain because the sky turned sideways and he could watch the stars disappear across the horizon at night. It wasn't noticeable during the day, but he postulated that there were other reasons for that and that he couldn't possibly know everything. He once again pitched his idea: If he secured the plowshare securely to the stump with nails and had the blade buried in the ground, and if everything was just right, when the earth rotated at night when he was asleep, the earth would revolve around the plowshare and dig the stump right out of the ground. After several minutes of thought he could find no fault in his logic, and so he began setting up his apparatus. When he was done he was cold, but he walked back home again with an inner satisfaction that he kept to himself.

The next morning as he prepared to go outside to the stump he was stopped by his father who was preparing to leave for Castletown. King Sigmus was just finishing his coffee when the boy whisked into the dining room for a piece of bread to take with him to the stump. King Sigmus looked up with satisfaction when he saw his son.

"Ah, good morning Bartholomew," he said. You are up early today."

The boy tried to snatch a loaf of bread and slip away without having to talk to his father because he was anxious to check on the stump and he did not want to be distracted.

"Wait a minute, my boy," Sigmus chuckled warmly. "Sit down and have something to eat before you sneak away, the stump will still be there when you finish breakfast, I trust." And then with a quick wink he reached for his coffee. "How goes the battle?" he asked.

"I have to get out there," Bartholomew said politely.

"You've been pretty busy lately," said the King. "Are you making any progress, or don't you want to talk about it?"

"Not just yet," said Bartholomew, "maybe later, maybe after lunch. I'll have to check a few things out."

"Run along then!" Sigmus laughed merrily. "Go about your business my boy." Then he smiled to himself as he watched his son, hastily shoving a loaf of bread into his pocket, run out of the room on a mission of his own.

With a heart full of confidence Prince Bartholomew ran out to the stump to make sure that the hole would not be too big, just in case the earth was moving faster than he had calculated. He ran as fast as he could and he felt the excitement grow with a certain sense of pride. But even before he made it to the stump he could tell that something had gone terribly wrong. It was exactly as he had left it the day before, nothing had happened! He felt a sudden pang in the pit of his stomach. Sure enough, the apparatus was just as he had left it. Nothing had happened. The earth had not moved even an inch. Anger, a ferocious anger rose up inside him and he felt humiliated. Suddenly he took out his anger the only way he knew how.

Next to the stump were the tools he had left on the ground from the day before. He reached for an axe, took it up, and started to attack the stump with vigor. The apparatus he cast aside in a heap. Then he delivered sharp blows to the frozen stump. On and on he hacked and chopped until his anger was spent and he was exhausted. His outrage had done little damage however and he threw down the axe in disgust. Then he sat down on the stump and tried to catch his breath.

A moment later he heard a voice. It was Abbot William. He was on the other side of the fence.

"Good morning, Bartholomew," he said.

Bartholomew could see that the Abbot had been watching him, and now he felt like a fool. He was ashamed of his own ignorance and he could feel the blood getting warm on his face. He looked down.

"Do you mind if I come over?" said the Abbot. And before Bartholomew could say a word, the majestic abbot leapt over the stone wall and came to the stump where the boy sat dejected. He put his hand on the boy's shoulder. "It was a well conceived plan," he said tenderly. "It is not your fault, Bartholomew, for how are we to know all the ways of the Lord?"

Bartholomew looked up and there was a tear in his eye. The Abbot saw it and his heart became filled with compassion.

"You are indeed a clever boy," he said softly. "You remind me of your father. But the Lord is clever too, Bartholomew, and so it is that He has plans that we can never fathom though He puts them in our heart. Never feel ashamed of your ignorance in front of the Lord, for He cares what is in your heart as well as what is in your mind."

When the Abbot was gone, Bartholomew stayed behind and sat on the stump for a very long time. After a while he picked up his tools and went home. King Sigmus was away to Castletown, but his mother was waiting for him when he came into the room to stand next to the fire. The Lady Kathryn was sitting in a chair and her hands were folded delicately on her lap when Bartholomew came into the room. She looked up and smiled, but it was a smile from which he had nothing to be ashamed.

"Come over here so that I can give you a kiss," she said in a way that always made Bartholomew feel happy.

The boy went to her and sat on her knee and stared into her beautiful eyes. He could become lost in her eyes and sometimes it made him cry.

"Would you like to hear a story?" she asked softly.

The boy nestled up close to her and she put her arm around him. He felt the warmth of her body and he relaxed.

"This is a story I heard when I was a little girl," she said. "It is the story of a stubborn man."

Young Bartholomew felt so safe and so content that he closed his eyes as his mother began her tale.

"Near the town of Peel there once lived a man, a very poor man, who worked the sea for herring. This man worked very hard, he worked and he worked and he worked and he almost never sat down, unless he was tending to his drift nets. Did he work so hard? Did he really work harder than other men? Some people openly said that he broke a sacred tradition and that his subsequent unhappiness was a curse. You see, in those days it was traditional for certain holes to be left in the drift nets for the herring boats. Now it was known that Finn Mac Cool liked to swim the coastal waters. The honored tradition was meant to ensure that Finn Mac Cool would never be caught again, for in truth a pact was made between the fishermen long ago and Finn Mac Cool, whereby they would always leave a hole in their drift nets large enough to swim through. In exchange, Finn Mac Cool promised never to cast his magic spells on the hard working fishermen, for in truth their job was hard enough already.

"Some people said that herring swam inside of his brain because all his thought was bent on the capture of herring. After many years of endless toil the man had saved enough money to move into a cottage built in the highlands. And after selling his meager hut and the land it rested on for what he could get, he moved away from the sea, far away from herring and haddock and driftnets and smoking, burning, reeking kipper.

"In his cottage on the hill he forgot all about the herring and the living, breathing schools of myriads upon myriads of mindless, senseless, cold fish, for herring no longer swam inside of his brain. But still he was not happy because he missed the one thing that brought him peace of mind . . . he missed his stone. Buried on the otherwise worthless property of his old hut, the worthless property he no longer owned was a thing of great beauty and solitary delight for the man. There was a large stone, buried in the ground and resembling the saddle of a horse. As a young boy, the man had fond memories of playing on this stone, and it was to this stone that many oaths were spoken and painful secrets revealed, for the boy came to this stone to be alone and to pray.

'Now that man had worked his young life away and he had worked very hard and endured many disappointments. He had sacrificed sweat and blood for the herring, for the sea was very dangerous. So now he was in such a position that he did not need to work as hard. And now there was time for other things. But everything now only reminded him of how hard he had worked to get to where he was, and the harder he remembered how hard he had worked, the more he remembered how much he missed his childhood. He sat on a chair outside of his cottage and looked out onto verdant glens and rolling countryside, but his heart was not there, he wanted to sit on his favorite stone once again where he could hear the sound of his own thoughts.

"And then he finally decided that he had to have his stone. He would go to the owner of his old property and ask if he could take the stone away, for why would anyone want such an old stone taking up so much of their precious property? So, picking up his walking staff he left his cottage and walked down the mountain to his old hut near the town of Peel and he whistled a familiar song to keep himself happy.

"As expected, the new owner offered to him his old stone gladly, for he was only too happy to be rid of it. The man had two draft horses brought in for the job. He watched eagerly as they were harnessed securely to the stone and he waited to see the stone come tumbling forward . . . but the stone did not move. Next the man bade the horses to pull harder, but still the stone did not move even an inch. The perplexed man scratched his head. Then he prepared to whip the horses to pull even harder, but that was when the owner of the horses stepped in and ended the expedition. And so it was that the man went away and he was very disappointed.

"Several weeks later the man returned with a new plan. He brought iron bars and lumber with which to pry the stubborn stone away from the earth. Some local boys he hired to dig around the stone so that it would loosen its grip upon the soil. The boys were healthy and hardy, and he put them to work. But after an entire day of strenuous digging around the stone it became clear that a new plan was needed, for even such intense labor did nothing to loosen the stone. He now knew that he needed to call in experts.

"Now the stone was buried beneath a structure of scaffolding and ropes and pulley's and levers and turning, spinning wheels. Men walked around the stone and shouted orders to other men that ran about and jumped every time a new order was given. After much effort and earnest hubbub, the stone had still not moved. Now the men began to spin around and jump up and down like the whirling, twirling machinery, but it was all in vain and soon their steam was diminished for any more useless enterprise. The captain of the demolition team said with much assurance, 'she will not move, of that you can be certain, for I believe that she is tethered to the earth itself. Find yourself another stone.' The man was heartbroken.

"Every day the man would come back to the stone and he would sit on it like he did when he was a young boy. The people would gather around their windows and watch the man as he sat thinking, and they tried to imagine what he could possibly be thinking about.

"One day the man went to the door of his old hut and spoke with the owner. He spoke long and the owner listened with increasing interest. When all the speaking and listening was over the man was happy. But it was not the man that went away that day; it was the owner, for the man had traded his beautiful cottage on the hill for his old tumbledown hut. Such is the story about the stubborn man and the stubborn stone."

When she finished speaking she looked at her son, but he was fast asleep. And so she sat with him and held his body closely until she too fell asleep.

The Flower Garden

All things pass even as the stars in heaven shall fall and like a candle extinguished, go cold. The process of becoming is also a process of death, and all that is in between is life. Powerful symbols define this process and sometimes we cling to these symbols for comfort because death is dark, and death is cold. And that is why life must be full of color and must reflect the light of the Lord, for such is the symbol of a rose. King Sigmus smiled every time he beheld the face of his beautiful wife, for the face of the Lady Kathryn was also like a rose.

Young Prince Bartholomew stood before an enormous Norwegian Pine tree and looked up to the top where he would place the star. The tree was easily ten feet high and towered over the cheerful boy like a giant monster.

"Can you reach all the way to the top?" said Bartholomew's mother, Queen Kathryn. Then she bent down and kissed him on the head. "Perhaps we should wait for your father," she continued. "He can lift you all the way to the top."

Bartholomew knew his father was strong, he had seen him carry huge packages, but he could not see any way he could ever lift him to such a height. The last few Christmas' he was getting taller even as their Christmas tree was getting shorter, but it was still a huge tree.

Queen Kathryn reached down and gave her beautiful son a big hug. She tried to pick him up but her strength had failed her, so she kissed him again and smiled.

"Would you like to help me cut out sugar cookies?" she asked.

"Yes I would," he replied. "Can we make animals?"

"Of course," said Kathryn. "I have some new cookie cutters this year. Would you like to make horses? I also have rabbits and birds because I know how much you like birds."

"Can Uncle Patrick come and help? I like him because he is always off riding giraffes."

Kathryn laughed. "Where did you hear such a thing?" she asked. "I did not know that Uncle Patrick rode giraffes."

"I heard daddy talking about it," said Bartholomew. "He said Uncle Patrick is always gone riding giraffes."

"I don't think so," said Kathryn with a growing smile on her face. "Uncle Patrick is a busy man. He travels all over in ships and carriages just to look at numbers. They say that he knows numbers that haven't even been invented yet. Do you remember the book he sent you from London?"

"But I want to see him, mommy. When can he come back to our house to play? He promised to teach me how to play the drum. Uncle Patrick said that playing the drum is all about numbers and that if I could play the drum I could understand many things about numbers that people don't even know. He said it is a secret, but that some people already know about it."

"We'll see," said Kathryn. "I've invited him to come and stay with us for Christmas, but he never knows if he is going to be busy until he is busy. Do you understand? Some people do things because they want to do them, but most people do things because they have to. It takes a lot of money to live, Bartholomew. Not everyone is a prince you know." And then she pinched his nose and made him laugh.

Later King Sigmus came home. He looked for Bartholomew, but the baking of sugar cookies with Kathryn had tired him out and now he was asleep on the floor near where his mother sat decorating some of the freshly baked cookies. Sigmus kissed her tenderly and pointed to Bartholomew with a smile.

"He's a real big help," he whispered with a smile. "How will that be, a King taking naps on the floor during a hurricane?"

"The boy's a dreamer," said Kathryn. "He wants to go off riding giraffes with his uncle."

King Sigmus laughed involuntarily but stopped himself lest he wake up the boy. "He will," he said with a twinkle in his eye. "And he will. But there is more to being a King than riding giraffes."

When Bartholomew woke up, he saw his mother and father sitting together eating cookies and smiling at him. It wasn't often that the boy saw his mother and father together when they weren't busy with something or other. This is how he liked to see them, when they weren't serious. They were even holding hands. Bartholomew jumped up and scolded his mother.

"You were supposed to wait for me," he said.

King Sigmus handed the boy a cookie with a laugh. "Do you want to know what happened to me?" he said.

"Is it scary?"

King Sigmus brought a finger to his chin and pretended to scratch. "Well," he said. "It could have been. I was driving home from Castletown, and wouldn't you know, a huge tree had fallen across the road, blocking my way. How was I supposed to get home?"

Bartholomew smiled. His father liked to tell stories, and he never knew where it was that his words would turn into stories, but they always did.

"Suddenly this wild looking woodchopper jumps out into the road hefting this huge axe!"

"Did he try to chop you up, daddy?"

"No, he didn't. He went to work on that tree and chopped it to pieces in two shakes of a donkey's tail. He called himself Hagen, Hagen the Woodchopper."

"Can he come here?" asked Bartholomew.

"Hagen spends a lot of time in the woods," said Sigmus. "He says there are monsters in there just waiting behind the trees, and that is why he has to chop them down."

Bartholomew started to laugh for he had finally realized that a story was being told. He was pretty good at stories too, for his age at least.

"Then where are the monsters supposed to live?" he asked his father calmly. "If Hagen the Woodchopper cuts down all the trees, the monsters will have to live here."

King Sigmus scratched his chin again. "Hum," he answered. "I never thought of that. I suppose you're right. I better tell Hagen to leave some trees for the monsters to hide."

The next day Bartholomew went with his father to Snaefell Mountain, near Laxey, to talk with some men about mining conditions and the moodiness of the men that worked there. They rode in their carriage and along the way Bartholomew played with a toy flute while his father looked over some papers he had brought along. The road was ruddy and deep ruts prevented them from traveling very fast. Outside the carriage Bartholomew watched the landscape change from woody to one of shrunken shrubbery and sparse foliage clinging to life in an almost barren landscape. And the higher they climbed into the hills, the more beautiful became the landscape below as if by viewing it from an elevation, they were seeing it the way God intended. Looking out the window always made Bartholomew drowsy and he would nod in and out of sleep next to his father as the soft rustling of paper coaxed him to follow his dreams as they waited patiently for him to nod off.

The men were complaining that the work was too dangerous and that they were being harassed by demons and ghosts. King Sigmus was always having to deal with these vestiges of folklore from the old world, folklore built up from ear to mouth, but the fears and apprehensions of the old world continued to exist and be reborn in every new tradition. It was impossible to separate one tradition from another as they were all part of a single thread that wove a discrete stitch through them all; it was important only to remember.

Bartholomew woke when the carriage shifted. His father was getting inside. He rubbed his eyes.

"You were asleep," said King Sigmus. "So I let you rest."

When they were driving back home, Bartholomew wanted to know about the men at the mine. He asked his father what they were so afraid of that they had to call him all the way from home.

"They're a strange lot," the King said shaking his head. "They see ghosts everywhere, Bartholomew. Some of the men are afraid to go back down into the mines."

"What is down there?" said Bartholomew: "Ghosts?"

"No, there are no ghosts down there," said the King.

"Monsters?"

"There are no monsters down there either," The King replied.

"Witches?" Bartholomew asked persistently. He had to know what was down there and he thought that if he just guessed it, his father would tell him the truth. "Is it witches?"

Finally King Sigmus turned to his son and told him the truth. "There are no witches," he said calmly though in truth he hated to say so. "There are no witches anywhere, there are no ghosts, and there are no monsters. These things do not exist, Bartholomew. Do you understand? In truth, only fools believe such things. The people here believe these things because they have always believed these things to be true. They believe it because they want to believe, so to them it becomes true."

Bartholomew asked no more about witches on the ride home. He looked at the passing countryside until he fell into another dream. He rested his head on his father's lap and let the rocking of the carriage carry him off to sleep.

One morning Bartholomew found his mother sitting alone in a chair near the window. She looked sad. Bartholomew watched her from around a corner. He wanted to surprise her. She was rocking back and forth in her chair as she sang, but her song was not sweet. Then Bartholomew saw that she was not singing at all, she was crying and her face was contorted with pain, not pleasure. He became frightened. He ran up to her and threw his arms around her.

"Are you all right, mommy?" he cried.

Kathryn immediately stopped crying when she saw her son. She did her best to dry her tears. But now there were tears in Bartholomew's eyes.

"Don't cry, silly," she said. "I'm fine now. Would you like to help me with some decorations?"

"I saw you crying," said Bartholomew still noticeably distraught. "Is it something I did?"

Then Kathryn reached out and put her soft hands on the boy's face to comfort him. "I'm all right now," she said. "It was just a pain, but now it is gone. Now tell me a story about ghosts, because I like to be scared."

"There are no ghosts," said the boy. "Daddy said that ghosts are just for silly people to believe."

"But don't you love to hear ghost stories, Bartholomew? I thought you loved them."

"I don't want people to think I am silly," he replied. "I don't need to believe in them anymore mommy."

Then Kathryn and her son went into another room. This is the room where she went to work on her paper things. She always loved to work with paper things and beautiful colors. Her face lit right up when they sat down. The table was cluttered with so many things: colored paper, scissors, glue, pins, brushes, shiny beads and glitter, and things Bartholomew had never seen before. The table looked like a mess, but the lady knew where everything was and what looked like utter chaos to the boy, was actually quite ordered to the boy's mother.

Kathryn picked up something she was working on. It was a paper flower. She folded the paper flower joyfully and tenderly as if it truly were a fragile flower with delicate petals. The joy could be seen in her eyes as they sparkled through their moistness.

"Our souls are flowers in God's garden," she said. "That is why I love to fold them, for God takes joy in our joy and sadness in our sadness. We are all flowers in God's garden, Bartholomew."

"Why does God have a garden?" said Bartholomew.

"Because flowers are beautiful," she said. "God's light shines on them and they shine back with beautiful colors. We are all like flowers to God, and that is why he wants us to live in his garden."

"What kind of a flower are you going to be, mommy?" asked Bartholomew innocently.

"I want to be a rose," she answered. Roses are the color of the blood of Jesus. That is why I like them so, for they remind me of God's sacrifice. Now let me teach you how to make one out of paper."

Though her hands were in pain and it hurt her to move them, she took great joy because she was doing something she loved. Bartholomew did not see her pain, all he could see was the love with which she spoke to him and the gracefulness of her fine fingers as she hummed a simple melody. Kathryn looked up from her work.

"Did you know that angels love flowers too, Bartholomew?" she said. "Angels take care of God's garden when He is away. You cannot see them, but sometimes you can hear them in the laughter of children for angels love to play with children. Angels watch us when we sleep."

Later that night a group of traveling musicians, troubadours, came to the castle for an evening of entertainment. King Sigmus and Queen Kathryn sat together on a loveseat while Bartholomew had a chair all to himself. Even the servants were invited into the room to enjoy themselves. There were jugglers and puppets, epic songs and comedies. There was a contortionist and a balladeer, a magician and a floor dancer. Chocolate was served and there was fruit-punch and tea and berries with cream. Roasted water-chestnuts were served. Bartholomew had never seen such a troupe and his eyes were fixated on the puppeteer and did not see Kathryn and the King leave the room. Several minutes later, King Sigmus returned without Kathryn and sat next to Bartholomew.

The next morning, Kathryn was not at breakfast when Bartholomew came down. He looked at her place at the table but there were no dirty dishes. He waited for one of the servants to come into the room. Maria came in with a place setting of silverware.

"Good morning, master Bartholomew. Breakfast will be served soon. Would you like milk this morning?"

"Where is my mom, Maria?" he asked.

"Miss Kathryn has taken ill this morning, master Bartholomew. I'm sure she will be down later," she said. "The King will tend to her needs. You are free to play today, and I am to tell you that a giant trout was reported in the Silverburn yesterday. Harold is going fishing this morning to catch that trout. Would you like to join him?"

"Maybe tomorrow," Bartholomew replied. "I am going to wait for my mom to get better first. Tell Harold that it is all right with me if he catches that trout."

Later that day Kathryn came down wearing her nightgown. Her hair was tied back and she wore thick slippers on her feet. In her hand was a small package wrapped with a tiny bow. Gingerly she came down the steps looking right and left for her son. He was in a parlor that faced the garden and he was lying near an open window, asleep on the floor. The sound of songbirds was bright and filtered in from the garden like a gentle breeze. The Prince had fallen asleep listening to their song. Kathryn sat in a comfortable chair and waited for him to wake up. She watched him sleeping and thought about how his life would be when she was gone. She had given him everything she could give. The last thing she would give him was a tender memory to look back on when his own life became hard or harsh.

Bartholomew woke slowly. He heard the voice of his mother before he saw her.

"Well well sleepy, are you going to try to stay awake long enough to say hello?"

Bartholomew smiled and yawned as the last images of his dream vanished from his mind. He stood up and went to his mother. She held out her hand and he put his own hand inside hers. She raised his hand to her lips and kissed it.

"I have brought you a present," she said. Then she handed him the package and smiled as she waited for him to open it. "I know it is not Christmas yet," she said. "But I wanted you to have this now."

Bartholomew tore open the package. Inside was a wooden flute. More than just a toy, this one was a real flute. He held it in his hands timidly. Then he looked disbelievingly at her.

"Yes," she said. "Go ahead and play it. "I have brought over a music teacher from England. Would you like to learn music?"

The boy nodded his head, but still he said nothing and it was true that he was still thinking. His mother had always been careful about giving him too many gifts. And she taught him that a gift well intended was a gift well given.

"I think you'll make a fine musician," she said. "Will you write a song about me someday?"

"I'll write six songs about you," replied the boy. "And they'll all be different."

The next day came another surprise. Bartholomew came running down the stairs for breakfast. Again his mother was not there. She was sleeping late, said Maria. The King also would not be there as he too was feeling under the weather. Maria said that there was a visitor there to see him and that he was waiting in the great-room. Bartholomew ran as fast as he could as his feet slipped on the newly polished floor. When he got to the great-room he stopped and poked his head around the corner to see who was there.

"It's no use hiding. I see you," came the familiar voice of Uncle Patrick.

Bartholomew ran up to him and threw his arms around him, giving him a big hug. "I thought you would not come," he said. "Tell me the truth now, do you really ride giraffes? I want to know because my dad says that only silly people believe in things like that."

Patrick started to answer, but he had to be careful. He knew how much his brother in-law loved his son and he didn't want to interfere. But he knew how upset he was now and he wondered if his own grief possibly was affecting his judgment. The love of a father for his son was special, but sometimes that love could appear harsh just when tenderness would be most appropriate. Kathryn had invited him knowing how her own condition was changing for the worst. Patrick knew that she had invited him for a reason, a reason that was implied but never spoken. He was there to heal her family.

"I give you my word of honor," said Patrick solemnly. "I have not ridden a giraffe today, and I may not tomorrow."

"You're just saying that," said Bartholomew with a big smile.

"I brought you something," Patrick said. "But you can't open it until Christmas."

"What is it?" Bartholomew asked with growing excitement.

"You really want to know? Do you really want to know what it is? Because if you feel that way about it, well then, in that case you may as well open it right now."

"Well, maybe I better wait for Christmas," Bartholomew said feeling guilty.

"Every day is Christmas!" cried Uncle Patrick. And with that, he reached around his back and brought out a box. "Open it up," he said. "It's all right Bartholomew. I brought you something else for Christmas."

Bartholomew opened the box furiously. Inside were a drum and a set of wooden drum sticks. He looked at his uncle with wonder.

"It never hurts to know more than one thing," Patrick said with a smile.

They talked about music and they talked about giraffes and horses and talking fish. And then Uncle Patrick said something to Bartholomew and he told him never to forget.

"Your imagination is your secret," Uncle Patrick said with a serious look on his face. "But listen Bartholomew, you can hide it inside real things and no one else ever has to know. And the deeper you hide it, the safer it becomes."

Bartholomew watched his uncle with great concentration, and together they were part of the same secret. Uncle Patrick made him feel important and he gave importance to his wandering imagination. Patrick continued.

"Some things you want to hide just for yourself. But then, if you ever want to go back to that place again you know where it is. This is not a bad thing Bartholomew. We all do it. This is how we hide things and still keep them close to our heart."

"I always thought secrets were bad," Bartholomew replied.

"Secrets that cause pain are bad," said Uncle Patrick. "But secrets that hide pain are not bad. Do you understand?"

Bartholomew nodded tentatively as he wasn't as fast to understand as Uncle Patrick thought he was.

"You will know many secrets in your life, Bartholomew. Some of them will be told to you and some of them you will learn. You must look into your heart to know which secrets are bad and which secrets be best hidden. The Lord has designed our hearts so that we will be able to make this distinction. In truth, this is what makes us all children of God."

"Do you believe in ghosts?" asked Bartholomew, but in his heart he already knew what the answer would be.

Patrick hesitated. In his own heart he knew that this was the reason he was here, this was the reason he was called. His sister Kathryn had trusted him with something special. He knew that he was being asked to give Bartholomew, Prince Bartholomew, the permission to dream. His heart went out to his sister and nearly broke. He would not let her down.

"I know that ghosts haunt my dreams," he began. "Ghosts haunt my waking life. These ghosts are quiet most of the time, but sometimes when things are quiet, we hear them in the wind and in the rain. But the ghosts that are in our mind are the most real of all, Bartholomew. I have no doubt about them for I see them in my life and in the lives of others. These ghosts are not trying to scare us, Bartholomew, for these ghosts are part of us."

He stopped for a moment as if lost in thought. Bartholomew waited for him to finish because he knew that Uncle Patrick always had something special to say. Patrick looked into his face, the face of innocence, and the memory of his own innocence came back to him and he continued.

"Some people ignore these ghosts, and it is only important that they not see them. Then there are those that see these ghosts everywhere even though they be absent. No man has all the answers, Bartholomew. I am glad that is so, for I prefer to look for ghosts and know that the world is still and will continue to be mysterious. There are those that would try to steal this mystery away from us and turn it into something else. I prefer the mystery. Yes, I do believe in ghosts, Bartholomew."

Later that afternoon Queen Kathryn, Bartholomew's mother, died peacefully in her sleep as the will to call her to heaven was stronger than her own will to live. Her passing was made easier for the King in that she was too weak to fight any longer and succumbed to death even before her final moment.

King Sigmus brought the news to his son. The King was strong, but the strength in his noble face was broken and the anguish and grief that he held broke through his strong exterior. When Bartholomew saw the look on his father's face he was frightened. He knew that something terrible, something beyond words had happened. King Sigmus tried to speak, he tried to tell Bartholomew the news, but he could force no words through his lips, and in truth, a piece of his tender soul was damaged that day.

Later that day when Bartholomew was allowed to see his mother, he could not look into her face. He was so utterly heartbroken that he could not even acknowledge the identity of the body that lay before him. He thought that if he did not look at her, did not see her face and her lifeless eyes, that it would not be so. He thought that maybe it could be avoided. Turning away without looking at her face, he left the room.

The household was in shock. Queen Kathryn was gone. No one noticed as Bartholomew walked past them alone in their private grief and went up to the room his mother used for working on her crafts. Bartholomew went to work. He remembered how his mother taught him to make the special flowers to be used as ornaments. In his mind he could see her still working diligently and lovingly at her favorite pastime. She had told him that she would like to be a rose, and that she would be a rose in God's garden. So, though his grief was profound, Bartholomew put it aside long enough to construct out of paper, a paper rose.

Before the day was finished, Bartholomew asked to see his mother once more because now he wanted to see her face again so that he would never forget her. This time he looked long and hard at her face. She looked different, or so he thought. But in truth, it was that Bartholomew had not noticed her slow, gradual acceptance of death as it destroyed her once beautiful body. Now her beauty was different, it was the beauty of a life well lived and lived with honor. Tears streamed down his face as he removed the paper rose he had made and set it on a table near her body. Then he folded his hands and said a prayer.

"Please God," he began. "Do not let my mother become a flower in your garden. I have made one for you to take, and if you would only bring her back you can have the one I made for you."

When the prayer was finished he left the room and went to his own room. Before blowing out the candle on his nightstand he searched his memory for a memory of his mother that he could take to sleep with him. He searched and searched and searched until he finally fell asleep with tears on his pillow.

He woke late the next morning. When he went downstairs the castle was busy with mourners and close friends coming to pay their last respects. Slowly and cautiously Bartholomew went into the parlor where the body of his mother lay in state. The lid of her coffin was open. When he saw the open lid the expression on his face turned from hope to bitter acceptance and when he looked on the table where he had left the rose, it was still there. But with this new acceptance also came calm as a wave of warmth surged through his face and for just a moment he thought he felt the gentle hands of his mother. Calmly he took the rose and put it in his pocket before leaving.

Bartholomew went to bed that night exhausted from an emotional upheaval that completely drained his energy. All through that long, horrible day he wrestled with emotions that gripped him like a lion. He felt no bitterness, no anger toward God as he had sometimes seen other people do. It was true that God had His own plans, and these plans were a mystery. Uncle Patrick had said that the mystery of life was not for us to know, but only to love. He said another prayer before sleeping for he was ashamed of what he had done.

"Oh Lord," he said. "Please forgive me for trying to trick you. I promise that I will never try to trick you again. My mom was in my garden, but now she is in your garden. Someday I will be a flower in your garden too, but I haven't decided what kind of flower I will be yet. Amen."

Then the boy crawled into bed and thought about his father. The moonlight pierced his window and landed on his face. Tomorrow he would give him a hug.

The Comet

One day Horse-Master Sorren was in the barn shoeing one of his horses from the team. He loved his work as he loved his horses. By pure chance the animal was spooked by a sudden sound carried on the wind. The frightened animal flinched, just a bit, but it was enough to cause Sorren to miss the mark with his hammer-stroke, smashing the hammer into his finger instead of the nail. When Sigmus asked about it, all Sorren would say was, "Tis a fitting punishment for some undeclared sin," and he chuckled knowingly.

One dark and chilly night young Bartholomew was roused from his bed by his father. King Sigmus stood over the sleepy boy of only nine years of age and whispered.

"Come with me, Bartholomew. There is something I want you to see."

The young boy's eyes opened wide and the aging King saw that he had frightened the young boy. He touched his son's cheek with his hand and it was warm. Then he smiled and gave a wink.

"Do not be frightened," he said. "We must not let the light in our eyes destroy the darkness. This is something you will like."

Young Bartholomew slowly crawled out of bed and put his feet into a pair of warm slippers his father held for him. Then he put on a nightgown over his bedclothes and followed his father out of the room. King Sigmus led the way. He carried a candle and the weak light barely illuminated their way through the long corridor of their castle. The boy followed closely behind his father and to the boy it seemed like they were tunneling into the very earth. So strange it was to be lurking around during the dead of night that the boy knew that it had to be something special.

King Sigmus led young Bartholomew through the garden gate. Starlight shone down on the beautiful flagstones enough for them to find their way to the center of the garden where a stone bench faced a grotto of flowers and water-plants. The dense foliage from the garden hedge blocked out most of the light from outside the sanctuary and they sat together in almost pitch blackness. Sigmus went down on one knee. He took Bartholomew's hand and pointed to a position in the sky. A tiny star burned weakly.

"Do you see it?" Sigmus asked.

Bartholomew looked to where his father was pointing. Sigmus was pointing with his finger, but all he could see was a faint star.

"Do you see it?" King Sigmus asked again. "Look closely son. It is not a star."

Then Bartholomew saw that it was indeed different than other stars. This one had a tail and was slowly moving across the sky against the panoply of the other stars. No more than a smudge against the night sky, the boy was fascinated though at first he could not say why.

"What is it, father?" he asked.

King Sigmus and Bartholomew continued to watch the fiery object and the King knew that this was a special moment. This was a moment the young boy would not soon forget.

"The astrologer tells me it is a comet," said the King.

"What is a comet?" Bartholomew asked without taking his eyes off the heavenly object.

"A sign," the King answered. "The astrologer tells me that a comet foretells of the future. See it as it blazes across the sky. This is surely a heavenly event Bartholomew, for it travels across the sky and passes between the spheres."

"What does it say?" the boy asked innocently.

The King laughed softly. Children were often the most charming when they were completely honest. His boy was honest and curious, and the King was proud of him.

"I do not know what it says," he admitted joyfully. "Fortunate is the man that has not learned all the secrets of God. For in truth, were we to know all the secrets of God, we would be too frightened to live."

"Will it hit us?" Bartholomew asked suddenly.

"No, it will not come close enough, unless I am mistaken." said the King. In truth, he was just a little apprehensive about it. "The spheres have been put in place by our Creator," he continued. "The universe is like exquisite clockwork. What it reveals or what it portends, I cannot say. But I do not believe that the Lord would carelessly bring wrath upon his people. Therefore Bartholomew, I choose to believe that it is a sign."

Father and son were quiet. Now the sound of the wind rustled the garden as it slipped through the hedgerow. The King shared a special moment with his son. He thought about his own father and how he wished he could be here to see him now. Finally Bartholomew looked at his father and asked.

"If the universe is really a giant clockwork, what does it do?"

King Sigmus furrowed his brow. He had never thought about it. He had lived his entire life without once ever thinking about the answer to this question.

"The universe doesn't do anything," he answered thoughtfully. "It just is."

Young Bartholomew was too clever to believe such a thing. "I think it must do something," he persisted.

"It is perfect," the King replied. "The astrologer informs me that the precision of the universe is limited only by our own ability to observe it, and that the beauty would only increase with our ability to more accurately observe it. This comet that you and I have witnessed together is a sign. The design of the universe was not invented frivolously, of that you can be sure."

They both watched the comet together and the mind of the King wandered. The gentle whirling and twirling of the night sky always made him feel safe and strangely humble. It seemed to him that the universe was great just the way it was, and it was enough for him just to look at it and be inspired. God had made it perfect and that was good enough for him. Perhaps his son would be different than he, for he was growing old while his son was growing young. Unlike him,

Bartholomew questioned everything. Alas, such was the fate of man that he should seek to understand that which was beyond the scope of his futile mind. Such was the fate of man that such futility should only inspire greater and greater leaps of faith into a new design that was being newly invented and molded from the fragments of destruction. And if he should at last discover the source of truth, what then?

When they were both ready to go back to bed, the King lit the candle and bade Bartholomew to follow quietly. He took him into the castle and down the winding steps into the cellar they went. The King opened a chest and removed a carefully wrapped cake. He smiled when he handed Bartholomew a piece. Then he took one for himself and closed the chest.

"This is a special occasion," he said with genuine mirth. "It's all right, Bartholomew," he said. "We are fresh off an adventure." Then he took a bite and smiled again.

The next morning Bartholomew woke late because he had spent the previous night dreaming about the secrets his father said were hidden in the perfection of the universe. He could not stop thinking about the strange comet and how it could break the design that his father said was perfect. To a boy of nine, such a statement can be a challenge, such a statement only makes him think harder, and his mind would not let it go.

After breakfast, Bartholomew went to the stables to look at the horses. One day soon he would have his own horse and he would give it a name, and the two would explore all the places that were left to explore on the island. Phillip the Horse-Master, charged with taking care of all the horses, was fitting a bridle to one of the carriage-horses, a black mare named Leona.

Bartholomew saw that Phillip was busy, so he went past him without saying a word and went into the stable. Phillip, a mild mannered Manxman, loved horses. He spoke to them tenderly and calmed them during a storm. Phillip liked to bring the horses into the stable so that he could examine them to see that they were healthy, and he could tell you the difference between the different grasses and their particular attributes for feeding horses. Phillip was careful, and it was a fortunate horse that stood beneath his ministering hands. Then he would let them roam in the pasture behind the stable where there was plenty of grass and clover for them to munch on.

The young Bartholomew went to the stall where his favorite pony stood munching on a barrel of oats. He went eagerly to the gate and looked in. The pony paid him no heed.

"I don't know what your name is," he spoke conversationally to the pony. "I'll just call you, Mr. Horse for now."

The pony did not look up or acknowledge his new name, but only continued chewing as if no one were even speaking to it. It did not matter that Bartholomew was a prince, oats were oats and a prince was a prince.

"You don't have to answer," chided Bartholomew warmly. "I know what it is like to be hungry . . . well, sort of."

Mr. Horse was not even a proper horse yet, but only a colt. There would come a time, Bartholomew imagined, when Mr. Horse would prefer to tramp across fields than to be penned up with a barrel of oats for company. The boy reached his hand into the pen and touched the hungry pony who paid not the least amount of attention to the young boy talking nonsense.

"Your hair needs combing," Bartholomew continued.

Then Bartholomew turned around and began searching the stable. There were six pens in three of which horses chomped on oats and hay or merely stood looking at the boy rummaging around. He was looking for a comb with which to groom his favorite horse's mangy mane. Then he saw a wooden bench against the back wall of the stable. There was a window above it and dirty light filtered through the dirty glass and shone upon the work-bench. On the table was a myriad of cutting and shearing and sharpening tools, along with oils and cleaners and ointments in glass containers. He found several brushes on the table and took the one he thought was best for his purpose. Then he went back to the pen where Mr. Horse stood, still focusing all his horse attention on the remaining oats in his barrel.

"Now I'm just going to brush your hair, Mr. Horse," said young Bartholomew innocently. "I know that there is no way for you to comb your own hair, but that is no excuse. Do you hear me, Mr. Horse?"

Bartholomew reached as far into the pen as he could, but he could not reach all the way to Mr. Horse's gnarled mane. The boy grew frustrated until he came up with another idea. Carefully he climbed onto the railing that kept the horse from escaping. As he did this he remembered his father's instructions for him not to play near the horses. His father had said that he was too young and that he could easily be hurt, for horses were ignorant animals. Bartholomew told himself that he would be careful and that his father surely would not object if he promised to be careful. How could his father say that horses were ignorant animals? Horses were good animals. Besides, all he wanted to do was comb his hair, and that was not really playing, was it?

Now the boy was able to reach the thick mane of the pony. He sunk the comb into the thick hair and tried to pull it through, but the hair was very tangled and the comb would not go through. He pulled down harder on the comb and suddenly he lost his balance and fell headlong into the pen still holding the comb. Mr. Horse was startled by the yanking on his mane and the presence of a boy falling into his pen. The horse became nervous and started to panic. Bartholomew tried to get to his feet as the horse started bucking in his pen. Bartholomew realized that he was about to be trampled to death and tried to climb out of the pen, and that is when Mr. Horse reared and threw his hindquarter into the boy, breaking his leg. Bartholomew cried out as he fell safely outside the pen. When Phillip came racing into the stable his heart broke for Bartholomew and his heart broke for the horse, because he knew who would be blamed.

The doctor finished checking the bandages on young Bartholomew's leg. Then he told the boy how lucky he was not to have been hurt more severely. King Sigmus stood near the window and waited for the doctor to leave. Then he came up to the bed and looked sternly at his son. His face was stern but also charged with concern.

"You are lucky," he reiterated. "What were you thinking? Did I not tell you to stay away from the horses?"

"I'm sorry," Bartholomew pleaded, and he knew that he had done something wrong. "I just wanted to comb his hair," he cried.

"You need to think about what you have done," said the King. "It is Phillip's job to care for the horses. He was not there when you were hurt." The King hesitated before finishing his sentence. Then he said. "I am going to give you a choice, Bartholomew. You will be punished, or Phillip will be punished in your place. The choice is yours. When I return, I will expect an answer." Then he quickly and confidently left his son's room.

The door closed and young Bartholomew watched it sadly and knew that when it opened again, he would be different and that he would be changed. He loved, Phillip. The last thing he ever wanted to do was to get him into trouble. He never should have disobeyed his father. And then a strange thought occurred to him. The sign that he and his father saw in the sky came back to him now. God knew everything that he would ever do and everything that he had ever done. Perhaps the sign was meant for him to remind him that he could never escape the consequences of his actions, and that in a perfectly designed world God could still do anything he wanted.

When the door opened again, he had made up his mind. King Sigmus stood next to the bed and looked down expectantly.

"Have you thought about what I said?" he asked.

Bartholomew did his best to sit up in bed, but the cast on his leg and the dull pain that permeated his entire body made it difficult. Propping himself on one elbow he did his best to look dignified when he said.

"I wish for you to punish me and not Phillip," he said with resolution.

King Sigmus withheld a smile though he was very proud of his son at this moment. He withheld a smile because there was still one more thing for him to do, and he did it now with uneasiness, a trepidation that he was unaccustomed with.

"I have thought about what your punishment should be," he said, trying to sound fatherly and kingly at the same time. "It should serve you best, and my punishment for you is that you should decide the proper discipline to be given to Phillip."

Bartholomew felt sudden pain in the pit of his stomach and the blood drained from his face. So unprepared he was for this that he could not even think of a way to respond but only stared at his father incredulously.

The King was conscious of the effect his words were having on his son, but he fought back the urge to temper them just yet. He continued speaking as if his young son were not in pain.

"The duties of a King are often mysterious and difficult to ascertain, and oftentimes your judgment must be your own moral compass. A King does not wish to punish his own people, Bartholomew. He does it because he must, do you understand?"

Bartholomew looked at his father and his eyes began to grow moist. His father truly was a King, and he was just a boy. His indiscretion now seemed so trivial compared to the vicissitudes and decisions that had to be made by a King.

"Do you see now, Bartholomew why it must be so? You could easily have been killed. You disobeyed my instruction to your own detriment. And who was it that was supposed to protect you?"

"I only wanted to comb his hair," Bartholomew said tearfully.

Then King Sigmus knelt down by the bed next to his son and took his hand. Now his eyes were moist too. He loved his son so much that it was sometimes difficult to teach him. The King squeezed his hand warmly.

"You are forgiven," he said softly. "I only wanted you to understand how the judgment of a parent can sometimes seem strict or harsh, but it is from love that it is given. It is not easy to punish, Bartholomew. But there will come a day when you will be called upon to deal out punishment. Do it from love . . . never from anger, Bartholomew."

Young Bartholomew reached up and put his arms around his father. He hugged him tenderly and took comfort from his strength. Someday he would have to live up to the expectations that were implied by his birthright and he knew he would need help. Then he let go of his father and asked.

"Why did you show me the comet, father? Did you know it was there all along? Did you know that I was going to break my leg?"

King Sigmus laughed heartily. He laughed because it was so much like his son and he laughed for himself because he was so happy.

"How wise do you think I am?" he asked with a smile. "No," he said, still smiling. "I think that was a warning of another kind. I think that even the Lord sometimes must discipline His children and He allowed you to break your leg out of love. No, I think the warning was for someone else."

"I do not like these mysteries," said the boy.

"Everything is a mystery, Bartholomew. To the Lord, everything is as one, but we must wait for the end."

The Monk's Bridge
(An Old Legend)

"Tell me the story about the Monk's Bridge," Iona said. "I love to hear you talk about the bridge."

"Alright," King Sigmus answered. "I'll tell you about it, Iona. But you must remember that I was not there at the time."

Iona smiled and waited for the story to begin. She knew how much the King liked to talk, but she also knew that the moment must be right . . . A story can only begin at the right moment, or any magic the story may have had would be lost.

"I was not there at the time," the King repeated for effect, "for how old do you think that I am?"

Iona laughed and clapped her hands together. "300," she said with a wink.

Sigmus wagged his finger at her playfully. "Now then," he began. "Let me tell you the story about the bridge, but mind your manners Iona, and do not make me laugh."

Legends surrounding the Crossag Bridge or *little bridge* as it has come to be known, dating back to the time of its construction in 1349 by the Order of Cistercian Monks, are many and are filled with much hearsay and rumor. The abbey supports itself partially with the yields of its farm and winery. Sheep are raised for their precious wool, some of which is used to make the white habits worn by the brethren of the Order; the vellum is used for writing the words that belong to the Order. The bridge was constructed to allow the packhorses to cross the Silverburn, a gently meandering river which flows from St. Marks and empties into the sea at Castletown. Carts laden and overflowing with vegetables constantly went across the uneven flagstones of the narrow bridge, and the slow creaking was the sound of the lives of most of the devout monks bent over in the fields doing honest work for the Abbot and for the Lord.

It was said that the sound of the Lord could be heard in the sound of heavy, fragrant, slowly-turning earth and the sound of roots being loosened from the soil. The vigorous monks in their quaint monastery lived on an island within an island, isolating themselves from the outside that they may live fully on the inside as a prayer is uttered in the naked darkness to one that is outside of all but inside of everything.

Brother Martin crawled on his hands and knees through the vegetable patch weeding and tending to the tender shoots. His large hands were gentle and delicate for such tedious work and the sweat beaded on his brow, but his devotion made such work for him a joy. He wore his monk's habit, soiled and dirty from working in the sun and heat. After working in the field he would wash up and don a clean habit. Rows and rows of onions and leeks and carrots and radishes grew together in separate rows where they could be watched closely. The monks also grew large leafed vegetables in another part of the field. Brother Martin liked to work beneath the soil, so he preferred to tend the roots.

Alongside Brother Martin was Brother Anthony, a small, darting man with quick movements and wandering eyes. Brother Anthony was always looking to see what was happening elsewhere, and sometimes he would miss a weed or fail to see a damaged leaf that needed tending. Sometimes he would pass by plants that could have been saved if only his attention had been singular. Instead, his mind wandered. And though he worked hard and devoted his time to God, his mind many times wandered from the soil to fields that existed far away from the gentle abbey. Some of the fields that his mind wandered into were dangerous fields that were wild and untended. Brother Anthony tended the wild fields of his imagination. His imagination was planted with strange and mythical plants.

The rows were planted close together and the space between the rows was only enough for a diligent monk to crawl through. And so the busy monks would bend their backs to the work and be completely hidden from view by the stems and stalks and rising foliage of the various plants. When Brother Martin and Brother Anthony were side by side on adjacent sides of the vegetable rows Brother Anthony thrust his head between the thick foliage and whispered.

"Have you heard about the bridge?"

His voice was so soft and so low that Brother Martin at first thought it was the sound of his own prayers he was silently reciting to himself.

"Brother Martin, Brother Martin?" he called. "They must not be allowed to build the bridge."

Brother Martin stopped working. Someone was speaking to him and he was slightly annoyed. Speech was strictly forbidden for all but the most necessary conversation. Idle talk was discouraged and disrespectful. The rules of St. Benedict were closely followed, the rules about unnecessary speech in particular.

"Brother Martin, I must speak to you about the bridge."

Brother Martin recognized the rat-like face of his brother and he recognized his voice because not all talk was forbidden. Brother Anthony continued whispering and his voice was rising with the intensity of his excitement.

"Brother Martin! The bridge will bring supernatural spirits from outside. Beware, Brother Martin that we may bridge the gap between the spheres of heaven and earth and suffer great punishment."

Brother Martin maintained his silence in spite of the urgency clearly coming from Brother Anthony. He did his best to ignore the entreaties of his fellow monk and not break his own vow with a careless word. In a few moments he was crawling away in search of new weeds to unearth and for the moment his anxiety was over.

The next morning and the morning after he was approached covertly and spoken to by Brother Anthony as he tended the fields. Each time he heard protestations about a new bridge that was being built by the isolated order of monks. Brother Anthony was terrified that the building of the bridge would bring terrible consequences.

And then, one night while the monks slept, Brother Martin was gently roused from sleep by Brother Anthony. He had his finger to his lips to admonish the startled monk from crying out. Then he pointed with his finger to the door and motioned for Brother Martin to follow quietly. It was strictly forbidden to do so, but finally Brother Martin could stand the constant harassment from Brother Anthony no longer, and he followed. Quietly leaving the sleeping monastery without being noticed, they were soon outside in the crisp evening air. When they were safely away from the monastery, Brother Anthony spoke.

"It is safe to speak here, Brother Martin. No one will hear us."

"What is the meaning of this?" Brother Martin answered angrily, while still trying to keep his voice down. "We will surely be severely punished for this."

"Not if you do not tell," Brother Anthony said with certainty. "No one will hear us and no one will suspect a thing."

"Speak quickly for my patience is short and your manner is vulgar and overbearing. I do not like being distracted in my work when we are in the fields. Tell me now what is so important that you must seize me in the middle of the night and tempt me to break my vows."

"You will see," said Brother Anthony. "For three nights now I have seen it with my own eyes, and now you will see."

"What have you seen?" said Brother Martin impassively. "I am anxious to return to bed."

"We have a visitor to our little bridge, Brother Martin. Did I not tell you that to build a bridge would bring danger?"

"What danger, and what visitor do you speak of?"

"Come," said Brother Anthony. "I will show you."

The impudent monks walked together in the moonlight. The path from the monastery led them through a grove of thick coniferous trees planted by the founding order of monks in the last century to mark the territory ceded to them in their official charter. Quietly and carefully, Brother Anthony led them through the darkness. Moonbeams splintered through the trees like needles, tickling the creaking trees to life in the eerie silence. Then he suddenly stopped and pointed ahead to the bridge that could just be seen dimly in the waning light. They came at last to the place where the little bridge, built with the very stones quarried for the monastery, innocently spanned the meandering Silverburn with its high, narrow arch.

"Look on the bridge. Do you see it, Brother Martin?"

The figure of a man, shrouded in a long, woolen cloak, stood alone atop the bridge. In his right hand he held forth a burning lamp, enclosing himself within the warm spectral glow.

"It's the Lord," whispered Brother Anthony. "He has been coming here every night. I think something is about to happen."

Brother Martin looked at Brother Anthony with confusion. "How do you know that is the Lord?" he asked warily, for he secretly feared the answer.

"Keep quiet now," answered Brother Anthony sternly. "You will see."

And then they heard the sound like the earnest swishing of sails being filled with billowy wind and like the wispy fluttering of great and prodigious wings within vast volumes of air being displaced in elegant and nimble strength. Then, gracefully descending from above, an enormous creature lighted upon the stone bridge where the mysterious man stood waiting. A moment later a second messenger descended from above and a secret meeting was convened on the bridge in the glimmering darkness made luminous by the brilliant emanations of lamplight. The light shone upon the airy messengers, and like a translucent membrane passed right through the upright wings as if they were made from slight, mellifluous flesh of heavenly firmament conceived.

The late night conference was finished and one of the messengers suddenly took flight and with a tremendous updraft ascended and disappeared into the starlight heavens. The second messenger remained a moment longer and was given to further speech until at last it too ascended into heaven with an upward bound. Now the bridge was deserted but for the solitary being alone within its own sympathetic radiance. The man, if indeed it truly such be, stood motionless in fixed meditation. At last the lamp extinguished and now the figure remained illuminated with an inner radiance that was blinding and glorious.

The following night Brother Martin lay awake in his bed after his prayers, thinking about the strange events of the previous night. He laid quietly, neither turning about in his bed or mumbling and uttering strange sounds like some of his brethren sleeping beside him. Then he noticed by the dim candle-light, Brother Anthony craftily slip out of his bed and leave the room unobtrusively. A few minutes later, Brother Martin also slipped out of bed and followed Brother Anthony because he had no doubt about where he was going.

Fortuitously, the sky was slightly darker than the previous evening and the extra darkness allowed Brother Martin to get closer to the bridge than he otherwise would have been comfortable with for fear of being discovered. For the second night in a row now he had disobeyed the rules of the Abbot by leaving the abbey at night, but he was not thinking about the consequences of his disobedience just now, though the punishment could and often times was quite severe for those few monks that sometimes ventured out. He firmly believed that Brother Anthony was concealing something important from him and he was sure that there was more yet to be revealed if only he kept his guard over him.

The moon was waning. Brother Martin hid in a thicket and peered through the dim light. He could see Brother Anthony standing on the bridge. The monk was alone but he paced back and forth with unusual trepidation as if he was expecting something to happen, and when it did, Brother Martin was not surprised.

Once again the sound of rushing air was followed by the lithe and graceful descent of another messenger angel. The angel spoke with Brother Anthony though the sound of their voices was lost in the intervening darkness. Their meeting was brief and soon the angel took flight again, leaving Brother Anthony alone. Brother Martin returned to the abbey in earnest, lest he be discovered by the object of his scrutiny.

The next night and the following night Brother Martin observed Brother Anthony stealing away into the night only to return again several hours later. Brother Martin tried to forget about the strange and haunting manifestation, but the more he tried to free his mind from the sight of angels, the stronger became the temptation to return to the bridge. He had told no one else about the manifestation and it was certain that this also was a sin, but he was determined to allow one sin to conceal another, more serious sin of which he was unable to control. Finally, when he could resist the temptation no longer, he escaped once again into the night and returned to the bridge. Crawling on his hands and knees through the bushes, he poked his head through the foliage and beheld a ghastly sight that would prove to be a turning point in his, all too short, life.

As before, Brother Anthony was standing on the bridge talking with the messenger angel. He stood in front of the angel and his back was facing toward Brother Martin. The angel towered over the gaunt monk made thin by a life of paltry, unsavory vegetables and tepid broth, digging in the dirt and searching the rows and rows of wilted vegetables for answers. Several feet taller than the monk, the angel had the bearing of authority and was a commanding presence in the pale starlight. Brother Martin felt a tightening in his throat. The air was charged with tension. His mouth quivered as the essence of fear permeated the very atmosphere with heaviness and dread. Though he wanted to escape, he could not take his eyes away from Brother Anthony and the uneasiness he felt as visceral pain.

And then without an inkling or subtle indication that anything was about to happen, Brother Anthony let his cassock fall to the ground and his nakedness became manifest in the star-lit darkness. The angel spread its sinuous wings and wrapped them around the naked body of the apostate monk, completely enveloping him in an amorous embrace. Brother Martin was horrified and frightened. Scrambling to his feet he ran as fast as he could back to the safety and protective arms of the monastery.

The next day while he labored in the field, Brother Martin thought that he heard the sound of whispering. He was too ashamed to search out the source of the sound, and he could only but keep his head down and not let the shame on his face show. Later that day while he busily harvested leeks from the rich soil he heard the familiar voice of Brother Anthony. Suddenly Brother Anthony thrust his head through the vegetable row and smiled broadly, proudly, and there was the slightest trace of lecherousness in his sated expression. Now, far superior to his fellow monks working lonely fields, sowing lonely lives for their lonely souls, he could barely hide his condescension. Brother Anthony's eyes were swollen and there was a sodden puffiness around his noxious mouth now stretched with a wicked grin.

"Did you see enough to satisfy yourself?" he asked.

"How did you know I was there?" Brother Martin whispered.

"The angel saw you," Brother Anthony replied coarsely. "She told me that you were there watching."

Brother Martin whispered to himself. "An angel cannot be a woman." Then he looked into Brother Anthony's face and condemned him. "You have committed a great evil," he said.

"Follow me tonight," he answered. "Follow me tonight and I will show you something even more beautiful."

Suddenly Brother Martin slammed his face into the dirt with such violent force that he became wobbly from the concussion and nearly swooned. Then he did it again before looking at Brother Anthony with confusion and a glazed expression. Brother Anthony quickly retreated as his fellow monk slammed his face into the dirt again.

Distinguished by their brown tunics, several lay brothers worked the fields along with the monks from the Order. They were not attached to the canonical office of the Order and could come and go as they pleased. Uneducated and mostly peasants, the many lay brothers that helped in the fields were educated in another office, the office of gossip. They were secular by nature and worked in the fields for money and so they were not often with occasion to speak with the religious monks only to disturb them from the lofty flight of their thoughts. Mostly they talked among themselves in hushed tones. They talked about sheep and carrots and sorcery.

This morning the peasants were in a stir amongst themselves. They were discussing something anxiously and they would occasionally pass knowing glances to the quiet monks working the fields unaware of the horrific discovery. One of the humblest peasants repeatedly made the sign of the cross and uttered silent prayers.

Brother Martin was working the field that morning and he was close enough to hear fragments of conversation between the excited lay brothers. A monk, one of their own, had been found in the Silverburn just beneath the little bridge. It looked like he had fallen according to those that had found him, but no one knew why he was there, whether he had fallen or whether he had jumped. Brother Anthony was not in his bed this morning and he was not present during Matins or breakfast. Brother Martin knew whose body had been found even without hearing the name.

That entire day Brother Martin could not prevent his mind from fixing on the events leading up to Brother Anthony's death. He prayed, but even his prayers were interrupted by pangs of conscience and remorse, as if in some way he was partially responsible, and were it not for his intransigent silence, Brother Anthony would still be alive. At Vespers, he could not command his own thoughts and his prayers were forced and insincere, for his mind had taken flight.

Brother Martin stood alone on the little bridge and prayed. It was after midnight and the stars were bright but for the patchy fog that rolled across the sky in waves. Completely overwhelmed by his experience, he could concentrate on nothing else now and his only thought was to see the angels and to speak with them and to know them. From them he would learn much about the secret places and secret hidden things of this world only too cleverly hidden from men.

The air was cold and damp. He waited and would continue to wait all night if need be. After about an hour of pacing the narrow bridge lost in lofty meditation, he saw a light; the light was moving along the path leading to the bridge. Then he recognized the figure of a man that walked solemnly and carried a lamp and he knew that this was the same man seen by Brother Anthony and himself. The man walked up to where Brother Martin stood and the lamp shone with such a glare that he could not see the face of the man nor even his features but that they were hidden behind an aura that surrounded his entire body. Then He spoke.

"How many vows will you break this day?" He asked sympathetically. His voice was not angry or intolerant, but mild and compassionate.

Brother Martin stared and tried to see through the dense light, for he wanted to see His face. Brother Anthony had said that it was the Lord. How could he know such a thing?

"Will you keep your silence now, young man? Is your vow now suddenly so important to you? Silence is a good thing, but you must listen to your heart for it is pure. The Lord's heart beats in all men."

"Who are you?" asked Brother Martin fearfully for a dreadful realization was awakening in his blood. "I cannot see your face."

"You could not look upon my face," the man answered. "I carry a light that others may find me."

"Are you a messenger?" Brother Martin asked weakly.

"I am a *message*," He replied.

Something ignited in Brother Martin's soul. So powerful was the surge that no mortal man can endure. The monk collapsed. "Forgive me!" he cried as he fell prostrate on the bridge in front of the man and wept bitter tears. "Strike me dead," he pleaded. "I am not worthy to be in your presence."

"Your Brother Anthony begged to be forgiven and to be saved. And yet, you beg to be destroyed. Is your sin so much greater than was his sin?"

"My sin is great," the monk pleaded with great difficulty. "My soul is rotten with sin for I am too weak to resist temptation. I run from sin but yet it seeks me out and strikes me at night with such tenderness that I am corrupted with thoughts of serenity and peace."

"Your soul is silent, and yet you speak. Instead, let your soul rejoice, for it pleases the Lord to hear men sing. It is good to live away from other men, but remember, the heartbeat of the world faintly beats in the hearts of men and a cold heart beats with the icy blood of separateness and separation. Though men may walk different paths, they don't live apart, and though the heavens turn above you, all men walk together."

Brother Martin would not raise his head and only tried to burrow down deeper into the stone as if the stone would hide his shame. He felt nothing. All bodily sensations were cut off and all that existed was his shame, his terrible shame.

"Rise, Martin, for you are not a worm. Go from here and sin no more, for even as I carry a lamp, so shall you become a lamp. If you want to keep your vow, speak only to me and you shall not want for speech, for silence is the language of God and the language of God lacks nothing."

And so it was that Brother Martin returned to the monastery that night and thereafter he had many conversations with the Lord, but to another man not another word did he ever utter again and the fruit on his lips was from another tree. The Abbot, when he saw Brother Martin's visage, knew that he was in a state of grace and he commanded that no one speak to Brother Martin unless he first broke his silence. Some of the brethren thought that Brother Martin had become a holy fool, for they had no personal knowledge of his new state of grace. But there were rumors that continued to develop about Brother Martin, rumors that would become legend after his short life on earth was ended.

It was said by some of the lay brothers and even by some of the monks from the order that Brother Martin was filled with an inner spirit that poured from his body like light and that to be in his presence one could feed off the always present calmness of his soul and be thus calmed as his calmness extended from his body like an aureole. Others said it was a state of grace and that Brother Martin must have done something to please the Lord.

Brother Martin humbly worked in the field until the end of his life, pruning, nurturing and giving life to the tender vegetables in his care. If anything, he became more humble as his reputation grew. Some thought of him as a mystic, and the Abbot never tried to dissuade those that came to the abbey just to be near him if only for an hour. After several years Brother Martin retired to a small hut near the little bridge, and there he lived an ascetic and sparing life like the anchorites and pillar dwellers of old.

Accounts of Brother Martin's death differ slightly, and though there is no definitive written record of his death, there is agreement about one thing in particular. It is taken as fact that Brother Martin knew the exact day if not hour of his death, and he went to it gratefully and gracefully like an expecting groom to his wedding.

On the day that Brother Martin died he was spotted walking across the little bridge, now known as *The Monk's Bridge*, in deference to Brother Martin about whom this legend still exists. Small birds flew around him and lit on his shoulder. Brother Martin seemed to be expecting something and he paced thoughtfully. He spoke to the birds in a strange language and he would hold out his hand tenderly that they may perch. Soon other creatures appeared from all around and gathered around the bridge on which he stood like a divine orator. He blessed the creatures and bid them farewell. It was the first time he had spoken in several years and now his voice was strange and otherworldly as if he spoke with different ears and different tongue. Then, the surprised monks saw Brother Martin say one last prayer, a prayer to the world. He whispered a faint prayer in the direction of Jerusalem. Then he sat down on the cold stone bridge and went to sleep. Many hours later, when Brother Martin did not move, they checked on him. He was no longer among the living. And so it was said that he left for heaven on that day and that he had come to greet his own escort. Clutched tightly in his hand was found his most precious possession. None could say what it was, for to the ignorant eye it was nothing but a nail.

The rest of that fateful day was filled with another supernatural joy, for the animals and small creatures came to gather around the solitary bridge in a last act of respect for their friend as if the passing of Brother Martin had sent a shock through the rich and fertile land that was felt in another plane of existence. The monks from the abbey could only watch with wonder and speculate about the strange bird that had flown from his nest, for our home is but a nest and one day we must all leave its comfort and take flight.

Hagen the Woodchopper

"On the Continent are vast forests of primeval gloom and utter impenetrability. The forest is growing, breathing, thinking . . . The people are afraid to go into these forests alone. Fear of the unknown is the most frightening, visceral fear known to man. And so it was that large groups of woodchoppers roamed the antediluvian forest and tamed the wild places, but some of the wildness they kept for themselves."

King Sigmus laughed heartily and slapped Baron Mc Mallory on the back. "Vast armies of woodchoppers you say? Just imagine a woodchopper on my little island. Now that is an idea."

Now when King Bartholomew was a little boy he liked to wander all over his castle grounds, which was actually more like a small village, and watch the different people performing their particular deeds. One of his favorite people to watch was Hagen the Woodchopper. It was true that Hagen the Woodchopper worked with his back, but he had special knowledge that no one else had, and he liked to talk while he chopped and chopped and chopped. Hagen the Woodchopper looked just like a woodchopper, which is why some folks thought he turned his occupation to the chopping of wood. No one really knew for sure however, because Hagen the Woodchopper was very reclusive and quiet, until he came to his occupation of chopping wood and then he would not stop talking.

Hagen loved to chop wood. He knew everything there was to know, and it is certain that there was nothing left to be known about wood and saws and axes and splitting, growing, harvesting, pruning, and burning. Hagen the Woodchopper was the preeminent woodchopper and there was no discussion about it. It is true that he also had a vast knowledge of tree lore. Ask anyone which was the best tree to gather warmth from, ask anyone which tree was the best to cook food with, in short, ask anyone which was the best tree to hang a witch from and Hagen, the Woodchopper would know the answer.

Not prodigious in height, Hagen was stout, brawny, and prodigious in girth. He had hair black as a raven, a full, ratty beard that was always collecting food and insects. His eyes, the color of coal, were distant and mostly devoid of intelligence, but he had a heart that could make up for all his shortcomings. It was said that King Sigmus hired him one day when a large fallen tree blocked the road and his carriage could not pass. Hagen the Woodchopper was just passing by when he saw the tree, and quick as the devil after service, he chopped the tree to pieces and cleared the way for the King. From that day forward, Hagen the Woodchopper had been pronounced woodchopper to the House of Sigmus . . . and he also caught rats in his leisure time away from sharp tools and sawdust.

Young Bartholomew first came to know of the woodchopper when his father took him along one morning to witness a new cutting technique developed by Hagen. Local woodchoppers all agreed that Hagen could chop wood like no other; there was not his equal to be found on the isle. The wood that he chopped was the most fragrant, pleasing not only to the eye but to the nose, wood that anyone had ever encountered. It was magical. His secret was carefully guarded, but to the young Bartholomew he admitted that, "only a warm heart can guide a cold axe."

Most of the good people that inhabit the isle are poor, but there is no dishonor for them to have to go without luxuries. In truth, there are no luxuries on the Isle of Man. Hagen, it was universally known, did not chop wood with the aim of living princely or with the intention of saving enough money to leave the island. He was quite literally, in his glory to live on this small island, and he would never want to leave as long as there was wood to chop.

One day while Prince Bartholomew was talking to Hagen as he went about his business, a business that had no set hours to worry about, he told the young boy a tale. He loved to talk to the boy because he was so curious to know all the things that most folk only wanted to keep secret because they were uninterested or because they were afraid to think about it. And the boy knew how to listen. Some other boys only wanted to talk and to brag all about their own adventures, but not Bartholomew. He wanted to hear adventures that were not like the adventures of the other boys his age.

It was: "A tale of the trees," to use his own words. "The trees are sacred," he said. "And do you know why?"

Prince Bartholomew could only shake his head and wait for an answer.

The young Prince was nine years old. He had deep blue eyes the color of an ocean and beautiful blonde hair that veritably shone in the light of day. He was a bright boy, forever curious.

"It is because the trees hold the precious souls of children," said Hagen the Woodchopper.

Bartholomew gasped. His mouth fell open and he stared at the woodchopper thunderstruck, but enchanted and eager to hear more. Hagen looked around to make sure that no one else would hear, and then he said.

"It happened very long ago that a boy, just about your age, was lost in the forest. The people could not find the boy because he had climbed up into a tree to hide from evil spirits. The boy was so scared that he could not speak and he could not hear and he could not come down from the tree. Sadly, the boy was not found in time. He died right there in the forest, but the trees were so upset, the trees were so heartbroken by the death of the young boy that they would not let his soul escape. They captured it and kept it safe, and so it is with all children that are lost in the forest. The forest does not protect the old and mature people that have lived a life happily. The trees protect the souls of the innocent, that they may live and experience the sound of birds and the feel of the wind. The forest is alive with the beautiful spirits of the children."

Then Hagen the Woodchopper hefted the axe high above his head and with one powerful stroke, split the log that he had prepared. Bartholomew was not afraid to hear such stories, and though they were sad, he thought them wonderful and they made him smile. Bartholomew was still smiling when he asked Hagen.

"Can you talk to trees?"

"I can talk to the trees," said Hagen with a wink. "But they don't talk back. I needs to guess what they want, for that is the job of a woodchopper."

"Are the trees really alive?" the boy asked sincerely. He knew that there were people living on the island that believed some things his father said never to believe, so he hoped that this was something that would be all right.

Hagen the Woodchopper lifted his tremendous leg and set it down on the log he was working. Putting his axe on the ground he scratched his face and pulled out a woodchip from his beard. He continued to scratch as he was thinking because scratching always helped him to think. Finally, he said.

"Everything is alive . . . in one way or another, even the trees. I'm not an expert on life, my boy, but it seems to me that there's a different kind of life, for life talks, and that is true. There's the life we can hear, like the birds and the animals, and then there's life that we don't hear, like the trees."

"Then how do the trees talk?" Bartholomew persisted. He wanted to know. He was sure that Hagen the Woodchopper knew the answer.

"They know," said the woodchopper. "They know it in their roots. They have roots that reach into other places," he continued, peering thoughtfully into Bartholomew's eyes. "They can feel the wind and they can hear the sounds that float through their branches. Their branches get smaller and smaller that they may hear fainter and fainter sounds, and they reach everywhere that they may know all things."

Bartholomew stood there with his mouth hanging open. He knew it! He knew that if he just asked, Hagen the Woodchopper would know.

"Look at my hands," said Hagen. "They are as callous as boot leather and as delicate as the wings of a sparrow. They got this way from work, for work is my life. The same way that the tree can know a thing through the wind and through its roots, so it is that I can know a thing through my hands, and when I put my hands to a tree, I know it."

One day when Bartholomew was in the stable watching a horse being shod, the cobbler said something curious. The cobbler was a decent enough fellow when he was silent, but sometimes when he came to talking he would plant bitter seeds where the soil was ripe. Bartholomew watched him closely as he filed the hoof, checked it with his fingers, and then nailed the new shoes on a black mare.

"Does that hurt?" said Bartholomew as the cobbler tapped the last nail into place.

Ed the cobbler looked at Bartholomew and smiled. "Doesn't hurt a bit," he said. "Don't know how the horse feels about it though."

Bartholomew laughed. Then he jumped up onto a railing that separated the horses and swung his feet under him.

"Do you talk to horses?" he asked politely. "Hagen the Woodchopper talks to trees."

"Had a horse one day, and he tells me that Hagen likes to chop more than just trees." And then he nodded his head agreeing with himself. "That's what I hear," he said looking serious and grave.

"What do you mean?" Bartholomew cried out with panic in his voice.

Ed the cobble put his hand on Bartholomew's head and messed up his perfectly combed hair, and then he sniggered. "I'm just teasing you," he said. "I'm sure that Hagen is a fine fellow."

"Hagen the Woodchopper knows more about trees than anyone else in the world," said Bartholomew now trying to defend Hagen against any doubters that would say something bad about him. He was sure that Ed the cobbler was making fun of Hagen, and that just wasn't right.

"You think so," said Ed the cobbler shoving a well-chewed pipe between his teeth and lighting a bowl of tobacco. Then he blew out a cloud of blue smoke and took the pipe out of his mouth. "Them woodchoppers is a tricky lot. All day with them sharp tools, cutting, hacking, chopping to pieces, it's enough to drive a good man to drink."

"Hagen the Woodchopper likes to drink pints of ale from Castletown. He told me so."

"See what I mean," said the cobbler.

One day Bartholomew spoke to the stonemason that was fixing the wall circling the castle. He stood there with a look of thoughtful concentration and there were numbers moving inside his head. Bartholomew mistook the stonemason's silent absorption for one of boredom, so he asked.

"Why does everyone do something different?" he asked politely because he didn't want to bother the man even though he smiled and seemed kind enough in his tranquility. "Someday I want to know everything, and then I won't have to ask anyone for help."

"That is a nice thought," said the stonemason. He didn't mind being bothered and welcomed a break even if it was just for a moment of conversation with a precocious child. "But if you know how to do everything, you may just not be really good at anything. Sometimes it takes a very long time to learn a thing, so how much longer to learn everything?"

"Maybe," Bartholomew agreed half-heartedly. "You could be right. I'll have to ask Hagen the Woodchopper to see what he thinks about it."

"Hagen the Woodchopper?" the man said curiously.

Do you know him?" Bartholomew asked.

"Not in the least," said the stonemason. "He's not the one that chopped up his wife, now is he? But, tell me lad, how hard can it be to split a log in half? Don't look for answers from the likes of woodchoppers if you want my advice," and then he stood up and resumed thinking.

Bartholomew went away feeling sad. Why did no one see the goodness of Hagen the Woodchopper? Why did everyone want to put him down? He went home and asked his father about it.

King Sigmus finished talking to a tall man with a book in one hand and a pen in the other hand. The man made a notation in the book, then nodded. He bid him farewell, then he turned to his son.

"How are you today?" he asked. "I have not seen you for hours."

"I've been talking," he said as if that would be enough for his father to know exactly what he had been doing. "Will Hagen the Woodchopper come back soon?"

"Hagen comes and goes as he pleases," Sigmus answered. "I let him do what he wants to do, unless I need him for something specific."

"Why do some people not trust him?" Bartholomew asked. "Some people say bad things about him."

"Hagen is a strange bird," King Sigmus agreed. "That is why I like him so much, Bartholomew. "He goes into the forest with his cart and is gone sometimes for days. Some people get to thinking, and the more they think, the greater becomes their mistrust. I don't know why, except that they don't like it when people are different than they are. Do you understand what I am saying, son?"

"Would they want everyone to be the same?" asked Bartholomew innocently.

His father smiled because he knew that it was a very important question. He wanted his son to learn things on his own, but he had to be careful lest he become impetuous and overbearing as he got older.

"Next time I see him, I'll invite him up to the house for lemonade," said the King. "I expect that Hagen is around somewhere."

And so he was. Hagen the Woodchopper drove his cart into the forest and disappeared into the darkness. The large, wooden wheels creaked and his cart rocked back and forth as he slowly went deeper and deeper into the trees. His horse was old, he was old, and it seemed to Hagen that the best things in life were old. He wanted to protect the memories of his craft against the invasion of those that would take it away from him and not show the same respect for his knowledge. That is why he went away from people, so that they would not pry into his business and make it their own. Then he stopped the cart and got out to look at a large tree. He smiled because he knew the tree.

He went into his cart and took out a small saw. Before him was a magnificent rowan tree, *witchwood*, the *bird catcher*. One of the nine sacred woods burned by ancient druids in [13]Beltane fires atop isolated hilltops on May Eve, the rowan tree was guarded by ancient dragons to protect against incursions from the *Otherworld*. The leaves of the tree are long and spiny like the bones of a small fish or the tiny hairs of a carnivorous flower. Hagen knew this tree and he had come back to it many times over the years. The wood of the rowan tree is precious and has many uses, some of which include the protection from sympathetic

---

[13] *Beltane Fire: A Celtic ceremony to celebrate the return of the sun. A Druidic rite of Spring using the nine sacred woods. Beltane fires were lit on May Eve. to bring prosperity and to proclaim the triumph of light over darkness and to bring the sun's light down to Earth.*

magic and evil witchery involving sacred plants.

Hagen looked at the tree. He could feel its power even before he touched it, for it had grown more powerful since the last time he came to it. Then he put his hands on the trunk and the life in the tree came to him through his fingers and poured into his body through the delicate lines of his fingertips. He caressed the tree and murmured a charm that the tree may know to whom it was speaking. When he found the branch that he wanted, after looking and scrutinizing nearly every branch, he put down his saw and reached into his knapsack. Taking out a long, slender knife, he spoke a sacred word to the tree before cutting the tip of his finger with the blade and letting a drop of his blood fall to the earth in front of the tree. Then he took the branch he wanted, said the sacred charm in reverse, and left the grove.

On the way back to Castletown, Hagen the Woodchopper stopped in Ballasalla to speak to King Sigmus and to see Bartholomew. His cart creaked as it rolled across the Crossag Bridge. He was carrying along with a secret package, a cartload of fine ash wood that he had taken from the forest. He came to ask the King if he wanted to have a new walking staff made for him from a piece that Hagen thought would be perfect for just such a use.

After speaking to the King about it, Sigmus knew what he wanted to do. Holding the wood in his hands firmly and feeling the strength that such fine wood carried, he turned to the woodchopper.

"No, thank you Hagen, but I do not want you to make me a staff from this wood." Then he smiled broadly. "I would like you to make one for Bartholomew. Would you do that for me?"

"I would love to," replied Hagen the Woodchopper. Then he smiled before asking. "Would you mind if I worked a charm into it so that he would never be lost in the forest?"

"That would be just fine," said the King. He knew what the people said about Hagen, but he had his own impression of him and he saw something different than most folk. In Hagen, the King saw honor and craftsmanship, and the King saw vestiges of the old world.

Before leaving, Hagen the Woodchopper stopped to talk to Bartholomew. He loved the boy like the son he never had and he wanted him to grow up and be as great as his father. He said nothing to the boy about the staff he planned on making for him; he would stop by one day and give it to him as an unexpected present. There was something good and powerful in receiving unexpected gifts, so much more for the one that gives them. The boy was climbing a tree in the garden when Hagen found him. Bartholomew quickly jumped down when he saw him.

"It's good to see you," said Bartholomew. "Have you come to work in the forest or are you here on a visit?"

"I was just off to Castletown," said Hagen. "But you don't think I could pass through these parts and not stop for a visit, now do you?"

"Have you talked to any trees lately?" asked Bartholomew. In truth, Hagen the Woodchopper was a hero to Bartholomew because he was always off on adventures. Hagen was different because he had real adventures, not the ones made up by some people when they wanted to feel important.

Hagen knelt down on one knee. He was a large man, a hulking man with strength enough for whatever came his way. He threw his knapsack on the ground before him and opened it up.

"Come here, my boy. I want to give you something."

Then he withdrew a small flute, a flute he had made with his own hands. Little bigger than the length of his hand, it was a flute to play simple melodies on, a flute that would listen to the sound of the boy's heart. It was only a simple flute, not one that was too fancy, but it was made by his very own hands. It was also made with a special piece of alder wood. Hagen had fashioned it with his own hands and crafted a special charm into the wood that would respond to the emotions of the song that was in the heart. He handed the flute to Bartholomew.

"I made this for you to play when you're off wandering," he said. "There is nothing better than to wander with the melody to guide you along. I knew this tree, Bartholomew. I knew this tree well. This was made from a very special tree, and I hope it still remembers."

"Remembers what?" asked Bartholomew somewhat confused.

"I told this tree that I would make use of it for a special person. And then I promised that this person would take care of it and always remember that there is power in remembering and that sometimes the memory becomes the thing being remembered. And then I asked this tree to store a special memory in the wood before I took it. I made this for you, Bartholomew."

Bartholomew stared with his mouth open and there was a special wonder in the way he looked that caused a tear to form in the eye of the woodchopper.

"What is the memory that is in this flute?" asked Bartholomew with reverence and awe.

"I asked that the tree remember what it felt like to live. I asked that the beauty of life and the sound of birds and the feeling of the wind to be remembered. And then finally I asked that the memory of the sound of laughter be remembered."

"Can I play it?" Bartholomew asked curiously almost as if he had been given a thing to be put on a shelf and stared at.

Hagen the Woodchopper broke out in to such a din of ferocious laughter that Bartholomew had to laugh along with him. Hagen the Woodchopper laughed until he cried.

The Sparrow and the Piper

Sitting near an open window one morning the sound of a bird caught the King's attention away from his kippers and eggs. He set down his cup and cocked an ear to the beautiful song of the nightingale. The song reminded him of a lullaby his mother would sing to him as a little boy when he would become frightened at night. The birdsong was so sweet and lilting that the memory of his mother completely overwhelmed him, and just for a moment he was young again. "Thank you," he said to the nightingale, and then he bit into a piece of toast with a tremendous crunch.

Slanting sunshine poured through the open window beneath which Prince Bartholomew sat in a chair and smoked a long pipe, and the curling smoke made the shafts of streaming light look thick and distant as a pinprick from heaven. His room was in the north tower and looked out over the large tract of rolling hills and heath-country adjoining the nearby property owned by the Cistercian Order of Rushen Abbey, granted in perpetuity to them by King Olave Godredson in the year 1134 of our Lord. The tall tower was covered and entangled with thick ivy like clutching, clinging fingers and a large oak tree grew alongside the tower like a sentinel. Bright tapestries and shiny coats of arms decorated the walls of his room, and it was there that his extensive collection of swords and sabers and lances and pikes, shields and fencing foils was kept. Thick rugs covered the floor to give comfort from the creeping dampness of the heavy air that blanketed the island and rolled in from the turgid sea. The Prince spent much of his time in his room, alone, and there he would study old books and manuscripts from Britton and Ireland. On cloudy afternoons he would throw open his window and let the sound of his flute waft into the open air. And when he entertained the fair sex he would take out his fine pens and parchment with which to render their beauty forever captured, and like a songbird, cherished, for the Prince was a dilettante and an artist in love and war.

A plate with the remains of a lunch of smoked fish and roasted potatoes lay on a table next to a tankard of ale. Now the Prince was relaxing in his favorite chair beneath the bough of a drooping oak tree that grew next to his window. Songbirds often perched on the branches from which he lured them to his window with clusters of honey and seeds.

The sweet sound of the enchanting songbirds filled him with intense joy. He had no idea how they could be so happy, nor would his appreciation of their happiness interest them in the least, for happiness is established in many ways and the myriad small creatures have no knowledge of anything else.

The Prince's eyes grew heavy. Inside the slanting rays of the sun he could see tiny atoms floating, being carried by the stream, and he watched the dancing interplay between the beams. The fragrant aroma from his pipe filled him with a relaxing, peaceful lassitude and he sank deep into his favorite chair. He blew out a smoke-ring and watched it drift slowly into the streaming sunlight. Then he closed his eyes for a moment. In that moment the smoldering pipe fell from his languid hand and hit the stone floor as his mind slipped beneath the wave of the rushing wall of sleep and he dreamed a remarkable dream accompanied by the sound of wood-thrush and veeries in his ear . . .

. . . *The fluttering warble of the white-throated sparrow sounded so sweet, like music or nectar from the voice of God. Bartholomew followed the bird as it flittered from branch to branch twittering its wonderful song. The bird was speaking to him, trying to tell him a secret. So beautiful and articulate was the song that the Prince knew that it was intended for him to hear, but just when he was beginning to understand, a cloud passed in front of the sun and a cold, dark shadow raced across the wispy meadow. Bartholomew tried to concentrate on the song of the bird, but suddenly its bright, clarion call was being absorbed into another sound, a sound that was harsh and violent. The cheerful song of the bird was now turned into a persistent hammering, a throng that only increased with rage and intensity. Soon the sound of the sweet song was lost in the din until Bartholomew was forced to cover his ears for the sound was now dire and horrible. Bartholomew looked up to see where the bird had flown but the sky had turned darker and an ill wind blew dust and debris across the tender land in a circling windstorm. And then he heard the sound of his favorite bird again . . . but the familiar voice was now different and had changed. The soft, delicate articulation had now become blaring and dead and was more like the sound of whining from an injured animal . . .*

Bartholomew woke from his dream slowly and there remained a lingering vestige of dread that he could not dislodge from his mind. It was as if he had seen a vision of the future, a vision that had no place for idle sleepiness and tranquility, but instead was filled with noise and reckless ambition. To prevent the oncoming melancholy from making him sad he went down to the stable and saddled his horse. Then he rode out to his favorite ledge overlooking the sea to Ireland, the island of the saints.

Most of the time Bartholomew felt very safe being isolated on such a beautiful island, but other times he felt that his tiny island was vulnerable in its remoteness. Sometimes it seemed to him that the horrors of the world could only reach him through dreams, and in this way evil had no boundaries. And then the beautiful song from his dream came back to him. It was a melody that no real bird had ever sung either in joy or sorrow. He could never forget such a melody. Suddenly he went into his saddle-bag and retrieved his flute. There he sat on the precipice overlooking the sea and rendered the sound of his dream into music. The music seemed to come to him not from his own mind but from another place and he was but a vessel, not a conjuror of sacred melodies. No, indeed, the melody was not the song of the bird, but the song of the Lord, for the Lord needs no instrument with which to make music but need only to breathe through the tiny throat of birds. And though each little bird in God's kingdom may one day perish, the song remains the same and shall continue evermore.

On the way back to his castle, Bartholomew stopped at an inn for supper. He sat down at a table and ordered a chicken and a pint of ale. Then he looked around the room to see if there was anyone that he knew. Two old Manxmen sat at a table smoking short pipes and eating from a plate of smoked herring and cabbage. A tall man in a frock coat read silently from a folio he had with him and waited for his tea to cool. A tired old Manxwomen fed her children and hummed an old nursery rhyme she had learned from her mother, and her eyes were far away though her children looked to her for more food. The rest were just a collection of miners and foul-smelling fishermen ripe with sweat and curses and stories of the sea. A man sharpened a knife at a separate table and nodded when the Prince saw him. Then with a wink he sheathed his knife and bit into a thick carrot. Oily smoke hung in the air like mist and mingled with the smell of strong spices and scorched meat. He decided to keep to himself and pretend that he was busy thinking, for the Manxmen have much respect for thinking men and for men who write words to be remembered that others may one day think.

When he finished devouring his chicken the inn had become much darker, and with the darkness came a corresponding darkening of conversation. Now the loud and confident voices of close-talking men had turned to whispers. Bartholomew wiped his mouth with a napkin and drained his glass. On his way out of the inn a man took hold of his arm as he passed by.

"You are Prince Bartholomew?"

"I am," replied the Prince.

"Do you know where evil creatures hide during the day?"

Bartholomew was just about to reply when the man continued.

"I do," he said. "They are hiding in my house. That is why I am here, don't you see? If I go back before it is dark I will surely see them . . . and I don't want to see them. That is why I drink."

Bartholomew left the inn with a queer feeling. He paid the old woman's bill before leaving without even knowing her name or giving her a second thought. The smoke had made him lightheaded and once outside the fresh air cleared his mind while the vague feeling of doom subsided. What did it matter that half the population believed in ghosts and wandering demons and witchcraft? What did it matter? It was fear that did the most evil and caused the most damage. The darkness, like a thick curtain, separates the things of this world from the things of the otherworld and from things that should not be spoken except in whispers and guarded speech. Men will talk about things in the night that they would never think during the daylight hours, for the darkness hides the work of the devil and the associates of the devil.

Yes, the world could be frightening, Bartholomew reasoned. But the Lord did not expect that we should ever face it alone, and just as man was never instructed to love himself above his fellow man, the fear that men too often felt was better put to action by fighting against those that would build their own island around their heart and not be moved to tears by the tears of children.

When Bartholomew arrived back at his castle the sun had gone down. One of the local deemster from Castletown was meeting with King Sigmus. Bartholomew walked past the open doors leading to the drawing room and he overheard their conversation. What he overheard made him stop in his tracks. The story, as Bartholomew would learn, involved the murder of an old Manxwoman named Hilda Bingen who lived in a little hamlet just outside Kirk Michael. She had been killed with a shovel by several savage blows to the head. Her husband confessed willingly to the crime but claimed that a demon had tricked him into the murder. He could not remember what the demon said to him but only that the murder seemed like a good thing to do at the time. The rest of the villagers were too frightened to leave their homes and locked and bolted their doors and shutters.

"Evil passes right through closed doors and windows," said the deemster. "Evil lurks everywhere, and we must keep watch. Our shores cannot protect us from the evil that is already here."

"Nonsense," the King answered finally. "The only evil that exists is the evil that is in men's hearts. I suspect that strong drink account for the voices in his head. Where is he now?"

"He is chained fast at Bishop's Prison," said the deemster. "The only voices he will hear now will be the sounds of his own lamentations."

Bartholomew lit a candle and sat on the edge of his bed. Talk of evil and murder made him sad. To him, the world that was his own was idyllic. The world was such a beautiful place, what need was there of murder and mayhem? Here there was plenty of earth to work and plenty of sunshine if one were willing to put their hand to something worthwhile. Too often good men ended their days in smoky taverns and pothouses. His father had said that evil exists in the hearts of men and such was the nature of evil as if evil also were natural. Suddenly his dream came back to him with urgency. If it was true what his father said, then this evil was also in his heart, the same evil that drove happy men to murder. This could not be true! Evil was a force that could be fought by strong men, and there was no reason to succumb to it without a fight.

Later that night after everyone had gone to bed Bartholomew led his horse quietly out of the stable and walked him to the road before taking the reins and riding cautiously to Kirk Michael. The sky was overcast and no stars helped light his path but he was not disheartened. Strange things sometimes happened after dark on the lonely roads and none too few Manxmen had come home with frightening stories and shaky hands finding courage again around the neck of a bottle. When he arrived at where he was going he led his horse off the path and tied the reins to a tree. From the elevated copse where he stood he could see down into the sleeping village below. A few faint lights winked from behind closed windows where the darting eyes of frightened children and watchmen wrapped themselves in warm blankets. He would quickly do what he had come to do and then he would hurry home again.

He took the flute out of his pocket and put it to his lips. Then he waited for his mind to take him to the place he needed to be. The sound of the sweet melody came back to him like a distant echo and the reverberations went deep into his heart as he played. In the distance he could hear the sudden shriek of a child. A moment later he began to pipe the enchanting melody again.

Little Penny Jacobson woke up suddenly from a bad dream. Her room was dark and outside of her window was an even blacker darkness. The twigs from a tree that grew outside her window had scraped against the window pane, and in her terror she thought that it was the sound of a monster. Now, in her fear she wanted to cry out for her mother, but her fear was so great that she became petrified like a stone gargoyle. Her eyes remained fixed on the small window that was her gate to the outside world. The wind blew and the twisted twig scratched against the glass again. Little Penny Jacobson brought her hands to her mouth and slowly put her thumb in her mouth for protection. Her tender heart raced. And then she saw a face, a terrible and frightening face in the window. It was a monster and she could see its huge pointed teeth and a long, red tongue. She sucked her thumb harder because that was all that she could do.

And then the window slowly started to open, first just a crack and then wider and wider. In a few moments the window was open enough for the monster to crawl through. The monster had crawled half-way through the window when Penny Jacobson heard a distant sound. It was the sound of a flute. When she heard the beautiful sound of the flute, her paralysis was broken. The sound had penetrated through to an inner spring of energy and courage and she screamed for her mother. When her mother burst into the room the monster was already slinking away into the night.

Prince Bartholomew walked his horse over the uneven and thickly rooted path of hungry, reaching roots. He watched the path warily and his tired body slumped in the saddle weakly. Suddenly in his path a great cloud of mist hung suspended, blocking his way around it. Bartholomew had no weapon with him, for he expected to cross paths with no one at such a late hour. He nudged his horse to go around the mist, but the mist moved until it was directly blocking his progress again. He felt the nervousness of his horse and he patted his neck reassuringly. Bartholomew pulled back gently on the reins and stopped in the middle of the path. He felt the presence of something unnatural and a cold shiver rushed through his body. Alone on his horse, long past midnight, he was truly alone and in harm's way. The atmosphere of the dark night became close and closed in around him. Bartholomew stroked his horse tenderly to calm his steady and timorous trembling.

"Easy now boy," he said softly. "There is nothing to be afraid of."

Bartholomew confronted the amorphous fog fearlessly. It had a cold, foul, septic odor that was wretched and evil. The cloud wiggled and pulsed in a sinister way, stretching and twisting like an unborn child trying to be born, trying to assume human form. Bartholomew watched the pulsating miasma and saw that it was trying to congeal, but it was as if his presence prevented such a manifestation and the mass only became more agitated. Slowly he reached into his saddle bag for his flute. The fog moved in an almost human way, for the fog merely disguised whatever hideous presence animated that terrible vapor from within. This was evil incarnate thought the Prince. He felt the sudden urge to strike out, to destroy the presence, and his mind charged with violent intensity. Instead, he brought the flute to his lips and played the opening notes of the lyrical melody taught to him by the bird of his dream. When the first sweet notes were brought to life, the pulsing mass became inert and it was as if the melody had transfixed it to the spot. Then it gradually began to disintegrate and dissipate into the night air. Bartholomew had no malice in his heart, no retribution, only contentment.

And so it was that Prince Bartholomew set out to rid his kingdom of evil and heal the wounds left behind from the creeping sickness of despair. Wherever tragedy would come unexpectedly into their little kingdom the people would expect to hear the beautiful piping, for the piping brought new hope when hope was lost. The true identity of the piper in the darkness was never known, but sometimes though a light be hidden beneath a bushel basket, the light still escapes into the darkness.

The Druid

Wisdom can be learned in many ways. There is wisdom of the mind and there is wisdom of the soul. Wisdom of the mind tells us what to do, while wisdom of the soul tells us what not to do. When we learn to do nothing we learn the wisdom of the heart, for God speaks to us only through our heart. There is wisdom of the earth as well, but when we acquire this wisdom we lose ourselves and forget everything we have ever learned.

One day, off together on a little adventure, Prince Bartholomew and his friend Sylvan rode away together out of Ballasalla heading north in the direction of St. John's and then onto Thort-y-Will Glen. The sky was overcast and windy, but the temperature was mild and the flowers were in bloom and the sweet smell of purple heather and clover filled the air. Bartholomew wore a green jerkin and red hose which he tucked into his black boots. He also carried a sword and two daggers tucked into his belt. Sylvan, the more austere of the two, was dressed all in brown as if he was trying to blend into the landscape and did not want to be noticed. He also wore a sword and carried a dagger in his belt, for they both remembered the assault on [14]King Sigmus that terrible day in England and they were acutely attuned to the prospect of being caught off guard. In their saddlebags they carried food and a few bottles of ale. Bartholomew also carried his flute for music was beginning to interest him again after such a long absence. The path gently sloped up into craggier and denser and darker thickets and copses. They were out exploring; off adventuring and in search of forgotten relics from ancient epochs. Standing stones were strewn over the entire island and it was Bartholomew's desire that he should know them all. Sylvan had boasted that he had seen and nearly captured a ringtail fox while exploring the terrain around St. John's near the foot of Slieau Whallian hill.

"Show me," replied the Prince.

Now they were picking their way along the path through the wooded area, but they did not expect to see the fox, for in truth they made more noise than a legion of corpses escaping the churchyard on All Soul's Eve.

---

[14] *Told in detail in the tale: "Young Bartholomew."*

One of the few places on the island that was deeply forested, they enjoyed the excursion through the undergrowth. Everything was different beneath the trees.

Then they unexpectedly came up on an old man crouched down over an elderberry bush growing off the pathway. He was carefully cutting the toothed, elliptical leaflets, avoiding the tender panicles and stuffing them into a small, leather pouch he wore around his belt. He looked up when they drew nearer. Deep wrinkles etched his weather-worn face like deep mountain crags. He had a warm, angular face that looked as if it had been carved from a block of cheese. Hair, the color of the sky before a storm, fell about his face carelessly beneath his large grey hat which kept his face in shadow. Sylvan nodded to the man and touched the tip of his hat. The man smiled, revealing surprisingly white teeth considering his obvious age.

"May the sun warm your sight," he said with a friendly smile.

"And to you as well," Sylvan replied merrily.

"Are you in need of assistance?" Bartholomew asked politely. He wondered what such an old man would be doing so far from his home and he wondered if he was not lost.

"I do not ask for help," said the old man with a sniff. "I offer help to those that would seek it from me."

"Well then, are you a healer?" asked Sylvan, patting his patient horse tenderly.

"Indeed," the man replied.

"And do you heal cows and frightened sheep?" Sylvan said with a pleasant, affable grin.

"I heal the world," he answered unequivocally.

"My friend here has a broken heart," Sylvan continued to joke.

"The world has a broken heart!" the man announced with such intensity that Bartholomew felt compelled to apologize for his friend.

"We'll be on our way," said Bartholomew. "We did not mean to bother you. " He was suddenly sorry that he had spoken to the man, for in truth he had no time for such ill-tempered men.

The old man continued to look at Sylvan quizzically, examining his heart even as Bartholomew tried to lead him away. For his part, Sylvan only looked at the man with a curious interest, like one would stop to watch the meanderings of a bee and wonder that it may avoid a particular flower.

"You are lucky," that man spoke directly to Sylvan. "You are lucky that your heart does not beat in this world, for if it did, you should surely die from pity."

"Thank you," said Bartholomew. "That was nice of you to say. And now . . ."

"Wait a moment," Sylvan burst in becoming slightly annoyed with his reticent friend. Bartholomew was so careful about drawing a confrontation, that he was often confrontational. "I think that he is trying to tell me something," he continued. Sylvan looked at the man closely and asked. "What is your name, and what do you know of my heart?"

"My name is Azuma," he answered. "You can see that I am old. I am older than any man you have ever heard of, that is true. I know your heart because I know all men's hearts. Such is my trade."

"It is your trade to know men's hearts?" said Sylvan incredulously. "How can that be possible? I have never heard of you, Azuma. Tell me about such a trade as a man could have in human hearts."

Azuma slowly rose to his feet. He was tall, but he hunched over as if he carried a terrible load on his back. "Do not be afraid," he said. "I have lived on this island for a very long time, and now I have become part of this island as a song becomes part of the soul." He looked at Sylvan and then to Bartholomew as if asking an unspoken question. "Would you like to come to my place of dwelling?" he asked. "What I have is not much, but I offer it to you in friendship. It is not far."

"Do you live in St. John?" asked Bartholomew. "Climb up. I shall give you a ride."

"I live in a cave," said Azuma. "It is dark, but it is warm. I go out to gather herbs and sniff the wind."

"Hermits living on the Isle of Man? You are the first hermit I have ever known," Sylvan said. "Are you fighting against the devil?" he asked. "I have heard that the devil attacks the solitary man."

"The devil disguises himself as a solitary man. Come, come with me," said Azuma. And then he trudged ahead, into the forest.

Bartholomew and Sylvan exchanged questioning looks and then they followed. After a few hundred yards through the forest they saw Azuma push aside the foliage of a large bush. The darkness of the opening to a cave was revealed. He turned to see if his new friends were behind him. Then he smiled and then went in. Bartholomew and Sylvan hitched their horse to a tree and followed. Outside the cave they stopped and waited.

"Is this the fox you promised to show me?" said Bartholomew. He secretly wondered if this were just one more experience that he would let his friend drag him into.

Sylvan shook his head slowly. "This is not my doing," he answered. "Perhaps we will learn something. Or better yet, perhaps we will have a story to remember."

Azuma brought out tea that he had made. Bartholomew took a sip but would drink no more of it. Sylvan drank the tea and thought that it tasted of strong root.

"It is earth tea," said Azuma as he watched Sylvan carefully. "It is very strong, but it will not hurt you. The earth has much to teach the patient man."

"And have you learned from the earth as well, Azuma?" said Sylvan.

"Much knowledge is frozen," answered Azuma. "This is knowledge that is woven into the earth. This kind of knowledge can only be passed on to one that has been prepared to understand it."

"Like you?" Sylvan countered.

"Yes . . . like me," Azuma said. "This is the reason I live in a cave. The knowledge I look for is not easy to acquire, and so I need not the distraction of men and the ways of men."

Bartholomew was anxious to leave. It was clear to him that this man was horribly and utterly foolish, and that he was trying to follow the ways of the peregrines and wandering saints of antiquity. Instead, he was just a dried up, odious, stinking old bear hiding in a cave. He looked at Azuma and then to his friend, hoping to draw his attention away from the spell being woven by the old man. Azuma noticed the change in Bartholomew.

"Your friend does not respect the earth, perhaps," Azuma said to Sylvan never once taking his eyes off of him.

"My friend is a prince," Sylvan responded. "And he loves the earth in his own way."

Azuma poked around in the fire with a long stick. He had almost forgotten his visitors were still there when Sylvan asked.

"Do you pray for the world, Azuma? I have heard that many solitary men such as you go off into the world of isolation so that they may pray for the world."

"There are many to pray for the world, as you say," Azuma replied. His eyes grew pale as he listened to his visitor and he was sorry for him. "Many that pray for the world do not know the world, and so for them it is an act of compassion. They do not know the truth, for they have no knowledge of what the world is. Many that pray for the world would lament their act if they knew the world the way I do, for they are proud and I am meek, and their prayer a petition and not a sacrifice. I am disappeared from the world though the world continues."

"Is the world really so bad that one must flee from it and hide away in a cave?" asked Bartholomew. He did not like this man and he wanted to be finished with him once and for all.

"The wise man knows that he cannot flee from the world," the hermit said to Bartholomew indifferently. "The wise man disappears into the world and is carried away like a wisp of smoke in a flow. The wise man suffers not the will to do, for he wants nothing."

"You say that only to sound wise in your obscurity," said Bartholomew. He knew of these men and their ilk, subtle in their ways of concealment, and he was dubious if not a little annoyed. "A wise man has no need for clever words."

"Perhaps you are right," answered Azuma. "My words are not intended to obscure, they are offered in friendship. Perhaps my words cannot penetrate where they are unwanted."

"What does your heart beat for, if not of this world?" Sylvan asked anxiously. He was becoming more and more drawn to the hermit and his strange words. "Can you heal the world from inside of a cave?"

"The world has been drenched in blood, but still it has not been healed from the infliction of the ways of men."

"So what do you do?" Sylvan begged. "Tell me, Azuma, what can be done?"

"In order to heal the world, you must go into the world and you must listen to the sound of the world. But the world I speak of is not the world from which you came. I am not of the world from which you came but am a shade, a mere shadow. What to you seems like isolation to me is complete immersion. The beauty of my world is not to be found inside the cave, but everywhere. One must first know the language of existence. Only then will you have the knowledge to heal."

"What language is this?" Sylvan asked. "I know of no language of existence."

Azuma smiled warily. "Another time," he said. "Leave me now for I am tired of talking."

Bartholomew led the way and Sylvan followed him out of the forest. When they were standing together near the horses Bartholomew stole a glance at his friend. Sylvan was lost in thought and his eyes were glassy.

"Pray we do not cross paths with this man again," said Bartholomew as he and Sylvan rode away later that afternoon. "I for one am glad that he lives alone in a cave. Alas, may he not enter again into the world of people."

Sylvan rode along beside his friend and he was silent. Deep in his mind the words of Azuma sounded, rising from within like rumbling reverberations from a subterranean chamber buried in his soul. He listened to these reverberations and he was stilled. There were legends and rumors of legends about great wizards, druids that could hear the sound of the earth and understand. It was said that these men could speak the language of the birds and the forests and that the wind spoke to them in the silent ebbing of the light when children slept and good men closed their door. To Sylvan, the sound of men was tedious as it was loud and threatening and full of hidden meaning; but most of all the sound of men was ignorant of the subtleties of the world and most of all the sound was the same. He had come to the island because the clashing of swords and the rattling of armor was pointless and offered him no hope that a truer world could ever be developed through such means. Here the sound of battle cries and the sound of flags unfurled in the wind was distant and could be ignored, but the sound of the wind through the trees also made a sound that might replace the sound of flags and marching boots. In Azuma, he had for the first time heard the stirring of something deep within him coming to life, fighting to be born. The sound of Bartholomew broke his concentration.

"Do not listen to these holy fools, my friend. They are only too willing to tell other men how they may live . . . but they do not live. Alas, it is all the same to me that these cave-dwellers come to this island, but do not be fooled into believing that they have something to teach."

Sylvan nodded with a slight smile, but he was lost in thought and merely answered, "Holy fools, holy words. The Lord speaks to those that would listen."

The next day and for the following days Bartholomew stayed at home and practiced his fencing technique with [15]Edward De Villet, who was now fully recovered from his wounds. Once or twice he went hawking, but mostly he spent his time close to home. Much of the time he spent in his magnificent garden, playing his flute and studying old manuscripts of the saints. Twice he rode to Castletown to see Sylvan, but he was not home and left no word of when he would return.

---

[15] *Edward De Villet: Sword Master to Prince Bartholomew.*

Then Bartholomew started riding into Castletown every day to see Sylvan. He would hitch his horse and walk around the wharf lost in thought. His friend had changed, and he knew that it was in part due to their encounter with Azuma.

Bartholomew came to a meadow on the outskirts of town leading to Ballasalla. A small grove of long-standing trees marked a spot where ancient rune-stones were to be found, and now it was a sacred spot that was left untouched by the slow expansion of Castletown. Once it had been a burial ground and the ancient hawthorn trees were planted to commemorate the rite and to represent that death is but a sojourn. The ancient druids would have worshiped in this grove and the legends still tell of a mysterious merging of time between the world of the past and the present time.

In the middle of the ancient grove he found his friend. Sylvan was standing there, still as a stone, and perched on his arm was a yellow warbler. He was unshaven and his clothes were dirty and looked like they had been slept in. To Bartholomew it looked as if Sylvan was speaking to the bird, but he quickly dismissed such a thought. Sylvan heard him approach, and turning to Bartholomew he raised his arm and the bird flew away. Then he smiled.

"Hello, my friend," he said in greeting. "What brings you here?"

Bartholomew clasped his hand. "It is good to see you," he said. Then he knew that his friend had not bathed and was still wearing the same clothes he had last seen him wearing. Something was wrong. "I have been worried about you."

"Worried? Why should you be worried, Bartholomew? There is no reason to worry about me. Did we not fight together once? You know my skills."

"How did you get a bird to land on your arm, Sylvan? Do you talk to birds now, but not your best friend?"

"Let us take a walk," said Sylvan.

Then they walked further into the meadow until they were far off the road. In the center of the meadow was a sunken hollow now overgrown with wild grasses and thick shrubs. This had once been a meeting place for ancient rituals. On a group of stones that had once been used as chairs in ancient ceremonies they sat.

"I want to tell you a story," Sylvan said thoughtfully to his friend. He stood up and stared into the sky. Then he fell into a dreamy muse and began to speak with an unfamiliar voice. "This story is called, *The Seven Fruit Trees*." He took a deep breath, and then he began:

"Once there was a respectable man who lived near a forest and tended his land along with his seven children. He was righteous and never missed a holy day of obligation. He worked hard and he shared the bounty of his labor with those around him. For each of his children he planted a fruit tree. In time the seven fruit trees bore delicious fruit, the best fruit in the village, and there was abundance and life was good. He would go into his grove of fruit-trees and speak to God, and there he would thank him for his bounty. Some folk said that the fruit from his trees was magic and that among its magical qualities was the ability to hear the lyrical voice of God.

"One year, one of his trees bore no fruit and the man quickly cut it down to preserve the integrity of his other trees. That year his yield was lessened with the loss of one of his trees, but he did not give less to those around him that were still in need.

"The following year another one of his trees stopped bearing fruit and became barren and the man quickly cut the tree down lest it infect his other trees. That year his yield was even less, but he still did not withhold his bounty from those around him that were still in need, and he took only less for himself.

"The man spent much time with his trees and he would watch them carefully and take care that they were not infested with flying, crawling pests and burrowing pests from beneath. The fruit from his trees was precious to him now, even more precious with the loss he had endured. And so it came to pass that one day while he was out tending to his trees, a raven landed in one of the branches and would not leave. He shouted at the raven and he shook his fist in the air, but the raven could not be persuaded to leave. Finally he threw stones at the raven and at last it flew away.

"The next year another one of his trees dried up and was barren of fruit, and he cut that tree down as well. That year a wanderer showed up at his house and stood in the road in front of his fruit trees waiting, waiting like an ominous raven. Finally the man became curious to know what the wanderer wanted that he should stand so long in front of his house.

'You must sow the seeds of your remaining trees,' the man exclaimed. 'Your trees are too precious to watch them wither and die. Sow them so that they may live again in other trees.'

"Angrily the man chased the wanderer away with curses and protestations. He would not plant new trees in his grove which was now sacred to him. The people need not watch him so carefully that they knew of his business and the business of his trees and he became angry that they should concern themselves with his life. The man decided to pull back from the villagers, and that year he gave less than what was needed and those in need looked to him for more, but he refused.

"The next year another one of his trees withered and was barren and was cut down, and the man cried. He went into his sacred grove with his remaining trees and he prayed. He worked tirelessly to tend to his remaining trees. He watered each one with the rich water from his well. On cold nights he would wrap blankets around the roots to keep them from freezing. And he spent so much time with his trees that he frequently found himself falling asleep beneath them. And then on one afternoon he woke to find that his tree was filled with noisy crows and that they were eating his precious fruit.

'Get away!' he shouted. Then he hurled stones until he was weak and exhausted. The crows were eating his fruit and there was nothing he could do to stop them.

"The next day he chopped down one of his trees because the remaining trees would be easier to defend and would not attract as many crows. Now he no longer gave away his fruit to those in need, for there was only enough for himself. What he could not eat, he saved and hoarded in jars which he hid away in a deep chamber beneath his house.

"One day he went to his grove and discovered that one of his trees had been chopped down by angry villagers. He looked in horror at his fallen tree, but there was nothing he could do to save it. Overcome with grief he lamented his terrible fate. Now he was left with only a single tree. He thought about it day and night until a new thought took hold of him.

"And instead of grief, a new passion awoke within him and he directed all his energy to save his remaining tree, for why did one need anything more than a single tree? His remaining tree became the expression of his life and he was content. He could not help others but he could help himself, for he was only responsible for none other than himself. But there came a year when only a single piece of fruit clung to his sacred tree. He watched the fruit mature and he waited anxiously for he knew not what to do.

"Finally one day in the crisp autumn air the fruit dropped from the tree and landed on the ground in front of the man. He picked up the sacred fruit from the ground and hungrily devoured it on the spot. Then he waited to hear the voice of God, but instead he heard only silence. From that day onward he was deaf to the sound of God even as he was deaf to the sound of the earth. He could neither hear nor speak, as he had been struck dumb.

"But he did not cut down the remaining tree though it withered and would not ever bear fruit again. It had become holy to him now. The tree changed and it had now become petrified. Now the man would only come to his sacred grove to sit by himself beneath the twisted and petrified branches of his one tree and ponder the meaning of his existence, and just as his tree had become barren so should he.

"Years passed away and the man learned to live in the silence of his world. He could no longer hear the sound of his own voice and soon he had forgotten that he even had a voice. In time he began to hear the sound of the world with a different sense, a sense that he was able to capture through long periods of observation and meditation, and the longer he looked at a thing the more distinct the sound came into his mind, for now the world spoke to him in a voice that was not his own. After many years the man now listened to the sounds of the world in the movement of animals and the passing of the seasons and he no longer remembered that he once had a voice of his own, and without a voice of his own he became the voice of what he could hear. And now for the first time in his life he was content because he no longer thought about the man that he once was; that man no longer existed.

"One day he was sitting beneath the one tree watching the wind slip through the tall grass that grew around his sacred grove. A tiny bird flew up to him and landed on the patch of grass where he was sitting. The man had become a great friend to the birds and they often sang for him in their own voice that only he could hear. And then the bird spoke to him in a new voice and he realized that he could understand their language.

'The [16]Axis Mundi has born a new fruit at last,' the bird said.

"The man smiled, but he could not remember how to speak. Then the bird continued.

'You have tasted the fruit of the world and now the world has tasted you. It is good. You have become ripe at last. Go into the world and seed it with the smile and with the deeds and with the words that contain you. You are reborn.'

"And then the bird flew away."

Sylvan looked up cautiously so that he could see the reaction of his friend. Bartholomew stared back with a curious expression on his face. It was clear that he did not understand or was disturbed by the story in some way. Sylvan expected as much from him however.

"It is not finished yet," he admitted. "I haven't really thought of a proper ending yet."

"You wrote this poem?" Bartholomew asked suspiciously. "What does it mean? " He would never have expected something like this from his old friend. There was more to Sylvan than he knew.

"Well, yes. But it is not yet finished."

"You have changed," said Bartholomew. He was truly concerned about the change in his friend and he wondered what could have happened.

"Do not fear change, Bartholomew. Remember, we do not change the world, the world changes us and so we selfishly inflict this change upon the world and imagine that the change came from ourselves."

"It is unhealthy for you to speak this way, Sylvan. Come, let us go hunting and wash our face in the cold stream."

---

[16] *World Tree.*

Sylvan smiled awkwardly. Then he took a step back from his friend. "You do not understand," he said. "I am now part of this change. My heart is no longer mine to control."

Bartholomew knew that it was useless to argue. His friend would surely emerge from this new phase in a week or two. Perhaps it was best to let him be.

The days for Bartholomew returned to normal. To take his mind away from the troubling predicament of his friend he threw himself into his normal activities with renewed enthusiasm. If his life returned to normal he thought possibly everything would settle down as well. He rode his horse, he practiced his fencing technique with De Villet, and he sat in his garden with Iona and told her stories and played music for her. Bartholomew did all these things again to restore his sense of stability, but he soon realized that his sense of stability was what was bothering him, and it was the slipping away of his friend that had brought it to the surface. If Sylvan could examine his own life so closely, so thoroughly, and so completely and still find it wanting, then why couldn't he? In truth, his privilege isolated him from the vigor's and rigors of everyday life; that could not be denied. He needed to find something to do. Yes, he needed some kind of work.

He began to study the history and to examine the complex lineage of past Kings, past treaties, past successions, wars, navel battles, proclamations, protestations and letters of renunciation until he was exhausted and confused. Surely he could never be expected to know all such history and the myriad workings and machinations that had taken place in older, more violent times. He examined the records of Tynwald and tried to understand how such clashing of cultures and such a complex mixing of peoples could ever live in peace. In the end he became despondent; there were just too many dates, too many references to dead and forgotten agreements. In truth, he had no great desire to know the history of history. He only wanted to protect the world of his father and leave no trace of dishonor behind after he was gone.

One day Bartholomew, while out riding, came across Hagen the Woodchopper. He of late liked to be by himself; he liked to be alone with his thoughts, but mostly he liked to be near trees. A couple miles outside of his castle there was a small copse hidden away in a sunken hollow. He often liked to allow his horse to nibble the grass while he lay on the ground and watched the clouds float above. Sometimes he liked to bring his flute and revisit sweet melodies he remembered, and that is what he was doing when he heard a loud chuckle, and turning his head, beheld Hagen the Woodchopper.

"Well, well now, my old friend. Your song tells more about you than your clothes."

Bartholomew rose and shook the woodchopper's hand vigorously. It had been years since last they had met.

"I knew you by your song," Hagen continued. "The wood knows the song of a woodchopper and the woodchopper knows the sound of wood. Aye, Bartholomew, I've hewed many trees since last we met."

Bartholomew smiled, for he was playing the very flute given to him many years ago, carved by the woodchopper himself. He was very happy to see Hagen again and he continued to shake his hand long and hard.

"It's good to see you again, Hagen. What a fortuitous meeting! An unexpected meeting . . . an unexpected friend . . . Tell me, what news from the trees?"

"The trees tell me that you are beginning to entertain some very strange ideas," said Hagen with a knowing smile and a wink. Then Hagen dropped his knapsack on the ground and shook his head and danced on his toes. "I'm growing old," he said. "I need to coax the blood back into my aching feet lest they walk away without a drop in them."

"What have you been doing, Hagen? I should like to drink a pint or two with you some afternoon. And tell me, do you still talk to trees with such cheerfulness you old sage?"

"The Isle of Man is no proper place for a woodchopper, Bartholomew. There are scores and scores of scores of trees to be hewn on the Continent, but this is my home and this is where I feel most close to my craft. Yes, the trees are few, but they are wise."

"Tell me, Hagen. Can you tell me how a man can know a tree? And can a man also know a bird, or a cloud, or the taste of the air and the smell of the seasons? I have a desire to know what secrets there are and if such secrets be known."

"That is a tall order," Hagen replied. "I must take off my boots if I am going to tell you these things."

And then he sat down and began removing his enormous boots and leggings. When he was done he wiggled his toes and laughed. Then he talked to Bartholomew in the way that he knew best.

"There are secrets of the earth and there are secrets of men. Secrets of the earth come from God and secrets of men come from men. The secrets of the earth are simple and they are easily known, even to a woodchopper. The secrets of men are complicated so that they remain secret. These secrets are evil, Bartholomew. Do not listen to the secrets of men."

"Can the secrets of men ever come from God?" Bartholomew asked.

"God does not keep secrets from us, Bartholomew. Secrets are the invention of men. There are hidden things and there are revealed things. The trees and the streams and the birds of the air do not try to hide the knowledge that has been given to them, instead, they only praise it by singing or by growing straight. It is only men that try to corrupt this knowledge and then hide it that they may acquire secret knowledge coveted by other men such as them."

"Magic?" asked Bartholomew, now comforted by the old wisdom and magic of Hagen.

Hagen went into his knapsack and withdrew an apple. He looked at it and then handed it to Bartholomew before reaching into his sack for another. He took a huge bite and nearly obliterated the juicy apple in one giant chomp.

"The knowledge and wisdom of God are inside this apple," he said, and then he took another bite. "There is no secret here to learn from. The apple is here to teach us patience, for in the wisdom of God patience is a godly thing. It is only the devil and men of the devil that would try to make the apple better. And it is only the secrets of men that would try to corrupt and go around the wisdom of God. Men such as this are not happy unless they improve on the wisdom of God. Beware of such men, Bartholomew."

Bartholomew thought that he had never tasted a better apple. He spoke with his mouth full and the juice ran down his chin. "And the cave dwellers and pillar dwellers and men of the wild . . . what of them, Hagen? They say that they listen to secret words that are spoken into special places and things. I know one of these men, and I fear that he has taken away my friend by his charm."

"Corruptors of nature," said Hagen, and then he spat. "Men that talk to the wind that they may change it, and men that see through the eyes of birds that they may learn hidden things . . . these men are corrupt. These men that sing secret songs and hide their true meaning beneath clever words are corrupt. The corruption is not in the music, the corruption is in how the music is made."

Hagen talked and Bartholomew listened and he knew in his heart that what Hagen said was true.

"When clever men learn the secrets of music and hide such secrets in special languages and symbols it becomes corrupt. These men, the boilers of salt! The music of the earth is written in the earth and in the heart and it takes no great man to sing such music. These men do not listen to the wind and to the trees, Bartholomew. These men speak to the wind and imagine that the sound they hear is the voice of God. But it is only the wind."

"Then it is not real, Hagen? Am I not to believe my eyes?"

"Yes, you should believe your eyes and you should believe your ears, but mostly you should believe your heart. There are men that can speak in tongues, Bartholomew. That is nothing new. There are men that can speak with birds, and that is also not new. Speaking to birds and speaking to God are very different things. The birds are all too eager to speak, but do not trust them. You may trust the songbird, but do not trust a carrion eater. Carrion eaters speak with carrion eaters."

Hagen stopped to lick the juice off his fingers. Then he spit out a mouth full of seeds and laughed heartily. "Do not be fooled by these silent men either, for they are also corruptors of the nature of nature. It is no great marvel to keep your mouth shut so that you may hear new things. These men would close their mouth and then claim that they were able to hear through their eyes or through their skin or through their stomach. Aye, I have known some of these silent men, oh, how loud they breath and how foul their exhalations. If I want to make a noise, I shout it out for the whole world to hear. The songbird does not sing to make me happy. Verily, the songbird sings because its song is more beautiful than a single lifetime. It would be wise to let these silent men have their way with their quiet words."

"It is good to hear such good judgment in such strange times," said Bartholomew. "It may just be that the chopping of wood is the most noble and good thing to do in all the world. I am glad that we will always have the wisdom of the trees to listen to when times are dark."

"But there are strange happenings in the trees I am sorry to say, Bartholomew. I've seen happenings that made my skin crawl and my fingers to reach for the axe. Let me tell you what I saw last night while I slept beneath the trees."

Bartholomew knew he was in for a story. He loved the tender woodsman and his stories and he knew that to be a good woodsman was to be good at telling stories, most especially after a drink. Bartholomew went into his saddlebag and brought out some beer and a wedge of cheese. He broke the cheese in half and gave it to Hagen. Then he opened a bottle of beer and handed it to Hagen. Finally he opened a bottle for himself.

"Now I am ready to hear your tale," he said.

Hagen smiled, took a long draft of beer, and then he was ready. "I was chopping some elder up in Kirk Malew," he said. "I bedded down there for the night right in the forest, cause even a woodchopper don't like to wander alone at night if he can avoid it. A bed of needles and a crust of bread, these are the luxuries of a woodchopper."

He stopped to scratch his nose and bite into the cheese. Washing it down with a drink from his bottle, he continued.

"Now, fairies don't bother me, and trolls I have never yet crossed paths with yet. I've seen creatures of the night though they crawl, fly, or ride the wind like a vapor. Now, the trees were restless, for the moon has special powers that be needed for the rites of witches and wizards. When magic be about, the trees listen but carefully and they shake with fear and sometimes anger, and they whisper across the entire forest in their secret, tingling, root-twitching way. The trees are alive with life and alive things, Bartholomew."

Hagen now got even closer to Bartholomew, for what he next had to tell he didn't want even the trees to hear, lest they become suspicious even of his wood-chopping ways.

"And then I was waked up in the middle of the night by such a din that I thought the forest was coming to an end. But when I looked to see what it was making such a din my eyes fell upon a Witch's Sabbath and wild orgy like the mythical orgies of yore or other intercourse with the devil. A blue mist filled the trees, a billowy, willowy, mist, and the sound was coming from inside the mist. The sound was the sound of piping, for there was a piping going on, a piping like the piping of Pan himself never piped."

Bartholomew had stopped drinking his beer and stared at Hagen the Woodchopper lest he miss a single sound from his mouth.

"Now I know it aren't a Beltane fire, but what was happening I couldn't even know. The moon was a-waxing last night, Bartholomew, a-waxing into an unholy constellation. Now they didn't see me or know that I was there, and I stayed out of sight. Hidden behind an old oak tree I spied on their pagan ritual to see what damnation they would bring against the forest. The blue mist was turning and turning around and I could see revealed shapes and pieces of dancing, naked bodies moving in and out of the wavering mix of mist and smoke and turgid nakedness."

Hagen now narrowed his eyes like he was trying to narrow his thought enough to remember clearly. The birds now were silent and all around them was the beautiful nothingness of a calmed forest.

"And then the mist started to clear. Now the terrible sound began to diminish, but when the mist cleared they were still dancing their unholy dance in the moonlight. But then a procession came into the forest, it was a procession of white robes and candles and they gathered around an overturned stone glittering in the moonlight with glowing lichen and sickly moss. I could feel the anger of the forest, building, and building in the sight of such wickedness. Suddenly a hairy, misshapen, hoofed Pan emerged into the circle, and he began to play his cursed pipe . . ."

"Are you sure it was Pan?" Bartholomew asked eagerly. "Are you sure, Hagen?"

The woodchopper scratched his head. "I'm not really sure of anything," he admitted. "The music was playing tricks with me. I could not escape the lure of the music. The sound was making me go closer and closer and I could not resist. Some kind of power had hold of me, Bartholomew."

"So tell me what happened then!" Bartholomew cried. He wanted to hear it all so that he would know the scope of such devilish acts.

"Everyone was dancing," he continued. "I saw a large owl perched on the stone, and everyone was dancing in circles around the owl. Then the ones wearing the white robes started to take them off, and I saw that they were women, beautiful women, and they were unclothed. They were unclothed, Bartholomew! Now I was becoming very nervous, and I knew it was time to get away before I too become spellbound by such perversion. But before I could leave, one of the women looked right at me and smiled. Her eye fell upon me like a dull hammer. A cold chill went up my spine and I ran away as fast as my legs could carry me or I fear I would have been the victim of a wanton sacrifice."

Later, when Bartholomew was riding back to his castle, he thought about all the things that Hagen had said. It is true that there was more happenings on the isle than he even realized. But what did it matter?

When he was almost home he slowed down and walked his horse across the Crossag Bridge. At the top of the bridge he stopped. This was his favorite spot on the island to stop and think. The Crossag was a bridge across more than just the gentle Silverburn, he thought to himself. This was like a bridge to another world, a quiet world, a bridge to the sacred world of his childhood. This was the entrance to a new world, a world of Christianity, while on the other side of the bridge was an ancient world of forgotten paganism and sleeping druids and fairies and whooping birds and vanishing monsters, talking trees, changelings, enchanted graveyards and a wealth of folklore to guide one through every part of life. This was the threshold to his life where everything was gentle and made sense, a world given to him by his mother and father. But he was somehow drawn to the other world as well, a world that was yet to be discovered, a world superimposed on his own world but too faint to see. Sylvan now belonged to this world. Alas, he would allow his friend the privacy he had earned and he would not seek him out again.

He looked into the gentle, meandering river. The Silverburn was indeed an important part of his life. Life too was like a gentle river, always flowing but never flowing backward. In truth, his friend was not lost to him. No, his friend was just following a different river. But Bartholomew smiled to himself as he nudged his favorite horse forward, because he believed that all rivers emptied into the same ocean.

The Abbot and the Bird

It is said that strong drink poisons, not only the body, but the soul as well. Wise is the man who tempers the one that he may save the other; but wiser still is the man who knows the difference.

The two riders bolted down the road from Ballasalla, kicking up a small dust-storm in their wake. A passing traveler or a wandering Manxman would have seen the smiles on their faces and heard the playful cackle in their voices as they thundered down the road. They could not have known what the two riders were laughing about or why they rode with such abandon; they perhaps would have only shook their head and gave a quick wink, for it was King Sigmus and Prince Bartholomew on their way to Rushen Abbey.

Through the south gate they steered their horses, and it was Bartholomew that was first. The exuberant Prince jumped out of his saddle and landed on the ground confidently and bowed to his father.

"What did I tell you?" he said with a tease. "Master Brendan cannot be beaten on the open road," and then he patted his horse on the flank.

"You're wrong," responded the King with a merry laugh. "I just don't like to arrive in a hurry. I leave that business to country gentlemen and princes and underlings."

"Alright father," Bartholomew conceded with mocking deference. His good nature shone through at times, for his nature was true. "That is your prerogative I suppose."

The courtyard at Rushen Abbey is large, bounded by the Silverburn on one end over which a stone bridge, the *Crossag* was built early in the 14th century to assist the monks, laden with overflowing vegetable carts from the field, in fording the gentle river. Many large trees offer much shade and shelter from the driving wind. A pebbled path winds and meanders through the trees for the monks during their contemplative walks and that they may be secluded for a few moments from their brethren. Many buildings, including a mill and a waterwheel, make up the Cistercian

Abbey built with large stones quarried by the silent, laboring monks. Like the rules of Saint Benedict, the rules are strict and simple, and little embellishment ornamented the austerity implicit within such an Order.

Abbot William came out into the courtyard to welcome his guests. He and Sigmus shook hands, as they were old friends. Then Sigmus presented his son.

"This is my son, Bartholomew," he said. "Have you met before?"

"That was long ago," the Abbot said with a wink. "It is a pleasure to see you again Bartholomew," he said offering his hand in friendship. Dressed in the traditional bleached wool and known as the White Monks, the Abbot looked as serious as that of the rules of his Order to which he was in charge, for his was a life of prayer, and a life of work. He had looked forward to meeting the young prince for some time now because the last time he was but a boy.

"The pleasure is mine," answered Bartholomew as the memory of the tree stump came back to him.

The Abbot turned to King Sigmus and briefly discussed some matters of which Bartholomew knew nothing. The Prince stood patiently and smiled, not daring for a moment to interrupt the conversation. He looked around at the buildings and thought of just how simple in architectural design they truly were. In a few minutes the Abbot addressed him personally.

"Shall we take a walk through the grounds?" the Abbot asked. "We have some very special trees of which we are exceptionally proud. I'm sure you would find them interesting."

Later they sat down for lunch at a shady veranda attached to the chapterhouse. A light meal of vegetable soup with lentils, tomatoes, and bread with cheese was served. The monks were used to very austere meals, but now and then they ate fish or pork on feast days. Bartholomew enjoyed the delicious cheese and listened to the conversation between his father and the Abbot politely. The Abbot opened two bottles of the famous brown ale the abbey was noted for. The abbey even had special glasses for serving their ale, for it was the nose that was particularly special and a challis glass was best. The Abbot poured him a glass and waited for him to taste it.

"My father speaks highly of your ales," Bartholomew said.

"Perhaps you would like to visit our brewery some day. Of course, brewing is not perfectly defined, and it was many a brew-master that found the right recipe through experimentation. Our techniques are constantly being modified. Over time we have learned much, but there is much left to be learned."

Bartholomew raised the glass to his lips and tasted the heady brew. He smiled broadly. "You brew this here in the abbey?"

The Abbot smiled. Then he resumed his discussion with the King.

"It is not enough to preserve knowledge," he said, turning to Sigmus again. "It is just as important that new knowledge be learned."

"And you get this new knowledge by studying the Church Fathers?" Sigmus asked. "Can nothing further be learned?"

"You have misunderstood me, Sigmus. "There is much that has been revealed through the scriptures, but we must go further . . . we must interpret the signs that have been given to us by those that only recorded divine revelation. Much that has been written was intended for later times . . . such as these times in which we now live."

"Then are there no new revelations?" Sigmus asked politely but without anxiety. "Are we doomed to go no further, William? Cannot our world, like an egg be cracked open, that new knowledge be learned and used for the betterment of all?"

"Spoken like a true King," said William. "You are a noble and just leader, Sigmus. The world could certainly be served better by leaders such as you. However, you still have not followed my line of thought."

Then the Abbot shifted uncomfortably in his chair and took a drink from his glass before he resumed speaking. He perfunctorily touched the silver crucifix he always wore around his neck to remind him of his station and of which he drew comfort. Glancing quickly at Bartholomew he saw that he had finished his glass. The Abbot filled it again while he composed his thoughts.

"The kingdom was never intended to be on this earth," he began hesitantly. "Of course we should do our best to relieve the suffering and injustice that living in such a world inflicts upon us all. But that is not the purpose of our life here on earth. These things of which you speak only serve to distract us on our true mission."

"Is it not enough to live righteously?" Sigmus asked hypothetically. "We are all servants, yes. But we must continue to seek . . ."

"There is nothing to seek," William said with a gesture of his finger on the table. "Everything we need is right here. Everything we need is here and now, Sigmus. That is what I am trying to tell you. There is no need to seek, for everything is already here."

"But you pray," Sigmus spoke up. "You live in constant prayer and supplication. Surely you are hoping for more."

"We do not pray for ourselves, Sigmus. We pray for the world. Our sacrifice is for the world, not of the world."

The King finished his glass and wiped his mouth. William and he often found themselves in heated arguments. Mostly it was Sigmus that could not understand the implicit meaning often hidden in William's words, and he would need to think about it when he was off by himself.

William poured the rest of the ale and looked at Bartholomew curiously. "Are you always so quite?" he asked casually.

"I listen so that I may learn," replied the Prince.

"Listen for the Lord," said William pointedly. "The Lord inspires us all in different ways." William was looking at Bartholomew, but he was speaking to Sigmus. "Yes, Bartholomew, much can be learned by listening. Sometimes when we are very quiet we can hear the voice of God speaking to us. That is how we learn."

Bartholomew listened to the Abbot and his voice went right through him. There was power in his voice not unlike the voice of authority that comforts us when we are weak. Bartholomew's mind began to drift. The conversation between his father and the Abbot was not to his liking, and the strong ale was beginning to make him warm. There was also power in nature thought Bartholomew. Instead, he began to concentrate on the sound of the birds. He listened carefully until he was able to isolate the sound of just a single bird. He thought the melody rather complex and he wondered what could be the purpose of such a complex melody when a far less complex melody would be just as effective for identifying the bird to other birds. His eyes wandered over the trees trying to capture the image of the bird with the poetic voice. What in God's green earth could inspire such a song? Often Bartholomew became inspired to write songs of his own. The beauty of the world can sometimes be contained within a sweet melody, and was itself, a gift. The Manxwomen sang songs in the fields, songs to comfort and bring strength. The men sang songs in the taverns and inns, but these songs were inspired to bring courage and were unlike the songs of the earth. The earth had its own songs and often it was the sound of a storm or the rattling of shutters in the wind that made the truest music. But then Bartholomew thought about the bird again. It had only one song, one song to serve the purpose of each and every new day. He sighed deeply. How much better it was to have a new song for each new day.

"Are you inspired by the sound of birds?" he heard the Abbot suddenly ask.

Bartholomew, completely carried away by the intoxication of the birds and by the strong ale, smiled broadly. His face was flush.

"Now I understand the reason why you and your brethren like it so much here," he said a little too thoughtlessly and his words sounded slurred. "Another glass of this and I should be seeing visions myself."

The Abbot sat in stunned silence. The blood drained from his face as the brashness of the young Prince offended the entire Order. He merely glared at the Prince with sadness before excusing himself, and leaving the table, left the King alone with his son. King Sigmus at this moment was deeply disappointed in his son, but he did not show it.

"It is time for us to leave," said the King.

Once back in their own home, King Sigmus allowed his disappointment to turn into anger. It started out as a tiny flame, but it continued to feed on something. The King dismounted his horse and handed it off to the stable master. Even before Bartholomew had dismounted the King was demanding an explanation.

"How could you say something so utterly ignorant?" he asked without restraint. "Have you learned nothing your entire life? Have I taught you nothing about etiquette?"

The King continued to rave, and the more he raved the angrier he became until his anger overcame him out of all proportion to his better judgment.

"Did you think the Abbot was an innkeeper, Bartholomew? Are you so used to being served that you cannot even think straight?"

Bartholomew blushed crimson, not from shame but from self pity. Never before this day had his father spoken to him with such vitriol, and it was as if he was being scolded for offences long since buried and forgotten. Or as if, only now had the true nature of his soul become known to his father. The King continued to vent his frustration to the dazzled boy.

"I send for the best teachers so that you can learn from their experience, I expose you to every kind of refinement, but your offish behavior, your brashness bubbles to the surface. Have you lost your mind, Bartholomew? Speak to me!"

A tear stung in the young Prince's eye, but King Sigmus didn't see it. Suddenly Bartholomew snapped the reins of his horse and bolted out across the lawn and out of the gate. He was soon out of sight as he disappeared around a bend in the road toward Castletown.

In a secluded area on the end of Bridge Street is an old inn called *The Commercial Street Inn*. The inn was old even before Bartholomew was born, and he would go there sometimes for a pint or a chicken if he was hungry. He was well known here, and this is where he was now as he opened the door and went in to the shadowy common room. He found a small table near the window and sat down noisily.

"Ale," he said to the innkeeper who was watching him closely.

After he had drained his first glass, he began to relax. He ordered another glass and then he packed his pipe. Through the window he could see children playing in the street where rainwater had collected in deep ruts made by carts carrying goods brought up from the wharf. They were covered in mud and yet they laughed and continued to play until they were pulled violently away by stern mothers hoping to buy goat cheese or a skein of yarn.

The inn was inhabited by several groups of men and fellow travelers sitting around pots of ale and talking in loud voices. Large candleholders, smoking and dripping wax, hung from the ceiling and pushed back the lingering gloom. Stale smoke filled the room and hung in thick clouds above the tables like the clouds of choking doom above a besieged city. At a few of the tables silent men watched from behind thick beards, deep penetrating eyes, and closed mouths. These were men that had come only to listen, and it was for the tales that wafted eerily through the thick smoke, the tales of sorcery and witchcraft, the tales of murder and mystery, that they came.

An old man with a deeply wrinkled face held up precariously by the stiffness of an old buttoned-up frock coat was talking. His eyes were fixed on a particular memory and he tried to articulate his fading vision. With his groping hands he tried to grasp the image in his mind.

"I saw it," he said. "I saw it as clear as I see you now."

"Tell us again," they all exclaimed as they sloshed their ale and swallowed noisily.

"Wasn't part of this world," said the man. "In and out, in and out, one moment it was there, and the next moment it was gone. I saw it."

"A wizard wouldn't allow himself to be seen like that!" shouted one of the men with certitude. "A wizard would just be gone . . . and you too if he had a mind to do you ill."

"Wasn't a wizard," the old man moaned. "I would have known a wizard in an instant. This was something different, something evil and monstrous."

"So it was a monster? Are you telling us that you were chased home by a monster?" they said.

The old man's head bobbled slightly as the memory was once again forced into his timid mind. "Could have been," he announced. "Aren't nothing else to call it. I seen my share of monsters lurking around after dark, and I tell you . . . could have been."

"Well I seen my share of monsters too!" said one of the men derisively. Everyone here has seen one if truth be told. The hills are full of beasts and spirits."

Then they were all talking at once and arguing about which one had seen the most monsters, which one the most hideous, the most cunning. It would have ended in endless bickering until the man shouted.

"Wait!"

The chatter stopped. All eyes fell on the man as he reached into his coat pocket and removed an object. It looked like a huge fang from a large animal. He threw it on the table angrily and said.

"I found this beneath my window the next morning."

Bartholomew smiled, for he had heard these stories before. Weak minds and strong drink was the playground of the devil. He too loved to hear stories, and on occasion would come just to pass an hour or two listening to such stories from which dreams come.

At another table a man sat close to a young woman and whispered in her ear with fat, quivering lips. He was hoping to bring her home with him for the night. She listened and contemplated his words with surprised expressions and grimaces. The man's greasy fingers pawed at her and stroked her hair at last disappearing beneath the table. The woman gazed right through him, but her thoughts were far away. Her eyes fell on Bartholomew inadvertently but quickly averted as she turned away. When her face turned toward him again, the Prince could not bear to look at her and turned away as a new distraction caught his attention.

A short man with high leather boots, a crimson waistcoat, and a bright green scarf tied around his head, a travelling jongleur that he was, rested his foot on a chair and balanced a large lute on his knee. With a wink he brought his hands up and began to render a melody. No one paid him heed, but the Prince now watched him intently. Though he looked old, his hands were deft as they danced across the silver strings. Suddenly he stopped and raised a curious eyebrow. A moment later a mysterious woman emerged from the shadow and stood behind him, resting her hands, ornamented with rings and shiny bracelets, on his shoulders causing him to wince with a smile. The mysterious woman, reaching her slender arms around the man, plucked a handkerchief from his waist pocket and daubed his forehead. With that, the man began another tune with the sweet accompaniment of his beautiful companion's softly lilting voice. Bartholomew was enchanted. Her fingers danced as she sang, weaving a magic spell in the dim light and he could not take his eyes off of her fingers, and though no one else in the room seemed to take any notice of them at all, the Prince thought that they played only for him.

The song was the tale of an enchantress and told a sordid tale of forbidden love and deceit. Verse after verse she wove her tale of woe. It was a tale in which an enchantress, a piteous forest nymph, did lure her young lover to his demise. Soon Bartholomew had fallen into the spell cast by the beautiful minstrel. He saw only her and everything else around him was buried beneath the lust ever growing in his young heart. The clever musician continued to play and the soft sound of his lute only beguiled the young Prince even further. And then the verses of the song became lost to the roaring sound of rushing blood in his ears. The woman continued to look at young Bartholomew and playfully tinkle tiny bells that were wrapped around her fingers. As she swayed from side to side her glittering earrings tinkled softly, but to the Prince the sound was sinking deeply into his ear though he strained to hear it. The Prince continued to drink from a glass that always seemed to be full though he could not remember asking for more.

Now it was darkening quickly outside his window. Inside the room men continued to talk and laugh and declare oaths of friendship, but the men were now changed and the Prince could not remember their faces. His head was spinning. How long had he been sitting here? He must have fallen asleep he thought to himself, and now it was time to leave. But then he remembered the beautiful woman. She was still singing! Bartholomew shook his head violently. There was a full glass of ale on the table in front of him. Now the room was filled with acrid smoke from the many men that smoked from long pipes and the greasy smoke from the kitchen roiling with the noxious scent of frying herring.

He stood up to leave and nearly fell down as the room lurched from side to side. Holding on to the table he steadied himself. There were plates of half-eaten food strewn across the table, but he did not remember eating. Then he felt the gentle touch of a hand on his arm. It was the barmaid. She looked expectantly at him and waited. Bartholomew reached into his pocket and brought out a coin and dropped it on the table. The barmaid recoiled and looked askance at him, but she did not speak. Feeling awkward, the Prince dropped yet another coin on the table without even knowing what he was doing. Then he started to find his way out of the shadowy room now become almost entirely dark. Before leaving, the Prince stumbled over to where the minstrel sang, smiling awkwardly before dropping a coin into a glass from which the minstrel was drinking. Then he moved to the door. The barmaid tried to stop him, to make him listen, but he brushed her aside and staggered to the door.

Once outside the cold twilight air filled his mouth with a jolt. He stopped to look around because he could not remember where he was or how he had gotten here. Then he started walking down the street, turning into a dark passage lost even to the starlit night sky. He looked up and when he did he fell over backward and hit the hard flagstone pavement with a thud. When he tried to get up a strong hand grasped him and pulled him to his feet. A moment later he was struck in the face with a tremendous blow that knocked him down again and he lay in a daze and felt quick fingers rifling through his pockets. When he tried to resist, a sharp blow from a boot knocked him back down again and he lost consciousness.

When he opened his eyes again he was in a strange bed. His head was sore and a dull pain throbbed behind his eyes. He closed them again and collapsed into the warmth of the bed and fell asleep again. The second time he opened his eyes the pain in his head was lessened if somewhat duller. He looked around to determine where he was. It was dark in the room but for a single candle which gave off a warm yellow glow. Carefully he slipped out of bed and put his feet on the cold floor. Slowly standing up he felt the dizziness return and confusion. Moonlight came in through a small window, and in the pale moonlight he saw the figure of a man, sleeping in a chair near the door. The man moved when he saw that the Prince was on his feet. Suddenly he jumped up from the chair and hastened to the Prince to steady him lest he collapse on the floor.

"Easy now," said the man. "Just lay back down for a moment, my friend." It was Sylvan, his dearest friend.

Sylvan set down a cup of steaming coffee on a table near the bed and waited for his friend to open his eyes again. He said nothing to wake him, but merely looked at his friend and smiled. Yes, he was impetuous to the point of recklessness, but he had a tender heart. But his recklessness this time had nearly gotten himself killed.

"Have some coffee," said Sylvan when Bartholomew at last opened his eyes again. "It was hot when I brought it to you. Are you up now, or would you like to sleep some more?"

Bartholomew gingerly cast off the covers and threw his feet over the bed. Then he reached for the coffee on the nightstand.

"This is ice cold," he complained.

Sylvan smiled. "I told you it was hot when I brought it to you, but that was hours ago. The sun is rising. Tell me, my friend, what happened to you?"

Bartholomew massaged his neck and tried to stretch the soreness away. The side of his face was swollen purple. "I was watching a woman . . . she was singing. I think that she did something to me."

"She did something to you, my friend," said Sylvan with a laugh familiar to the Prince. "She bewitched you. Does every woman in the world bewitch you?"

Slightly embarrassed, the Prince mused. "That is not what I meant to say, and you know it."

"I had been looking for you all day," Sylvan said. "First I went to the castle, but I was told that you rode off in a furry after an argument with your father."

Then Bartholomew remembered. He remembered the way he had acted and he remembered the act that provoked the argument in the first place. His father was reprimanding him justly, so it seems, but he did not want to listen. Remembering at last, he was ashamed of his actions, but all he could say was.

"I feel like I have been trampled by a horse."

"You were trampled, but not by a horse," answered Sylvan. "By the time I finally found you I was nearly too late. I found you on the ground being beaten and I managed to chase the attacker away. Then I brought you here and put you to bed. That was yesterday."

"I was a fool," said Bartholomew. "Thank you, my friend. Thank you for watching over me in my folly. But tell me now, why were you looking for me to begin with?'

"There is something I want to show you," Sylvan answered. "I have found something that I think will delight you, but I must show you."

"Well, what is it?" said Bartholomew with growing interest.

"Are you well enough to ride?" asked Sylvan hesitantly.

"Well enough," answered Bartholomew, who was now anxious for action lest he dwell on the intricacies of his own stupidity.

After a light breakfast, the two riders trotted away from Castletown and headed north, toward the interior. Sylvan led the way with Prince Bartholomew following close behind and nursing a terrible headache. The ride to Ballafayle Cairn, outside of Kirk Maughold near Ramsey, would take them several hours to reach and pass through many parishes, so Sylvan brought a few things to eat and some water in his saddle bags. The fresh air continued to revive the Prince, but the bruises he had suffered during the attack were deep and his jaw was most sore, appropriate he thought for it was his mouth again that had gotten him into such trouble.

Near midday they rode down into a forested glen ringed with large willow, one of the seven sacred trees, and ash, a tree associated with healing and magical properties extending its roots into the ground, the air, and into the Otherworld. Inside the ring of trees were the ancient remains of an old stone wall, now overgrown with lichen and fallen into ruins. Sylvan jumped off his horse and motioned for Bartholomew to do the same. With an uneasiness brought about by his bruises and the long ride, the Prince followed, only too happy to be off of his horse.

"I know this place," said the Prince reluctantly. "I have already been here."

"Come with me," Sylvan answered. And then he disappeared into a thick copse of trees that extended far into the glen.

Further back, nestled between the large trees, was an ancient cemetery or burial ground, surrounded by stone slabs protruding from the ground. Sylvan went past the cemetery and jumped up onto a mound of earth that enclosed the cemetery. On the other side of the cemetery he jumped down and disappeared. Bartholomew quickly followed because in truth, he had never seen this before.

When he came down on the other side his friend was sitting down in front of a small pool of water no larger than a few cubits. This was a hole in the ground now filled with water from a deep cistern. Bartholomew sat down next to his friend and stared into the pool for a moment.

"An ancient pool," Bartholomew finally said with disappointment. "You wanted me to see an ancient pool of water?"

Sylvan smiled, for his friend did not notice and it was in his nature to be cynical and slow to understand. "I found this," he said finally. "It is special. Look at the water."

Bartholomew looked down. The surface was calm and reflected the image of the overhanging trees."

"Wait for it," Sylvan said patiently. "Keep still and wait for it Bartholomew."

Bartholomew continued to watch the pool, but still nothing was changed. Gradually he began to become attuned to the sound of a single bird singing sweetly from an overhanging bough. The song of the bird soothed his mind and made him more receptive to the sound of the world around him. And then the water became dark as the reflection from above faded. Now the smoothness of the water was replaced by a shimmering, a shimmering undulation in the water that was not unlike the tiny vibrations of the wind through the soft hair-like petals of the wood hyacinth in the thick scented air before a violent storm. And as the pool became more opaque his vision became more attuned to the surface of the water until the vibrations of the one, reflected the reverberations in the other. Each new thought brought a new vibration to the surface causing him to plunge further, deeper into the pool. His mind was not his own now as a new thought was being written into his soul. A song was being sung, but the song was not his own. Deeper and deeper the music of his soul took him and the song was reflected in the vibration in the water. Long this sensation lasted though time did not move. Then his mind slowly began to clear until the surface of the water once more became a reflecting, silver mirror. His breath came back to him and he felt weak from an inner emotion newly revealed.

Prince Bartholomew was jolted out of the trance to which he had succumbed. Something inside of him revolted and pitched him out of the void which was sucking him down. His friend Sylvan was watching him intently, expectantly. The tension that was between them was unbroken as neither one wanted to break the spell. After several minutes the feeling diminished and the Prince broke the silence.

"Tell me about this thing," he said plainly as his senses slowly came back to him and he let out a long breath of air.

"Everything in the cosmos, Bartholomew, everything in the world is one thing. The world is a liquid just like the surface of the pool and everything is communicated together. It's the spirit of the water," Sylvan said eagerly. "It's the spirit of the world. Did you hear it?"

"What are you saying, Sylvan? Are you saying that the water is alive?"

"The surface of the pool is like a mirror, Bartholomew. It is sensitive to your gaze, and like the gossamer wings of a tiny water creature, it is sensitive to your thought."

"But my thoughts were emptied into the depth of the pool," responded Bartholomew. "And I too became empty."

Sylvan leaned back and chewed on a stem. "The soul is a mirror," he said.

"The soul is the mirror of God," responded Bartholomew quickly by way of defending his own faith. "I see the truth now where once I was ignorant."

Sylvan would not relent because he still did not believe that the Prince understood what had happened to him. "God does not need a mirror to look into your soul," he said.

"The mirror is for us," Bartholomew countered. "The mirror is for us that we may see into the mind of God. Go back home now my friend. I will meet you there soon."

When Sylvan was gone and Bartholomew was alone he sat for a long time and thought about what had happened to him. He knew that he was alone, but somehow he felt exposed, and that he was not alone. God knew what was in his soul, that he believed, but what about Satan, did he know what was in his soul too? He thought once again about what the Abbot had said to him earlier . . . that morning? The Abbot had said that if one was very quiet they could hear the voice of God speaking to them. He looked at the pool again and he began to feel ashamed about the way he had acted that day. There would be a deep bruise on his face to remind him however. At last he picked up a small pebble near his shoe and pitched it into the pool, disturbing the water. Then he got to his feet and went to his horse.

On the road back to Castletown he rode with reckless abandon, for now he felt alive, he felt a strange exhilaration that came with certainty of a new action. This is how he was. Instead of going to Castletown however, he turned along the narrow path leading to the abbey just as the sun was going down. They would be singing vespers he thought to himself.

Bartholomew walked his horse slowly and respectfully along the path leading up to the monastery. Constructed in strict accordance with the requirements of the Order, the monastery consisted in a set of buildings constructed in rectangular form and oriented according to the sunrise with the chapterhouse at a right angle facing north. The stone buildings were constructed of hewn stone, uninviting, stern, and mostly dark, for candles were not lit without purpose lest the dark places be immersed in shadow. He hesitated before entering the square. In the chapel he could see faint light coming through the narrow windows and he could hear the faint sound of chanting monks. The quadrangle was lined with shade trees and was rather large. Outside the courtyard Bartholomew tied the reins of his horse to a tree and entered the cloister, moving along the darkening cloister walk. This is where he had met with the Abbot and his father.

Not wanting to disturb the Abbot during the divine office and not knowing what else to do. He sat down and rested against the strength of an old oak tree and bent his ear to the sublime music coming from inside. In a few moments he was asleep.

The soft sound of a man's voice woke him. A bright light was shining in his face. It was dark all around him now. Then the light moved away from his face and he could see the outline of the Abbot, wreathed in the soft light from the lantern he carried. The Abbot spoke softly, for he recognized the Prince.

"You are hurt," he said plainly, but there was compassion in his voice.

Prince Bartholomew relaxed. A feeling of wellness and calmness overcame his tired body. He no longer felt the pain in his face.

"I am not hurt," he answered. Then he looked at the Abbot and felt the calmness of his presence, but he remained silent.

The Abbot waited patiently. He did nothing to make the Prince feel that there was anything out of the ordinary happening. The cloister was quiet and peaceful. A solitary bird sang from a high bough. The Abbot smiled warmly.

"Saint Francis loved birds," he said. "So did our Lord. With all the wild places in which to perch, and yet it comes here."

Then the Abbot paused. He looked at Bartholomew and he could see that he was waiting for something and that he knew not how to begin. The Abbot was a very wise man indeed.

"The birds speak in the language of God. Do you believe that, Bartholomew?"

The Prince was about to answer when he realized that the Abbot was not finished yet, and that he was waxing philosophical. Bartholomew found this a very welcome distraction, for the sound of the Abbot's voice was comforting. He wanted to hear the thoughts of the Abbot; for the moment, his own thoughts were unimportant.

"I tell you, Bartholomew . . . the birds are born to be happy. That is how they were created. It is their very nature to be happy and to sing. The Lord loves them, and He is pleased to listen to their song, as am I."

Then the Abbot did something startling: he raised his head and whistled in the language of birds. He whistled, and an unseen starling hopped on to a lower branch just above their head. The starling twittered and the Abbot twittered back to the starling. Then the starling flew away and the Abbot looked down to Bartholomew.

"There is a story I heard once," he began. "It is told that one day our Lord, while walking along the road west of the Sea of Galilee, stopped to rest beneath a large cypress tree. In His pocket He brought out a crust of bread to eat because He was very hungry. A tiny sparrow was perched on a branch just above our Lord's head and chirped as our Lord was eating. [17]The friendly bird hopped down and landed on the ground in front of Him. The Lord, not wanting to deny the hunger of even the lowest of His creatures, tore off a small piece of bread and fed it to the bird. The bird flew away at once to eat the tiny morsel. Soon there were many birds surrounding the Lord. He fed them all, and yet His hunger was relieved."

Bartholomew smiled, for the story was familiar to him. "I do not understand," he said. "Are we to go hungry, so that others' may eat?"

The Abbot smiled back. "To the Lord, we are all like the tiny sparrow, Bartholomew. If one were to seek the nourishment of our Lord, how much the better for the entire world?"

"I want to apologize to you," Bartholomew said suddenly. Now he felt compelled to speak. "I was a fool, but now I understand something. Yes, there are many forms of intoxication. Indeed, there are many forms of temptation. I have experienced some of these temptations. And while I experienced the intoxication of the body, I did not understand that there is also another form of intoxication, the intoxication of the spirit."

"Have you experienced this also?" asked the Abbot.

"Yes I have," Bartholomew answered. And then he rose to his feet and inclined his head in deference to the Abbot. "Thank you," he said. And then he left the cloister quietly and led his horse away from the abbey before mounting for the ride back to his home.

---

[17] *Jesus asked, "Are not two sparrows sold for a farthing?" And again, "Are not five sparrows sold for two farthings?*

Alliesian Cog and the Magic Candle

"Pity the weak man whose faith is tested, but fear for the strong man whose faith thus be tested. I say this to you Iona because I have been tested severely. Only pray for me Iona, for my faith is tested every day."

*Our soul is like a tiny flame burning sweetly
that we may follow when our thoughts darken,
for the light of our soul never fades completely
and the voices of the angels forever hearken."*

The Isle of Man is a lost island of demons and wizards steadfastly preserving the magic of the power of words and the power of belief. Saints and sinners have come to her shores in search of answers and have found only deeper questions. Sleeping gods are sometimes woken by the murmur and incantations of restless men wandering the windy, wispy, landscape protected by towering cliffs jutting from the sea. Many a man has drown in the frigid waters and stories abound of the peril of lost sailors being pulled from her waters by miraculous hands. On the Isle of Man, even the stones talk to one another. It is the spirits that are jealous and intolerant of speech.

On the west side of the island near a high and craggy cliff where wind from the sea blows persistently across the sharp, jagged cliffs, sets a cottage. This is the cottage of Alliesian Cog. No trees grow on this precipice where his cottage rests against the edge of the island like a broken hand clinging for safety. Some day the cottage will be blown into the sea and disappear, but until such a time, Cog remains steadfast. Like many that come to the island, Cog is something of a mystery and little is known about him for certain. Rarely does he leave his home, and when he does it is cause of much discussion and discourse when his inner thoughts be translated into language. And it is also a rare event when one is able to share a pint with him at a local inn, for he does not mix much with other people.

Cog is an expert on angels. In truth, if truth can be learned from him at all through his obscure speech, he speaks to angels on a regular timetable. He calls them and they appear. Cog knows some of the angels by name and it is from them that his vast knowledge is derived.

The people shy away from Cog because they are afraid of him. Most people only watch him walk along the high cliffs near his cottage in the twilight hours, plodding along with his hat and his walking stick. They watch him and they wonder, but not aloud. Talk of spirits and angels turns most men's hearts to stone as the subject brings out memories and mysteries of all manner of supernaturalism and other things carefully buried. They say that the island is still alive with evil spirits and angry gods and it is no weak-minded Manxman that wishes to stir up trouble.

No one truly remembers when Cog came to The Isle of Man, for he has lived here for many years now, settling at last on the lonely cliff by the sea. Like many, the history of his life has become mixed with hearsay and rumors, for many are the men that come to the isle to escape other demons. The stories about him are as numerous as they are horrible to hear. There is however a consensus about certain facts and it is the veracity of these facts that account for his aloofness and unwillingness to mix with the people of Man. Moreover, it is exactly for this ability to dissolve into folklore that he came to live here in the first place.

There was a time when Cog was married to a beautiful woman whom he worshiped like a precious object and kissed tenderly each first light of daybreak. They lived happily in a small village of the Habsburg Empire. There was a small pond on the edge of the village where they would walk together and throw seeds to the birds. Together they raised a few sheep the wool of which they sheared and wove into beautiful rugs and blankets. Cog was also a talented smith. He forged his metal into knives and scissors and shears and blades for working the earth. These tools were admired by noblemen from afar and Cog earned a good living even after paying his taxes to the duke. During some of his free moments he made elaborate tools for working the fine wool they collected, and these he made into presents for his beautiful wife, Alliena.

Alliena loved her work and there was not a day she would not fuss over a particular aspect of her craft that she was always improving with the new tools given to her by her husband. Alliena worked her craft out of love and she poured her soul into each of her creations before giving most of them away to other people of the village in greater need than her, for in truth she was very generous.

Most of the villagers were poor, earning their living from working the soil or the raising of lowly animals. Their hands were hard, their mind was slow, and their tongues were sharp, for they were uneducated and ignorant of most of the ways of the nobility and the conveniences and frivolities afforded to people of class. Their clothes were simple and coarse to withstand the intense labor in the field and the damaging rays of the sun, so they were justly bewildered by the fine and delicate wares crafted by Alliena.

Into the blankets she made, Alliena wove in wonderful patterns and pictures. Alliena was a gifted woman, but in truth it was from her generous heart that her gifts were sown. Sometimes she adorned them with symbols and mysterious designs with special colors because she loved to think and daydream about her forthcoming life in heaven when her time on earth was over. She and her husband loved to talk about heaven. In heaven no one would ever be hungry again and no one would need to fight in wars and die alone on freezing battlements. In heaven, her husband had said, never an angry word would ever be uttered for anger could not exist in the presence of the Lord.

During the long, dark nights, warm and safely behind locked door, by candlelight Alliena would work with her needles and wool and she would listen with rapt attention to her good husband as he would talk about heaven and the angels. Alliena was not a learned woman, for it was not proper for women to study writings and have knowledge of matters not relevant to domesticity. It was hard in such times to get enough food to eat, so there was no time for pointless and profitless endeavors. Books and manuscripts were written by men and they were to be studied by men. The realm of words was ecclesiastical, and it was not for blacksmiths and sheepherders to have occasion to own private books lest it lead them to thoughts of their own. It was true that some thought, if allowed to kindle in the weak mind of uneducated men, could rage across the countryside like wildfire. In this way heresies and dangerous philosophy had slowly penetrated into the narrowest, lowliest hovels of the empire. So the people were kept busy and mostly they were too tired and cold to turn their mind to subjects they could not understand. In this way, folklore became a secret language that only the simple men and women huddled in smoky rooms listening to stories from toothless men, truly understood. Alliena's husband was different. Her husband was a hard worker and his hands were black and calloused, but he was also wise and he had many friends across the land that knew about his vast knowledge of angels and angelic power. They would travel across the Continent on foot, through the dense and dangerous forests, across vast untamed land to hear him expound about angels. Often they would arrive during the nighttime hours and their arrival would cause a stir amongst the sleeping peasants and drowsy dogs of the village.

"Listen," Cog would speak to her tenderly. "The angels will come to us if we call to them because they love us. They guide us and each of us has been assigned an angel to watch us. We do not have to see them to know that they are there, do you understand, Alliena?"

Alliena smiled and looked up from her needlework. Silently she acquiesced and Cog continued with greater tenderness.

"The angels are terrible in their virtue," he continued. "And that is why we cannot bear to stand in their presence, Alliena, for when we sin the angels are near and we are burned by their virtue. Angels have knowledge of the truth, but we must come to this knowledge through our experiences here on earth. This is our mission. Sometimes this knowledge is given to us, Alliena. This is what revelation is."

"Can the angels fight the evil that is in our land?" said Alliena suddenly. She stopped sewing and looked at her husband for an answer. "There are witches everywhere, why do the angels not fight them?"

"There will come a day when the [18]Principalities will come down and wash away the filth from our good land. They watch us, Alliena. They watch out over our cities and villages, and they wait . . ."

Alliena watched her husband expectantly. She felt safe in his presence because of the goodness in his heart. His vision was clear enough for the both of them and she followed him confidently through the frightening and trying times in which they lived.

"What do they wait for?" she asked.

"It is complicated," he answered. "I believe that there are forces of evil that also watch us and wait for a chance to lead us to perdition. [19]Abbad

---

[18] *Principalities. The seventh order of angels in the hierarchy of Dionysius.*

[19] *Abbadon. Angel of destruction and of hell, or the bottomless pit.*

on, the angel of destruction, waits patiently."

"And how are we to know if an angel is a good angel or a bad angel? How can we ever know?"

"Do not worry, Alliena. I will always be with you and I will protect you from evil. I will deal with the angels."

And so it was that Cog dealt with the angels, for he knew their names and he knew how to contact them. One day while he was chopping wood to feed his stove an angel appeared to him and told him of a time of great sorrow that would soon befall the village. Being only a ninth order angel, the angel could not intervene but only warn Cog to beware lest he be swept away in the maelstrom.

Cog was vigilant with his words and with his thoughts. Every night he would read to Alliena stories of the saints and martyrs and how they were tested. He would sing softly to her as she would work the magic into the blankets she wove, for love is magic and the love was in her hands. There was not much to eat during that long winter and every day Cog would go off into the woods to hunt. He would crouch down into the snow and he would wait for a chance to surprise an unsuspecting animal that was also trying to survive the bitter winter. Sometimes he would come home with a quail or a rabbit, but many times he would come home with only a song in his heart to lessen the pangs of hunger. Sometimes he would fall into a deep state of relaxation and his mind would drift away from his body. During some of these moments he would talk to angels. And then he would walk home with no memory of his conversation or only fragments that would need to be pieced together. Alliena would always know that he had spoken with the angels and she would not speak to him until his mind had returned to their tiny home. She could see vestiges of dreaminess in his eyes and she would not wish to break the spell of enchantment. They had enough flour however and they enjoyed making bread and drinking warm cider with their evening meal. The winter moved in and they huddled closer together through the long, cold nights.

The next morning after visitations from the angels, Cog would be anxious to tell his wife everything he remembered. It was only after a night of sleep that the memories would begin to return to him like air bubbles rising to the surface on a pond of fronds. Then he would relate to her what had been given to him. And so it was that other believers would travel for days just for a chance to hear Cog speak his broken speech about things he only half-remembered.

One very cold winter day Alliena trudged out through the deep snow carrying one of the blankets she had made. She was bringing this to one of her neighbors who had recently delivered a beautiful baby girl. The blanket was very special to Alliena and she waited for a special occasion to make a gift of it. The birth of a new baby was just such an occasion. She had decorated it with an intricate Celtic knot-work symbolizing the power of unity.

That winter proved to be a hard and portentous winter. Wind and snow scoured the hamlets and villages in the domain of Duke Mac Millan, lacerating the tiny hovels of the frightened people. Wolves patrolled the edges of the village and threatened the livestock, and hunting parties were organized to fight them back into the wild. Hunting was poor, and even rabbits were hard to come by. In that cold and bitter winter, some of the people died from fever.

The weak and infirm were among the first to die including the beautiful baby girl with the lovely blanket woven by Alliena. Soon after the baby was buried in the churchyard, Alliena delivered a baby boy of her own. Cog was proud and went through the village telling everyone about the beautiful baby given to him by the Lord. Cog was enraptured with his baby, so it is possible that he forgot about the poor child that had barely settled in the grave when he went to that bereaved hovel in such a state of joy. Is it true that some sins can never be forgiven? Is it true that some indiscretions can never be rectified? Can it be true that the world be balanced so precariously against the tiniest sin that could destroy her? Cog never meant to elevate his happiness over the grief of those less fortunate than himself. But sometimes the nature of happiness causes people to become indiscrete against all their better intentions, and if it were not for this beautiful quality the world should perish from utter shame.

Isabel Merrywurt was a horrible and terrible woman it is true. She was jealous and petty, she was quick to anger and retribution, she was selfish, cantankerous, vile, full of vitriol and stupid if the complete truth be known about her. She owned practically nothing. She was poor and her children suffered the more for her bitterness and despair. In part, her selfishness can be explained by her complete and utter hopelessness in the wake of her tragic fate so common among the wretched poor.

When despair and despondency become too great of a load to bear, the bitter person oftentimes turn in new directions to look for answers and to place the blame where it can be made personal and real. This is what Isabel Merrywurt did in order to make sense of her own disgust for herself and her condition.

Into this cauldron of iniquity and despondency is added the responsibility of raising yet another child, a child of God. Who among us cannot agonize over the fear of a hopeless mother trying desperately to feed her children? Who could not sympathize with her anguish over how to feed her family when her own husband did not have enough to eat and began to wither away like a slowly dying plant? Isabel's condition, no matter how dire, did little however to excuse her own corrosive nature, for this too is the work of the devil. And with the help of the devil, Isabel Merrywurt appeared in front of the local constable and denounced Alliena as a witch. That Alliena had also lost her own child on that cold and fateful winter was seen as evidence of her guilt, for according to Isabel Merrywurt, she had given her own child to the devil in a witches' Sabbath.

Alliena steadfastly maintained her innocence, for she was no more a witch than the tears of her baby an ocean. Sadly for Alliena however her fate had been sealed the day she was denounced, for innocent persons were never denounced and to be denounced was to be guilty. Cog told the investigators that they were making a mistake, but the word of the husband of a witch is worthless. He pleaded with them to reconsider the hateful words of a bereaved woman looking to blame someone for her own ill fortune, but they would not listen. Cog was not even allowed to talk to her or to see her. He went through the village tearfully lamenting his fate, but the people were afraid of him now and they remembered the strange visitations during the night and they wondered about him.

Cog walked the empty streets in a haze. He could not sleep and he could not eat, but all he could do was to think about the horrible treatment his wife was soon to endure. How could this have happened that a good act, an act of charity, could turn out so wrong? Alliena's love had been returned with hate. Alas, such a bitter world it had become. He went into several taverns and was chased away. The people did not want him around anymore; he was marked. No one would listen to him. The world had turned its back on Cog, but it would be his dear wife that would suffer for it.

Slowly Cog walked to the edge of the village. There was a little stone wall that acted as a boundary and kept the sheep from escaping, for the wall belonged to an old farmer whom Cog had been friends with when there were sheep. Now there were no more sheep and weeds grew up through patches of snow and bent against the bracing wind. It was dark. The night sky was filled with bright stars. Cog sat on the stone wall and drew his coat tightly around him to stay warm. He looked at the stars. The heavenly sphere was mysterious and beautiful as the wandering stars like clockwork danced across the sky and recorded the events on earth. He knew that there were messages in the stars and he knew that [20] Wormwood would fall from the sky without warning. No, he could not read the messages in the stars. Perhaps there was nothing in the stars. Perhaps the world had already ended. And that is when Cog did something desperate and full of despair. He took off his coat and threw it away in the snow. Then he lay on his back on the frozen wall beneath the starlit heaven and went to sleep.

Alliena fell in and out of tortured sleep. She lay against a stone wall, her legs manacled to cold steel chains. She clutched tightly to a lice-infested blanket worn thin and frayed at the edges. In her tormented sleep she still worked her beautiful designs into her own blankets. In her dream she was taking one of her blankets to a house that was lit up warmly and bright. She knocked on the door and she could see people inside, but they could not hear her knocking and she was left knocking and waiting to be heard . . .

Cog opened his eyes. He was confused, for it was morning and the sky was beginning to brighten. He tried to remember why he was so confused, and then he remembered and he wondered if he was dead.

"You are not dead," said a familiar voice. It was the voice of an angel. It was the compassionate voice of his companion angel, Ariel.

Cog was nestled safely in the arms of his guardian angel, and he was warm. His coat was wrapped around his body and the angel held him close and shielded him from the wind.

"The dark night of your soul has passed," said Ariel. "Do you feel better?"

---

[20] *Wormwood. The name of a star in Revelation 8. It falls from heaven and poisons the rivers and springs.*

"You have saved me only to suffer greater anguish," Cog answered.

"All must suffer," said Ariel gently and Cog could feel his arms tighten slightly.

"Is it necessary that we should suffer, Ariel? Tell me true and assuage my broken heart."

"The world of blood is wrought with pain and suffering. Rejoice that you may live."

"Is my soul so important to you then?" Cog said painfully.

"A lost soul is like a lost sheep. Better that it had never been born than to be sacrificed on the altar of pity. How much more beautiful it is to save a lost sheep than for the entire herd to perish by wolves and be martyred."

"I do not understand you," said Cog.

"There is more sadness in store for you," said Ariel. "You may be weak in body, that you be strong in spirit."

Then the angel was gone and Cog was warm and sober in the morning light. He put his coat on and walked back to his home, and his warm breath crystallized in the morning air.

Burgomaster Eckert sat at his desk and pretended to look at the writing on a piece of paper set before him. His lone, drooping eye lazily scanned the paper before rising to fall on the body of Cog who stood before him obediently. He was in an unpleasant position, having to defend the actions of the Witchmaster General, and he did not want to bother with it. The husband of the woman being tried for witchcraft, Cog was not likely to see the justice. Oh, if only the woman could just die and be done with! He had to feign compassion however, for that was his role in the proceedings, and as Burgomaster he was charged with running a village free from witchcraft.

"You would not recognize her now," the Burgomaster said. "The devil has been exposed and she is a vessel for evil. Pray for her soul, Alliesian, and do not come here again."

Cog had to do something! He tried to make the Burgomaster understand.

"I can care for her," he pleaded. "She will . . . I will take her away from this place if that is what you want."

"Then you would seek to spread this evil to another unsuspecting village?"

"No, no of course not," Cog quickly added.

"Then you still deny that she is a witch!" shouted the Burgomaster, slamming his hand on the table with such force that Cog nearly fell over from fright. "You best be on your way," he continued. "You best be on your way, for now I am beginning to suspect you."

Cog prayed day and night until he became sick and feverish, and it was during his darkest hour that the angel Ariel appeared to him near the window. The angel was luminous and shone translucent in the dim light. The angel floated near the rafters and looked down upon him. Cog looked up to the angel and his grief was so great that he could only cry.

"I do not cry for myself," Cog said mournfully. "I cry for my wife."

"Protect your grief for it is beautiful," said Ariel. "Only guard your soul that it not be fortified with vengeance."

"I do not need protection," Cog answered through his anguish. "My wife needs protection, not I."

"You cannot protect her," the angel Ariel answered. "I cannot protect her. Rejoice in the wisdom of the Lord, for the wine is more precious than the cup. I have come to protect you."

"Can you not save her from such injustice?"

"There can be no justice on Earth," said the angel Ariel. "Much is hidden above [21]The Curtain."

---

[21] *The Curtain. This is the partition between earthly and heavenly life.*

"Do you know the future?"

"I know all things," the angel Ariel answered.

"Then tell me what to do?" Cog pleaded with intensity. "Surely you must know everything that will happen."

"I do know what is going to happen," Ariel answered. "But I do not know what is in your heart."

"What is in your heart?" Cog answered angrily.

The angel Ariel vanished. Cog looked at the window where the angel floated. He stared at the window as if he were waiting for something, waiting for another sign. He stared at the window in vain and waited for the angel to come back.

 Soon her interrogation began. During the long and thorough process of interrogation, most consorts of the devil were made to remember their own guilt with the aid of professional methods printed in manuals like the Malleus[22] Maleficarum. Sometimes the consorts of the devil had a much harder time remembering their guilt and during these times drastic measures were taken to save their soul.

Finally Cog decided to murder the terrible woman who had accused his wife, for it was the only way he would be able to live with himself. That the woman could live when his wife must die he could never accept. He paced back and forth through his lonely house. He had forgotten to light the stove and his house was freezing, but he could not remember why he was so cold. Such was the mind of Cog. Back and forth he paced for hours trying to decide whether or not to burn her house down or to just strike her dead with an axe. The longer he thought about it the greater his passion became until he was no longer cold though there was frost on his table.

Cog reached for an axe that he kept next to the door. He could not lift it. Then he saw that the angel Ariel was preventing him from raising it off

---

[22] *Heinrich Institoris' Malleus Maleficarum, The Witch Hammer. Published in 1486. A handbook of interrogation methods involving torture to obtain confessions from witches.*

the floor.

"I will not allow you to do this," said Ariel.

"Let go of the axe," Cog demanded. "You have no right to stop me."

Then Ariel put his hands on Cog's shoulders and held him fast. "I will not allow you to do this to yourself," he said again.

Cog struggled within the grasp of the angel Ariel and they wrestled until Cog was exhausted. Finally Cog slumped to the floor despondently, defeated.

"You would wrestle with me all night, but you would do nothing to save my wife."

"Do not judge the wisdom of the Lord," Ariel said with sympathy. "And do not try to guess the future, for only the Lord knows."

By now the passion of Cog had abated and he no longer sought vengeance on the woman. He looked at Ariel and could only wonder why he cared so much for him.

"I will not harm the woman," Cog said at last with a sigh. But the angel was already gone.

On April 6, during an intense interrogation, Alliena remembered the events leading up to her apostasy and subsequent pact with the devil. The events were carefully recorded and entered as evidence against her. Cog would never see her again. When the news was given to him that Alliena had perished during questioning, he threw away his soul, for he had no use for it any longer. The Lord had broken him completely. Gathering a few possessions that he stowed into a pack, he went into the street in front of his house, and there to his own demise, he cursed the name of the Lord and walked away without looking back.

Cog spent his first night alone, in the thick forest at the edge of the village. With him he carried enough supplies to last long enough until he found another village where he could find work. With him he carried a broadsword he had forged specially for himself before leaving his own village. Should he be accosted on the road by hooligans and robbers, they would taste the product of his skill with steel.

He threw down his pack and went to work building a fire. Soon he had a good fire going and he went to work roasting a rabbit he had caught earlier that day. This night Cog said no prayer before dinner because he could not bear to think about divine matters. He fell asleep as the fire continued to blaze.

Sometime during the night he was awoken by the sound of growling and of the snapping of angry jaws. He jumped up and threw some more branches on the dwindling fire until it was once again raging. Then he looked in the snow directly across the perimeter of where his camp was made. The fire cast wavering light that reached to the edge of the forest, but it could not penetrate the inner blackness. He looked down. There were footprints in the snow. These were footprints from a large animal. "Strange that I was not attacked in my sleep," he muttered to himself.

He looked up to the sky and sighed. The clouds were thick and covered the canopy of stars completely. Cog was truly alone now. The angel had left him and the wilderness he now traveled was colder than anything he had ever known.

Alliesian Cog wandered the Continent for several years, doing odd jobs and living off the land. He could easily find work when he told the people that he had some skill with metal. But everywhere he went the people were suspicious of him and watched him like a hawk. Sometimes they asked him to help with the forge. They fed him when he asked, but only reluctantly and with the intention that he would soon leave. His thoughts narrowed until the only thing in his mind was the desire to stay alive.

At last he came to the Isle of Man aboard a fishing vessel. His beard had grown wild and his hair was now turned white and he came to the new land as a new man. The Continent was being scoured of witches, their familiars, and every manifestation of evil, and like a pestilence sweeping across the earth the scourge killed everything within reach. Cog knew that he would be safe and out of reach on the Isle of Man, but he also wanted to be close to the spirit of his lost wife. For now, the Isle of Man was a haven, a sanctuary where women were not tortured and the devil was not feared.

The Isle of Man is not large; it is only 12 miles wide at the narrowest point, but Cog at first wanted to be near the sea where he was not closed in. He had a fear of being captured and forced into smaller and smaller compartments. His fear was the fear of being in enclosed places because the smaller and smaller his compartment became the closer he came to himself. The sound of the sea was comforting and sometimes at night he could not hear his own cries.

The first time Cog saw them was on a cold and rainy night. The sound of the storm had woken him and now he could not fall back to sleep. Demons, it is said, can hide within the shadows of ordinary matter. These shape-shifting demons can make themselves invisible to ordinary perception, and it takes a special form of perception to see them in their horrible disguise. These demons are not themselves made of matter. They are incorporeal, as their corporality exists in another, obscure and distant plane of existence. And so they control their own fatal, disembodied spirits from a world that intersects with our own world through the shadows and amorphous vapors of the otherworld.

For years Cog had wandered the brutal edges of a world lit by fire, a world fading in and out of holy epiphanies and savage cruelty. This netherworld of horror is where Cog spent his life, so it was only too natural that he should one day wander too far and unexpectedly glimpse the world where black shadows move. Or was it only that the horror that was his own life had made him more sensitive to the evil and unholy machinations for which the hearts of men are but a battlefield? Cog had seen his share of horror and grief in his life it is true, but he was not prepared for the horror of being confronted with a demon the night it stole into his small cottage.

Cog did not know it but demons have no fear of soulless men. Demons have no fear of soulless men because they are unprotected, they are easy, and they are beyond hope. Soulless men offer little resistance. For several nights now Cog was restless and slept fitfully, sometimes waking several times, suspicious, paranoid, always apprehensive. Each time he would systematically look around his dark room, peering through the blackness, hoping to find something to explain his nervousness. He knew that if he only kept his eyes open he would be safe. He would sometimes pass through the entire night alert, frozen and paralyzed in his cold bed.

And then he saw something peculiar. It was a shadow near the window that moved ever so slightly against the backdrop of the night constellations. The shadow would shift and a star would disappear as if the blackness of the shadow were more empty than the night sky and the night sky had fallen into a great abyss. He froze. The star swallowing shadow seemed to grow. He tried to cry out, to speak, but his mouth would not open and his body trembled.

Then the shadow began to slowly move across the floor toward the bed. There were no sharp edges to the apparition, but instead it remained an amorphous mass of nothingness. Directly for him it came, slowly, purposely, inexorably. Cog nearly died from sheer panic until at the last moment he jumped out of bed and ran from the house. The open air and the night sky made him feel safe. He slept no more that night, and each and every night afterward he wondered . . . he wondered if the shadow would return and what would happen if he were asleep. Cog knew that he was being watched, he was being stalked, but he could not understand what or why this was happening to him now.

After a fortnight he was near exhaustion, for he could sleep for only minutes before waking in a panic to search the house for the shadow. He knew that he had to find a way to stop it; he had to find a way to kill the shadow. But how does one destroy something without body, without substance, without form? What tools, what weapons could be used against such a monster? Cog knew that he needed help. Cog knew he needed someone to tell him how to fight such a foe. So, taking his coin purse and a sharp dagger, and filling his pipe with a load of tobacco, he locked his door and began walking to Castletown.

Cog was afraid to travel at night for how could he see the shadow? If the shadow was where the monster lived he would never see it. But he was no less afraid to travel during the daylight, for there were shadows everywhere, and that is where the shadow hid. The path to Castletown was well-trodden if narrow. Cog loved to walk through the woods and through the moors and meadows of his homeland, and everywhere he traveled he traveled by foot. His legs were his freedom. Cog was swift and surefooted. An oak staff he carried for balance and for sweeping away snakes and other serpents from his path. When life became too difficult or too unbearable for him to cope, he would start to walk and soon his mind would clear and his anxiety would be left behind in the dust from his pigskin boots. No, there would be no other travelers this day. The people would be in church.

He arrived in Castletown by late afternoon without incident. After being cooped up in the house for so long it was good to be on the road again wandering the pathways and byways of his new home. Now he needed to find supper and a bed for the night. Tomorrow he would look for a sorcerer to help him deal with his problem.

On the outskirts of Castletown there is an inn, an inn not usually visited by outsiders. It is called *The Blacksmith*, and it is owned and run by a wizened old codger named Todd. Todd is an old blacksmith, hence the name of his establishment, *The Blacksmith*. He had burned his hands beyond recognition in an accident long ago, so now he no longer works the forge. Instead, he only works the oven. On his hands are two large gloves which he always wears to protect them. They say that the sight of his hands are enough to cause the ladies to faint, so he keeps them covered. But take pride in his cooking he does, because even with destroyed hands he can still roast a fine leg of lamb and it takes no great skill to work a tap. The people that come to his inn are a different sort in all certainty. Todd doesn't run the cleanest establishment, but he is quick with a drink and he doesn't ask too many questions of strangers. Some folk prefer to just stay away from *The Blacksmith* altogether. So much the better, for the regulars prefer it that way. They say that bad things sometimes happen at *The Blacksmith*.

Entering the dimly-lit inn, Cog stepped through the smoky haze and brought his staff down with a dull thud on the wooden floor. The curious eyes of a few oafish and vulgar woodsmen fell on Cog and summed up his worth for buying drinks and giving a good story. One of the men stood up by way of introduction and belched loudly. Then he sat down again and resumed his eating. They were none too impressed with Cog.

The innkeeper, Todd, shouted from behind the counter where he was drawing a tankard. "Are you looking for food?"

"Aye," said Cog, trying to sound as harmless as possible. "And a bed for the night. I don't need much, and I don't mind mice and noise and spiders either."

"Sit down," said Todd unceremoniously. "I'll bring you a pint and then you can tell me what you want to eat."

Cog sat at a table in a dark corner near the window and took off his hat. He laid his staff across his lap and loosened his coat. Then he started to fill his pipe when Todd came over and set down a large glass of beer.

"I like bread and meat," said Cog. "Bring me what you have."

When Todd returned with a large plate of steaming food piled high Cog asked him. "Pray tell me where I can find a sorcerer, if you can. That is, if you believe in such things as such."

"A sorcerer, you say?" Todd replied with a laugh. "That isn't hard. Castletown is full of sorcerers. A sorcerer and a saucer full of secrets, they're burning witches for nightlights on the Continent. But witches are safe here."

"I have a job for one of them if they be willing."

Later that night after all the men folk had went home, Cog turned over in his bed and opened his eyes. He could not sleep. Todd the innkeeper had continued bringing him drink after drink after drink until he was fairly drunk. And the smoke was so thick! Cog was not a drinker, nor the rowdy sort, so the evening was disruptive to his digestion and now he felt sick.

The lamps were still burning outside and the weak light filtered through the open window. The air was cold and damp, heavy as they liked to say on the island. Sounds of the night filled his small room where creeping predators sometimes came close to the inn. He lay there for hours, falling in and out of a fitful sleep, waking every few minutes completely disoriented. Then his mind focused on the sound of the wind. The sound was distant and ethereal, luring him to follow into the darker realms of slumber. He was being carried by the wind aloft and floating without the need for his body, floating, following a silver thread, always moving away. And then he lost consciousness. Now the air got heavier.

Slowly he came to realize that he was awake and that he was staring at a shadow against the wall near the window. How long he had been staring at it he could not remember. The demon had followed him to Castletown. But now he was so exhausted that he could not remain awake. Try as he may, he was going under . . . He snapped his eyes open an instant later. The shadow had moved closer. Now his throat was tightening, choking off any attempt to cry out. He stared at the shadow . . . opening his eyes desperately he saw that the shadow was even closer.

And then in one giant leap it was on him, pushing him down like a giant rock. Cog was paralyzed, unable to move or to cry out. He struggled in his mind, trying to break free of the tremendous force that was crushing him, choking him. Cog was shaking violently, contorting, twisting and thrashing about. And then he saw the creature above him pushing him down with hideous and terrible hands, horrible destroyed hands. He was straining against incredible power clawing at him with such hideous hands. The monster was speaking . . .

"Wake up! Wake up! Come out of it!" It was Todd the innkeeper.

When Cog left the inn later that morning, Todd the innkeeper took him aside. "You asked me about a sorcerer," he said softly. "Now you listen to me and I'll tell you where to find one . . ."

Cog stumbled like a drunken man across the uneven flagstones that paved the narrow lanes of old Castletown. Built close together, the shops and houses rising like a stone barricade carved through the twisting streets crammed everything together, making it hard even for a cart to pass without difficulty. Dogs barked and were kicked aside, babies cried and their tiny voices were drown out by the incessant shouting of their intolerant mothers searching for fish oil and fresh linen. Built around the castle, the town crouched obediently against the stone battlements of the medieval edifice. And even as the castle had fallen into disuse, the town only crouched lower. The street was crowded with determined women carrying packages and footmen escorting docile old men. He was looking for Schemer's bookstore on 9, Arbory Street. There was a small shop just above it where a cunning old woman sold candles and beads and other assorted paraphernalia. He would find his sorcerer there.

Cog entered the shop at street level. He went through a shop heavy with the odor of scented candles and the hint of herb which was just beyond his recognition. The shop was stocked with soaps, candles, white linen, beads, pottery, glassware, rugs, wall decorations, etc. Walking and finding his way through the narrow aisles and alcoves, he finally found the back stairwell told to him by Todd the blacksmith. No one took notice of him as he ascended the creaking stairs and went up to the top floor. At the top of the stairs was a door left partially ajar. Carefully opening the door he went in.

Raggamot looked up from his task and saw Cog standing silently, patiently, waiting to be acknowledged. He had a thick glass lens protruding from his eye, held in place with heavy, drooping eyelids, and in his hand was a long, thin stylus he was using to set a jewel in place. His actions were slow and methodical. He had a long nose that tapered at the end like a beak and slow, murky eyes like the eyes of a dead crow. And his fingers were delicate. Cog thought that they looked oddly feminine and had never experienced a day of honest work.

"You're a jeweler?" said Cog, not so much as a question as an observation. "Todd never said that you were a jeweler."

"Does that disappoint you?" Raggamot answered flatly. Then he sighed. "Yes, I am a jeweler. Now, thank you for coming." Then he put the lens back in his eye and bent his head to his work.

"Wait!" Cog fired back. "I was told to come here. Todd the blacksmith told me to come here. He said that perhaps you could help me. That is . . . if you are a sorcerer."

That made Raggamot smile. "I am many things," he said. "Some things I do for the world, and other things I do for myself. And then, some things I do for other reasons."

Cog anxiously asked: "Do you know anything about demons?"

Raggamot smiled again. "If you have spoken with the blacksmith, then you know that I do. Now tell me then, which demon is it that you are concerned with?"

Cog told Raggamot what he knew. He told him about his flight from the Continent and how he was being pursued by the shadow demon. He was surprised by how much Raggamot seemed to know, nodding his head and asking probing questions that only Cog had knowledge of. When he was finished with his story, Raggamot was satisfied.

"You have forgotten something important," Raggamot said. "You have failed to tell me how and why you lost your soul."

Cog looked up suddenly, completely startled. He looked closely at Raggamot, and now the hair on the back of his neck tingled.

"You have lost your soul," Raggamot continued. "Or, it seems more likely to me that you have thrown it away. The demon that is following you is following you for only one reason. You have no soul, Cog. You are marked. The demon that is following you is an ally of Lucifer. Without a soul, you are free to be plundered. That is why you are being followed. You are dead. You are dark matter, devoid of light. Tell me about when you died, Cog."

Cog was furious. "What on earth are you talking about?" he shouted.

Raggamot was confident. "You have cursed the Lord. That is a sin of separation. It is a sin that is different from all other sins because it separates you from your only possibility of redemption. You have turned your back on God and have abandoned his saving grace. Now, do you remember?"

Then Cog remembered the day he cursed the Lord. It was on the day that he learned the terrible fate of his dear wife. Yes, he was out of his mind with anger and ire for God at the time, but surely the Lord would not condemn him for such a sin of passion. But Raggamot would not listen.

"You do not understand," he said. "The Lord did not throw away your soul, you did. This is your fault, Cog."

"What am I to do then, am I damned forever?"

"You have to fight this demon," said Raggamot. "It is your demon, your personal demon that has been assigned to you. Your soul will not return until you defeat this demon."

"But how can I defeat such a demon?" Cog pleaded. "It hides in the shadows and lurches out at me when I try to sleep. My strength is almost spent trying to keep it at bay."

"Tortured flesh weakens the body and strengthens the soul, but a tortured soul draws unholy power from the flesh and weakens the soul. To deny the flesh, one must torture the soul. Do you understand? The way for you to destroy this demon is to let it come to you," said Raggamot carefully. "You must let this demon enter you. Only then, will you be able to fight it and to kill it."

The words of the sorcerer were plain. Cog understood them even as he was horrified by their implication. But he was desperate and pleaded with the sorcerer to do more. "You are a sorcerer, Raggamot. Why can you not kill it for me?"

"Understand this, Cog. The demon you must face is part of you now, and you can never escape from it. When you cast away your soul, you were no longer part of the world of men. The earth shall be your private hell until you come back into the light."

"Tell me what to do," said Cog with resignation. "I will do anything."

Raggamot got up from his chair. He was wearing a long robe tied with a white braided belt. He went to the door and closed it. Then he went to the window and gazed out for a moment. Cog thought Raggamot had forgotten about him when the sorcerer suddenly turned around and began to speak again.

"The world was divided long ago between matter and things not made of matter. There are things that are, and there are things that are not, do you understand? All that is of this earth is made from things that are. But there are other things, Cog. The spirit does not belong to the world of things. The spirit belongs to the things that are not. The spirit is light. The light is the spirit of God, and all that is not light is not from God. We are trapped in our bodies of matter, but our spirit is part of God. To fight this evil you must first accept it, and then . . ."

"And then what?" Cog broke in frantically with growing uneasiness.

"I can help you kill it, but there may be some unexpected damage."

"How so?" begged Cog to know. "Tell me Raggamot!"

"Do you remember Todd the blacksmith?" Raggamot asked slowly.

Cog answered tentatively, almost in a whisper: ". . . Yes."

"Have you seen his hands?" asked Raggamot peering into Cog's eyes sympathetically.

"He is a blacksmith," Cog said defiantly. "He burned his hands in a forge."

"No, Cog" said Raggamot with conviction. "You are wrong."

"His hands were burned in a forge," cried Cog with mounting horror, "and that is why he is no longer a blacksmith."

"No, Cog! I was there. I know because I was there when it happened. Why do you suppose that he sent you to me?"

Slowly the realization set in and Cog knew that Raggamot was speaking the truth. He looked into the eyes of Raggamot and suddenly he was terrified because he knew beyond a doubt that he was in the midst of a true sorcerer. Raggamot saw the expression and knew that Cog would do as he was instructed.

Cog went back to his room at *The Blacksmith*. He ate a small supper and went to his room without talking to Todd. Locking the door behind him he took off his clothes like a man doomed to die. Every movement seemed dour and foreboding to him now and was charged with purpose. He thought about his wife and what she must have undergone during her ordeal and he wondered if her last moments on earth were peaceful as she succumbed to death. His eyes were full of tears now. He could not save his wife, but if he could save himself he would be able to prolong her sacred memory in his heart. At last he could wait no longer. He crawled into his bed and went to sleep and his heart was heavy.

He woke with a start. It was daybreak. He had slept through the entire night! Cog jumped out of bed and ran to the window to pull up the shade. It was morning! He felt refreshed as the first night of uninterrupted sleep in a fortnight revived his aching body. Then he remembered the shadow. Why had it not attacked him when he was most vulnerable? Sitting down on the edge of his bed while still in his nightshirt, he tried to understand why the shadow did not come. The conversation with Raggamot came back to him now . . . but that was yesterday. Today he felt much better. Today he felt much stronger.

He was beginning to tell himself that perhaps he had dreamed the whole thing up, and that is when he saw something move, something that was just at the edge of his vision. Dread suddenly filled his body and he knew that his ordeal was not over and he knew what it was that he had to do. Turning his head slowly, he saw the shadow. It was near the window. Suppressing his urge to flee, he waited to see what the strange apparition would do. He waited. The shadow didn't move. He waited for several minutes, and still the shadow did not move.

"What are you waiting for?" he said.

Still the shadow did not move, but he could see that it was alive in some strange way. It was pulsing like a heart.

"Come and get me!" he shouted. "I'm waiting," he said with frustration.

Then the shadow did move. Now it was moving slowly toward him. As the shadow came closer and closer, it began to assume a distinctly human form as if the mere proximity of Cog was causing the mass to transform. Cog was terrified. He couldn't move, even as his impulse to move was urging him to escape. He was frozen in place by his own acceptance of the horror. The shadow moved across the floor like an amorphous fog and stopped directly in front of him. It now had the definition of a man and there was no doubt to Cog that he was facing an evil manifestation. Cog trembled. Then the creature reached out an arm toward him. Slowly the limb extended, reaching, probing, feeling with long, tentacle-like fingers until it was almost touching him. He tried to cry out but his body did not obey him now. Closer and closer came the groping fingers until it touched his leg. An icy sensation shot through his leg as the creature reached right into his body. Then the creature reached for his arm to pin him down and hold him in place. Cog knew that the creature was about to crawl directly into his body. He felt icy fingers, fingers like blades sinking deeper and deeper into his body, growing stronger and more forceful the further it went. Then Cog raised his eyes to where the creature's head would be. The mouth of the demon opened until it was impossibly large, large enough to swallow Cog's entire body. And when the demon rose to its full length it towered over him like a hungry bird of prey. Then the head came down to engulf him and that is when he felt something inside of him break loose.

Suddenly a burst of energy surged through his body and ignited like a bolt of lightning. Cog was ignited. Twisting, ripping his body away from the icy pinions of the creature that was now half way submerged in his body, he detached himself and flung his body headlong through the window with a crash of shattering, splintering glass. His body landed on the ground beneath the window, lacerated, bleeding, and in such a state of wild frenzy that the pain was temporarily eclipsed by the survival instinct to escape from the parasitic creature. Never looking back, he ran from the inn like a man possessed.

Cog ran from the inn to save his life without realizing that he was being chased, not by the specter, but by an angry mob of men from the inn intent on capturing a dangerous madman bent on destruction, for Cog was truly a disturbing, menacing creature himself now.

Unaware of anything except escape from the inn, Cog ran like a spooked animal. The blood from the many cuts and lacerations on his body covered his nightshirt with bright-red streaks of crimson. To the mob that was falling far behind him now he must have seemed like a dangerous lunatic. In truth, Cog was out of his mind now and he was obeying an older law. He left the road and ran through fields and across pastures, frightening the livestock with his terrible howling.

And then he collided headlong into a black carriage. The collision was so violent that Cog was pitched into the road and nearly trampled by the team. He landed on his back, still howling, as the team of horses, frightened by his terrible cry, reared and nearly caused the carriage to spill.

The door of the carriage was flung open sharply as a well-dressed woman jumped out to access the situation. She found Cog, still dazed by the impact and covered with blood, trying to get to his feet. His eyes were wild. The woman stepped into the street and held him down with both hands until the coachman came to her assistance.

"Easy, easy now," she said softly, somewhat shaken up herself. "You are badly injured. Do not try to get up. I will help you. Do not worry."

Just then, the mob which was now about six men from the inn arrived panting and wheezing. They were all shouting and screaming and trying to get the attention of the well-dressed woman that was shielding Cog from them.

"Move away, my lady," said one of the most belligerent men. "You are protecting a madman. Let us take him away from here and deal with him in our own way."

The lady was self assured and regal. "What has he done?" she asked with authority.

"The man has broken a window at the inn. He tried to escape without paying his bill," said one of the panting men still breathless from the chase.

Cog tried to get to his feet again, but the lady gently pushed him back down. She was adamant.

"This man is hurt," she said forcefully. "I will pay his bill when this is over. But for now, all of you be on your way!"

The word of the lady carried weight, and soon all of the men turned around and walked away without speaking. Then the lady spoke with her coachman.

"Help me get him into the carriage, Sorren," she said. "I want to speak with this man."

Cog allowed himself to be helped into the carriage. He was still stunned and offered no resistance. Then the lady got in beside him and pulled the door closed. She looked at Cog and tried to smile, but she could see that he was badly hurt.

"There is no telling what those men may have done to you," she said. "You are safe now. If you are guilty of nothing more than breaking a window, I will not allow you to be condemned."

Cog looked closely at the woman, and though he was still dazed he could tell that she was important. Briefly he fell asleep as the stress weakened and he began to relax. He opened his eyes when he heard her speaking again.

"Do you have a story to tell?" she asked. "Or, are you hiding from a story?"

Her voice was so gentle, so soothing and reassuring that he started to cry. He felt like he was falling.

"Sometimes it seems like the world is a very dark and lonely place," she continued. "Sometimes the problems of life just weigh us down until we are crushed in the road beneath the wheel."

Cog looked into her eyes as she spoke. They were pale blue and full of empathy as if she were very sensitive to pain.

"You talk like someone that understands," said Cog meekly. "But how could you understand? How could you possibly understand the depth of my sorrow?"

The woman watched him intently and let him speak to her and pour out his heart without judgment. She knew that grief was a process and that part of the process was being able to let go of the ghosts that followed.

"How could you understand my curse?" Cog continued. "Sometimes my fear is so profound that I cannot move. But even the pain is better than death, because I am a dead man. I am a dead man, my lady, and yet I live. The Lord has cursed me. But in truth, I deserve nothing less and that only adds to my grief."

"What were you running from?" asked the lady. She knew that he was not running away from a broken window.

But her question had an immediate effect on Cog. He suddenly changed as the memory of his flight came back to him and he remembered what he was running from. The memory burned and he began to fidget and shake. Clearly in a state of panic, the lady put her hand on his arm to calm him. Just then there came a cautious knock on the door. The lady opened the door enough for the coachman to see that she was all right.

"Is everything all right, Kathryn?" he asked.

"Yes, thank you Sorren," she answered. "Please wait until I am finished here. My errands can wait a bit I think."

Slowly Cog realized who this woman was. The recognition was slow, but now his temper was changed.

"Are you Queen Kathryn?" he asked, but he knew in truth that she was.

"I will have my coachman bandage your wounds," she said tenderly. "But tell me your name. And pray tell me how you came to find yourself lurching through windows."

"Please save me!" Cog begged. He just knew that Kathryn had come to save him. She had come just in time to save him from the mob. He could see it in her face, her expression as if she too were in pain. "I can't run anymore," he cried. "Just let it come to an end. Just let it be over."

"Tell me your story," Kathryn said tenderly.

So Cog indeed told her his own sad story without leaving anything out. He told her about his wife and her ordeal, he told her of his blasphemy and his encounter with Raggamot. Then he told her of his narrow escape when he thought that he would surely die. By the time he was finished, the life was drained right out of him and he was more despondent than ever. Kathryn was moved by his story. The wretchedness of his life nearly moved her to tears, but she did not want to let her emotion show in the face of so much despair. He looked pathetic. He was an utterly defeated man and she knew that he was balanced on a narrow edge between life and death.

"Listen to me carefully," she finally said to Cog. She was speaking to him now like he was nothing more than a frightened child. "Though we are weak, the Lord is strong. There is nothing that the Lord cannot do and there is no evil that the Lord cannot defeat. We must try to be strong and fight evil where we find it. The Lord will help us because he wants us to fight and he wants us to be strong. Do you understand what I am saying?"

"I've tried," Cog whimpered. "I've tried to be strong, but I can't fight it any longer. There is no chance for me. What hope do I have of fighting such evil?"

Kathryn had never seen such hopelessness before. She knew that without hope, the Lord cannot do His work. She knew that the Lord needed hope in the world, for evil could not abide where there is hope. But Cog was completely shattered now. He had already given up. She looked at him, how strong he must have one day been and how weak and pathetic he was now. Kathryn knew that the Lord could do anything and that the weak and infirm would be given special grace. Then she had an idea. Perhaps she could give him hope; perhaps she could give him enough hope to fill his empty heart. She reached behind her seat and pulled something out of a bag. It was wrapped in fine tissue paper. It was a beautifully decorated candle, a candle she had found in Castletown and was bringing home to put in her little boy's room. She held the candle in her hand and said a silent prayer. Then she turned to Cog.

"Listen to me," she said to him. "This is a magic candle. It was given to me by an angel. I speak with angels, Cog. The angels are here to help us and we need not be afraid of them."

Cog's eyes opened wider. He looked into her face. Then he looked at the candle for a long time as if he were weighing the possibility, because he too had once spoken with angels. Then he looked into her face again to see if she was smiling.

"Angels are messengers, Cog. They know what is about to happen, and even if they cannot always intervene for us, they are there to pray for us and to give us hope. Do you hear me, Cog? Through hope, God is able to experience the beauty of His creation."

Cog watched Kathryn and he became transfixed by her tender words and by her graceful charm. The weight of his ordeal was beginning to fall off his shoulders. He did not know that someone like Kathryn could exist in such a world of terror and pain.

"Take this candle," she said. "Take this candle with you and put it in your room. Then, if the shadow should ever come to you again, you need only to light this candle. The light from this candle will destroy the shadow, Cog. Light this candle whenever you feel frightened. Let the tiny flame guide you as it did Job. The light is the light of the Lord."

Then Cog slowly took the candle from the hands of Kathryn. He received the candle from her hand, and then he brought his head down to her hands and kissed them.

"Hope is a gift for us from God. Hope is the language he has given us to talk to those in need."

Cog tried to speak, but he could not find the words. His eyes were moist.

"I have a son," said Kathryn. "His name is Bartholomew, and he is a prince. Some day you will meet him. When you no longer need this candle, I ask you to give it to him."

Cog waited each night for the shadow to return. Each morning he would wake holding the magic candle tightly. He would go out of the house and he would carry the candle in his pocket, and he would be ready to strike the match at a moment's notice should the need arise. Every action taken was taken with the help of the magic candle he carried with him. Soon the magic candle became part of him and he no longer had to think about it. After a while he stopped worrying about the evil that looked for him because he had been safe for so long. After several years passed, years which saw the passing of Queen Kathryn and the construction of a new abbey, Cog was truly a new man, a changed man.

One day while Cog was out weeding his onion patch he saw an unfamiliar person coming up the hill to his cottage. The man wore a long coat, carried a stout walking stick, and had on a large hat that cast his face in shadow. Leaning against his garden spade, he waited. When the man was still several paces from Cog, he stopped. Cog waited but said nothing for the business of any man is sacred to him on his own property.

"Heard rumor that you talk with angels."

"Do I know you?" Cog inquired.

"Any of these angels have a name, per chance?"

"What is your business with me?" Cog shot back curtly.

"My business is witches," he said defiantly. "I'm a witch finder. I travel all around looking for witches, and when I find them, I burn them."

Fury rose up inside of Cog and a deep rage threatened to explode. Obviously this witch finder did not know to whom he spoke. He needed to be careful lest he be overcome with rage and bludgeon this man to death where he stood. Cog had no sympathy for this man, only apathy. The past was done and he had no desire to relive it again. The man continued to speak.

"Do you know, or have you ever known any witches? Your coastline is very dangerous. Some people say that it is protected by magic. This is only an inquiry, and of course you may refuse to answer."

Cog knew what it meant to refuse to answer. His wife, Alliena, had also refused to answer . . . at first. Fear began to cloud his reason. He looked

long and hard at his interlocutor, and just for a moment he had the
impression that he was looking at a real witch, a real witch come to
terrify him all over again. The man to whom he spoke was an impatient,
imposing and evil man, the kind of evil that, like poison, had eaten him
alive from the inside-out until nothing remained but a skeleton of what
once could have been a man. Now an unnatural fear of death surged
through his body and he nearly collapsed. The memory of his wife's
torture haunted him anew and now he feared that he would be
discovered and brought back to the Continent in chains. They would
interrogate him and he would confess just as his wife had. And then the
vision was gone and Cog answered.

"No, I have never known a witch," he said as his voice trembled.

"Witches can be cunning, you know. Sometimes they disguise
themselves as God-fearing women. They could even take on the guise of
an angel, I suppose."

"I know nothing of witches," said Cog weakly.

"They're burning witches like timber in Württemberg. I have heard that
it looks like a razed forest. The smoke was spectacular they say. But
there is much more evil throughout the land, and I fear that this is only
the beginning."

Then there came a day that he left his house to go hunting without the
candle because he had forgotten to bring it along. Hiding in the rushes,
he crouched down and waited for his chance to shoot a quail he was
watching. It was a bright morning, the air was sharp and he was feeling
fine, but just then a cloud passed over and blocked out the sun. A
shadow raced across the earth rapidly and it swiftly passed across where
he crouched. The shadow came like a plague of locusts riding a demonic
wind. Suddenly a chill went through his body and he remembered that
he had left the candle at home on a shelf. All his fears and
apprehensions came flooding back to him in that instant. He started to
twitch nervously. Directly in front of him the quail walked into the
small clearing that was to be Cog's target. Cog saw the quail, but he
could not lift his arm to shoot. He was so frightened that he only
crouched lower into the rushes. Two other quail came out into the
clearing. Cog watched them and heard their nervous chattering, and he
thought about himself. He was being hunted, and he was hiding, afraid
to come out. Suddenly the urge to flee came over him with such

intensity that he fairly exploded out of his hiding spot and ran home as fast as possible in the midst of an eruption of frightened, agitated birds.

Cog lived in a small stone cottage on the edge of a cliff looking out over the sea. His cottage had a private bedroom and a fireplace where he could cook his meals and heat his home during the cold months. The home was dim when he entered and went directly to the shelf where he had put down the candle so that he would not forget it. Once the beautiful candle was in his hands he felt safe again. Taking the candle with him, he went into the kitchen where he stored his food, and sat down at a little table which was placed against the wall and where he took his meals. Still winded from his speedy return home, he needed a few minutes to calm himself. On the table were the remnants of an aged cheese and a crust of bread. He reached for the cheese, and then he opened a bottle of beer that was still on the table. Finally he began to relax.

Outside the cottage a lost bird crashed into the window with an ominous thud. Cog raised his head hastily; he had fallen asleep. Now there were long shadows slowly moving across the floor as the sun was beginning to set. He rubbed his eyes. Suddenly something stepped out of the shadow near the window. At first the shape was nebulous and undefined, but Cog knew painfully well what it was. He sank deeper into his chair as a strange calmness swept through his body. This is what he had been expecting for a long time now, and he was prepared. Soon the creature would begin to take human form, and then it would come for him. Cog waited with a sense that finally he would take charge of his life and he would exorcize this demon from his life once and for all. Reaching into his coat and pretending to be looking for something, he carefully and surreptitiously removed a wooden match. Then the demon attacked.

Cog struck the match across the table confidently and held it to the candle that was carefully concealed in his other hand. Kathryn had given him the confidence he needed to destroy this demon. The creature was already upon him when the first rays of light from the magic candle filled the room.

Suddenly the demon was blown off his body with tremendous force as if a hurricane had swept through his house. The light was so intense that he had to shield his eyes at first. But then the radiance lessened as another wave of light swept across the room. Wave after wave of light poured into the room and he was washed in a brilliant luminosity of warmth. The demon was expunged in the terrible and righteous light. Cog knew that he was free at last. His eyes filled with tears. Overcome by the power of the Lord he fell back in his chair in complete supplication. As his body fell against the back of his chair, his head snapped back and his mouth fell open, and the last breath left his inert body.

He saw that the light was rising from his room, ascending into the infinite sky beyond his tiny home. Upward into the sky like a turning staircase, the heavens were revealed to him. He could see angels carried on wings floating and flying in majestic circles, caught in the heavenly light. On the staircase ascended a countless multitude of persons being escorted by brilliant heavenly angels. Higher and higher the heavenly spectacle disappeared beyond his vision. Then Cog felt himself being drawn upward into the spiraling splendor. He floated effortlessly and peacefully into the stream of heavenly light. Then he looked down and saw his body and he realized that he was leaving earth forever. He saw his house and then he saw his tiny island disappear into a sea of nothingness. And then he realized that he was being escorted by an angel. The radiance penetrated his vision and asked him to be calm. But the voice of the angel was familiar to him and he knew innately that it was the lady Kathryn, the woman who had saved him. They floated together on the divine ether and the face of the lady Kathryn was beautiful and serene.

"You cannot stay here," said the lady Kathryn. "You have been given a gift, but your life it not yet over." Then she smiled radiantly and her voice was pure. "It is not for us to know the future, Alliesian. I can only show you a small part of it, and then you must go back again."

Then the lady Kathryn told Cog to look ahead. She motioned with her hand and Cog saw what was intended for him to see.

"Look!" she said forcefully as the sweep of her hand revealed two small figures ascending the staircase escorted by an angel. "You have suffered greatly on Earth, Alliesian. Behold your wife and your infant child."

Cog saw his wife and their child ascending to heaven and his heart was overcome with joy. Alliena looked as beautiful as the first day he first beheld her beauty. And there was his son, his little boy Steven who had died so young and so innocent of worldly sin. He could see their faces and they were transfixed by the power of the Lord. Cog watched them as they ascended into heaven and his heart nearly burst.

"This is what you were brought here to see," Kathryn said joyfully. Then she looked directly into Cog's face and he recoiled from her magnificent splendor, for he was guilty before the Lord and was ashamed. In that moment he knew that his heart had been broken for a reason and he wept bitter tears and begged the Lord to forgive him. "There is still work for you to do one Earth," she said. "Go back and be strong in the power of the Lord, Cog. I think that you will not need the candle again. When you return to Earth, you are to put out the candle with your hand, and when you open your eyes you will be reborn into a new world. Farewell, Cog."

And then Cog was standing next to his body. Clutched in the right hand like the sword of Saint Christopher, the light continued to shine. Slowly, Cog reached out and snuffed out the candle between his thumb and forefinger.

And so it happened that one day while Prince Bartholomew was out hunting he stopped at the local tavern for a pint. He took his tankard with him to the window where the light was best and sat down. A few tables away he could see a man sitting alone in the shadow. The man was smoking a pipe and was looking directly at him. He had long, stringy hair that hung about his shoulders and a narrow, hawkish face that pulled his craggy skin tight and left his face with myriad silver etchings like traces on pewter. His eyes were dark and glassy. His facial movements were slow and methodical like an animal emerging from a long hibernation. Bartholomew tried to pay no attention to the man, but in truth the man made him uneasy. After a few moments the Prince got up and took his tankard over to the table where the man was still watching him intently. Bartholomew set his tankard on the table. "Do you mind if I join you?" he said.

"Please do," answered the man. "You are Prince Bartholomew, are you not?"

Bartholomew nodded. He was well known across the island, but there were those for whom his aristocratic bearing meant little.

"The angels are fond of you," the man said categorically.

"How do you know this?" asked Bartholomew with a smile. He was charmed even as his suspicion increased.

"They told me so," the man responded with certainty. "My name is Alliesian Cog. Call me Cog if you prefer. The angels visit me in my house. I call them and they come to me sometimes."

Bartholomew could not resist a smile and he could not hide it. He turned his head and pretended to cough.

"You think that I am trying to amuse you, perhaps?"

"No, of course not," Bartholomew said apologetically. "But tell me Cog, what do the angels have to talk about?"

Cog tamped his bowl of tobacco down with a silver tool he kept in his pocket. He did not mix well in polite society, which is true. He was accustomed to being scoffed at and ridiculed, but he expected something different from the Prince. He knew that this prince was different.

"You would be surprised to find out how wise the angels are," said Cog. "The angels live forever and they do not forget anything." Then Cog lowered his voice. "The angels know everything, Bartholomew. They have knowledge of all things. The Lord has allowed them to know these things about us. Do you understand?"

"I do," Bartholomew responded as he took a long draft and then set his tankard back on the table.

"I don't think that you do," Cog replied. "If you did understand, you would be far more impressed by my words."

Bartholomew shifted in his chair. He was not accustomed to being corrected so unequivocally by persons he did not even know. "Then allow me to fill my bowl while you explain further," he said.

"Many of the angels were cast out of heaven, you see. But some of them remained because they did not try to defy God. Those that remained chose to serve God and they were allowed to be messengers, messengers of God. But even as messengers they decided to take certain people into their confidence, for they were eager to share their vast knowledge of our world. They were vastly proud of the work of God and they wanted to share their joy. I am one of those that have been taken into their confidence, Bartholomew."

Bartholomew lit his pipe and blew out a puff of aromatic smoke. Then he took the pipe out of his mouth. "You are a fortunate man, Cog. But tell me; is it really true that you talk to angels? I have heard rumors about you over the years. They say you speak to the angels."

"I do," said Cog without hesitation. "They are all around us," he continued. The world is full of angels, Bartholomew. They are here to help us you know."

"And why should we have need of help, Cog?"

Cog laughed. Then he blew out a thick smoke ring and said. "Is it really so bad to admit that sometimes we all of us need help? The world is a dangerous place, Bartholomew. There are demons that would like to do us harm."

"There are men that would also like to do us harm, Cog."

"No one knows that more than I do, Bartholomew. You can believe me when I say this. It is true that some men can become possessed by the demons they own. I have seen this myself. I have known some of these men."

Bartholomew was becoming reflective. "I have heard that angels are beautiful," he said.

"And so they are," Cog answered. "In truth, the angels are messengers, and there is much they have to tell."

"And why would the angels want to tell us anything?"

Cog smiled warmly, revealing his teeth as he could not suppress a smile. Clearly he eagerly wanted to talk and only waited to be prompted by Bartholomew.

"Tell me Bartholomew," he said, "tell me what you think that this world is."

"Now you are trying to be funny," said Bartholomew. "Just say what you mean, Cog. There is no need to be obscure with me. I have no reason to doubt your word."

"I was not trying to amuse you," said Cog. "Listen to me Bartholomew. The world is a battlefield. The world truly is a battlefield, and we are being attacked from positions from which we have no defense. The angels and the demons are waging an ongoing war in the hearts of men. They are fighting for our soul, Bartholomew. But your mistake would be to believe that your soul belongs to you. It doesn't, it belongs to God. You are the guardian of your soul, but your soul is separate from you and is not part of you. Do you understand?"

Bartholomew nodded his head but kept silent. He had never met a man like this before and something about Cog made him anxious in a strange way. He could see that this man was very passionate about his ideas and he could not but think that he was a man that had undergone much pain. Cog slowed his speech down and narrowed his eyes on the Prince even more directly.

"God knows your every thought, your every move, he knows everything you say and everything you do. This is because you are part of God, Bartholomew. And that is why the angels want to help us fight against the evil that wants to use us for the purposes of evil."

Bartholomew had never heard anything like this. He suspected that Cog was part of a Gnostic movement, or part of another, even more secret society that had gone underground after being declared heretical. He nevertheless was very interested in what Cog had to say.

"And you learned this from an angel?" he asked directly.

"There are many angels," Cog replied.

"Yes, I suppose there are."

"Some of the angels have been allowed to live on Earth, Bartholomew. Did you know that?"

"No, I did not know this," said Bartholomew slowly and with some degree of discomfort. The conversation was going in a direction he did not like. "How do you know this?"

"We cannot hide from God, Bartholomew, just as we cannot hide from the truth. We know the truth in our heart, because our soul belongs to God, and God is the truth."

"Why are you telling me this?"

"I have seen much evil," said Cog. "Without knowing, I have even spread this evil. I have been the tool of a great evil. But now I have confronted this evil and I am free."

"I am happy for you," said Bartholomew.

"And so you should be," Cog said with a genuine smile. "You should be," Cog repeated, "because I was saved by your mother. I knew your mother many years ago. She is the one that led me to the truth."

And so Cog told Bartholomew the whole story of his life and how he had come to the Isle of Man. He told him about his wife, her trial and execution, and how she had been forced to admit to being a witch. He told him about the candle and he told him about his vision of the afterlife. When he was finished, he felt relieved though he had no reason to fear the consternation of Bartholomew.

"But you said you talked with angels," said Bartholomew.

"I was saved by an angel," Cog replied.

Then Cog reached into his pocket and removed the candle he had saved throughout the years. He looked long and hard at the candle. It was partially burned and the wick was black. Parting with it was hard for him to do, for now he was truly on his own. Then he brought it to his lips and kissed it before handing it to Bartholomew.

"This was given to me by an angel," he said. Then he stood up slowly and left the inn without another word.

Bartholomew remained in stunned silence. There were so many questions. He felt himself becoming emotional. Of course Cog was just a tired old man, and tired old men told stories. Bartholomew examined the candle. Cog had said that this was intended for him and was a lasting gift from his mother. Another candle on the middle of the table glowed faintly in the hazy light. In his hand he held the candle from his mother. Then he slowly reached out his hand to the burning candle on the table, but just before the wick from the magic candle touched the flame, he stopped.

No, he would not light the candle now. He did not need to light the candle to feel its power. Perhaps he would never light it, for most of his demons stayed at a safe distance from him now. Yes, his mother had been beautiful according to his father. His last memory of her remained painful. He now knew that there was a special kind of beauty that could never be seen but only experienced. Then something that his mother used to say to him came back to him like a gentle echo of her beautiful life. "Remember, Bartholomew," she would say. "Through hope, God is able to experience the beauty of His own creation."   And it was in that moment that a light seemed to kindle inside his soul, and if his soul truly did not belong to him, he believed that the Lord would allow him this one moment of indulgence.

Hypatia and the Silver Grotto

There are magic pools and magic mirrors and powerful sacred spaces buried within the earth to summon up our passions, just as there are buried emotions that, once called up, can never be satisfied or contained by our own individual nature. And once possessed, we are slowly devoured, once possessed we are drawn inextricably to our downfall. Our nature can sometimes be corrupted for evil just as nature incarnate can sometimes be conjured from without, for the spirit of nature is part of the world, above as below.

One day while Prince Bartholomew was out wandering the wild heath country around Peel he stopped at an old ruin that caught his attention. The site was neglected, overgrown with weeds and scrub brush, and were it not for the remaining standing stone, Prince Bartholomew would have missed it entirely. Fierce tangled weeds clung to and twisted around the stone, covering the ancient symbols and runes with strangling vegetation and holding it to the earth with sharp, gripping thorns. The tortured stone looked odd and strangely out of place though it must have been many hundreds of years chained to the earth. The Prince jumped down from his horse and knelt on the ground to look closely at the stone. Worn from the cold and rain and unbroken wind that swept across the island, the stone had aged with time and was now a thing ancient, forgotten and silent, and whatever secrets it once held were now faded and lost.

Thick brambles of black-cherry and sweetbriar and bracken surrounded the stone on three sides and merged with the hillock. The stone, still visibly adorned with faint, tiny runes and faded symbols scratched from hands long since turned to dust, seemed to be a marker and protruded out of a hidden burrow that penetrated further into the hillock. Prince Bartholomew carefully pushed aside the prickly thistles and crawled through an opening to a hidden grotto just behind the stone and partially buried within the tangle. He crawled deeper into the grotto until he came to a pool of water that bubbled up from an underground fountain and filled a shallow stone basin with fresh water. Tiny seeds of flotsam and grains floated on top the water. The Prince cupped his hands and scooped up the crystal clear liquid, bringing the cool water to his lips. It was sweet and refreshing. The Prince took another drink from the pool because he could not quench his thirst. Finally he bent down and put his lips into the water and drank deeply. When he was satisfied he lifted his head and stared into the pool.

The water shimmered and reflected the dense foliage surrounding the hidden pool like a mirror. Thin rings of gently undulating ripples spread out from the center of the pool like a heartbeat. Prince Bartholomew stared deeply into the glassy, glazing mirror with a smile of pure joy and his eyes became glazed, for the pool was a pool of enchantment. He suddenly had the desire to embrace the entire world. Instead, he only lay on his back and fell asleep.

When he awoke he brushed off a bug that was tickling his nose. He felt revived, from what he did not know, but he had an urge to sing. Then he remembered the pool. Looking directly into the pool he suddenly noticed something that looked familiar. It was a face, but it was not his own face; it was the face of a woman.

He smiled. The face was gazing up at him out of the water. She was beautiful and strangely beguiling the way one is drawn toward the forbidden pleasure of vice. Thin lips and ivory skin behind which large, watery emerald eyes, mysterious as an ancient oracle, looked up, and she smiled faintly with a secret she guarded vigilantly. Bartholomew knew that she must be an ancient goddess and it did not occur to him that she should be looking up from the water. She smiled enticingly as he continued to look down into the glimmering pool.

"What is your name?" he asked eagerly, for he was falling under a powerful enchantment.

"My name is Hypatia," answered the beautiful nymph.

"Hypatia," he repeated blissfully and the words tasted sweet.

"You have tasted from my pool, and now you belong to me," she said, and her smile seemed to grow. "You shall be my lover and I shall be your mistress. Do you love me?"

"Are you a goddess?" Bartholomew inquired passionately.

The water stirred as a gentle breeze, licked by the sweet scent of hyacinth from distant fields, slipped through the grotto. In the pool the face of

Hypatia became even more beautiful and alluring as her pride swelled. Bartholomew wanted to kiss the water.

"You may call me your goddess," said Hypatia, "I am your goddess and you must obey my wishes, for a goddess is very jealous and a goddess does not share her love. Go from here now. You can show your love to me by loving that which I love. Go out and kiss the wind, then return to me tomorrow and I will appear to you."

Bartholomew went away in a state of bliss. The enchantment had not dissipated but had only burrowed deeply into his soul. When he was almost home, he stopped his horse on a knoll just outside Ballasalla. The horse came alive beneath him. Then he slowly emerged from the dream beneath which he had fallen. His horse waited patiently.

Suddenly a gust of wind blew across the plateau and went through his hair, whipping it around and across his lean and youthfully questioning face. He remembered Hypatia's instruction to 'kiss the wind.' What did she mean, and how was he supposed to kiss the wind? Next to where he sat a large oak tree grew. He could see the motion of the wind as it passed through the tree, and the individual leaves turned and flickered as the wind passed through, but he knew that the wind was not a separate thing but a thing without separate identity. The wind could no more be kissed than could the separate colors of a picture be appreciated in isolation. His mind wandered as his eyes took in the beauty of the sprawling countryside beneath him. It was all beautiful and needed no further context. Nudging his horse, he went home in a thoughtful mood.

Later that day while King Sigmus joined in with some of the servants in a friendly lawn game consisting of the striking of wooden balls with mallets, Bartholomew sat in a lawn chair drinking tea and watched the fun. In truth, he was thinking about Hypatia. Iona came running across the lawn when she spotted him sitting all alone. She smiled bashfully, for she was outside of her standing when she said.

"Come join us, Bartholomew. We only just started."

Bartholomew smiled back at Iona. Her innocence and playfulness always made him smile, for she was a happy girl.

"Perhaps another time," Bartholomew responded. "I am tired from my ride, and I only want to drink my tea. Go along, Iona. Enjoy yourself."

Iona ran away giggling to herself as if Bartholomew had said something positively amusing. Bartholomew blushed, for he always imagined that Iona was teasing him for some reason that he could never understand.

Dark clouds passed over the castle silently. The room was pitch-dark when Bartholomew slipped out of bed and walked to the window. He was restless and he needed fresh air to clear the bad dreams from his mind. Throwing open the shutters he felt the cool wind as it swept across his face into the room. The stars were bright and he lingered at the window, taking deep breaths of the refreshing air. The bracing air continued to blow across his face, but he no longer felt the coolness for the air passed right through him as from another open window. Several minutes passed in which he did not move a muscle and he stood still as a stone, petrified and insensate while the wind whipped through his hair and nightshirt. At last he emerged from his oblivion, and as the presence of his body became known once again to him he only became more distant and alien to his senses as if they belonged not to himself, but to someone else.

The next day Prince Bartholomew crawled through the tangle until he once again reached the hidden grotto of Hypatia. He carefully pushed the floating debris from the surface of the water and stared into the glimmering inkiness. Small ripples gently rose from the depth, once again revealing the intoxicating face of Hypatia. Bartholomew breathed a sigh of relief.

"You have done what I told you?" Hypatia inquired.

Prince Bartholomew studied her beautiful face and only smiled at her question. Hypatia spoke sweetly to Bartholomew as if he were no more than a child.

"I have another task for you to perform for me. It will make me happy and bring you much closer to me, for I am inside of you now. Can you feel my presence?"

"Come closer to me," Bartholomew replied listlessly, for the enchantment was growing more powerful by the moment.

"We shall be together," Hypatia reassured him. "But first you must prove to me that you can love the things that I love. Leave me now.

Leave me now and speak to the trees. Listen to them for they are wise, and do not be fooled by the spoken words and the wisdom of men."

Like a lingering scent delicately carried along on a silken zephyr, Bartholomew left the grotto under the power of Hypatia's gentle words. He rode away and did not recover his senses until he was almost home again. The powerful muscles of his horse bore him effortlessly, and were it not for the sound of his own breathing he would not have known the graceful horse beneath him was not his own body. When he dismounted his noble steed he nearly fell to the ground for he had lost his legs. A stable hand took the reins from him and led the horse away as Bartholomew tried to recover his sense of balance.

Bartholomew sprawled out on a sofa and sipped tea. He took off his boots and closed his eyes for a moment. King Sigmus poked his head into the room and then entered when he saw his son. In his hand was a freshly sharpened feather pen and his fingers were stained with ink.

"There you are," he said. "Are you unwell, Bartholomew?"

"No," he replied. "I was just resting. Is there something you want me to do?"

"Well, yes," Sigmus said. "I wonder if you would ride out to the abbey for me. I have need of a certain book and I do not want to delay my work. The Abbot will meet you at the gate."

"I would be happy to do so," said the Prince.

"You may stay for a glass of ale, or two," said Sigmus. "But do not delay longer than that. I do not really need it for an hour or two."

Prince Bartholomew rode away feeling cheerful. The mission was to his liking. The Abbot welcomed him with a smile and a handshake. Then he handed Bartholomew a book wrapped in a leather rucksack and tied with a cord.

"Perhaps you would like to join me in the garden for a glass of ale?" he inquired, for he knew only too well the Prince's liking for the thick, black ales produced by the monks.

After the second glass, Bartholomew excused himself politely and said that it was time for him to go. He thanked the Abbot for the delicious ale and bid him farewell.

On the way back to the castle, Bartholomew stopped his horse near an old oak tree that left a large bough overhanging the road. The strong ale had gone to his head. Carefully he jumped off his horse and stepped off the path and sat beneath the large tree to be out of the sun. He sat down and leaned his back against the gnarled trunk, for the oak was many years Bartholomew's senior.

After a few minutes he felt better. He was about to stand up when he remembered the instructions of Hypatia and that he was to speak to a tree. Having no reason to prolong the ritual, he decided to speak to this tree, for if there was nothing to learn from an old oak there was nothing to be learned from a mere ash. He addressed the tree.

"I am Prince Bartholomew. Speak to me some of the wisdom you have acquired from your long life on earth."

In response, he heard the cackling of a raven somewhere in the distance and the twittering of a wren nearby. A light breeze blew through his hair. He tried again, for the enchantment had clouded his reason.

"Tell me what it feels like to live and tell me if you fear death."

His horse snorted uncomfortably. She whinnied and danced from side to side, no doubt wondering just who it was to whom the noble prince was speaking so eloquently, and made uncomfortable by his eccentricity.

"That you may speak to me in private, I will draw closer," said the Prince.

And then he went up to the tree and wrapped his arms around it in an embrace not unlike a traveling minstrel for his lady. Bartholomew dug his fingers into the porous bark and laid the side of his head against the elder trunk. If anyone would have seen the Prince in such a disgraceful posture they would surely have thought him mad, but fortunately for the Prince, his indecorous demonstration of reverence was never witnessed by family or Manxman.

At last he fell to the ground in a fit of weeping. Overcome with exhaustion, the Prince could not resist the penetrating presence of the enchantress Hypatia as she burrowed deeper and deeper into his consciousness. The Prince would surely have fallen asleep now but for the soft whispering in his ear like the silent burrowing of a clever earwig.

"Wake up Prince Bartholomew. Are you listening?"

The Prince raised his head but he was still groggy. His eyelids were heavy and he had to fight to keep them open. "What?" he said aloud and the sound of his own voice startled him. Then suddenly his head snapped back up. "Is someone speaking to me? Show yourself."

"You must be quiet," the soft voice purred. "You must be quiet or you will never hear me." Then the thoughts of the tree filtered into Bartholomew's mind like sunshine brings forth life through a tender leaf . . . and he listened.

When Bartholomew arrived back at the castle the King was impatiently waiting for him. Bartholomew walked casually across the lawn and when he reached his father he would have walked right past him. The angry words of Sigmus stopped him.

"Where is the book you were sent to bring back?"

Bartholomew looked at him with an expression of utter confusion. He stared blankly at his father, but he did not see him.

"Are you alright?" Sigmus asked, now becoming increasingly concerned. "Bartholomew, are you alright?"

The Prince looked straight ahead into empty space. "What?" was all he could say.

With the help of two servants, Sigmus carried Bartholomew to his room and put him into bed. Bartholomew put up no resistance but only turned over and went to sleep immediately. Iona came up later with a tray of tea but Bartholomew was unresponsive, so she left the tray on the table and left the room wondering what was wrong with the Prince.

The next day Bartholomew came down for breakfast as if nothing had happened. The servants looked at him with curiosity, but he only smiled at them and wished them a good morning. King Sigmus was eating an egg and looked up when his son entered. No amount of questioning could uncover the reason for his strange behavior, so Sigmus decided that it was probably just a normal reaction of a young man in the folly of his youth and that it would soon pass. He gave it no more thought.

After breakfast Bartholomew went off by himself and did not say where he was going. He did not say where he was going because he was not going anywhere in particular but was merely walking. Behind the castle is a large expanse of woodland and spongy meadow bordering on the primary grounds attached to the abbey. Trees were left to grow large and old. Owls patrolled the sky and perched in ancient oaks. Oftentimes Bartholomew walked here and a path had slowly been created over the years, beaten down by measured feet on many an afternoon excursion, and this is where he went.

Prince Bartholomew lay on his back in the middle of a small cluster of trees. He listened attentively to the wisdom of the trees and enjoyed their playful singing, for not all trees are solitary creatures. The world around him receded until all he could hear was the patient, languorous, sluggish sound of the noble trees of summer, singing of the sweetness of the sun and the permanence of soil.

Iona stood near a large tree and searched for the Prince, for she had seen him traipsing through the fields and she knew where he was going. In truth, she was worried about Bartholomew and even though she was but a servant, her eyes followed the Prince with pleasure and her heart rejoiced to be near him. Then she saw him laying prostrate in a small grove of trees and she became worried.

And so Iona went up to the Prince slowly and timidly, for she did not want to interrupt him if he truly intended only to take a nap in the shade. She stood next to him and as she looked down she could see that his eyes were closed and his breathing steady. Of course, he was only napping. The young servant tried to sneak away quietly but the Prince was roused by her very presence. He opened his eyes and Iona could see that they were distant and obscured with an inner emotion. Iona looked into his murky eyes and suppressed a laugh. He was handsome, yes. But he was also peculiar and comical.

"Are you feeling quite well?" she asked awkwardly, for she had no reason to be there.

"Perfectly well," answered the Prince with a yawn. "I was listening to the trees, Iona."

She laughed suddenly and then caught herself and blushed at her own indiscretion. She was a good girl, a loyal servant, but she was also a young woman and subject to the same torments of all women.

"You don't believe me?" asked Bartholomew nonplussed.

"Ah . . . what do the trees know?" Iona said. "You were sleeping, tell me true."

The Prince sat up and held his knees with his graceful fingers entwined. Then he cocked his head slightly. "The trees speak to me, and I listen," he said.

"Well, I have never heard them," said Iona with feigned mockery and she smiled and pursed her lips.

But the Prince had forgotten that she was there and his eyes began to glaze over as if the state out of which he had only emerged was calling him back again. In a moment he was gone. Now what Iona saw made her very uncomfortable and she feared for the Prince. He was falling under a spell or act of sorcery. Iona gathered up her hem and ran away. When she was gone, the Prince closed his eyes and lay back down beneath the sentient trees.

After a couple of days the Prince was unrecognizable to everyone that he met, and he stopped even his normal conversation with those with whom he lived. He was often seen walking among the trees and most often asleep beneath them. The household, all of whom were very fond of the Prince, was apprehensive and talked to King Sigmus, but he only scoffed, for Sigmus was convinced that Bartholomew suffered from a common malady . . . he was in love.

On the third day Bartholomew saddled his horse and rode away without a word. He rode to Peel, for he was no longer able to resist the consuming allure of Hypatia.

The face of Hypatia appeared on the shimmering pool like a lost melody remembered, and Bartholomew sighed audibly. The smile on her face was radiant.

"You have done well," she said. "You will make a wonderful lover, for you love me do you not?"

Bartholomew was speechless. The enchantment of Hypatia had taken his will to live and now he was content to be controlled by the will of Hypatia.

"There is one more thing you must do for me," she announced. "To prove your love I now ask you to bring me to life in your world. Your love can do this, my prince. But I am a jealous lover, so you must abandon your love of all things except me. You belong to me now and you must worship that which I love."

Prince Bartholomew nodded. He was ecstatic, in a state of surrender, for the enchantment of Hypatia was too powerful to resist.

"If you love me," Hypatia continued. "You must worship me. I can only live through your worship, my prince. Tell them that Hypatia, Earth Goddess, is alive in all things and all things come to life through her life. Hypatia is life! When you have resurrected me, I will appear to you in the flesh. Go now. You have seen that there is no life for you without me. Go now and proclaim Hypatia!"

Bartholomew rode back to his castle and this time he did not stop on the hillock overlooking his home. He put his horse in the stable with a bucket of oats. Then he went to his room because he was too exhausted to stay awake.

He woke late in the day. The sun was going down. Then he realized that he had fallen asleep. His father had gone to Castletown on business, so he ate a light meal of ham and leeks and then decided to go for a walk. He had a strange desire to speak, but the words would not form in his mind and a prevailing confusion clouded his thoughts. Only the thought of Hypatia was clear. He had the desire to tell everyone about Hypatia and how wonderful she was. Suddenly he shook his head from side to side violently. No, that was not the way it was. There was something wrong, something he had to change if only he could remember.

The Prince went into the garden and sat down on a stone bench near the grotto at the center of the labyrinth. If only he could think straight he would surely know what to do but his thoughts were as twisted as the sculptured walls of the labyrinth and they only took him further and further from himself.

From the kitchen window where Iona washed up the dishes she saw Prince Bartholomew go into the garden and then disappear within the thick hedge. Then she had an idea. She poured a tall glass of lemonade and decided to take it to him in the garden. On a tray she also put a slice of bread and a wedge of cheese, for she did not know that he had already eaten.

She found him at the center of the garden. He looked up, startled that anyone would have followed him and when he saw that it was Iona he relaxed. Bartholomew looked tired, distraught, confused, and it saddened Iona to see him this way. She wondered what terrible problems he could be dealing with.

"I brought you something to drink," she said finally after an uncomfortable silence.

The Prince looked up and started to smile, but something prevented him and he only scowled.

"Would you like to try it?" she said.

Then she went up to where he was sitting and put the tray down on the stone table. Suddenly a new thought occurred to her and in her wildest imagination she would have never thought she could have done such a thing.

"Close your eyes," she said. "I want to give you something special."

Prince Bartholomew did what he was told, because he could think of nothing better to do. He closed his eyes and waited. And then unexpectedly he felt the soft pressure of Iona's lovely lips against his own lips. It felt like the tiny flutter of a dove or the beating of a broken heart. And then he felt her soft hands against his face and his eyes filled with beautiful tears, for when he opened his eyes he beheld, not the face of Iona, but the enchanted face of Hypatia and his heart was elated and his dream a reality.

Iona opened her eyes and stared into the eyes of Prince Bartholomew and it was a beautiful moment turned frightening. His eyes were alive with passion, ignited and burning with uncontrollable ardor. But it was the expression on his face which caused her blood to turn cold, for he looked right through her! She tried to back away but suddenly she felt the strong hand of Bartholomew on her arm, gripping, holding her fast. Now her fear was turned to terror.

"Hypatia," Bartholomew said laconically and his eyed bore into her like a hawk. And then he smiled and moved closer to her. "Hypatia," he said again.

Iona struggled to break free. "Please let me go," she begged but she knew that Bartholomew was possessed and that his will was not his own. She pulled her arm away violently.

And then Bartholomew recovered his senses. He let go of her arm, but his face still bore a dull, uncomprehending expression that Iona took with her as she quickly retreated from the garden.

Iona ran up to her room and locked her door. Then she sat on the edge of her bed and cried. She cried for herself but she also cried for Bartholomew. It surely was not Bartholomew she had only just escaped from. Something terrible had happened to him.

Never before had Iona been so frightened. She was all alone, because no one would believe her if she were to suddenly announce that the Prince had been taken over by an evil spirit. And it was an evil spirit, for she could think of no good spirit that would take away a man's soul. Her cheeks were flush and her little heart was beating rapidly. But she knew that she could not hide in her room forever and that she must soon come down to attend to her chores, so she glanced at herself in the mirror that rested on her chest of drawers and tried to smile, and to put on a brave face. She brushed her hair with a horse-hair brush and then she went downstairs to begin preparation for tomorrow's meal.

When King Sigmus came home it was late and the castle was quiet and dark but for a few candles left burning. Iona was there to greet him. She asked if he would care for a cup of tea before bed but the King refused politely.

"I am very tired," he said. "Have you seen Bartholomew since this afternoon?" he asked.

Iona didn't want to lie to the King, so she said. "He went into the garden tonight. But he has not come inside again yet, so I cannot tell you more."

The King was perplexed. "He is still in the garden?" he said, wondering if he had heard her right. "At this hour, Iona?"

"I think so," Iona replied.

"Is he alone?" the King countered.

"Would you like me to find out?" said Iona awkwardly, for she had no desire to go back into the garden at this hour.

"Never mind," Sigmus answered. "I will see him tomorrow. Good night, Iona. Are you going to bed now?"

"Shortly," she said. "I will put out the lights."

Later, after Iona had put out the candles and was on the way up to her room, she heard Bartholomew come in. By starlight she could see his outline but the expression on his face was cast in shadow.

"Bartholomew, is that you?" she whispered, even though she clearly knew that it was. She just had to speak with him again, to hear his voice, to search for a clue to his strange behavior, and she had waited all night for him to come in.

The Prince walked up to her slowly and warily before going down on one knee. "Forgive me, for I have frightened you," he said.

Iona could see that he was changed. "Get up," she scolded him softly, but secretly she was flattered. "Get up before someone sees you."

"Only if you say that you forgive me," the Prince insisted.

Iona could not hold back a smile of relief, and the Prince saw it.

"I saw that!" he said triumphantly. "Now I can sleep tonight in peace, for the lady's honor is restored."

Iona could not believe the change in Bartholomew. There was no trace of his sullen, distant melancholy, and he was even charming again. She sat next to her mirror and brushed her long, chestnut hair by candlelight. The Prince was recovered! Thank the Lord.

But when Bartholomew closed his eyes for the night he was visited by phantoms and terrible dreams. His dreams were alive with a presence, a terrible, heavy and foreboding presence. The presence was all around him, pushing him down beneath a terrible momentous force. His dreams were his thoughts, and as if in some way his mind was being probed and extracted, leaving only the faint ghost of a dream to represent what was once his own thought, he was lost to himself.

The next day when he came down for breakfast, Iona watched him surreptitiously to see what kind of mood he would be in. She was cutting bread in the kitchen when she heard Bartholomew's voice in the next room. Picking up a kettle of freshly brewed coffee, she went into the dining room as casually as possible.

Bartholomew sat at his usual chair and his head hung down limply. Iona came in briskly and set the kettle down on the table, looking carefully at the Prince. The sound of her dress woke him from a stupor and he raised his head slowly. He looked awful: his hair was disheveled, his eyes were swollen, and he was unshaven and still wore the same clothes from the night before. Dark, puffy circles under his eyes made his once beautiful face seem sunken and sallow. Iona gasped when she saw his face.

King Sigmus looked up when he heard Iona gasp. He was busy with his breakfast and seemed unconcerned about the condition of his son. But perhaps he was just not as perceptive as Iona.

"Is something wrong, Iona?" he said.

Iona smiled sheepishly. After a quick glance at Bartholomew she looked away. Then she picked up a dirty dish from the table and went back to the kitchen.

In a small alcove attached to the kitchen is a dining area where the servants take their meals and drink tea when they are not busy. Sometimes they tell stories, and sometimes they munch in silence or in silent meditation. They relax and they gossip and they tell secrets that bring wry smiles to their faces, for such servants know much more than what is seen and what is heard in the daylight hours, for so it is that the words spoken in earnest echo through the corridors long after they are uttered.

Iona sat at a chair and looked out the window. The bright sunshine poured through the window and illuminated her young face like beauty caught in polished alabaster, for there is a timeless beauty that can never fade but only rise up again like tiny white flowers after a springtime shower. Her worry only made her more vulnerable, more innocent, and more beautiful, for the emotions of a young woman capture the beauty of the griminess around them of which they are a precious stone in a setting of gloom.

Maria was there. She was much older than Iona in years as well as experience, and she was King Sigmus' most trusted servant. It was Maria that truly ran the day to day operations of the domestic side of life in the castle. It was to Maria that the servants turned for comfort, for she was wise in ways that were never spoken about except in quiet alcoves and hidden corners. She knew the folklore of the island; she knew the superstitions, the tales of pride and the tales of woe. Maria was an old crone, that is true, but she was gentle and she was kind and she was loyal to those around her.

"Come now, Iona," she said. "Tell me what is on your mind because I can see that you are upset by the lines on your face. Yes, I can read them like tea leaves."

Iona turned to Maria, her elder and her friend. Ah, surely Maria already knew what was in her heart.

"I am afraid of witchcraft," she said. "Can witchcraft find us in our own home, even in our own bed?"

"Why do you worry, Iona? You are surely not possessed by witches, for you are protected by the King. How could witches find you here?"

"There is someone else," said Iona. "It is not I, but another for whom I fear."

Maria smiled and took Iona by the hand. "A man, is it?"

"What do I do?" Iona pleaded.

"Men are easily possessed by witches," Maria said pointedly. "Men are easily controlled by their own weaknesses . . ."

"Yes, but what can be done to save him?" Iona interrupted.

"Perhaps if he is weak he should not be saved," Maria speculated out loud.

"Please, Maria."

"There is an old legend," Maria began. "In this old legend there was a handsome prince. He was well loved, and two powerful witches each wanted him for their own. One of the witches wanted him for a toy, and the other witch wanted him as an object to be admired. They both used their magic to control the prince. Each witch would counter the other witch's magic with even more powerful magic of her own. In the end, the prince was so altered from the magic that he was no longer desirable and so the witches quickly forgot about him."

"I will never forget about him," said Iona passionately.

"Then you must fight for him," said Maria. "The magic of witches is powerful, but it can be destroyed. Is that your wish, Iona?"

Iona nodded her approval.

"Find this witch!" Maria said forcefully. "All magic can be defeated. All magic can be defeated with sacrifice. Self sacrifice is the most powerful magic of all. It can never be defeated."

Later that day Iona chanced upon Bartholomew in the long corridor. She was carrying towels to a spare bedroom and Bartholomew was wandering, lost in his own thoughts. When they met, Bartholomew quickly spoke.

"Would you like to join me for a ride, Iona? There is something I would like to show you. The ride would do you good. Please come."

Once again, Bartholomew was changed. And now he no longer looked pallid and spent but instead looked vital and alive. Iona looked and saw only the old Bartholomew, the Bartholomew she knew before yesterday. Iona smiled warmly. She was happy to go with the Prince. She wanted only to be near him, to be in his presence, to laugh when he laughed and to cry when he was sad. Iona was in love.

"I have chores to do," she chided the Prince. "Who will tend to my chores if I am not there? Perhaps the King will want some tea and I will not be there."

"Maria can boil a pot of water, can she not?" Bartholomew said.

Iona smiled. "And what will I wear?" she said, but her mind was already made up.

"Wear what you have on," said the Prince.

Iona burst out laughing and she could not stop. "I am wearing a dress, silly," she said, not waiting for Bartholomew to answer.

Soon they were riding away together. Iona now wore riding-hose and a scarlet cape. She rode with Bartholomew and gingerly held him around the waist though she wanted to hold him tight.

Iona didn't often travel away from the castle. She was a servant, not a princess. Now, riding with Bartholomew over the rolling hills and deep glens with the wind blowing through her hair, she felt alive; she felt free and her face beamed with joy. She would gladly serve the King with a life of service for moments like this made her feel important and she imagined, just for a moment, that she could be loved even as she loved the Prince.

But as Bartholomew galloped across the lushness of his homeland he had other ideas, for he was still buried beneath the weight of Hypatia's powerful magic and he had only brief moments of lucidity in which he could use his own mind, for Hypatia was not all-powerful and the Prince was not nearly as weak as he seemed. However, even now he was riding to Hypatia to fulfill his promise to deliver the innocent Iona to her, but he could not gather the forces necessary to counter her powerful intention which she worked through him though he were nothing more than a shell. Buried deep in his mind was sadness, for he knew that he was doing great evil and he wanted no harm to come to Iona.

As Bartholomew brought his horse to a walk he relaxed because he was near the fountain of Hypatia and he could feel her presence most acutely.

Iona loosened her hold on the Prince and tried to determine where she was. They were off the path leading to Peel, but she did not recognize the area in which they now treaded slowly and methodically. Down into a gradually descending ravine Bartholomew led his horse and the two riders swayed side to side as the horse proceeded into a wild overgrown tangle of old growth and wild heath country infused with twisting vine and sharp thorn. An atmosphere of dread emanated from the soft ground like poisonous vapors from an evil miasma. Iona wondered if they were in an ancient graveyard or burial ground. Then Bartholomew stopped his horse and jumped down. He looked up to Iona and smiled, but his smile was not happy, but one of anticipation.

"Let me help you," he said thoughtfully, and lifting her down his strong hands held her gently.

Iona allowed herself to be helped, but she was becoming slightly anxious. In front of her was an old stone sticking up from the ground, partially buried and covered with thick vines. She looked around curiously before asking.

"Is this a cemetery?"

"This is on old ruin site," he answered. "Follow me, Iona. I want to show you something special."

Then Prince Bartholomew dropped down to his hands and knees and began to crawl into the dense undergrowth. After a few feet he motioned for Iona to follow him. Then he disappeared completely. Iona laughed half-heartedly and then she followed the Prince. When she came to the end of the burrow she saw the Prince looking down into a basin of water.

"Look," he said. "This is the fountain of Hypatia."

Iona crawled up to the edge of the fountain and looked down. The water was still. She looked to Bartholomew.

"You must drink from the fountain," he said, and then he smiled. "It is alright, Iona. Drink from the fountain. You will see."

Iona put her trust in the Prince. She believed that he would never hurt her and she only wanted to help him. Again she glanced at

Bartholomew. He was waiting anxiously for her and she could see his impatience. Still she hesitated.

"Please, Iona. You must drink from the fountain or you will not see her."

And so Iona bent her head down and brought her lips to the edge of the fountain and she drank. The water tasted foul. Then she noticed a feeling of pressure against her ears and she felt herself becoming hot with fever. Suddenly a wrenching pain in her stomach caused her to swoon and she became dizzy. A voice was inside of her head speaking to her, cursing her, shouting at her. The pain increased as the voice in her head became more vicious. She tried to ignore the voice but it was becoming louder and louder and she felt like something was trying to crawl inside of her skin. Then she collapsed and began to writhe on the ground, tossing her head from side to side.

Bartholomew watched in horror. This is not what he expected to see. He could hear Iona whimpering as she struggled against an invisible foe. And slowly his mind began to clear, and like the warm flow of blood into a frozen organ his senses started to return. Now the sound of Iona became unbearable to him as his heart broke from the shame of what he had done to her. He crawled to her and held her head in his hands desperately. But her body had gone limp and her head hung down like a broken doll. His mind continued to return to him and with each moment his anger and fury grew as he became cognizant of the treachery of Hypatia.

He looked down at Iona. Her body lay motionless and her mouth fell open. She was dead. "No, no, please do not die!" he cried with anguish. "Iona, come back to me Iona."

Suddenly his fury erupted. His blood turned to ice and he took his vengeance out on Hypatia. He crawled slowly out from the burrow. Then he went to where his horse was tethered to a tree and retrieved his sword from where it hung from his saddlebag. Walking slowly to the stone which marked the grotto of Hypatia the energy surged through his body. Then, with systematic violence, he smashed the stone with his sword causing sparks to fly off in all directions. When he became too exhausted to strike the stone with his sword he threw his body onto the stone and tried to dislodge it from the ground. Finally he was able to tip it over. Next he looked around for a large rock and when he found one he pummeled the stone until it cracked.

He crawled back to where Iona's body lay. Then he brought his lips to her forehead and kissed her. But then he saw her eyes flutter and then open. She was alive!

The Prince threw his arms around her and held her tight. Tears of relief filled his eyes. He held her and could not let her go and it was in that moment that he realized what she had done for him.

"Oh, Iona," he said tenderly. "Thank you for believing in me. I knew you were there, but I could not get to you. I could feel you there but I was helpless. Now I am free."

"I'm tired," said Iona with a sigh. "Will you let me sleep for a while?"

And so Prince Bartholomew lifted Iona from the ground and held her and cradled her in his arms while she slept, rocking her and caressing her face. He watched her as she slept and slowly his heart was captured by her innocence and her charm, and the Prince's heart was once again conquered with a love that would last him until the end of his days

The Witchwood Door

"Tell me Iona: Can one's soul become old? Can one's soul become sick with grief? Oh Iona, in truth the soul can become crippled with age just as a man is thus crippled."

"Our soul is given to make us strong," she answered the King proudly. "Truly, our soul comes from the Lord."

"My soul is so tired, Iona. My soul is weak."

"The weakness is not in your soul," the servant said. "The weakness is in your heart."

In the heart of Castletown stands an old brick house tucked away within the narrow and winding lanes and byways of this royal, coastal town. No one remembers who first built the house, for through a series of strange fires, questionable transactions and misplaced documents going back over a century, the information has been lost. What sets this house apart from all the other old houses that speckle the town however, is the door. Surely one of the most remarkable doors ever to have been carved, the door has taken on an aura, a mythological reputation that has grown stranger with each new telling. Each new generation has claimed the mystery inherent in that door as their own until the legend of the door has become a manifestation of those that would want to claim it for their own, and the legend has become richer and richer through a gradual transmutation.

King Sigmus first showed it to his young son as they passed by in their black ebony carriage. The boy could have been no more than seven or eight years old at the time. The streets were so narrow that they had to creep along slowly to avoid crashing into discarded objects and children playing, for not many carriages passed by and the children loved to look at it. The King pointed out the window.

"Look Bartholomew," he said as he pointed to the house. "Look at the door. I think that it is the greatest door I have ever seen."

Bartholomew quickly climbed over the seat and jumped on his father's lap. He peered through the window and smiled even before he knew what he was looking at, for Bartholomew was an enthusiastic boy. What he saw was a large, oaken door flanked on either side by an enormous rowan tree the sides of which were embedded into and formed the very frame of the door, as if the roots had hungrily grown into the very substance of the house. It was magical and impossible. On the center of the door was a carved symbol. Two large snakes were twisted into a strange patchwork of braided Celtic knots, one devouring while being devoured by the other. The snakes were intertwined in such a way that they defied the nature of the space on which they were carved and emerged from a dimension that came from an inner surface concealed.

"Do you like it?" asked King Sigmus.

Bartholomew hesitated before he answered as if he needed to think about it before he could answer. The boy was curious, for the door made him uneasy.

"Who lives there?" he asked.

The King was surprised by the question. "What do you mean?" he said. "The door . . . Look at the door, son."

The carriage continued to pass by slowly. Bartholomew continued to watch the house until it was out of sight. Then he looked at his father with a questioning look.

"Does a bad man live in that house?" he asked. "I think that I don't like that house. I do not like the door, father. It scares me."

"There's nothing to be afraid of," said Sigmus with a cheerful laugh. "It's just a door, Bartholomew. Forget about it if you want."

King Sigmus could not have known the lasting impression that door would have on his son. He could not have guessed the obsession to which his son would devote so much of his time pursuing. The mind of a young boy is easily captured, and so it was with Bartholomew.

Bartholomew thought about the door often. He would lay in his bed at night and try to imagine what could possibly be happening on the other side of that door. And then he would fall asleep hoping that his imagination would take him to that place for him to wander through the lonely hours of the night. There had to be a secret he believed, and one day he would know that secret. Every time he and his father were in Castletown, he would beg his father to drive past that door, for he was no longer afraid of it now. The house seemed to be abandoned, but though they never saw a person anywhere near that house, Bartholomew knew that it was not abandoned, and that behind that door was a person. He even imagined that the person behind that door was looking at him at that very moment, and the thought excited him.

When Bartholomew was older, he would take trips to Castletown by himself and he would go to the house with the strange door. By this time he had come to name the door. He called it *The Witchwood Door*, for he was convinced that the maker of that door was once a druid. Sometimes he would sit atop his horse, transfixed, and he would stare at the door for an hour. Once he even sketched it into a notebook that he kept in his saddlebag. Sometimes he would stop at one of the local inns and inquire about the house or the whereabouts of its inhabitants. No one knew, or if they did know they would not say and he would have to go away even more spellbound. On one day, the owner of a local pub drew a pint for Bartholomew when he stopped in to quench his thirst before riding back home. He listened to Bartholomew for a minute, and then he said.

"There have been stories passed around about this house, and that is true. But no one really knows for sure. Used to be said that an old sailor lived there. Some folks say he was a pirate. They say that he came home from a voyage out to sea and that he had been gone many years. They say he brought home boxes and crates a plenty. Then one day was spotted two giant trees, one on each side of his door. Folks say that the trees were there to guard his house when he was gone, but none ever saw him come home and none ever saw him come out. Some folks say that he is still in there."

"Is that what they say?" said Bartholomew as he took a long draft from his glass nearly emptying it in one gulp. He finished it off before dropping it on the bar with a loud thud. "Interesting," he said, pointing to his empty glass. "What do you say? Tell me, when did all this happen?"

The innkeeper took Bartholomew's glass to the tap and refilled it. Then he came back rubbing his head as if the memory were so close and only needed to be dislodged.

"I first heard this story from my father, and he first heard it from his father. Like I say to you, no one really knows for sure."

Bartholomew had heard this before. This was a typical tale and he was bored with its predictability. His disappointment set in even before he finished his drink. "I don't understand," he said. "You said that those trees protect his house. How do they do that?"

"Those are not trees," said the innkeeper slowly shaking his head as he wiped a stain from his bar. The man spoke softly as if he were afraid they would be overheard.

This was unexpected. Now Bartholomew suddenly was interested again. Reaching into his pocket he threw down a piece of silver, surely more money than the innkeeper would see all day.

"Then tell me," said Bartholomew eagerly. "What are they?"

"Those trees are demons," said the man decisively. Then he swallowed hard. "Brought back from the Orient they were. They say that the sailor was a wizard, and I reckon that he was. Those trees are his familiars. You best stay away from that house, and don't even look at that door if you want my advice."

Bartholomew thanked the man for his advice. Then he left. In another part of town was an even dirtier, even darker and rundown tavern. Ducking beneath the carved sign over the door that was broken and left swinging in the wind, he went in and was surprised at the wretchedness of the place.

"What do you want?" came a low growl from within the smoky interior.

Bartholomew turned and started to leave, but then he stopped. If need came, he could certainly take care of himself. He never traveled without a weapon.

"It's Prince Bartholomew!" someone shouted.

"I'm looking for information," said the Prince. "The house on Kirk Arbory Street, the one with the door made from trees, tell me, does anyone know anything about it? If you talk, I'll buy drinks."

A commotion arose throughout the tavern. Bartholomew knew drunken chatter when he heard it. Finally someone spoke up.

"Sure, I'll talk," he said. "That is, if you still want to hear."

"Then let's start drinking, and you can start talking," said the Prince to a rousing volley of drunken cheers.

The man that spoke was old. His face was wrinkled and destroyed from the sun. His nose was swollen, pock-marked and ugly, but he smiled, for even without teeth he could still be content.

"Legend has it that the trees were here before the house, even before Castletown was built. And as the town was built up around the harbor, the house was built up around the trees. The house itself is a harbor, and those trees are ancient berths to another place, a place that reaches farther than the sea. Those trees have always been here. Some folks say that they were here before the island was brought up from the sea."

"And the door?" Bartholomew asked impatiently. "What about the door?"

"That is not a door," he said. "It is a wall."

"What are you talking about?" Bartholomew demanded. "I have heard this all before, but I do not believe it."

"He's right," said a short, paunchy man stepping out of the shadow. "Let me tell you a story," he began. He looked around cautiously, taking everyone in with his eyes, as if they too were now included in his story. "The pirate that lives in that house was a wizard. No one disputes that far as I know. They say that after coming home from the reach after so many years his face was old and wrinkled and ugly. He was getting old and he feared getting old more than anything. His young wife waited for him every day hoping he would come back home, and when she finally saw him she recoiled from his ugliness. He assured her not to worry. He had brought home a formula. He had found a magic potion that could make him young again. That is when he planted those two rowan trees you see guarding his door, but the enchantment needed one more thing to make it true . . ."

"A sacrifice?" said Bartholomew sarcastically. "Is that what it needed, a human sacrifice?" He was almost able to predict what the people would say.

There was a murmur through the crowd. Some of the men were starting to grumble. Arguments erupted and he could hear shouts and curses. But the man was not finished with his story and he raised his voice the loudest.

"She danced naked in the moonlight, that's what she did if you want to hear what happened! Her skin was so pale that it glowed silvery in the moonlight as her tender feet danced and fluttered like the wings of nymphs. The story goes that his young and beautiful wife was made to dance a dance of rejuvenation in the moonlight. She danced without a stitch of clothing if you can even imagine such a thing. The gods love pretty women, but they like them best when they are unclothed."

"So do we!" shouted a drunken man nearly falling out of his chair.

"Then the old wizard took his young bride back into the house and closed the door for the last time," said the short man. "And so it is that the old wizard and his wife don't get old . . . no . . . that happens to the trees. It is the trees that age, and that is why they can never come out of that house again."

"Are you telling me there was no sacrifice?" Bartholomew asked with barely concealed derision. He was becoming irritated again. "Tell me, how can the trees do such a thing without a sacrifice? There is always a sacrifice."

The men all looked at one another with surprise. Then they thought for a moment before the room exploded in a fury of yelling and cursing.

"Yes, yes I believe there was a sacrifice," one of the men began. Then he belched and reached for his drink. "I think it was the devil . . ."

Bartholomew had heard enough for one day. Now he was getting angry. He left the tavern and jumped up on his horse. He was just about to ride away when a voice stopped him.

"Wait," said a very old man that suddenly appeared beside him though Bartholomew did not recognize him from the tavern. The man motioned with his finger that Bartholomew was supposed to come closer. "Go to the House of Keys," he said. "Ask them about Kelly Bournam. Ask them to tell you what happened to Kelly Bournam. Tell them to look in their books and tell you what happened to that poor child."

"Can you tell me?" Bartholomew asked.

"I could, but you wouldn't believe me. Go to the House of Keys, Bartholomew. Ask them about it." And then he turned and walked away slowly.

Bartholomew rode to Castle Rushen to petition the Keys. The 24 Keys were not in session on this day. Bartholomew was able to talk to a member however. Captain Edward Christian received him in a small antechamber. Tea was served because Prince Bartholomew was a dignitary and was always treated with respect by the Keys. Bartholomew wasted no time in declaring the reason for his visit.

"You want to know about Kelly Bournam, is that right?" said the Captain. "This is most unusual, you do understand."

Bartholomew nodded. He had gone too far to turn back now. "Can you just look it up in the records?" he said.

"In which records would that be?" the Captain replied.

"Death records," said Bartholomew. "She did die, did she not?"

Edward Christian left the room to find the records while Bartholomew waited. Almost an hour passed while he paced back and forth and regretted his damnable curiosity. Then Edward Christian returned with a book under his arm. He looked frustrated and his face was moist from perspiration. He dropped the book on to a table like a man dropping a heavy load.

"Do you want to tell me what this is about?" he said brusquely all the while trying to hide his growing anger.

Bartholomew looked questioningly for he didn't know what to expect, but he did not expect derision. "I was told to ask about this person," he said. "I don't know who the man was."

Edward Christian sat down on a red divan facing the Prince. "It seems that you have indeed dredged up a name from long ago, a name best forgotten I should think."

Bartholomew looked on quizzically but said nothing. Edward Christian continued.

"A rather curious entry indeed. I shall read it in its entirety." And then he read the document carefully.

Kelly F. Bournam, maiden name unknown, born September 12, 1416
Married June 10, 1433 to Ambert P. Bournam
Died June 17, 1438
Cause of death: Extreme old age.
The body was examined by Thomas Watten. His report contained the following notes:
Plague-like sores, festering open wounds, signs of apoplexy. Strange marks covereing her body, indicating possible possession by the Devil or consorts of the Devil. Due to the shrunken, twisted limbs and emaciated condition of the corpse, nothing further could be learned. The deceased is survived by her husband who is currently lost at sea and unavailable for purposes of identification.
Bournam House, the family estate survives in perpetuity through escrow accounts administered by Hermeodotous, Bradda Head. Port Erin. The body was given to Hermeodotous for special burial services contained in her will.
Note: Kelly Bournam was found mysteriously, unclothed on her doorstep between two gigantic Rowan trees which framed her door. No explanation could be ascertained.

When he was finished reading, he waited for Bartholomew to say something. He waited patiently, but the Prince was lost in thought.

"Is this what you were looking for?" he asked. "It sounds like the poor girl did indeed have a terrible life . . . the little of it she lived that is."

Bartholomew rode back to Ballasalla feeling uneasy. He spent some time shooting arrows to take his mind off the growing realization that was trying to surface. Later that day he went for a music lesson at the home of his music teacher. They exchanged a cordial handshake which was customary for Bartholomew, and then they sat down to play a duet together. Nothing more than a practice etude used for the purpose of instruction, the piece was fairly simple and allowed the musician the opportunity for ornate flourishes. The etude was traditional, a fragment from an old folksong that Bartholomew had played many times. But his mind would not allow him to concentrate to come to the place his music teacher was trying to lead him, it just seemed dry and pointless. When they stopped to compare a discrepancy in the sheet music they were reading, Bartholomew asked Gustav Wilhelm.

"This music is old, Herr Wilhelm. Is all music about holding on to the past?"

"Quite the contrary Bartholomew, you misunderstand me. Music is about bringing the past into the present and making it relevant once more with a new generation. One should never dismiss the past so easily, my friend. But tell me, does this music sound old to your ears?"

"Pardon me, Herr Wilhelm, but this music sounds dead."

Gustav laughed warmly and brushed aside Bartholomew's impertinent remark. He liked the young Prince and he was aware of his willfulness.

"It is not proper for a young man to think so keenly about death," said the Music Master. "The deeper you contemplate death, the closer it comes. Believe me Bartholomew. It is far better to think about life."

"Does death seek us out then?" asked Bartholomew. "Should we hide from death that it not find us?"

"Hold on, dear Bartholomew!" the Music Master broke in. "What has come over you today? Death is not a thing. Death is not a thing like life, but the gradual giving back of what one has taken. When we immortalize our beautiful thoughts with music, we are helping to sustain that . . . which is life. The study of music is not meant to resurrect the past, my friend. It is to honor the past."

"But tell me," said Bartholomew with feverish intensity. "If we can hold on to life hard enough, if we can find a way to capture the essence of that which is life, can we escape death?"

"I am a music teacher," said Gustav Wilhelm nervously. "What you are asking me should more properly be asked of a man of God. These thoughts are not thoughts that can bring you answers, Bartholomew. These thoughts will only harm you. I suggest you study the music of life and leave the music of death to the angels."

Bartholomew went to his room and waited for tea to be brought. He went to the window and opened the shutters. Standing at the window his mind wandered and became lost in abstraction. Alone in his room he felt small while the entire world was present just outside his window. It was there, and it would be there when he was gone and turned to dust. What purpose could it serve to know the world? There was so much to know, so much to learn about the world, but even then, it was impossible to know more than a pencil sketch of a few things . . . that was all. A soft knock at the door broke the spell that he had surrendered to. It was the young servant Iona, bringing his tea.

"Thank you Iona," he said.

She nodded and turned to leave. Bartholomew started to close his door, but then he stopped.

"Iona!" he said as she was already walking away.

She stopped and turned around. "Yes," she replied. "Is there something else you want, Bartholomew?"

Bartholomew stepped into the hall. He didn't really know what he wanted to say. His overzealousness had caused him to leap before he knew what he was doing. Embarrassed by his own foolishness and afraid he would frighten the poor girl, he tried to turn his back on her.

"Are you all right, Bartholomew?"

And then he asked. "Would you want to live forever, Iona? Tell me true."

"No," she said with a smile. "I would not like that at all. Is that what you wanted to ask me, Bartholomew? Such a strange question for a man like you to ask." And then she giggled again and had to control her laughter lest the Prince think she was making fun of him.

Bartholomew beseeched her. "But if you did, Iona. Think about if you did. You could be beautiful forever . . ."

Iona gasped. She was surprised at her Prince, but his flattery was unintended so she had to forgive him. She could see that the Prince was upset about something and needed to be alone, for this was another one of his moods.

"The world can only have so much beauty," she said modestly. "Ugliness teaches us to admire the beautiful things in our world for they are fleeting indeed I should think. True beauty does not perish at the end of life, Bartholomew. I would want to see all the wonderful things that are to come, for this world will go along just fine without me. To live forever would be a curse." Then she smiled respectively and went on her way leaving Bartholomew alone in the hallway.

'Alas,' she was probably right thought Bartholomew. 'Why do I waste my time with such drivel?' He drank his tea quietly. Then he went to bed and found his dreams to be comforting, but near morning he was woken by the song of a bird. And when he woke up, he had a new thought. After eating a large breakfast he went to the stable and saddled his horse for a long ride. He packed some food and a few bottles of beer in his saddle bags. Then he rode to Port Erin to find this man named Hermeodotous.

The house sat alone on top of a high seaside cliff overlooking crashing waves and nesting peregrine falcons of Port Erin Bay. A narrow path, or what had once been the remnants of a narrow path, led up to the large stone house. Perhaps no one had used this path for many years thought Bartholomew curiously. Walking his horse carefully over the uneven and rock-strewn path leading to the cottage he wondered what sort of man he would find. After checking at several shops along the way he had finally found someone that knew the man of which he spoke. The owner of a pub in the harbor where Bartholomew had stopped to ask directions knew of the man he sought. He opened the door to his pub and went outside motioning for Bartholomew to follow. Then he pointed to the top of the cliff at Bradda Head across the bay.

"There it is," he said. "Hermeodotous lives in that there cottage."

Bartholomew gave the man a coin and turned to leave. He mounted his horse and prepared to leave.

"If you want my advice," the man suddenly said as if the idea had only just occurred to him. "If you want my advice, you will not go there."

"Why not?" Bartholomew asked. "You just pointed it out to me. Why did you show me where it was if you didn't want me to go there?"

"You look decent enough," the man said finally as he clutched his pipe in his large hand. "Something strange about that house," he said. "I wouldn't go there alone."

Bartholomew looked down from his horse. He waited for the man to continue, wondering if it was worth his time to stay and listen. After several moments passed without a word, he finally decided that the man possibly knew something about it.

"Can you tell me why?" he asked. "If there is something you can tell me about that house I would welcome whatever it was."

"No one has ever seen him," he said cautiously. "Not a soul has seen his face or heard his voice, and that's a fact. Some folk are strange in their own way. This one is a mystery. Ain't no sheep on those slopes. No chickens either. He don't grow nothing they say. He don't needs to grow nothing. I'm asking you then, what does he eat?"

"How do you know he is there?" said Bartholomew. "If no one has ever seen him, how do you know he is there?"

"Unholy business," said the innkeeper, "Tis unholy business. At night is when he comes to life. At night is when he moves around, and you can see them. Lights shooting from his windows like slippery lightning I tell you, slippery lightning."

Bartholomew remembered those words as he rode up to the olden stone cottage on the cliff. The two-story house was very tall and compact. The construction was aged pepper-stone fitted and mortared in the old way. Gothic arched windows protruded from the house and were in stark relief to the moldering stone walls that dripped with salty dampness brought in from the sea. The tall gambrel roof was pitched sharp as a needle and small dormers protruded like peeping afterthoughts and made the house look dangerous and sinister. In front of the house was a circular driveway that came up to the entrance under a canopy with

Ionic columns to support such a large structure. The flagstones were in disrepair and weeds had cracked and overtaken the careful symmetry, leaving only irregular stones in its place. Jumping off his horse, he tied the reins to a column and went up to the door. A large brass knocker was attached to the oaken door. Feeling the coolness of the metal, Bartholomew gave a loud knock and waited to be admitted.

After several minutes it was clear that no one was coming to answer his persistent knocking. He turned and looked around to see if there was any evidence of habitation. Not a sign showed the smallest evidence that anyone had ever lived in the silent house. Bartholomew decided to walk around the back of the house to see if there was anything of interest to him there. Between the house and the cliff where a steady wind came up from the sea was a small patio area surrounded by hearty trees that acted like a canopy and shielded the center around which a table and chairs were positioned. Then Bartholomew noticed that there was a man sitting at the table. He was looking in the direction of Bartholomew as if he had been waiting for him the entire time. Dressed elegantly in black doublet over a white shirt with puffs and a white ruff collar that surrounded his head with fiery points of red jewels, he looked aristocratic and daunting. He sat with his legs crossed, revealing bright red hose and black pantofles with a silver buckle and a red rose covering his feet. A thick, black belt around his waist held a scabbard and sword and a leather purse. He had a narrow, Flemish face with a short, well-groomed goatee, hollow cheeks slightly blushed, and wavy black hair that fell about his shoulder. He was looking intently at Bartholomew as he approached cautiously.

"Welcome to my home," said the mysterious man. "I have been waiting for you."

Bartholomew bowed respectfully in deference to the man in his own home, as was his custom. "My name is Prince Bartholomew," he said. "Pardon my intrusion, but I was merely trying to see if someone still lived in this house. You are . . ."

"Lord Hermeodotous," the man said proudly. "I am the lord of this estate." Then he waited for Bartholomew to resume speaking. When he did not, Hermeodotous said. "You are surprised to see me. I can tell by your expression that you did not expect to find me."

"I have heard that you are . . . a very private person," Bartholomew said. "It is said that you are very reclusive, so you can imagine my shock when I should find you at home on the very first visit."

"Do not explain," he said with a casual wave of his elegant hand. "I have my reasons for remaining private, and the remoteness of my house perhaps helps me to exaggerate my own uniqueness."

Bartholomew saw that on his hand was the most exquisite ring he had ever seen. The ruby was strikingly polished and fairly radiated with brilliance. His eyes were drawn to it.

"It is a family heirloom," said Hermeodotous. "I have known many jewelers in my time. But tell me, Bartholomew, what brings you to my home?"

Bartholomew didn't really know how to begin. He never really expected to talk with Hermeodotous. In truth, he didn't even expect that there was such a man.

"I saw your name in the death registry for Kelly Bournam," said Bartholomew. "You are Hermeodotous, are you not?"

"Yes, I am," he answered with a smile.

Bartholomew looked annoyed. "But how can that be?" he asked. "The reference was to a man that lived in 1438. How old are you?"

Hermeodotous laughed. "Do you think I am a wizard, Bartholomew? Look at me young man. Do I look old to you? You must understand . . . I am Hermeodotous VI."

"Of course," Bartholomew agreed. "The death certificate said that the Bournam House of Castletown would remain in perpetuity, and that the executor would maintain the estate in all matters."

"That is true," said Hermeodotous. "I am the executor."

"And yet you conduct all your business from this house?"

"Yes I do. I like my privacy, as you can see."

"This is none of my business," said Bartholomew as politely as possible. "But do you know anything about the history of the Bournam House?"

"Tell me what you would like to know, Bartholomew. I know everything about the house."

"I'm interested in the door, Lord Hermeodotous. What can you tell me about the door?"

"Ah, yes the door. It is an exquisite door indeed. Solid wood, carved from between two magnificent trees. The door is remarkable indeed."

"And the trees?" Bartholomew asked with growing interest.

"Rowan trees," Hermeodotous answered casually. "I should think that you would know that. I do not know just what you are asking."

"I'm talking about magic," Bartholomew announced suddenly. "I'm talking about black magic."

Hermeodotous raised an eyebrow. He cocked his head and looked at the Prince thoughtfully for the first time. His gaze was penetrating.

"Bournam had a wife, a young wife," Bartholomew continued. "By all accounts, she was a dazzling beauty. She died horribly, Hermeodotous. She died of old age, and if her death certificate is accurate, she was hideously deformed. There is a contradiction here. Do you know what could have happened to her?"

"I was not there," said Hermeodotous with a lack of concern. "Remember Bartholomew, I am Hermeodotous VI. But you must have a reason for coming here. Surely you would know that I could not possibly know the answer to your questions."

"Yes, of course. But tell me Hermeodotous, why is this house being maintained in such a fashion? Why do you not sell it?"

Hermeodotous smiled and even tried to conceal a snigger. "So Prince Bartholomew," he said. "The truth comes out at last. You think that the black magic you referred to is coming from me. Is that correct?"

Bartholomew gasped and backed away like he had been blown by a powerful wind. Hermeodotous continued to speak.

"You have brought your suspicions to my door. You have brought your suspicions and you have implicated me. I say, you are a very resolute man, Bartholomew."

"There is something evil about that door," Bartholomew said almost like a plea. "I cannot rest until I find out what it is."

"And if you do find out, what then? What happens when you determine that it is not evil?"

"Corruption of nature cannot but be evil."

"Is it evil to live forever, Bartholomew? Tell me then, if our soul be immortal, why not our body? And if our body should perish . . . are we the more noble by the act of dying?"

Bartholomew stared at Hermeodotous with a growing understanding. The more he spoke, the more certain Bartholomew became of his suspicion. An understanding was beginning to develop between the two men, an understanding that was implied, not spoken. Bartholomew feared to say the words that would verify his suspicion, so he only looked around the edges. Hermeodotous decided to penetrate Bartholomew's thoughts and find out where they were focused.

"What if I told you there was no reason to die, Bartholomew? What if I told you that dying served no purpose? Tell me then, would you consider me a necromancer?"

"How old are you? How old are you really?" said Bartholomew through tightening lips.

Hermeodotous laughed out loud and looked at Bartholomew with knowing eyes. "There is only one Hermeodotous," he said. "But why do you look so pale, Bartholomew. You suspected me all along, did you not?"

"What are you?" Bartholomew said apprehensively. "Are you a wizard?"

"You could call me a wizard if that would help you to understand. That is a name that has been used to scare people. Yes, some would call me wise, but I do not like the word wizard."

"Are you not afraid to admit such a thing to me?"

"Tell me, why should I be afraid, Bartholomew? I have not told you a thing yet. Anyone can claim to be a wizard, and there is nothing unlawful about that."

Bartholomew threw his hands in the air. "Then what?" he said.

Hermeodotous rose from his chair. He walked to the edge of the garden and looked out to sea. The warm air blew through his hair and made him look absolutely wild. Like the air itself, he seemed to waver like something airy, incorporeal. He spoke into the open air as if Bartholomew was not standing beside him.

"I am a member of a society, Bartholomew," he said didactically. "I am a member of a very secret association of men such as myself. I tell you this because as you know, there are many secret societies abroad and I am not revealing anything by telling you this. Ours is a very old tradition, Bartholomew, much older than you can imagine."

"And the Bournam House is connected to this society. Is that what you are saying, Hermeodotous?"

"In a manner of speaking, yes," he said sternly. "You see, the society of which I am a member, have come to identify qualities of nature that go unnoticed except during the most extraordinary circumstances, such as during a thunderstorm or an astral alignment. This is what we do. We are men of learning foremost and we have made some startling connections between the physical world, and the non-physical world. Do you follow me?"

"The non-physical world?" Bartholomew repeated suspiciously. "Are you a neo-Platonist then, Hermeodotous?"

"Oh yes, Plato's world of forms," Hermeodotous answered with a smile. "That is a very good guess, Bartholomew. I see that you are a man of learning as well. For Plato, this world of forms was a mathematical abstraction, real, but only insofar as the rational mind that could advance an explanation. Plato believed in perfect forms, believing everything else to be but an imitation. But for the members of my society it is more real than the ground on which you stand. Would you like to see it?"

Bartholomew was becoming more and more uncomfortable. Perhaps he had made a mistake in coming alone. He found himself face to face with something that frightened him. He spoke cautiously.

"Is that door part of all this?" he asked carefully.

"It is," Hermeodotous answered. "Do you want to know what lives behind that door, Bartholomew? Would you like to see it?"

Bartholomew stared but was silenced by a revulsion that was rising up within his mind.

"Come Bartholomew, where is your sense of adventure? This is a secret that I know you would appreciate. Has your curiosity, the very same curiosity that has brought you to my door, suddenly become sated?"

"What is behind that door?" Bartholomew finally said.

"Why don't you find out, Bartholomew. I don't think the door is even locked. Go and find out."

Later that night when Bartholomew lay in bed thinking about his conversation with Hermeodotous, he was haunted by an uneasy feeling that something bad was going to happen to him. He had discovered a secret that perhaps should never have been uncovered. The room was dark. It was late into the night and the servants had gone to bed hours ago. The sound of the wind outside his window was getting louder though he wasn't expecting a storm during the night. Bartholomew knew that sorcery was practiced on the island, but he never expected to confront it directly. Magic was a part of the history of the island and it was present in almost all of the lore that was known and taught to eager children. He turned over in bed and faced the window. Faint starlight peeped in from outside. Suddenly he noticed something that he had been listening to for a long time but had only just crept into his consciousness. The wind was making a particular sound, a sound that seemed to whisper to him. It was whispering his name. He held his breath to be certain it was not the faint beating of his own heart, but there it was again. He pulled the covers up to the top of his head to block out the sound and that is how he fell into a fitful sleep.

Bartholomew was woken during the night by the sound of furious knocking on his bedchamber door. The knocking was persistent and anxious. Scurrying to the door as fast as possible he opened it. His servant Sorren stood there in his nightshirt. His eyes were dazed and bloodshot and Bartholomew could see that he was distraught.

"What is it, Sorren?" he asked.

The poor man was shaking. He could speak only with great difficulty. Reaching out imploringly he said.

"There is something in the castle, sir. Something is here."

"Calm yourself and tell me what you are talking about," said Bartholomew reassuringly.

"There is a wind loose in the castle, a terrible wind sir. I felt it only a moment ago, yes I did."

Bartholomew opened the door wide and motioned for Sorren to enter. "Come in here and tell me what you are talking about," he said. "Now then, tell me about this wind. When did you see it, and tell me where you were."

Sorren was a servant but he was also a friend to Bartholomew. The two of them had hunted together and Bartholomew had taught Sorren how to read. He knew that Sorren was no coward, so whatever it was that had spooked him was something to be taken seriously.

"I didn't see it, sir. I felt it just a few moments ago while I was up in the north tower. That is where I felt it."

"What were you doing in the north tower, Sorren?"

Sorren started to answer, but he was so nervous that his words sounded incoherent and jumbled. He tried to speak.

". . . I was just . . ."

"Never mind," said Bartholomew. "I do not need to know what you were doing. That is your business. But tell me about the wind. Tell me truthfully, for you have nothing to fear from me."

"I was in the tower," he began. "I had a candle with me to see through the darkness. Suddenly I feels a gentle wind, a wind like the breath of a baby, in my face. That is when my candle begins to waver and I thought it would go out."

"As you know Sorren, there are drafts in the castle and sometimes the wind blows with such great force . . ."

"It was not that kind of a wind, sir. This wind was unnatural. I stood still and did not move, but it was the wind that moved all around me and I can all the time feel a gentle touch of air surrounding my body and prickling my skin."

"And then you came running here, is that right, Sorren?"

"No sir," he replied. "In truth I was too scared to move, so I just hided myself in the darkness and cupped my hands around the candle."

"And then, what then Sorren?"

"That's when I saw the vapor, sir."

"The vapor? Speak up Sorren! What vapor?"

"I knows magic when I see it, sir. This was magic, bad magic."

Bartholomew was getting frustrated with having to drag everything out of the man with such an effort. "Tell me about it, Sorren. I need to know everything you can remember."

"It was green like the color of trees in the springtime. There it was, but there was a hidden fire inside and the edges, they glowed like swamp light. I watched it move and it moved along the floor slowly, changing shape and shifting direction like it was looking for something."

"Or someone?" said Bartholomew.

Sorren looked down in shame. "I hid from it," he said. "I escaped and then I came here to tell you."

"You're safe," Bartholomew assured the frightened man. "It was looking for me, not you. Sorren, tell me now, where did it go?"

"I looked. It turned to smoke, Bartholomew. Then it was gone, disappeared into the air. It disappeared right into the air."

"Go back to bed now, Sorren. You're safe now my friend."

Sorren relaxed now that Bartholomew had taken charge. "What are you going to do, sir?" he asked.

"I'm going to the north tower," said Bartholomew with purpose. "I'll get to the truth of this, Sorren. Of that you can be sure." Then he smiled reassuringly to Sorren and whisked out of the room.

The north tower is a circular tower gained by climbing a long, circular staircase. The stairwell is narrow, little more than a tunnel carved through thick stone as it ascends toward the topmost chamber. Torches were fastened to the walls but were seldom lit, for the tower was never used but for secret, private purposes known only to God.

Bartholomew slowly ascended the narrow staircase. He carried a candle in his hand, and in his other hand he held a dagger lest he be surprised and suddenly overtaken. His heart was racing. Now he knew that he had penetrated too far into the mystical world and that it was brought upon him by his strange obsession with *The Witchwood Door*. He could not think about that now however, not until the specter was expelled from his home. The faint light from his candle made his own face glow eerily in the darkness, and now he was himself a ghost, a ghost chasing a ghost.

At the top of the tower is a chamber. Bartholomew entered the chamber and found that it was empty. There were windows facing out from the castle. Bartholomew saw that they were closed. He went to a table and set down the candle. On the table was a book. Sorren must have left it behind. Bartholomew picked up the book and opened it. Now he knew what Sorren was doing up here and why he was reticent. It was not a written book, but a book being written. It was a book of poetry that Sorren was writing. Bartholomew put the book on the table. No, he would not intrude upon the secret thoughts of his friend and loyal servant.

Bartholomew walked around the tower. "Show yourself," he said out loud. "Do you expect me to wait for you now?"

And then he noticed movement near the window. At first it was amorphous, a wavering fog left over near dawn, but slowly it began to congeal into something solid, something dense. As expected, the form slowly turned into the form of a man, and in a few moments Hermeodotous stood before him. Though his body looked solid, it had a quality of airiness and seemed to be merged with two alternate worlds at the same time. Bartholomew's fear and apprehension now turned to anger.

"What do you want?" he said angrily. "You have scared my servant half to death."

"But I see that you are not frightened," Hermeodotous responded. "That is good. I see that you are a very special man, Bartholomew."

"Do you think that you could harm me in my own home, Hermeodotous?"

"There is much I could do," he said. "But the real reason I am here is to make you an offer."

"You travel in strange ways, Hermeodotous."

"Count Bournam would like to meet you, Bartholomew. He has invited you to his home, and I am here to extend that offer to you."

"Has Count Bournam risen from the dead?" Bartholomew said derisively.

"I asked you before if you wanted to know what was behind the door that so interested you, Bartholomew. But as you will remember, you chose not to answer."

"If Count Bournam is alive, tell me, why did he not come here himself?"

"The Count does not like to leave his home," said Hermeodotous. "He prefers the hearth to the heath in truth. Now then, will you come?"

"I will not," said Bartholomew. "Your magic does not interest me. Take it away and come to me no more."

"Are you not tempted, Bartholomew? There are things for you to learn that would certainly be irresistible to you. Would you like to travel the way I do?"

"In the name of Christ, I ask you to depart from this castle now!"

Hermeodotous laughed. "I am not a demon," he said. "There is no reason to evoke the name of the Lord. You ask me to leave, therefore I will leave. But remember, Bartholomew. Now that you have this knowledge, you can no longer be safe."

"What does that mean?" demanded Bartholomew. But the shape of Hermeodotous had already dissolved into the empty night air.

Bartholomew could not sleep the rest of that night, and all the next day he paced his room trying to decide what to do. He knew that he could never be free from this menace and that he would constantly be haunted with new fears and apprehensions. For the first time he began to consider the possibility that what Hermeodotous said was really true. An involuntary shiver went through his body. Then his decision was easy and he started to make preparations.

A dog barked nervously as a large cloud passed over the moon. Bartholomew crouched down in the darkness and opened the shutter on his lamp enough to see through the almost pitch blackness. He waited behind a tree just outside the Bournam House. Even in darkness he could sense the evilness of this house as if an atmosphere of doom surrounded the very space itself. Taking a few deep breaths to steady his nerves he went slowly up to the door. Come what may, tonight he was to be finished with this wretched house. The darkness made what he was about to do easier as his invisibility somehow justified his intrusion. Just a faint beam of light guided his footsteps to the door. He set down the lamp and reached for the knob. It felt cold to the touch. Slowly he turned the knob until he felt a soft click. The door was not locked!

Suddenly he was overcome by such a wave a nausea he nearly collapsed. The feeling of terror was visceral, and like a knot in his stomach twisting tighter and tighter he nearly doubled over in pain. No, he could not enter the house. He had not the strength to push the door further. Then his vision faltered and the door seemed to spin. He took his hand off the door and stepped back. Then, reaching for the lamp, he turned the flame as high as it would go. Finally he did what he had come to do, and with a sudden calculated movement he smashed the lamp into the door. It erupted into flames. Bartholomew was blown backward by the intense burst of heat and fell to the ground.

The Witchwood Door burned. Bartholomew knew he should run, but his eyes were transfixed and he watched it burn without the power to look away. The flame engulfed the door like liquid, becoming watery and unstable as the flames snapped and licked at the night air like jaws. Bartholomew thought that the flame resembled the outline of a man. He feared for what he had done. Crawling away on his hands and knees he tried to escape the burning door. When he was almost to the street he looked back once more. He watched as the flames died, or by some power had become absorbed into the door and finally were extinguished. He turned his back on *The Witchwood Door* and did not look back. When the last flicker of fire was extinguished, the cloud passed to the other side of the moon. Moonlight pierced the night sky and came to land on the smoldering door.

Prince Bartholomew came once again to the stone house on the cliff and reined his horse. As before, there was no sign of life. He knocked at the door for several minutes before walking once again to the little patio in back of the house. Sitting down at the stone table he waited. The wind blew dead leaves about and they settled on the table. Bartholomew could not understand the veritable feeling of decay that rose up within him, and he shuddered. Then he heard a voice. It was the voice of Hermeodotous, but it was thin and weak.

"Congratulations to you Bartholomew, you have destroyed me."

Bartholomew turned his head, and there he was. The change was astonishing. Though he still wore the same clothes as before, now they seemed worn, frayed, and served only to hide but not to ornament his once beautiful body. And now his acute, Flemish face was emaciated and ugly, burned almost beyond recognition. His body was shrunken and his skin was transparent, revealing swollen blue veins like thorns tracing his hands and face. His hair was completely white. He staggered toward Bartholomew and Bartholomew's eyes were drawn once again to the brilliant ruby ring.

"Have you come in good will to wish me farewell?" said Hermeodotous. "Do you like what you see?"

Suddenly Bartholomew felt a surge of remorse, and just for a moment he regretted what he had done. He spoke quietly, and with growing sympathy.

"No one should live forever, Hermeodotous."

"How long have you known the truth?" Hermeodotous asked. He sat down next to Bartholomew, but to the Prince he was but a wisp of smoke.

"You forgot something," said Bartholomew uneasily. "You forgot to bury yourself. Where are they interred? You forgot to bury your ancestors, Hermeodotous . . . Count Bournam."

Count Bournam laughed and his fragile body nearly collapsed. "Yes, yes indeed Bartholomew."

"Why did you invent such an elaborate illusion?" Bartholomew asked.

"The illusion extends further than you know, Bartholomew. But let us part as friends, for in truth I have no desire to kill you after what you have done to me. Soon I will be gone and the world will forget about me. In truth, I am weary of eternity."

Still Bartholomew was uneasy. He was not satisfied. "What happened to your wife, Count Bournam?" he asked. "I will not rest until I know the truth."

"You would not want to know the truth," Count Bournam replied pointedly. "Some things are better left unknown."

"I will not let this stand," said Prince Bartholomew defiantly.

But even as he spoke the image of Count Bournam began to fade. In a moment he was gone, leaving the Prince alone with a gnawing desire to know the truth.

The Prince rode to Castletown as fast as possible for it was getting late. Dismounting his horse in front of the Bournam House he went to the door and pounded. No one answered. He pounded again, but this time instead of waiting he kicked the door with a tremendous blow until it gave in, and then he entered. Once inside, he closed the door behind him and went forward.

He took a step and then he stopped and listened. It was quiet, too quiet he thought, deathly quiet. The shadows were lengthening for the sun was setting fast. Dull splinters of light pierced through the drawn curtains and illuminated the fine particles of dust stirred up by the Prince's intrusion. Everywhere the furniture was covered with oilcloth. The house was deserted. Thinking that he had made another mistake he turned to leave, but he had a queer feeling that he was being watched and he continued his investigation. He stepped through the great-room into an anteroom and stopped. On the floor before him two corpses lay in a thick layer of dust.

Faces down, the corpses were lying close together as if death had come suddenly and swiftly. Prince Bartholomew stood over the ghastly finding and like a tableau in death, he could not help but think he was seeing something planned, something arranged. Carefully he put his boot on one of the corpses and turned it over. He was shocked to find that it was a woman. He knelt down next to the corpse to get a closer look. The face was mummified with thin, translucent skin drawn taught over dissolving bone. He shuddered. Then he heard a footstep.

"Do you like what you see, Prince?"

Prince Bartholomew stood up and faced Count Bournam who watched him through the archway. Bartholomew looked at the second corpse and then at Count Bournam.

"That presumably is you," he said. "Is this a proper burial, Count?"

"Look carefully at me," said the Count. "Do you like what you see?"

Prince Bartholomew looked but said nothing.

"Now, turn and behold my wife, Kelly Bournam." The Count pointed his finger like a specter. "Turn Bartholomew, turn and face my wife."

Slowly the Prince turned around. At first he saw nothing until the voice of the Count said: "Come my dear."

And then into the waning light Kelly Bournam stepped into the room. Her beauty was overwhelming and unnatural. The Prince gasped audibly.

"Do you like what you see, Bartholomew?"

She was unclothed and seemed to glide into the room like an angelic apparition. Such perfection, such heart renting perfection the Prince could not have imagined. She wafted through the room within a glorious nakedness that was proud, unashamed. A tear formed in the eye of the Prince for had never beheld such utter beauty. Kelly Bournam danced and gently pirouetted through the waning gloom and the Prince stood captured in her strange aura."

"Does she look dead to you?" said Count Bournam. "Now, turn and look at me!" he demanded. "Look what you have wrought."

Prince Bartholomew tore his eyes away from the beautiful apparition of Kelly Bournam and faced the Count. His ugliness was even more striking now.

"Tell me, Prince . . . is it evil to want to live forever with this?" and he pointed to his beautiful wife with his once elegant hand.

The Prince once again drank in the splendor of the beautiful Kelly Bournam and his heart ached for her.

"Now, look at me again, Bartholomew. See what you have done. Look at me and see the evil you have caused. See me as my beautiful wife now sees me. I have hurt no one in this life, of that I give you my word. The evil here has been committed by you."

Prince Bartholomew's head fell down in shame, for he knew that the Count spoke the truth.

"Yes, I am a wizard if you would prefer to use that word. But now you have destroyed me Bartholomew, as you have destroyed my wife. To make up for this evil you will do as I order . . . you will kill my wife and me."

"No, I will not do that," the Prince said through clenched teeth.

"You will," the Count insisted. "When you have considered what you have done, you will do as I ask, of that I am certain. But this time finish the job that you started. It is not the door, Bartholomew. No, the life is in the trees. I saved our spirit in the trees outside of this house. When you kill the trees you will release us from this agony."

"No, no, no . . ." the Prince continued to say.

"You must poison two large nails with the essence of the deadly nightshade. When the moon is high you must drive the nails into the trees. Only then will we be released. You must make this sacrifice. This you must do."

The Baroness

Iona asked the King: "Am I in any of your stories?"

"Would you like to be?" the King answered.

"Only if it is true," she said.

"Love and death are true," the King said. "Every other thing in life happens because of these truths. Do you agree, Iona?"

"Only if it is true," she answered playfully. "And don't forget sacrifice," she added.

"We sacrifice for love," the King said by way of explanation.

"Strange it is that we should die from love," Iona said with a sigh.

"Indeed."

Prince Bartholomew galloped proudly into the lush courtyard of his castle; a single feather stuck up from behind his ear like the plume of an eccentric peacock. Sitting elegantly in front of him was The Lady Alacourt, the beautiful baroness and daughter of The Honorable Lord Alacourt, Baron of Willifort. Her hair was flaxen and lay in ruffled tresses about her bare shoulders. A smile adorned her rosy cheeks for she was out of breath from the exhilarating ride with the Prince, well known for his intrepid riding habits and liking for pretty women. Prince Bartholomew was her escort while she visited the isle, accompanied by her father, for it was also well known the Prince's handsome face and wild escapades and the ladies were eager to be thus entertained.

All the servants came out onto the lawn to catch a glimpse of the beautiful baroness; Fritz the gardener was there, John, the horse master, even Sorren came out of the castle to have a look, for all were eager to see the beauty from England.

Bartholomew jumped down from his steed and then lifted the Baroness valiantly, holding her high above his head before setting her down like a feather on the soft lawn. All the delighted onlookers applauded, and as they were so fond of the Prince, they were able to share in his pleasure as if it were their own. Taking the lady by the hand, Bartholomew bowed elegantly before disappearing with the lovely Baroness into the inner garden.

The Baroness had come to the isle looking to find magic and instead had found love. Every day the Prince would take her to isolated glens and sacred wells, for he knew them all, and he would describe to her the folklore associated with each place, evoking once again the spirit of the very place. He would tell her stories of water nymphs and forest spirits and changelings. He would show her stones that marked sacred wells where saints once passed and Pan had abandoned or been chased away. The Baroness was eager to hear them all.

Each day King Sigmus and Baron Alacourt rode away together in the King's black carriage and they would be gone until late. No one knew where they went; the King left no information of his dealings with the Baron and the servants were instructed to maintain their ordinary schedule. Other days they would lock themselves away in the King's rooms and not emerge until dinner would be served or they would take dinner in the King's chamber. The Baron had important business to attend to and the King was assisting him. Day after day passed and the King would be gone until late in the evening, coming home only when darkness was fallen. Unusual as it was for the King to be gone so much, the servants thought nothing of it, and the Prince was utterly distracted. They trusted Bartholomew to make the time spent by the Baroness worthwhile and pleasurable. Several splendid days passed this way and the Prince even began to neglect his falcons and books and swordplay; he was truly smitten.

Iona brought a tray of drinks to the garden where the Prince and the Baroness sat talking in hushed tones. She was a cheerful girl, always eager to hear about the exploits and vicissitudes of the courageous Prince, always eager to tell him that things would get better when he was disheartened. Secretly she admired the Prince and wanted to be ever near him, for she thought him beautiful; and to the King she was like an angel. Iona was sensitive to the mood within the castle as a flower is sensitive to the ever changing light and she would go from room to room bringing her own kind of light when the world became gloomy. Such was her propensity to bring cheerfulness wherever she went, she did not attempt to do these things, these things were part of her character. When she set the tray down on a stone table the Prince asked.

"Where is my father, Iona? He promised to meet us here for a drink."

Iona looked at the Baroness and smiled faintly. "The King is not feeling well," she said courteously. "He asked me to offer his apology and say that another time would be better."

Bartholomew took a drink from Iona and handed it to the Baroness. Then he accepted one for himself. "We'll have to find something else to do," he said before clinking glasses with his companion. "Cheers."

Iona left the garden feeling uncomfortable. She wanted to explain to Bartholomew that she was worried about the King, but she did not want to alarm him in front of his guest. When she was back inside the castle she went up to the King's chamber and knocked tentatively.

King Sigmus sat up in bed when Iona entered. She could see that he was very weak and his eyes he had to struggle to keep open. His hair was damp with perspiration; he had a fever. Although the King was in a state of decay he still had an air of dignity that no sickness could hide.

"Did you tell him?" he asked.

Iona nodded. "I told him you were ill," she answered.

Sigmus coughed. "No, no," he said through a fit of coughing. "You must not tell him that I am ill. He does not need to hear this right now. Tell me Iona, was the Baroness sitting very close to him?"

"Yes, my Lord. They were sitting very close together, but I did not linger."

"You did just fine," Sigmus answered. "I did not expect you to spy on them, Iona. You are a good girl. The Baroness comes from a very powerful family, Iona."

"Yes, I have heard, my Lord."

"Bah, why should you care about such a thing? All families are important, are they not? Thank you for coming, Iona. You may go to your room now if you like."

Iona studied the King for a moment, trying to decide whether she should speak. His words were troubling. Finally she asked.

"Are you going to be alright, my Lord? I could bring you something."

The King tried to laugh. "No, no Iona," he finally said. "There is nothing that I need. Now, give me a smile before you leave and remember what I said to you."

The Baroness appeared early the next morning for breakfast. She and her father, Baron Alacourt, were staying in a remote wing of the castle and took most of their meals in private, for the Baron had business to attend to on the isle and was away from the castle often. Bartholomew was already there waiting for her, but the King still had not appeared. The Prince greeted the Baron with a handshake. Then he took the pale hand of the Baroness and kissed it reverentially. He seated her next to his own chair and exchanged light conversation with the Baron. Soon after, Iona announced that the King would not be present for breakfast. He was still under the weather. Presently breakfast was served and Bartholomew proved that his appetites also included food, for he was known for his voracious appetites.

Later, after coffee was served, the Prince and the Baroness left together. The Prince announced that they would be gone the remainder of the day; then, he and the Baroness were gone. Iona watched them ride away together from a window, but she could only think about the King.

The high cliffs near Port Erin are dangerous but beautiful, composed of long, metalliferous slates rising out of the turbulent sea. Out to Bradda Head the Prince rode across the lush plateau, fragrant with yellow gorse and thick grass. He took his companion there to see the spectacular view. The coastline for as far as the eye could see was dotted with inlets and rocky bays with jagged coastline churning up vaporous haze rising into a watery mist that obscured the horizon. The Prince jumped down and caught the Baroness as she fell into his arms.

"This is where I like to come and think," said the Prince, spreading his arms out before him.

They stood together near the edge of the cliff. The Prince held the lady's hand, for her own protection.

"And what do you think about?" asked the Baroness. "Tell me," she teased. "What is there to think about that you should need to ride all the way to the edge of the sea?"

Bartholomew looked into the Baroness's eyes and saw that they were glittering with joyfulness. He put his arms around her waist and kissed her.

"The Baroness is being imprudent, perhaps . . ."

"Please call me Teresa," she interrupted him playfully. "You are a mystery to me."

"My whole world is a mystery to me," Bartholomew replied with a laugh. "You live amongst the world of men and politics and family ties, a world of ambition and obligation and hidden desires. But I live on an island of spirits, an island of vaporous thoughts. It is not so easy to live among men when one lives among the spirits."

Teresa smiled and then kissed the Prince. "Tell me more about these spirits you speak of," she said. "I want to see them."

"You would not want to see them," Bartholomew replied. "It is enough to know that they are here."

"Have you seen them?"

"I have," Bartholomew answered.

Teresa squeezed the Prince's hand playfully and pursed her lips. "Were you frightened?" she asked.

Bartholomew smiled at the question. She was so coy, but he loved her skilful manipulation. "Of course I was frightened," he admitted.

"Not I," the Baroness chided. "I am not afraid of anything, even you." And then she gave him a quick peck on the cheek and turned to face the sea.

That evening a great dinner was planned in honor of the Baron Alacourt. His business was complete and he would soon be traveling back to his home with the Baroness. It was known that the Baron was fond of feasting, so no effort was spared in seeing to the occasion that it would reflect favorably upon the statesmanship of the King. Certain rumors however were stirring by the time Bartholomew and the Baroness returned from their afternoon together. The Prince left the Baroness with her father and went up to check on his father. When he went in the King was sitting up in bed, reading from a large folio that was spread out on his lap. He was dressed in his nightshirt and his hair was in disarray.

King Sigmus looked up from his reading and Bartholomew could see that his face was drawn and his eyes bloodshot and weary. Bartholomew looked incredulously at his father.

"Are you not feeling well?" he asked politely.

Sigmus rubbed his tired eyes and tried to smile. "I am a little under the weather," he said. "It is nothing. By tomorrow or the next day I will be fine."

"Is there anything I can do for you?" Bartholomew asked. "Would you like me to escort the Baron on business?"

"No, no," Sigmus uttered enthusiastically. "Please, do not bother with that . . . but . . ."

"Yes. What is it?" Bartholomew inquired.

"You could escort the Baroness. I'm sure that there is much that would interest her on our little island. The Baron can look after himself. You go ahead and show the Baroness a good time."

When Bartholomew closed the door, the King lay his head down on his pillow and went to sleep. He was exhausted unto death, but he could put on a brave face for short periods of time. Now however, he was finding it much more difficult to pretend; all he really wanted was to sleep.

Later that evening after the candles had been put out and the servants had gone to bed Bartholomew walked alone through the dark halls thinking about the Lady Teresa. His mind was captured in her orbit and he could not escape; he was slowly being drawn closer and closer to her by an inexorable force. Finally, after roaming for almost an hour, he could wait no longer; he had to see her, he had to speak to her, to touch her and to know that she felt the same way about him.

Stealthily he walked the corridor leading to her room. He walked without making a sound. Tapping lightly on the door like a chick breaking through a fragile eggshell, he waited silently, impatiently. After a couple minutes passed he grew nervous and started to walk away. Then he heard the soft click of the latch on the door being opened and the door opened a crack. The Lady Teresa's head appeared in the opening of the door and her eyes opened wide when she saw that it was the Prince. A moment later the door opened swiftly.

"What is wrong?" she said, alarmed by the Prince's sudden appearance.

Bartholomew held a finger to his lips in a plea for her to keep her voice down. Then he tried to calm her with a smile.

"I just had to see you again," he said. "I was afraid that I would never see you again after tomorrow."

The Lady Teresa took hold of Bartholomew's hand and tried to gently pull him into her room. The Prince resisted and an expression of sadness crossed his face.

"Come with me," he said to her. "I want to show you something beautiful."

Hand in hand the two lovebirds ran down the dark halls barely concealing their happiness and enhanced by the boldness of their rendezvous, made haste out of the castle and into the pale light from an evening sky. Once they were past the glow of the burning night-lamps, Bartholomew picked up the Lady Teresa and threw her up into the air, catching her in his open arms and kissing her passionately, held her close.

"Come with me," he said with growing excitement.

They ran down a flagstone path until they came to the road leading to the abbey. The stars were bright and they could see flickering lights burning from behind open windows in the distance. Teresa was breathing hard when they finally stopped. Bartholomew pointed.

"That is the Crossag Bridge," he said, "*The little bridge.* It was built by Cistercian monks long ago."

The bridge was constructed out of stone. It was narrow, being built to allow cart traffic across the Silverburn by industrious monks hauling vegetables and barrels of ale. Walking onto the bridge from the narrow road they went up to the middle where it rose to a peak and stopped. Bartholomew looked over the side and waited for Teresa to join him.

"I love to come here," he said. "This is a very special place for me."

Teresa looked down into the water. The gently flowing water coursed over and around large stones that lay embedded in the riverbed. Starlight glittered on the moving water and the sound of gentle gurgling was soothing and strangely inviting.

"There is an old legend," said the Prince. "It is said that this bridge once was the meeting place of angels. It is said that this bridge connected Heaven and Earth and that the Lord once stood here."

"Is it true?" Teresa asked eagerly.

"No, it is not true," Bartholomew replied. "It is merely an old legend, a myth . . . a fantasy."

"But it could be true," Teresa insisted. "If it is a legend it could be true. You told me that you have seen spirits, so why cannot angels also be true?"

"The old spirits never leave this place, Teresa. The old spirits are part of this place. There is nowhere else for them to go."

"Then the spirits won't mind what we do," said Teresa seductively. And she moved closer to Bartholomew and put her arms around him. "If anyone is watching," she said with a laugh. "They will surely have a new legend to tell . . ."

Bartholomew slipped through the door near daybreak. Beside him was the Lady Teresa. Trying to come in surreptitiously they however were too intoxicated with the power of love to worry about how much noise they were making. Iona came down the stairs swiftly when she heard the door close. Her face was ashen; she had not slept all night. Her movements were slow and anguished. She approached the Prince with noticeable trepidation as if she feared what she must now do. Bartholomew looked curiously at her. He was embarrassed to be caught coming home at such an hour in the company of the Baroness, an unmarried woman. Iona looked deeply into his eyes, but she did not speak.

"What is it, Iona?" said Bartholomew. "What is wrong?"

"Your father . . ." was all she could say before she broke down in tears.

Prince Bartholomew left Iona and the Baroness standing there and bounded up the stairs in a frenzy. He ran to his father's room and burst in without knocking. King Sigmus lay in bed and his eyes were closed. Bartholomew at first thought that he was dead, for his skin was chalky and pallid. He ran up to his father and knelt down beside his bed. Then he took hold of his hand as it lay outside of the bedspread. It felt cold to the touch. Then the King opened his eyes as the warmth of his son's flesh brought him back to the world. The King spoke; his voice was weak, but it was proud.

"I'm sorry, my boy," he said. "But I am becoming too weak to pretend any longer."

Bartholomew was horrified. His throat tightened and he had a hard time getting the words to come out.

"Father, what happened?" he said. "How long have you been sick? I didn't know, I didn't know," he uttered tearfully.

"I didn't want you to worry about me," he rasped. "I didn't want anyone to worry about me. You're young," he said. "You should not waste your time fretting over an old man."

"How did Iona know?" said Bartholomew.

"I told no one," said the King.

"You need a doctor," Bartholomew said hopefully. "You need a doctor, why have you not called for a doctor?"

"I have a doctor," said Sigmus slowly. And then his eyes glistened remorsefully when he said. "Lord Alacourt is a doctor, Bartholomew. He is not a baron. No, he is not a Lord. There is no such place as Willifort."

Bartholomew was stunned. His mouth fell open and he looked at his father in disbelief. "The Lady Teresa . . ."

"She is not a baroness," the King said sadly.

"She lied to me," Bartholomew said softly.

"I lied to you," said the King. "I am sorry, my son. Do not hold it against the lady, for I know that you are fond of her. When I saw how attracted you were to her, I just couldn't tell you."

"But he is leaving here today!" Bartholomew cried. "You need help."

"There is nothing more that I need," said King Sigmus. "Now that there is no need for lies let me die gracefully, my son."

Bartholomew's eyes filled with tears and he could not bear to look at his father. Slowly he rose to his feet, and like a man condemned to die, walked out of the room without closing the door.

The carriage was loaded and ready for Castletown. Sorren was harnessing the team when Bartholomew came walking up from the forest connecting the castle with the lands held by the abbey. Lost in thought, the Prince came up to wait for the doctor to leave. When the doctor emerged from the castle holding the hand of his daughter he did not make eye contact with the Prince, for he was ashamed. The doctor let go of Teresa's hand when she saw Bartholomew standing there. She ran up to him and would have embraced him had not his expression stopped her cold. She looked at the Prince, but it was not the person she had known, it was not the same person she had embraced only hours ago. She let her arms fall to her side and waited for Bartholomew to speak. He looked at her and there was pity in his eyes.

"You lied to me," he said directly and without emotion. He looked at her and there was a palpable expression of grief on his face. "You broke my heart," he said through clenched teeth.

The lady Teresa could not bear the terrible eyes of Bartholomew and she hid her face in her hands. She did not look up when she heard the final words of Prince Bartholomew.

"Goodbye, Teresa," he said.

King Sigmus was awake, propped up with a pillow when a slight knock at the door was followed by the entrance of Bartholomew. He stood in the doorway and looked at his father. Iona was there, reading a passage from a book she held in her hand. The angry expression on his face had melted along with his self-pity, and he saw before him something special, something sublime, and something beautiful.

He went to the wall and took a padded chair and brought it over to the bed. Then he set it down next to Iona's chair and sat down. He smiled awkwardly for he was ashamed of himself. His throat was tightening, strangling him. Then he cast his eyes down and said.

"Please keep reading, Iona."

And so Prince Bartholomew spent the next two days at his father's side, listening to his sporadic conversation, his ramblings, his anguish. King Sigmus withered away slowly and inexorably until at the end he could not even open his eyes. Bartholomew sat at his side and watched as the man that had been his father became unrecognizable and pitiable. Bartholomew could do nothing to alleviate his pain, so instead he talked to him even though he could not respond. He did not sleep but only nodded off a few times during the long night. Iona was there beside him. She brought him food even though she knew that he would not eat. The Prince would look at her and smile faintly to acknowledge her and she would take the tray back to the kitchen.

The death of King Sigmus was long and excruciating to watch. Bartholomew held his hand and prayed for a quick end to his suffering and he suffered along with his father. The King's breathing then became shallow and Bartholomew knew that the end was near. He brought his father's hand to his lips and kissed it gently. Suddenly King Sigmus opened his eyes. Bartholomew looked at him but the King was looking beyond his son at something else in the room, something that was near the ceiling. His eyes moved as they tried to follow something that Bartholomew could not see. And then the King took one last breath and let it out slowly and a meaningful smile appeared on his lips.

When Bartholomew emerged from the King's bedroom Iona was sitting in a chair beside the door. She stood up when she saw him come out and she knew that the King was dead. Then she looked into Bartholomew's eyes; they were wet with tears and he trembled with an inner anguish that Iona could not bear to watch. She went up to Bartholomew and put her arms around him tenderly and his sobs were buried in her beautiful hair. Bartholomew cried tears of redemption, for his father had given him something he would never be able to repay. He cried on Iona's shoulder until he was utterly drained, but then he felt the deep inner trembling of Iona and it was like the feeble flutter of a tiny sparrow. In that moment something changed within Bartholomew's heart and his own pain was lost to the pain of another. He felt her hot tears on his shoulder and he became strong and resolute for her tears had saved him, her tears had brought him back to life. Then he stroked her beautiful hair and with each passing moment he became stronger and more determined. And so it was that on that terrible day, Prince Bartholomew became a King.

The Third Knot

"There are three gifts that the Lord has given us to teach us humility," said Bishop Jacob one morning as he and the King sipped tea and chatted casually.

The King raised his eyes and waited.

"The first gift is sickness, for when we are sick we are often brought to our knees.

"True," said the King.

"The second gift is fear, for when we are afraid our thoughts are turned from what we hope to gain, and are focused on what we hope to save."

"Interesting," said the King. "I would not have thought of that."

"The third gift is grief."

The King frowned, but he remained silent.

"Grief teaches us to love that which is lost. When we learn to love that which is lost we come closer to God, for His loss was our gain."

On the western side of the island near the high cliffs overlooking the sea, an old forgotten cemetery molders beneath the heavy sky and slowly turns into the dust from which it came, for no one comes to the gloomy cemetery anymore and no prayers comfort the wallowing spirits interred. A solitary yew tree crouches over the fallen and untended gravestones now overgrown with creeping weeds and clinging vines, shielding the plot from untoward eyes, and with the exception of King Bartholomew, would but be completely forgotten. In truth, no one remembers the dead souls buried beneath the forlorn tree and the dead have passed out of all hope of memory.

The crumbling ruins of an old church litters the windswept plot now overgrown and devoured by the dense yellow gorse and speckles the top of the plateau like the broken cemetery markers that lay as vestiges of a elapsed world silent but for the faint whispers of expiring saints. The yew tree, singular and massive, stands alone, old beyond reckoning but dating perhaps to the time of the saints, and was most possibly planted by St. Columba or Brendan the Navigator of Clonfert who set out on a long sea voyage to find the Garden of Eden.

To the superstitious Manxmen, this is a forsaken place, a cursed place, and it is better if the sole of their feet never touch such woeful soil in sport or in pursuit of adventure. Spirits and disembodied souls of the damned, bound to this place by powerful magic, roam the windswept highland and bring terror to those who wander too close. And though the bishopric has cleansed the moribund soil, the Manxmen still avoid coming near. The folklore of the Manx have turned this once sacred place into a place of horror, a foreboding and pestilent wound, and so it disintegrates into oblivion unheeded and unloved.

On a cold September afternoon beneath heavy scudding clouds, King Bartholomew stepped carefully around the tangled markers making sure not to disturb them and set down his rucksack against the old yew tree. His respect for the dead was enduring and unending, for he had seen his share of short and precious lives going unfulfilled and unsatisfied to the grave. Then he straightened his back as he stretched out his arms into the air and smiled. He loved this isolated plot and came here often when he wanted to be alone and even the dead did not harass him. In truth, it was the mighty yew tree that inspired the King.

Not exceptionally tall, the tree stood only several times the height of the King. However, it was the manner in which the tree had become integrated with the cemetery that was truly extraordinary. The crafty yew tree had quite literally extended its groping undergrowth downward and buried itself into the decomposing soil and had born itself anew with even more agile roots that rose once again along the trunk to merge with the main body of the tree, building and recombining with successive layers. In the course of countless centuries, the tree had renewed itself with the nutrients of its own body and had become hollow inside of a flowing muscular skeleton of sinewy, bone-like flesh.

Polished by the incessant wind that swept across the plateau, King Bartholomew, now in his sixth year after the death of King Sigmus, put his hands on the trunk of the tree and felt its warmth and smoothness within the veined protrusions that like tightening skin on an aged body reveal an inner network of structure. He wondered if some form of awareness or embryonic sentience existed within such a colossal artifact from antiquity, forever bound to the world of man. Alone, this solitary tree had survived the ebb and flow of centuries like the gentle inhalations and exhalations of a newborn child. It would survive forever until the end of days. Unlike other trees, this tree communicated to him something of an alien . . . otherness.

Bartholomew looked down at the stone markers now merged with the shifting, undulating soil and extending out at strange, puzzling angles. On some of the stones faint etching was still visible. Through the years, Bartholomew had studied each and every stone that remained, but he was never able to decipher the cryptic writing. He no longer cared what the writing said. His interest now was different and he accepted that some things could never be known to him.

The King walked amongst the stone markers and a peaceful sensation washed over him, a feeling of acceptance of the world and the ways of God. The dead were no more part of this abandoned cemetery than were the feeble memories of a child part of the woman who bore that child; they were forever lost, fleeting vestiges of what once was and did not intersect with the world of men. Thoughts like this always made him tired and it was by giving into the lethargy brought about by these thoughts that the King truly felt at peace.

King Bartholomew sat down and rested his back against the tree. He felt the solidness of the ancient sentinel and took comfort in it. A moment later he brought out the flute he had brought along with him. It was an old flute given to him by a woodchopper when he was a boy. The melody he played made him drowsy, and soon he was asleep.

When he awoke there was a strange man standing in front of him. The man was silent and waited patiently for Bartholomew to awake. Still groggy from the remnants of sleep the King was slow to comprehend the unusualness of the man before him now. He shook off the torpor with difficulty.

"What do you want?" he finally said to the man.

"I want to live forever," the man replied even though he knew that Bartholomew was not really asking him such a question.

King Bartholomew blinked several times. "What is your name?" he asked, slowly rising to his feet. "I thought I was alone."

"I thought I was alone," replied the man thoughtfully.

The man held a long oaken staff like the staff of a shepherd or the walking stick of a wandering monk. His white hair was long and hung about his shoulders unkempt. A long cloak covered his body and hung to the ground. Tied to the belt that went around his waist was a bag, cinched tight with a string. His face was old and wrinkled and his eyes were distant and steely. The man fixed his eyes on the King.

"My name is Renatus[23]," he said. "I am the keeper of the cemetery."

"I did not know that the cemetery had a keeper," answered Bartholomew, staring curiously at the strange man. He looked at the vagabond and wondered that he did not take better care of himself. "It looks quite deserted and disordered. This cemetery is abandoned. There has been no keeper here for many years now, to my knowledge."

"You do not understand what it is that I do," Renatus replied. "If you did, you would respect this cemetery more than you do." Renatus looked around the cemetery quickly as if to survey his realm. Then he turned his attention back to the King. "What you see is only part of what there is to see. I do not come before you to judge, as have you judged me. It is the hidden things in this world that are often the most important."

"I am sorry," said Bartholomew. "If there are hidden secrets buried in this place, it is not for me to unearth them."

"You would never unearth them," said Renatus. "The secrets are not buried in the earth, but have been born from the earth. The secrets are buried, but they not dead. The secrets of which I speak are all around us."

"Are you a speaker of riddles?" asked the King curiously. "The dead do not speak, but yet they are the giver of secrets . . ."

---

[23] *Renatus. Ancient Roman name meaning 'born again.' This really is intended to be seen as a metaphor of the concept of Pantheism, and is to be seen as a vestige of Greek Pantheism. Pantheistic: All=God, God=All. Renatus is the numen of the cemetery, a manifestation of the earth or earth-spirit.*

"The stones speak," said Renatus. "The trees speak, and yet they are not heard. Our voices are swallowed by the earth and yet they speak, for those who will listen."

"There has always been much talk of hidden knowledge," said the King. "This knowledge is secret so that it must be hidden. Is this of what you speak?"

"What has been buried must become manifest again. The cemetery is not a place of death, but a place of life. [24]The life is the light. I am the keeper of the light."

"I do not understand your words," Bartholomew said. He looked the man up and down and fixed his stare on his eyes. "What are you trying to tell me?" he said finally.

"Darkness falls on the earth like snow. Soon it will be covered and even my light will not be seen. The world is a cemetery. If you wish to escape into the light you must learn a lesson from this tree. It becomes reborn even as you must pass through darkness to see the light."

The Renatus pointed a long finger at the King. He looked like a specter and his skin had turned pale. Suddenly he smiled.

"The cemetery is no place for those who refuse to live. If you wish me to be your guide, you must first die."

King Bartholomew stood rooted to the spot. The conversation had left him utterly mystified and now he wanted to ponder the strange words of Renatus without having to speak. He was the King, and yet he felt powerless and insignificant in the presence of this man who acted as if his words were easily understood, as if an implicit understanding

---

[24] *Manichaeism heresy. This religion based upon the writing of Mani sees the material world as evil, devouring the light. Men were given an evil material body by Satan. In the beginning God created the worlds of light and darkness and the two were separate. The spirit is trapped inside of matter and must be released from the evil of materialism. The light is the spirit and is trapped inside the bondage of matter and must be released. A dualist religion based upon reason, not mystery. In order to free the light from the pollution of matter, all earthly pleasure had to be denied. There were severe ascetic monks that disappeared from the world to practice their form of asceticism in caves.*

existed between them. But an understanding did not exist. His words were foreign and obscure. If he wanted, he could have ordered the man to stop. But, perhaps the man would not stop and then he would be left in an awkward position. Instead, he just looked at the keeper and waited for him to do something. And then the keeper turned his back on the King and slowly walked away dissolving into the heavy atmosphere of the moist earth. In a moment he was gone and Bartholomew remained, wondering if he had been visited by a ghost or an apparition of the harrowing souls captured below.

The King spent the next hour examining the stone markers again. He was now even more interested in the history of this cemetery than ever before. When he returned home to Ballasalla he would ask Bishop Jacob, but for now he wanted only to examine the crumbling stones in the hope that he had missed something even after all these long years.

The cemetery was laid out without attention to order, and at the center of the cemetery was the massive yew tree that arched its stately boughs over the small plot like giant wings or the caress of a protective mother. A large raven perched high above and watched silently as the King picked his way through the perished field. Graves were situated in all directions without rhyme or reason like scattered seeds across the shifting earth. The headstones were chipped and weatherworn by centuries of bitter cold and rain and the writing was mostly worn away. On some of the stones however, faint scratches could still be seen.

Bartholomew dropped down to his knees to read the inscription on a headstone that caught his attention. It was not the writing that caught his eye however; it was the particular symbol that was etched across the grey stone. The figure was that of a serpent, swallowing its tail. Beneath the symbol was an inscription that was too faint to read but appeared to be Coptic[25] in origin. He brought his hands to the stone and ran his fingers across the symbol. As he did so he felt a memory coming back to him and slowly be began to succumb to the memory.

When he was just a young boy, he and his father had ridden into the hills to speak with a hermit that lived in a small hut scratched into the side of the hill. His father had said that the hermit lived in exile and that he was an anchorite and a heretic, but that he would be safe. Being just a young

---

[25] Coptic. *Egyptian Christianity brought to Egypt by St. Mark in the 1st century.*

boy he did not understand what the word meant. When he asked his father he was told only that he was hiding because of something dangerous that he believed. Once outside the hut, King Sigmus left the boy outside and went into the hut alone. Several minutes later he came out carrying something in his hands. It was a book. On the cover of the book was a symbol. Now Bartholomew recognized where he had seen this symbol before. It was the symbol of a serpent devouring its own tail.

When Bartholomew was back in his castle he quickly stormed into his father's library and closed the doors behind him. The library had been kept just as it had been when King Sigmus built it. Only rarely did he come here now for his endeavors were turned to the soil and to the earth and that of riding and physical exertion. The ancient writing passed to him through his father had largely gone unused, but now he was anxious to learn what was buried within the dusty manuscripts.

The library faced the outer garden and through a window streamed the late afternoon light. The walls were paneled with rich, dark oak. Candle holders were positioned in several places so that much light could be applied during the darkest hours. He took off his riding cloak and threw it on a chair. Then he walked across the thick rug that covered the smooth tiled floor, over to the bookcase. Lighting a lamp, he carried it to the bookcase and held it aloft so that he could read the titles buried within the deep shelves. His eyes scanned the volumes and folio's quickly, passing over the familiar books that he had seen many times before, the treasured copies diligently produced by quiet monks and ornately embellished with bright colors and pounded gold leaf, the lives of the saints, and the writings of great philosophers. He was looking for something quite different now, but perhaps his search would be in vain. Mostly the shelves were filled with account books and registers of common law and applicable exceptions to such law. Also among the shelves were several hagiographic tomes and accounts of the lives of the saints and books of apologetics, for King Sigmus loved the saints and prayed to them frequently during his life. After several minutes he was becoming exasperated. Oh well, what did he really expect?

He walked over to a large velvet chair and sat down. Placing the lamp on a small table he pulled out his pipe and packed it. A light tapping at the door brought him out of his muse.

"Come in," he said softly as he lit his pipe.

Iona came in quietly and her light feet glided across the thick rug like they were suspended on wings. Her shy gracefulness always made the King smile. Whenever he was feeling down, the very sight of her would make him regret his despair. Iona was the finest jewel that one could ask for. And yet, she could not see her own special nature beyond the capacity to love and to serve.

"I saw you come home, and I thought that perhaps you would like a cup of tea . . ."

Bartholomew started to say something, but Iona continued.

"So I brought you some." She came over to where he was sitting and carefully set down the tray. Then she turned to leave.

"Wait a moment!" Bartholomew suddenly said as a new thought occurred to him. "Iona, come and sit with me for a moment. I want to ask you something."

Iona smiled and then went over to the King and sat on his knee. Bartholomew smiled broadly and almost forgot what he wanted to ask. He kissed her on the forehead tenderly. Then he took her hand.

"Iona, do you ever remember my father reading books that are not kept in this library?"

"The King had failing eyesight near the end of his life. I remember that when he would read, he would fall asleep in his chair. Then I would cover him with a blanket and put his book on the table next to him."

"And what was he reading . . . when he would fall asleep?"

"The saints, my lord . . . he was always dreaming about the saints."

"Did he talk to you about the saints, Iona? Did my father try to teach you about the saints?"

Iona stood up and walked to the center of the room. Then she turned back to Bartholomew, but she did not speak. She was searching her memory. The King did not interrupt her or ask her a question. He waited for her to say something. A minute later Iona tried to explain to

Bartholomew what she remembered.

"There was one book he loved to keep with him. I remember now," she said with excitement. "It was covered with calfskin and it had pictures."

"What kind of pictures?" Bartholomew asked with growing excitement. "Think Iona, what did the pictures look like?"

"They were pictures of trees," she said.

Bartholomew stood up suddenly and set down his pipe. He squinted as if he wanted to capture a faint memory that could not be seen clearly. "Pictures of trees?" he asked. "Tell me about the pictures, Iona."

"The pictures, they were very strange," she began. "The roots grew through the ground and went up to become the branches, and then they went back down again into the earth like roots. The trees appeared to grow into themselves. I laughed when he showed me the pictures, but the King only smiled and said that the pictures only represented something that was deeper than even the deepest roots."

"Where is this book now, Iona?" said Bartholomew, feeling the rush of excitement through his blood.

"I don't know," she answered sadly, for she could see how excited the King was becoming. "Perhaps it is hidden," she said.

The following days and nights Bartholomew searched the castle for the hidden book. He looked in all the places he knew that his father liked to be when he was at home. The castle had many rooms and anterooms attached, and it was a long and exhausting search when Bartholomew returned once again to his father's chamber. After Sigmus died, Bartholomew had his room kept exactly as it had been. He could have taken over the Kings chamber, and it was his right to do so, but he preferred to remain in his own, if somewhat smaller, room in the tower.

But now he stood outside his father's chamber again. He was convinced that he had missed something, something however small that could act as a clue to the mystery that was taking shape inside of his mind. Stepping into the empty room he looked at the massive four-poster bed and thought about his father. His father had also been his friend, a friend he could never replace. Now there was a huge hole in his life that he could never fill with mere distractions, for the distractions only served to remind him how alone he truly was. If not for Iona he would perish from loneliness.

Next to his father's bed was a sunken stair turret leading up to the tower where his father sometimes went to read and meditate upon his kingdom. Bartholomew had been up to the tower many times. There was nothing there except a stone bench and a brazier. He would not go up there again. But, on the wall inside the turret was a large tapestry that always seemed oddly out of place. Bartholomew looked at it now. Why would such a tapestry be relegated to such a dark and unsatisfactory place? He went up to the tapestry and looked long and hard. It was that of a fair maiden, confined to her bower. She was looking sorrowful and forlorn out of a window. Outside the window was . . . Bartholomew looked closer. It was a tree.

Suddenly King Bartholomew took hold of the tapestry in both hands and violently tore it from the wall. Then he threw the tapestry on the bed and went back to the wall. He examined the wall very carefully. The stones were fitted together closely and snugly. The wall had been constructed very well he thought. First he tapped on the wall with his fingers. Then he pounded with his fists. Finally, in an act of desperation he threw all his weight against the wall and heaved with all his strength. The wall moved!

Pivoting inside on a crafted track with block and tackle, the wall smoothly receded, revealing a deep chamber of shadows. Rush lights were fastened to the wall on iron brackets. The King took one down and lit it. Then he went forward and thrust the flickering light into the darkness. There was a narrow winding stairwell leading up in the shadows. He pondered for a moment and then he knew that this staircase was probably built during the initial construction of the castle and was intended to be a secret room or possibly a hiding place. The staircase was fashioned directly beneath the original flight of steps into the tower and ran along the same pitch. Both were expertly hewn together by stonemasons and fit together thus entwined. Bartholomew smiled thoughtfully for he had heard many legends about secret rooms and subterranean chambers, and now he had found one. The steps were roughly hewn and were very narrow. Without further delay he went forward and ascended the hidden stairway. He counted hundreds of steps, but at last he came to the top which was ended beneath a thick trapdoor. The fumes from the rush lights were making him woozy and his eyes were stinging. He pulled back an iron latch and threw the trapdoor open into the inner chamber with a reverberating crash. Then he crawled up into the secret room.

The first thing he noticed was that the room was round, probably much the same dimensions of the tower above. The flickering light revealed that along the wall large iron rings were embedded into the stone. He set the rush light on the floor. Then he took hold of the iron rings and slid them out of the wall and as he did, afternoon light poured into the room bringing it to life again after a long winter hibernation. After he had removed all the key-lights, he was out of breath even as his excitement grew.

Everything was covered with a thick layer of dust and every movement caused more dust to float into the air. Soon the room was pierced through a churning haze of dust particles caught in the streaming light like a thunderbolt from heaven. He closed the trapdoor so that he would not fall through the open hole to his death. Then he looked around.

The walls were bare of adornments, and with the exception of brackets for torches and rush lights, they were solid stone. Around the perimeter of the room were storage crates and wooden chests. There was also an old wooden desk pushed tightly against the wall. Bartholomew walked over to the desk to see what it contained. The desk was covered with dust. Fragments of tallow candles and dripping wax covered the desk where they were presumably left to burn down. A letter opener lay in the dust next to an empty goblet that had once held wine. In the dust were tracks where scurrying rats had darted about looking for food. The desk had a single drawer. Bartholomew opened it. He found a letter. It was sealed with the seal insignia of the King and it was addressed to none other than he.

Bartholomew picked up the envelope. It was heavy as if it contained something other than parchment. The seal was that of his father's ring, now his ring, and it was sealed in red. He went over to stand in a thick beam of light that filtered through the key-light. Then he tore open the envelope. Inside were a handwritten letter and a key. He held the letter up and held it in the light; it read.

Bartholomew
Dear son. I leave this letter for you to read, for when you find it I will be gone. You have found my secret. I knew that one day you would come here at last.

and it is now yours to either embrace or abandon as is your will. I have kept this room secret from you for my own reasons. In truth, I did not want to influence you unfairly. Now I am gone and it is your choice what to do with that which I shall put in your hand shortly. With this letter is a key. This key is your last chance to abandon this present and if you should chose to do so it would perhaps be best. I struggled with my better judgment, which was to burn this cache and all its contents, but alas, I could never do that. But I warn you, for if you should choose to accept what I offer, you will be troubled. It is not my wish to trouble you, but sometimes the truth needs but be preserved in great trouble and to great peril. The key opens the chest beneath the south keyhole. Inside is a myriad of knowledge, forbidden knowledge. Inside this room lay the heresy of many centuries. I have tormented my mind for many decades with this secret knowledge and I cannot say that it has made me any happier. The choice is yours to make, but I beg you that before you open this chest you will leave this room and sleep on your decision. I love you son. May the grace of God continue to bless you. I pray that, God willing, I will see you in heaven.
Sigmus

When Bartholomew finished reading the letter, he kissed it. Then he read it again. He then looked at the key. His father had given him a difficult choice to make, but of course, there was no other choice than to open the chest. He tucked the key away in his pocket. Yes, he would honor his father's wishes and he would sleep on it.

That night the King was visited by terrible dreams. Once he woke up in a feverish sweat. He shot upright in his bed in the throes of a devilish dream. The room was dark and he could see nothing but faint outlines in starlight. A strange apprehension gripped him and would not fade even though he had awoken from the terrible dream. He slipped out of bed and donned his robe. Then he went to his chamber pot to relieve himself. Around in circles he walked through his dark room but his terror only began to build. He was suffering from an attack of panic. When he was a child he would have them occasionally and he would be paralyzed with a feeling of impending doom, but that was many years ago.

The feeling of sleep had left him now, expunged by an even greater feeling of uneasiness, so he lit some candles and took up his pipe. Then he went to the window and opened the shutters. Cool night air streamed in and filled his stuffy room. Now his mind began to clear and he knew that the apprehension and terror of the night was triggered by the discovery of the secret room and that he would have no peace until he opened the trunk. His father tried to warn him in the letter. It was still many hours till daybreak but his mind was caught in a powerful grip and was being rent between two opposing, opposite desires. The desire to open the trunk was powerful, but an opposing fear of what he would find would not leave him and grew more powerful. Part of his fear was that he would learn something that would change him forever, and that some new thought, some new idea would turn his life upside down. What would he be then?

Suddenly he realized the source of his apprehension. It was the strange man in the cemetery. He had completely forgotten about him. Now he knew what he would do. Setting the pipe down on the window ledge he went back to his chest of drawers and dressed for the day. Putting on a warm riding cloak he left the castle and went to the stable to saddle his horse. The guards opened the gate for him with a smile and a nod, assuming no doubt that he was late for a tryst, and he set off down the road by the light of the moon. The cool air felt brisk and soon he was revived and all traces of his dull apprehension vanished.

When he was once again standing at the edge of the cemetery the sun had not yet risen. The nocturnal sounds were all around him for he was a stranger at such an early hour and the creeping, prowling creatures of the night were unused to such intrusions. The gravestones and markers were lost in darkness, so he sat down next to his favorite tree to wait for the sun to come up. To pass the time he took out his pipe and smoked in silence. He relaxed comfortably against the trunk and watched a curious fox prowling near the edge of the cemetery. The fox crouched down and darted to and fro along the perimeter, but it would come no closer. It fidgeted and danced around the edges of the cemetery. Bartholomew fell asleep watching the curious movements of the fox.

He woke into the light, and before him stood the Keeper. Once again, Bartholomew was groggy and could not rise to his feet right away as the vestiges of sleep were heavy and slow to fade. The Keeper watched him silently without the slightest impatience; he could have waited for a thousand years. Bartholomew had never felt so relaxed before, so profoundly saturated, and he had not the slightest desire to move. His body seemed to sink into the earth. A strange lethargy had come over him but he succumbed to the feeling with submissive pleasure. Several minutes passed this way until Bartholomew realized that he was indeed awake. Slowly and awkwardly he rose to his feet.

"Is this cemetery so precious to you now that you come here to sleep?" said the Keeper with a radiant smile.

Bartholomew still felt weak, and like the aftereffects from a powerful sickness, he was slow to respond. Instead, he pointed at the man, for his speech had left him.

The Keeper continued to speak. "Yes, this is a peaceful place. The peace comes from the earth. Can you feel it?"

Bartholomew did feel it. Comforting warmth seemed to come from the ground and spread through his body in waves. The waves had permeated his body to the core. He still could not speak and looked imploringly at the Keeper.

"Do not worry," said the Keeper. "What you are feeling is overwhelming at first, but soon you will become used to it, and then you will know why this place is special." Then the Keeper smiled again. "But, you already know that this place is special."

"What . . . are you?" Bartholomew said finally.

"I am the Keeper."

Now Bartholomew looked into his eyes fiercely. He was regaining his strength. "What is it that you are the Keeper of?" he asked. "I thought that it was for the lost souls buried beneath that you kept this place, but now . . ."

"No," the Keeper agreed. "The souls of this field have no use for my skills. It is not for them that I remain. Yes, the earth yields much fruit, but not all the fruit of this world comes from the earth. For such is the fruit of the world intended for this earth that the earth is the womb of the world."

The Keeper said these words confidently and calmly and there was nothing false in his voice. King Bartholomew saw passion in his eyes, but that passion was frightening to him though he could not say why.

"Are you talking about the tree?" said Bartholomew. "I have heard of tree worshipers and the worship of trees. The ancient pagans revered the trees, and they planted them to mark sacred places. Are these the lost souls of tree worshipers that you keep?"

"I do not keep the souls of men," said the Keeper. "I guard the souls of trees. The men buried beneath are the past Keepers of the faith. It is the life preserved that we worship, for much knowledge is preserved in life."

"Is this just such a sacred tree then," said Bartholomew, "that you should worship in perpetuity?"

The Keeper went around King Bartholomew and touched the tree affectionately. "You do not yet understand," he said without reproach. "It is through such passion and dedication that the soul of the world is preserved and renewed."

"But you are the last of your kind," said Bartholomew. "Your dedication will end in sorrow."

"It is not my dedication that I was referring to," the Keeper answered cryptically. Then he looked at Bartholomew with a peculiar expectation and a silent understanding between them became manifest in that moment.

Something awakened inside of the King like a memory long forgotten or slow to emerge, or a memory dredged up from a deep recess. At last Bartholomew understood what the Keeper was saying. He now looked at the Keeper differently as an inner revulsion took hold of him, for he was slightly troubled by his revelation. "How old are you?" he asked suddenly as the realization of what the Keeper said filled his uneasy mind.

The Keeper smiled. By way of explanation he only said. "The Tree of Knowledge bears fruit only that it should be eaten. That the fruit should thus speak is difficult to understand, but there is much to be learned from forbidden fruit. Seeds must be planted, for the soil is the substance from which all knowledge becomes manifest."

"And so you are like a serpent eating its own tail," Bartholomew proclaimed calmly but with the certainty of a king. "I have seen the markings on your gravestones, the scratches, the tiny writing. This symbol is unknown to me. I thought the saints cleansed the isles of such heresy, but I can see that I was wrong."

"The saints were not able to undo what cannot be undone," said the Keeper. Remember, the house built upon rock will not sink into the sand. Instead, it will be blown away with a violent wind."

King Bartholomew left the Keeper to ponder his own words. Soon he was riding away beneath the bright skies of a new day. The words of the Keeper stayed in his mind and only made him more uneasy the further he rode. After riding hard for a quarter of an hour he brought his horse to a halt on a ridge overlooking a glen within a deep ravine. The beauty of this place always made him stop, if just for a moment, to take in the splendor of his kingdom. He mused; one did not have to grant the existence of an eternal soul to the trees to appreciate the power of the earth to produce God's glory in all things. It was enough only to see these natural wonders and be moved. As a King, he had promised to preserve the beauty of his kingdom against all form of hostility be they from man, or from heretics from the past.

He jumped down from his steed to stretch his legs. The path was trampled soft though it was abandoned and mostly unused. The people did not come too close to this place, for it had a queer reputation and the superstitious Manx had very long memories. Tall grass grew in spotted clumps just off the path.

Up ahead on the path coming directly toward him came a slowly moving wanderer. He walked methodically and turned up a small cloud of dust. The King watched him interestedly and wondered what he could be doing in so remote a place as this. When the man was close enough, Bartholomew greeted him and asked if he wanted a ride. The man looked up slowly. His face was very old, lined with deep crags and crow's feet. He had a full beard that looked like it had never been trimmed. He carried a walking stick made of strong oak. When he heard the salutation of the king, he looked up and considered.

"I have no need," he replied dryly. "Thank you, and good day to you."

"My name is King Bartholomew," said the King. "Pray tell, where are you going on such a fine morning?"

The man took a breath and let out a long exhalation. He looked up in defiance. "I am gathering herbs," he said angrily. "It is important that I find them before the sun sets."

"Are you a wizard?" Bartholomew asked, for the man had the manner and bearing of a wizard. He was dressed in a long, grey cloak and a bag was tied around his belt and gathered together with a string. Sprigs of cut herbs hung from his waist and gave off a pungent aroma and made it difficult for the King to breathe.

The man nodded his assent with a wry smile. Opening his arms wide for the King to see, he revealed the various plants and herbs from his work. He touched his hat with an expression of finality.

"Tell me, wizard. What is in your bag?" the King continued. He was not yet finished with the man and wished to question him further.

"Wind," answered the wizard.

"So, you are a purveyor of wind?" said Bartholomew with barely concealed consternation.

The wizard had made a move to walk around the King, but he suddenly stopped. Then he turned and slowly brought his eyes to those of Bartholomew. They were dark cobalt blue. The wizard narrowed his eyes and peered directly into the beautiful eyes of the King. He raised his walking stick and said. "Have you need of wind?" Then he reached for his bag and untied it from his belt. Next he loosened the drawstring and removed from the bag, a knotted rope bearing three carefully woven knots. Holding the rope in his hand he held it up for Bartholomew to see. "Have you a need for wind?" he repeated with an implicit challenge in his voice.

"I see a rope with [26]three knots. Have you woven the wind into the rope, wizard?"

"Untie one knot and come to expect a formidable wind. Untie two knots and the wind shall blow across this land with wrath and dominance and the myriad creatures shall flee . . ."

"And the third knot?" Bartholomew interrupted him impatiently.

---

[26] There is much folklore based upon the idea of tying the wind inside of magic cords. Often, the wind was purchased by fishermen as a charm against evil fates.

"I would never untie the third knot," replied the wizard. "The third knot would unleash a hurricane of unbelievable magnitude."

King Bartholomew was in a slightly mischievous mood after his morning with the Keeper. He was alarmed to see the extent to which magic and magic charms were woven into his kingdom like a silver thread. His father had taught him to respect the old traditions of the people, but sometimes his consternation caused him to act impetuously, for such was his nature. He reached into his pocket and brought out a coin. Handing the coin to the wizard, he said.

"Untie one of the knots."[27]

The wizard took the coin and put it in a small purse he kept tied to his bag. Then he took the rope carefully and untied one of the knots.

"Just a moment," said the King suddenly as a new thought came to him. "Untie two knots."

The wizard looked up unexpectedly as if he needed to reaffirm the King's request. Bartholomew cocked an eyebrow and smiled. When the wizard finished untying both knots he looked up, but the King was already gone.

King Bartholomew nudged his knees into the side of his horse affectionately and rode away in a cloud of dust laughing despite himself. When his horse came thundering over the next hill he was met with a gentle breath of wind in his face. He smiled and slapped the rump of his horse playfully. "Home girl, it's almost time for lunch . . . and a bucket of oats for you too."

The King was in a wonderful mood now. Kicking up dust he cantered along the path and felt the freedom of the open road. Bluebells and pansies, heath bedstraw, posies, goose grass, white roses, dandelions, purple sage and creeping bracken grew along the path, filling the air with deep scent and floating, wafting pollen, chased by dancing bees and

---

[27] *I see this as the mirror of the temptation of the esoteric knowledge sought by Bartholomew. In this instance, he is tempting the Lord through his thirst for knowledge and his impatience, and he feels justified in his temptation, for the Lord is more powerful than magic.*

curious insects. Wild hare nibbled the undergrowth and trembled with perpetual fear with each new sound or shadow from above. Swooping, diving birds searched for an unwary insect. Squirrels darted in front of his horse and leapt from tree to tree. Past old oak trees and copses of closely growing evergreen trees he thought about how beautiful his home was and that it was worth fighting for. The rolling hills and dales were dotted with blue and purple heather and in the distance he could see grazing sheep and circling crows.

He did not notice when the wind first became stronger, but now it was unmistakable. Choosing to ignore the obvious, the King rode ever on but the wind only became stronger and his horse began to labor beneath the strength of the building zephyr. Ahead he rode ever into the coming storm and the further he rode the greater became his antipathy for wizards and magic and superstition, but his antipathy was draining away his jovial mood and he was becoming morose. Debris filled the air making it difficult for him to see the path. 'It's just a rush of air,' the King thought aloud. 'It will soon blow itself out.' Further ahead he could see streaks of grey and black curtains of dust being pushed ahead of the wall of wind, but still he denied his own eyes and his own senses. 'Tis but a passing cloud,' he thought, and he rode the rest of the way home with an increasing feeling of weakness.

The castle became entangled in a gale-storm of turbulent wind, but the King only slept in his bed amidst the powerful tempest. The servants, and even the craftsmen and guildsmen of the castle, were nervous and waited for the King to emerge from his afternoon nap. The King had come back to his home in a sour mood and had gone directly past the waiting pages with rolled up messages and sealed letters, to his room. Now the talk turned to whispers as the older servants and cronies remembered old tales half forgotten and gathered around tea tables and in darkening alcoves exchanging stories and folk wisdom.

By the time Bartholomew came down from his afternoon nap, the castle was captured in a silent uproar. Each servant had a different opinion about the ominous wind. The stable master had cautiously quartered the animals against the onslaught of the evil wind. The blacksmith was convinced that an enemy power was at work, most probably a wizard from the Highlands of Scotland. A visiting pastor from a nearby parish was declaring that demonic forces were loosed upon the land. The servants wondered if it was safe to go outside and if it would be safe to breathe the air.

King Bartholomew listened to the concerns of his people before assuring them that no harm would ever come from a little wind, and that it was quite normal after all. In a side parlor the King met with one of his deemsters. The deemster was worried that strong magic was involved with the strange wind and that something terrible was surely about to happen. The King told no one about his encounter with the wizard earlier that day. He thought it was better left unsaid. When the deemster was gone the King rubbed his head for it was throbbing with a dull pain. The nap had only made him feel worse. Something was gnawing at the edge of his consciousness, but his headache and the business about the wind had distracted him completely. He went to the kitchen and asked for a bowl of soup. When he was finished eating he went to his room to smoke.

Relaxing in a comfortable chair near the window he busied himself with his pipe. Holding a burning brand to the bowl, he puffed the sweet leaf and blew out a cloud of rich, blue smoke. The sound of the wind outside was incessant. Outside his window the wind swept across the soil in powerful eddies that scoured the landscape and pushed debris across the land in destructive waves. Bartholomew puffed away, but even his pipe could give him no comfort, no respite from the pain in his head and the nagging thoughts that tried to break through, pecking and pecking and pecking. Soon the steady howling of the wind captured his attention and he was slowly lulled into a muse, a stupefaction to which he could not resist. An hour later he was asleep in the chair when the sound of heavy pounding on his door revived him. An anxious servant waited for the door to open and began speaking even before the door opened all the way.

"The wind is getting stronger!" cried the anxious servant. "Shall I send for a wizard?"

"Nonsense," Bartholomew answered. And though he was annoyed by the petty fears and protestations of the people of his kingdom, he loved them in all their kindhearted ignorance. "Just go about your business, Pater. Surely there is going to be a storm tonight, nothing more. Tend to your business and do not worry."

When the servant was gone, Bartholomew considered his words more thoroughly. There was much fear in the unexpected; he knew this to be true. Therefore, it was important for him to always try to act in accordance with what the people expected from their King. But what need did he have of wizards dashing about, speaking strange words and hammering out strange incantations with dead fish? Such wizardry only diminished faith in the Lord, and he would not have petty sorcerers questioning the wisdom of the Lord. In that instant his mind recoiled and he left his room and hurried into his father's chamber. He locked the door. Pushing the recessed door open again he ascended the stairway. The keystones were still on the floor when he had dropped them . . . was that yesterday? He could see moving streaks of black and grey wind as it swept past the castle, casting forth a grainy, diffuse light with an eerie, supernatural quality. He ignored the wind. Then, removing the silver key from his pocket, he inserted it into the keyhole of the trunk left for him by his father. He turned the key gently until he heard a soft click of the inner mechanism as it snapped open.

Bartholomew was unprepared for what he saw, and he gasped when he saw it, and stepping back he almost fell through the open hole in the floor. But then he quickly steadied himself. Walking up to the open chest he reached inside and removed a large book bound in calfskin and bearing the symbol of a serpent devouring its own tail. The calfskin was dyed forest green and the symbol, raised in relief, was red. He held the book gently in his hands, almost afraid to open it. A cold chill went up his back, for he was probably the only living person in the world to know about this book. Wiping the sweat from his brow he smiled awkwardly. Then he opened it.

All night and into the next day King Bartholomew stayed in that room pouring over the manuscript. He lit candles and brought food and wine with him, for he did not want to leave and he did not want any of the manuscripts to leave the tower until he had thoroughly examined them. All night the wind howled and circled around the tower, but his mind was now completely absorbed and the power of the words would not lessen their grip on his mind.

When Bartholomew finally emerged from his father's chamber he was met by anxious servants and an even more nervous stable master. Iona was among the worried servants who wanted comfort and expressions of confidence from the King. The land was being scourged by an implacable and impossible wind . . . even the animals were too frightened to eat. Could the King not see that something had to be done? Could not a wizard be found that would save them? Bartholomew, distracted as he was, and not realizing the scope of the dilemma, was not able to access the situation properly. He simply blurted out the first thing that came to mind.

"I will go," he said to them for comfort. "I will go and talk to the wind, if that is your wish."

He had no intention however of doing so. Instead, he only wanted to show them that he was a man of action. He wanted them to know that in a time of crisis, he would not be afraid to act.

And so, in the middle of the second day of wind, the guard opened the gate and King Bartholomew walked silently out from his castle, into the windswept and razed fields of his estate. And there he went, a solitary figure braced against the turbulence of a supernatural storm. From an upper window Iona watched the King walk out into the squall, and secretly she feared for him.

Constructed in the 10th century and built with a commanding position, the castle was built as a garrison, protecting the harbor from invading ships and marauding pirates come to take freely from the isle's bounty. Now, no longer acting as a garrison, the castle still quartered vigilant troops acting on the King's orders where war rooms were maintained, strategies discussed, courtiers quartered, and sorties could be launched with precision. With the sound of the portcullis closing slowly behind him, the King trudged along the main road leading away from the castle. Taking a less traveled road, he then walked until he came to a little stone bridge built over the Silverburn, the Crossag. He went over the bridge without stopping even for a moment to reflect, a thing he was prone to do since childhood, for there were many legends and stories of elves and monsters and angels surrounding the bridge and he liked to imagine the wild inspiration that could evoke such stories in the mind of men. The path now began to rise. The King bent his back to the wind and trudged forward. Impossibly, the wind pushed against him at every twist and turn of the path. Then he went around a corner along the path and through a narrow copse of evergreen trees until he stepped out on the other side like an explorer to a new world. The sound was deafening, the trees were bent forward, and he emerged into an open area away from the trees into a blast furnace. There was nothing to stop the steady surge of the driving wind now. But the King was hearty and the King was stout. He stood still as a stone. All around him he could hear the rush of wind and see the streaking debris of leaves and dust and grass filling the darkening sky with an eeriness that, for the first time, made him stop and take notice. He sat down in the middle of the field with the sound of the wind in his ears, but he thought only of the book. Thoughts lingered, unresolved in his penetrating mind.

"If a thing be said, that which was said is not that thing; if a thought be thus spoken, that thought can never be thought; if an action be thus harmful, that action is harmful to the bearer of such harm; but if a thought never be thus uttered, and if an action be not taken, that thing be not from God."

The King tried to understand the cryptic words when another verse from the book came back to him.

"If you chase the wind till the end of the day, you meet the new day with the wind at your back; but if you should seek to alter the wind, you shall be blown out to drift on an endless sea and the wind shall drive you from your home."

The essence of the book was too clear he mused. The duality that was the essence of existence, the demarcation between being and becoming, was an illusion and a lie. This knowledge, thought to be so dangerous and heretical, was as such, hidden by the very nature of its own incomprehension. Instead, the teaching was delivered in succinct parables and epigrams which were themselves obscure and incomprehensible. The power of this knowledge was not so easily obtained however, and that is why the teaching was difficult to make use of. For in truth, once this knowledge was understood, the power that could be used from the application of such knowledge became trite and superficial.

Bartholomew hated such esotericism that sought to treat every thing as a single thing, a single, incomprehensible manifestation of the breath of God. This philosophy saw the world as a single exhalation from the word of God. Now he looked up into the driving wind with new eyes, a new perspective, and now he knew that it had been wrong to tempt the Lord with such demonstrations even for one with a heart as imperfect as his own.

He went back to his castle and had to wait for the portcullis to come up, for the blowing debris made it difficult to see him clearly and his plodding gait through the storm was slow and measured. Wearily, he stood and waited. Looking up to his castle he thought about the life that it contained between such thick walls of stone, thick 12 foot walls of fitted stone. Of course he knew that the castle was not impenetrable, and often what was inside was more dangerous than that for which the castle had been built; that often the danger that was contained inside was very difficult to identify. Ideas went through stone like cannon fire through gossamer. The real strength of a castle was blood, not mortar.

He went past the guards and anxious servants and officials and he could see deep concern in their eyes though they hesitated to speak. He had nothing to offer them, no words of wisdom, no words of encouragement, so silently he went past them without a word. To his father's chamber he went and closed the door behind him. Then he went through the passage, up to the secret room and collapsed into a chair thoughtlessly. He closed his eyes for a moment to relieve the growing sense of panic that was beginning to rise up again. He had an almost visceral feeling of dread now, but he would not allow himself to waver in his faith.

That night with the sound of the wind lashing against tiny castle and amidst the silent terrors of his people, the King prayed for strength. He prayed to the saints that they might intercede on his behalf. He prayed without end until he fell asleep. In his sleep he was given a wonderful dream, a terrible dream, and as he dreamed his terrible dream the good people of his kingdom prayed for the King . . .

Bartholomew dreamed that he lay in a field of tall grass and white flowers awash in fiery radiance. The sun warmed his hands, but his feet were planted in the earth and he could not move. He shouted, but the voice that came from his mouth was not his own voice, it was the voice of thousands of children and old women and old men together lamenting the cold. He took great, gulping breaths and his lungs were now become the succulent foliage of thousands of trees and shrubs and bushes. A woodpecker pecked vigorously at his limbs for they were the limbs of countless trees full of gathering, groping birds and swinging, climbing, leaping animals. And now his ears were the ears of all the world and he could hear many voices in his head, only it was not his head but the head of all people and all creatures living or dead, growing or disintegrating back to the soil in which he now grew. 'I'm alive! I'm alive!' he shouted, but no one heard him because they were inside of his head and his heart and his bones, and they were as much a part of him as he was of himself even though he be whole. 'Leave me alone!' he shouted, and in response it began to rain. The rain cooled him down and the wind rushed through his hair, only his hair had turned into grass and he could feel small creatures walking over him and eating him. Then he began to sing, but the words were not his own and he could not understand the song, for it was not his voice but the voice of a peasant. Then the peasant began to cry and his head was filled with different voices, but he could not remember the sound of his own voice so he became the voice that was not his own. Then leaves started to grow from his head and the sound of the leaves drown out the sound of the multitude of voices that belonged to him now. Again he tried to shout, to scream that he was a person, but this time only bitter cold wind came out of his mouth and froze the tender stalks around him.

He felt himself sinking into the ground and suddenly his arms were reaching to heaven for they were now become branches with tiny, reaching fingers. And now he could feel pain and suffering, but it was not his pain but the pain of others and he could experience this suffering only as a growing weakness . . . a mournful sadness that included all the voices that for a cacophony of confusion and terrible integration in his mind, only became stronger. But it was not his mind now because it included unrecognizable emotions he was not familiar with and attributes that were not yet defined by emotions.

Finally everything became dark. The light from his world became dimmer and dimmer and as his world began to dim, his senses diminished until he slowly dissolved into nothingness. He tried to shout, to scream, to make his presence known, but now he had no identity, no discriminating attributes with which to classify him against the bitter world. In another moment he would be gone . . .

When King Bartholomew woke he was sweating profusely and his heart palpated wildly. The King sat up in bed and breathed a sigh of relief, for in his mind he had surely escaped something mortally dangerous. Now he would never be able to sleep, for the terrible dream so distressed his sense of wholeness, and now he was a part of something that was itself, whole and yet undefined. "I exist! I exist!" he cried, forcing his eyes wide open against the closing darkness around him. Then he shouted into the blackness of his room a cry of victory. "I exist, by God I exist!" He jumped out of bed and staggered to the window. Opening the shutters he let the cool air rush into the room. Then, into the darkest night he prayed.

"Oh, Lord of light, I abandon the darkness. Oh, great mystery, I yield to the journey. My spirit flows like a river to the ocean that is eternity. I do not yield my soul just yet, for I am weak. But if the journey be mine, I pray my soul once forgiven shall be stronger in the light that Thou have thus separated . . . and bless my separation."

On the third day of the storm King Bartholomew crossed paths with the wizard from whom he had exacted such a terrible gift. The price of the King's foolishness had been high, for the people were frightened. The wizard came to rest along the edge of the cart path. He waited. With a look of exhaustion on his face, the wizard looked dour as if the energy from the storm had come from his own body and he was slowly being consumed by the manifestation of his own power. The King stopped in front of the wizard who looked like he had been waiting on the exact spot for three days. There was fear in the eyes of the wizard. With his hand resting on the pommel of his sword, the King looked angry and menacing. The wizard feared for his life. Bartholomew uttered no form of greeting; he merely held out his hand in expectation. The wizard took the rope from his bag and held it out to the King. And then unexpectedly, Bartholomew said.

"Untie the third knot, wizard."

"What!?" exclaimed the wizard with surprise and utter disbelief. He could not believe what he was hearing. "Have you lost your mind?"

"Untie the third knot," the King repeated without hesitation. He was dead serious.

The wizard let out a sigh of resignation. "Be it on your own head," he said with sadness as he prepared to capitulate with the King's demand. Then he untied the third knot. When he looked up, once again the King was gone.

From the safety of the castle, Iona could see the slow progress of a solitary man struggling against the wind as he tried to make it to the castle. It was King Bartholomew! Dust devils and swirling eddies of stinging sand surrounded him like an aureole and lashed at his body. Several times she saw him fall or blown over by a tremendous gust of wind that threatened to blow him off the face of the earth, but he labored on and soon he was waiting for the guards to open the gate for him. Iona ran down to the entrance hall to hear what news would be forthcoming.

King Bartholomew came in from the storm and threw back his hood from his face. His eyes were watery and his face was red from the sand.

Then he took off his cloak and handed it to a waiting servant. He looked weary and stunned, and to the careful eye of Iona, he looked frightened. His unsuccessful attempt to perish the wind had only yielded a greater and more ferocious storm, and he did not know what to do, for secretly he expected the wind to blow itself out and he was surprised when it only became stronger. The captain of the guard was there. He stood waiting for orders. At first it looked like the King would not speak and that once again he would retire to his chamber for private contemplation, but suddenly he raised his head resolutely.

"Take two of your best men," he said to the captain quietly. "Go swiftly to Castletown and bring back a wizard. Do not fail. Go!" he commanded emphatically. The captain turned on his heels and strode away with purpose.

The King now addressed the remaining crowd that had gathered around him. He seemed to have taken strength from his decision, for now he no longer looked frightened, but there was a look in his eye of regret and remorse as if he blamed himself. The people loved their King. They would never blame him for bringing wrath upon their home, for it was the King's home just as well. He raised his hand and motioned for silence even though no one had uttered a single word.

"Do not despair," he began. "This evil wind that blows across the land is not the wind of the Lord. This is an evil wind, a portentous wind. This is a tempestuous wind. There are times when all men must decide where to put their faith. There is a time for every woman to look into her soul and decide if her soul shall perish in infamy or go gently delivered up to the Lord. I will not rest until I have brought down this evil. Go about your business and guard your soul against temptation, for evil follows from evil, as like follows from like, as righteous action follows from prayer."

King Bartholomew left the room and went swiftly to his father's library. Stepping inside, he closed and locked the door. Then he went to the bookcase and ran his fingers across the volumes coming at last upon the book of his choice. It was a book often read aloud to him by his father, a book that brought him much comfort. He took it back to his chair and sat down to read. Outside the wind raged and blew flying debris and dust and dirt and the fragments of snapped trees against the walls of his castle but he only studied carefully the lives of the saints.[28]

The guards returned later with the wizard. The King was informed of their arrival and waited eagerly for them to present the wizard. When they did, the King was again surprised, for the wizard looked nothing like he was expecting. The wizard was dressed in red leggings and a red tunic. He wore a thick belt around his waist from which several bejeweled pouches hung. His posture was dignified and confident. He rose from his chair when the King entered and bowed at the waist.

"I am at your service," he said politely and then he lowered his eyes and waited for Bartholomew to speak.

"Are you a wizard?" the King asked directly.

"Well, yes," the wizard answered sheepishly, for he was very proud of his status and never expected to be asked to confirm his own position.

"I do not approve of sorcery," said Bartholomew. "You are to leave this castle at once, and you are to tie the wind. That is my command. Do you understand?"

A royal guard stood near the door and waited for instructions from the King. These were the only people that were present in the room. The wizard blushed when the order from the King came. He began to hedge his bet.

"My lord . . . it is no small thing to tie the wind. Or course you must understand, for you are very wise."

King Bartholomew stared the wizard down, and it was the wizard that was becoming uncomfortable now. He backed up a step from the King. Bartholomew saw his reticence to commit to such a task and he rightly guessed that the wizard would try to diminish his own power.

"If this storm is the product of sorcery," he said carefully, "I may not be able to work the wind. There are powers beyond which I cannot control. I can only try . . ."

---

[28] *Most likely from "The Golden Legend," of Jacob de Vogagine, medieval hagiographic material with an emphasis on miracle tales. Written in 1260. From 1470 to 1530, it was the most printed book in Europe.*

"You practice the art of wind-working in Castletown, do you not?"

The King was stern and did not take his eyes off the troubled wizard who now seemed to grow smaller before the King. He held him in his gaze like a bird of prey and his eyes saw inside. The wizard smiled uncomfortably. Then the King passed judgment.

"You are to leave this castle and go out into the storm. You are a wind-worker as you have practiced your trade unmolested. You have practiced your trade on my people to your own end. I expect you to work the wind! If you fail me in this . . ." the King's voice trailed off and it was evident to the wizard what the implication of his words meant. Then the King turned his back on the wizard and the royal guard led him away.

Soon after, King Bartholomew was seen leaving the castle again. In the direction of Rushen Abbey he trod the dusty road and he was soon swallowed by the storm and disappeared from sight. His progress was slow and methodical as he kept his head down to shield his eyes against the wind. Finally he entered the protection of the abbey as the sky grew more ominous and asked to see Bishop Jacob. The Bishop was in his cell and had to be gone after by one of the monks. The King was led to a small antechamber. When the Bishop entered they shook hands like old friends.

"It must be important for you to venture out in such a storm," said the Bishop. "I have never seen a storm of greater ferocity. There is something supernatural at work, I fear. Are you well, my friend?"

King Bartholomew released the Bishop's hand and looked into his face. It was calm and peaceful after his many long years of service and asceticism. His austerity had made him wise in the ways of judgment.

"Has something happened?" Bishop Jacob asked with insight. He had known Bartholomew for many years, and his faults as well as his great strengths were known to him.

A small table was placed in a nook below a leaded window. The King sat down and motioned for his friend to do the same. Pale light filtered in through the thick glass and only made the King's flesh look pallid. He swallowed hard, and then he told Bishop Jacob the tale of the wind and how he had tempted the Lord. He told Jacob about the wizard and the knots of wind and how he had offered the wizard a coin to untie the wind. After he was finished he waited for an admonition from the bishop. Instead, he heard something he never expected to hear.

"I do not reproach you," said Jacob thoughtfully. [29]"I cannot judge you with malice for I have dabbled with sorcery myself, in my youth, before I came to this island."

The King's eyes opened wide, for he was shocked to hear such news. But he said nothing, and he waited for his friend to continue. Bishop Jacob watched the King to see what his reaction would be. Of his experiences in his youth he had spoken to no man except the abbot of the abbey that he served. The King waited with patience and did not press him with questions. Jacob knew that the King was a good man and was not a man to judge unfairly the past follies and indiscretions of other men, for he was quick to judge himself most severely.

"I was raised far from these shores," Bishop Jacob began with earnest. "My mother and father sent me to be instructed by the 9th earl of Marsh, a somber and serious man that I could form no attachment to. He was a master of the black arts. I wish to say no more about that right now, however. The earl trained me and prepared me for an occupation in the art of sorcery. With the grace of God I escaped his clutches, for the Lord wields even greater power. Yes, Bartholomew, I have seen the working of sorcery and I can attest to its power."

"Can you stop the wind?" asked King Bartholomew cautiously.

"No, I cannot stop the wind," Jacob answered honestly. "I am not a sorcerer, and I condemn all form of sorcery."

"Tell me, what can I do?" Bartholomew said with acceptance. He was frightened by what he had done, and he looked to his old friend for help.

"The Lord has worked his power through the saints," Jacob continued. "There are many stories of such manifestations of power. Consider the life of [30]St. Cyprian of Antioch. He was a great sorcerer of renown, and

---

[29] *Taken from the autobiographical notes of Bishop Jacob. "The Life of the Yellow Kestrel."*
[30] *A heathen magician of Antioch. Said to be the most powerful sorcerer of his time. He had dealings with demons and employed the power of the devil, and*

some say the greatest sorcerer of the day. The evil that he worked cannot be overestimated, for he had help from many powerful demons. He renounced his art when he discovered the power of Christ, and the Lord used him thereafter."

"He was a great man," Bartholomew said reluctantly.

"St. Maughold was not a great man, Bartholomew. He was a robber, and he would have killed St. Patrick but for the grace of God. It was not until he was rescued by the power of the Lord that he was able to do great deeds."

"That is true, that is true," King Bartholomew repeated resolutely.

"And it was St. Patrick that bade him to bind himself in chains and throw the key into the sea. Then he was told to set out in a coracle without sail or even an oar, trusting in the wisdom of God to send the robber to these shores where two of St. Patrick's disciples were already established. The key to Maughold's chains had been recovered in the mouth of a fish, and so it was that St. Maughold went into the mountains to pray and live the life of a hermit before being called to the service of God, for which he later became a saint. This is the way of the Lord, Bartholomew."

King Bartholomew looked meekly into the penetrating eyes of Bishop Jacob, for he had a great respect for the man. He spoke timidly, as if his mind were incapable of further speculation.

"The storm cannot last forever." he said passively, almost beseeching the good man to come to his rescue.

Bishop Jacob became fiery as an inner storm surfaced within his soul. He took hold of the King and shook him violently to rouse him from a draining stupefaction. "No, Bartholomew!" he exclaimed with fervor.

---

called upon the devil to win the virtuous heart of a beautiful woman, Justina. He could not capture her because of the power of Christ which she called upon with the sign of the cross. Cyprian was converted to the power of Christ when his magic was unsuccessful. When he renounced the devil, he was attacked by the devil and only escaped after making the sign of the cross which the devil could not endure. He later became bishop of Antioch and was beheaded along with St. Justina in the Diocletian persecutions at Nicomedia, September 26, 304

"That is not the way. You must fight for this land and the Lord will help you. This is your battle to fight and this is your pilgrimage to take. You must save this land. Take strength in the words and deeds of those that have come before you. Arm yourself, Bartholomew. Arm yourself with the power of the Lord!"

Then Bishop Jacob held the King in his arms gently and told him where to go to find the staff of St. Maughold, the holy relic that would bring him strength to fight the evil that was sweeping across the land. King Bartholomew took council from the bishop and he gained strength from his wise words, for they were words of action.

And so King Bartholomew left the abbey alone. He was filled with purpose and he gained strength from every step. For almost an hour he walked through the storm until he came to a little stone church nestled in a small grove of cypress. Bartholomew picked his way through the whipping, swaying trees until he came to the door of the church. He went in and closed the door with difficulty. It was very dark inside the church. Removing from his cloak a small candle given to him by Jacob, he gave himself enough light to penetrate the darkness to the front of the church near the altar.

Holding the candle forward he could just make out the outline of the staff that was held in the hand of the statue of St. Maughold. Placed in a recess in the wall of the church and framed with ornate carvings of an oak tree on opposite sides of the saint and coming together into a canopy over his head like a halo from heaven, the saint held open his arms in contrition, for he was once a great sinner. The statue of the saint was carved, but the staff was said to be that of the saint and it was a treasured relic.

Bartholomew sat down in the first pew to rest. He held the candle aloft and did not take his eyes off the saint. Like the saint before him, King Bartholomew knew that he was also a great sinner, and that his greatest sins were sins of omission, for to deny the power of the Lord was a great sin. Suddenly the words of the Keeper came back to him. Almost forgotten, the words struck him like a chord.

". . . The world is a cemetery. If you wish to escape into the light you must learn a lesson from this tree. It becomes reborn even as you must pass through darkness to see the light . . ."

The King continued staring at the statue. Like the roots of the yew tree, the roots of the church grew around the sinner like a halo, and the protection was everlasting. Then King Bartholomew knew what he would do. Rising to his feet with determination, he went to the statue and removed the staff. And before leaving the church he said a silent prayer. Outside the storm continued unabated.

Not long after leaving the protection of the church, Bartholomew was attacked by beasts and birds. He could see them circling around him, giant, black crows. Their raucous cackling could be heard above the howling of the wind and the King battled them fiercely with the staff of Maughold. He stood tall and knocked them from the sky with his great strength. Perched in trees and laying in wait they attacked him from all quarters, but he persisted.

"Be gone, foul scavengers and pickers of bones!" he shouted to the sky. "Be gone, legions of hell, be gone carrion eaters. Take your silent death, take your black souls and be gone!"

He walked and walked, fighting his way across the windswept land and he grew weary from his struggle. Pangs of hunger surged through his body, for he had not eaten that day. His breathing was short. Beads of perspiration ran into his eyes. Suddenly he stopped and turned around. His acute sense of hunting and an instinct for death revealed to him now that he was being watched. The chalky sky and the blowing sand made it difficult for him to see anything clearly. He continued on for a few steps, but then he stopped and suddenly spun around again.

Only a few yards away, crouched down close to the ground was an enormous beast, a vicious, [31]black dog. The dog bared its teeth and a terrible growling came in low, tight bursts. The beast was poised to attack. Bartholomew saw those terrible fangs and he trembled. Then he looked into the beast's eyes. They were black as night, the color of emptiness, and they gleamed faintly with a ghostly light from the darkening sky. King Bartholomew stared into those hopeless eyes and he knew that they were unreal, a specter without form. He drew

---

[31] *Mauthe Dhoog. A spectral beast that haunted to towers and battlements of Peel Castle. It attacked anyone that saw it and killed them outright or else drove them mad. During excavations of the castle, along with the remains of Bishop Simon of Man, died 1247, the remains of an enormous dog were found. This could have been the feared hellhound of Peel Castle.*

strength from his knowledge that he would not be defeated. Then he threw back his cloak and prepared himself.

When the beast attacked Bartholomew was ready. Lunging at him with those unearthly, luminous eyes, the beast took three giant leaps toward him, snarling wildly. But Bartholomew now wielded the staff of Maughold, and an explosion of radiance emanated from the staff, striking the oncoming beast like a surging breaker. The creature recoiled and backed away slowly, snarling and grinding its teeth with frustration. Bartholomew took a step toward the beast and the beast backed away further. Then the King raised the staff high above his head to strike the beast dead, but he did not strike, for phantoms cannot be killed by men.

"Away!" Bartholomew shouted, thrusting the staff toward the cowering beast fearlessly. "Be gone!" Then he turned his back on the beast and continued his journey unopposed by neither man nor beast.

The King carried the staff like a pilgrim through unknown lands and he did not waver. The sky above churned black and grey but the silent pilgrim made progress unto his destination. Into the face of the storm he now walked and his clothes were whipped and torn by the fierceness, but he would not turn back. And as the sun sunk at last beneath the horizon and the wind turned cold he reached the edge of the island to a plateau high above the turbulent sea below.

King Bartholomew stood at the very edge of his kingdom and the storm lashed him violently. Into the storm he faced with steadfast determination, for he had come to the edge of his kingdom to lay his claim. He held the staff of Maughold aloft into the storm and shouted for the entire world to hear.

"In the name of God, I release the power of the Holy Spirit to cover my precious kingdom once delivered with the strength of St. Patrick, with the grace of Christ!" Then King Bartholomew, once deceived, but now in righteous glory, raised the staff high above his head and with a single powerful thrust, drove it down into the earth.

Then the King turned his back and walked back to his home. The wind now began to abate, and by the time that he reached his castle, the storm was destroyed. When King Bartholomew came around the last turn in the road leading to his castle he came upon the wizard he had brought from Castletown. The wizard fell down at his feet and pleaded for his life. The King reached down and took the wizard by the arm and ordered him to rise.

"Do not fear," he said to the powerless wizard. "I release you. Go in peace and practice the black arts no more."

In the years that followed, the children used to go to the edge of the island to see the place where King Bartholomew stilled the wind. It had now become a shrine. In the very spot where Bartholomew had plunged the staff of Maughold into the earth there now grew a tree, a single, large oak tree, for the oak tree is known for strength.

𝔄 𝔓𝔢𝔫𝔫𝔶 𝔣𝔬𝔯 𝔘𝔫𝔞 𝔚𝔞𝔱𝔱𝔩𝔢𝔴𝔬𝔯𝔱𝔥

"If you could have any wish granted Iona, what would it be?"

"I would bring back the children," she answered.

"That is a beautiful wish," the King said. "But what if you could only bring back one child, one single child, how could you choose?"

"No," she answered. "I would never choose one child over another."

"But if you had to Iona . . . what if you had to?"

"I would refuse to speak," she answered.

"You would refuse?" the King asked with growing interest.

"Yes," she answered with conviction. "And in that way, the Lord would answer for me."

𝕴ona entered the King's chamber with his breakfast of eggs, ham, bread, cheese, and tea, for even a sick King was indeed a hungry King. Bartholomew was under the weather this morning and could not get out of bed without great difficulty. The fox-hunt of the previous day ended poorly for Bartholomew when he was thrown from his horse, a thing that had never happened in local memory. Now the King was on his back, bruised and sore but none worse for the wear. Iona had insisted that he should remain in bed and rest for the better part of the day, and if he felt better by afternoon, perhaps he could take his tea in the garden. The King, only too willing to comply lest he be asked to do something he was surely not up to, agreed at once.

"Blueberry preserves," said Iona. "I hope that will make you feel better, Sire."

"Thank you Iona," said the King. "You always did know how to make me feel better. "Before you go, would you please bring me my star charts that are on the window-sill beneath the astrolabe?"

Iona looked inquisitively at the brass instrument then brought her King the star charts he had asked for. She hesitated for a moment in case he would be asking for anything else, but her only looked at her and smiled. It was the same smile she had seen for years, thankful and tender but devoid of any actual joy. The King smiled at her because he was her King and it was important for him to do so. She smiled back and left the room briskly.

In the pantry she poured herself a cup of tea and carried it out to the garden to relax for a while and listen to the singing of the birds. The castle had one of the finest gardens on the island and the most particular and exotic birds were only too happy to peck at seeds and sing for the King or Iona if she was there.

Iona sat on a stone bench still cold from the morning chill. This was her favorite place to be alone. This was her secret place to be alone with her own pain and her own passions and her own dreams, but were it not for tiny finches and sparrows her voice would vanish from this world unheeded. Only occasionally did she ever feel sorry for her own choices. She was the private servant to the King; there were many that would gladly trade their own life for her own. But to be so lonely in a world of such abundance . . . It made her smile at her own folly sometimes. Alas, but such is the weakness of a woman's heart, and it is in such weakness that the cold and steadfast reason of authority and power can sometimes break down.

She sat on the bench with one leg coyly placed over the other and the dappling sunlight played on her dress, and to Iona, the tattered and frayed edges and faded color was once again made whole in her memory. The way Iona held her tea made her feel beautiful; it brought back memories of when she was beautiful. And she truly was beautiful as a butterfly in a meadow of bright yellow flowers. That was when she first set her heart on the young King Bartholomew, following the tragic death of King Sigmus, and she was enthralled by his handsome, unassuming power to make all that set eyes on him blush, oh, but for that fateful day. . . .

On the festival of St. Patrick it happened. People from villages near and far were there. Children played with toy snakes and chased one another through the fields and meadows. Food that had been carefully prepared and blessed was abundant and each dish was nibbled and judged to be good by the good people of Man.

Iona was there and helped with the food and preparations for when the King would speak. Everyone debated and argued and thought about just what the King would say, and so it was that the debate about words far exceeded the very words that were yet to be spoken. It was thought an ill omen to be surprised by words, so everyone tried to anticipate the King. This was great fun to the good people of Man, and debates sometimes raged far into the night to anticipate a word that may or may not be spoken the very next day.

Iona was very young and very beautiful. The people of Man thought that she would marry a rich man and have many children. Iona would blush at such outlandish gossip, but she knew that the power of gossip could change the very nature of nature and she hoped they were right. Her father had died on the reach and her mother had died from grief. But Iona was strong and found strength with the small children to whom she became a teacher of happy songs and nodding lullabies to put them to sleep and make them forget the monsters invented by their parents. And at night, Iona put herself to sleep thinking about being married to the King. When the morning sun came peeping through her window the next day she would forget her dreams and go off to find the children.

So it was with great anticipation that Iona waited to see the King on that day. In her dreams the King had already spoken, and with a slight smile on her milky face she waited to hear what he would say today. But, before the King had even uttered a single word the news spread that a child had fallen into a hole.

Everyone including the King rushed to the spot. In a small field near the *Whispering Stone* was a deep hole in the ground that had gone unnoticed. Little Una Wattleworth, a child of no more than six summers had fallen in after trying to shout to a monster the other children told her was hiding down there. Now they could not see her and they could not hear her so they ran for help.

Everyone was sick with fear for the child. There was nothing to be done. Any movement near the hole only knocked more dirt into the hole. The King was frantic. He ran from side to side and clenched his fists but he could come up with no plan to save the child. Una, whose name meant, *a lamb*, was swallowed alive by the darkness inside the hole and not a sound of her could be heard. The children were crying and the women were wringing their hands, and Iona prayed through her silent tears.

The King became even more frantic when a group of men with shovels and spades ran to the hole with the intention of digging around it and saving the poor child that way. The King stopped them with an anguished gesture and looked to the women for help. There was nothing that could be done, and on that festive day so long ago, Una Wattleworth left the Isle of Man.

The King knew that he had to say something to the exhausted and grief stricken people, but he was utterly speechless. His mind did not compassionately become numb like the anguished people in his care. In his own mind all the images and memories of his own happy childhood bubbled to the surface and inflicted greater and greater grief. Finally he spoke. He spoke with power, but the people would later say that it was not the voice of King Bartholomew.

"In all the infinite wisdom of heaven, tell me why?"

Then his voice faltered and he was silent. The people waited for him to speak again but the King was wrestling with something in his mind and the people could see that he was desperate for words. So visibly shaken was the King that he fought hard to contain his tears if only to console the child's mother that stood before him now. He held the mother with his trembling hands and spoke to her with resolve.

"It was an accident," he said. "Do not blame yourself. The Lord works in mysterious ways and you can be sure that there was a reason that she was called home at such a tender age."

The King stopped. He could say no more to comfort the woman. Many children had died to be sure, and she would never be forgotten. But the next words that were spoken by the woman froze the heart of the King and would not allow him rest for many years to come.

The woman looked deep into the eyes of the King and spoke. "There are no accidents," she said without emotion.

That is the day that King Bartholomew died along with little Una the lamb, thought Iona. And that was the day that the King's obsession became her own obsession to help him the way she had helped the children she was so fond of.

The King went to the well every day for a long time after the child was buried. He would stare into the deep blackness and he would wonder how the child's mother could have uttered those frightful words, and to the King they were an omen. If everything truly is preordained, then the King's tears have been purchased with counterfeit money and he would discover the truth should it take him the rest of his life.

It happened one day that another mother had taken her small child to the well to see the spot where her friend had perished and to say a prayer for her. The little girl went to the edge and looked down. Then she took something out of her pocket. It was shiny. The child whispered something and then threw it into the well. The mother was surprised.

"What was that for?" she asked her child.

"The child looked up to her mother with a meek smile. She took her mother's hand and said.

"I wanted her to have some money when she got to heaven, mummy. Now she can buy a piece of candy."

That is how the legend of the wishing well began, and it is said that to this day one can still see the glitter of coin and polished rock glittering in the deep. And so after a while the King no longer went to the well to think, but his need to believe never faltered.

The Fox, the Hare, and the Angel

"A lion ran after a man, who was running after a fox that was running after a cat that was running after a mouse that was running after . . . the lion that was running from the mouse."

The Manxman looked up. The King was smiling.

"Alright," said the King. "Congratulations, I do not understand."

"The lowliest creature of all can sometimes be the bravest."

The King asked: "Are you talking about the man?"

"I am talking about the mouse," the Manxman replied.

King Bartholomew's loyal servants waited anxiously for news of the trial. They gathered around themselves and talked. None could remember the last time a Manxman had been tried for sorcery. Of course sorcery was practiced, but seldom was it ever tried in court, and almost never in front of a King. The accused had been denounced. It was infrequent that a Manxman ever informed against another Manxman, and it was said that on the Isle of Man: Good may follow from wicked sorcery, but good sorcery was wicked.

And then the saints sailed into the turbulent waters around Man, and with them they brought the power of Christ. The Manx insisted that demons and wizards still roamed the island and sailed the dangerous coastal waters. And so it was that the Manx prayed to the Lord to protect them from the demons and wizards and the pagan gods still hiding in words and the faint scratches on stone. They prayed for the power of Christ that it be stronger than the power of the earth.

In another part of the island King Bartholomew stood up to deliver his judgment in front of the assembly. He wore a long, white ceremonial robe, the Royal Vestments, that went to the floor so that his feet be thus disappeared even as Manannan Mac lir made the island disappear in mist. In his right hand he held a ceremonial sword, held aloft. This, the Royal Blade, had been touched by Patrick the Saint when he blessed it with his words and then cleaved a loaf of bread to symbolize the power of the Lord and that it be sustained from the bread of the earth. These symbols, contrary as they may be, became the symbols of a proud people cleaved from the world with the sword and sustained with the bread of Christ.

The local deemsters gathered and waited patiently for the verdict to be handed down from the King. The trial was over and everyone was anxious to get back to work.   Before him stood a downtrodden Manxman, accused and proved guilty of the crime of sorcery. Izaak Kelly, his head hanging down like an over-smoked herring, had been accused of and found guilty of hexing his good neighbor's vegetables. The accused was seen by the plaintiff, Hilda Gruden, gathering dust outside of her home and was also witnessed scattering a substance over the neighbor's turnip patch. Izaak Kelly was witnessed walking past the plaintiff's house on several occasions, and it was noted that his hands were thrust in his pocket as if to hide secret objects and witch-dust. Hilda also testified that when she went into her turnip patch to investigate, she was overcome by a strong desire to sleep, and it was only her strong belief in the mercy of the Lord that kept her from falling asleep and being carried off by crows. Later the crows got into her vegetables and pulled them up by the roots and destroyed what they could not eat. Now Hilda Gruden is so frightened of turnips that she nearly faints whenever she sees one. Izaak Kelly, being a simple man, admitted that he did covet the plaintiff's vegetables, but he said that he only wanted to look at her magnificent turnips. And he was merely brushing the dust from his cloak. His only plea was a plea for mercy because he knew that he would be pronounced guilty. The King directed his gaze at the lowly Manxman and he felt sorry for him, but mostly he felt sorry for what he now would have to do, for truth be told, the King was very dubious of sorcery. The laws of Man were written long before his birth however. What right did he have to alter the laws of a people immersed in law?

"Izaak Kelly," the King began with firm resignation though his heart was troubled. "I find that you are guilty of sorcery and that by your own admission you did so bedevil your neighbor's turnips with witch-dust. It is my judgment that you are to be sent to the Bishop's Prison for a period of six months six days and six hours, for you did so practice evil, and that you are to repent and promise not to practice sorcery ever again. But first you will reverse the cursed spell by which you did so hex one Hilda Gruden. You are ordered to walk into her vegetable garden, and with your left foot thus you are to step into the garden until your foot touches the soil. You will then back away from the good woman's house until you come again into the street where you will once again brush the witch-dust from your feet such as the lifting of the earth be undone. You will do this in compensation for your malevolent act, for like affects like and a thing reversed is a thing undone."

The prisoner was led away peacefully and the local deemsters showed signs of relief, for in truth the King could have ordered death for the lowly Manxman. They congratulated the King for his just punishment and they congratulated themselves for placing their trust in the King. Then they went away for a cup of strong drink. Izaak would be led away to the prison, and there he would repent and return again after half a year a returned man. There would be a celebration with new oaths taken and they would dance and light candles and kill a chicken to welcome home the new man, because a new man returned from prison was a new man returned to life.

Sorren opened the door to the carriage for the King to step in. He lowered the newly polished step so that the King would not have difficulty. The King could open the door for himself for he was still a young King, but Sorren liked to make life for him as easy as possible.

"Thank you, Sorren," said the King. "Would you drive back to the castle slowly? I feel the presence of an ache in my head. It feels like lobsters are trying to break into my skull."

King Bartholomew sunk into the comfortable seat and let his head fall back into the cushion. He hated to deal out judgment even though it be just. The hardest thing for a man to do, the King thought, was to judge the actions of another man. Woe to the man that make his peace with the Lord though he has condemned his own brother unjustly. He always prayed before he passed judgment for the Lord to grant him discernment and that he not be tempted by tiny prejudices and unnecessary retribution. The process often made him sick. The sickness would not be in his mind however, oh that it were, for that would be a process he could work through and by the power of his mind explicate without difficulty. The sickness more often went to his heart. The sickness of heart is a more difficult sickness to heal. Time does not heal this sickness. Time only washes over this sickness until it becomes buried deeper and deeper into the soul.

Outside the slowly moving carriage he watched the tranquil and tender landscape of brushed meadows and grassland and he felt calmer as he could see that which was worth protecting and smell the goodness of his kingdom in the myriad wildflowers and natural heath-country. The gently rising and falling hills hid away the huts and hamlets and cottages of the good people of Man. The King loved them all; he loved them for all their superstition and folklore and he loved them for their unselfish wisdom. These were the people he served. These people, immersed in witchcraft and charms and the comfort inside whispered words, were dear to him, and as their King he would try to honor their way of life though it be different than his own.

The carriage arrived at the castle, and when Sorren opened the door the King was fast asleep. Sorren touched him slightly on the arm, but he did not shake him.

"You are home," he said softly. "Would you like to rest here a bit longer?"

Bartholomew opened his eyes with a start. Slowly he got out of the carriage as he shook off the vestiges of the lingering opiate of interrupted sleep.

"Thank you, Sorren," he said listlessly, for he was not yet awake. "You put me to sleep with your peaceful driving. You can put the carriage away if you will. I will not be going anywhere today."

King Bartholomew went inside with the intention of going to his room for a nap, but Iona was there waiting for him. In her hand was a towel, and in her other hand was a cup of bees wax which she used to polish the furniture. The castle smelled of fresh cleaning. She resisted a smile though she was happy to see him because she knew how melancholy he became when he was called to pass judgment.

"Would you like me to fix you something to eat?" she asked.

The King took off his cloak and hung his hat on a hook next to the door. It was another cloudy day and the gloom penetrated into his home.

"You may light some candles," he said to Iona. And then a moment later he replied. "I am not in the mood for lunch, Iona. Thank you for asking, but in truth I am very tired."

"I will heat some water for you to take a bath," she said thoughtfully. And then she started to walk away to make preparations.

"Wait!" said the King.

Suddenly he no longer felt tired. The thought of Iona going through all the trouble to prepare a bath for him so that he might soak away his melancholy troubled him. He thought about Izaak and he wondered how long it would be before he would be able to soak away his troubles in the bath. His servants were so good to him that it often made him feel guilty that he should be so fortunate. Then he had an inspiration.

"There is no need to do that, Iona," he said. "I feel much better now. In fact, I am going to surprise you for dinner. Do not even think about it. Sit in the garden if you choose. I am going hunting, and I will bring you something special for dinner."

Then the King ran up to his chamber and changed into his hunting clothes. Changing his clothes made him feel like he was changing from a man of authority to a man of no consequence, an ordinary man. He felt like he was changing his skin and that a new man, a second man existed beneath his weighty garments. A weight fell off his shoulders even as the weight of his garments fell to the floor. When he was finished changing, he opened his window to let some fresh air into the room. At the door he suddenly stopped and returned to his dressing cabinet. He looked at himself in the mirror and smiled. Then he pulled open the top drawer and reached his hand beneath carefully folded undergarments. Slowly he pulled out a pendant and chain and held it and felt its warmth. Whenever he held it the beautiful memory of his mother returned . . .

When Bartholomew's mother died, he was left alone with her for a moment. In that moment he told her that he would always love her and cherish the memory of her tender smile. Then he took a small pen-knife from his pocket and carefully cut a lock of her beautiful hair. He kept that lock of hair until he had fashioned out of silver, the leaf from the [32]ro

---

[32] *Rowan tree. Its name is linked with the Norse word 'runa,' meaning a charm, and the Sanskrit 'runa,' meaning magician. Charm Magician. Rowan magic*

wan tree forged for him by Abel, the blacksmith.

Abel the blacksmith was a heavy, hearty, hulking man with large hands and a large mouth that he used for cursing and singing when the mood struck him. He forged and pounded metal, but he also made jewelry when his arms became tired from hammering the fierce blows with his hammer. It was Abel that taught Bartholomew the beauty of hard work and hammered things. And it was Abel that helped the young boy fashion the pendant out of a silver cup that the boy had given him.

When Abel was ready to pour the molten silver into the leaf he and the boy had designed, he motioned the boy to come closer. The blacksmith was wise through all his grimy blackness and oil-smeared face. He knew that the boy was fashioning a charm, though the boy would never think to call it that. The mould was split into two pieces which the blacksmith would carefully mould together. He asked the boy.

"Do you have something that you would like to add?"

Bartholomew nodded nervously, and then he removed the lock of hair from his pocket. The blacksmith was not heartless and he was not stupid. It took him only a moment to know what it was. And so on that day Prince Bartholomew and Abel the blacksmith forged Queen Kathryn's lock of hair into the form of a leaf made out of silver . . .

King Bartholomew felt his heart racing. The memory always gave him pause to think and to take stock of his own life. No one but he and Abel the blacksmith knew the meaning of this pendant, and the good blacksmith had taken the powerful memory to the grave. Bartholomew would wear the pendant around his neck when the memory of his mother came back to him or when he felt like he needed extra luck. This last vestige of his mother never failed him. He kissed the pendant and then he put it around his neck before leaving the room.

Before leaving the castle he went into the kitchen to find something to chew on and give him strength. The kitchen maid Eda Murphy was sitting at the table working. Eda Murphy stopped peeling potatoes long enough, when she saw the King, to wring her hands and sigh. She loved the King and she loved his kindness. The trial had frightened her, for

---

provides powerful expressions of forewarnings and foreknowledge. It seems likely that Bartholomew learned this from Hagen the Woodchopper.

she was an old woman, a woman steeped in the gossiped lore of busy servants and steam and boiling potatoes.

"Some of the servants are afraid my lord," she said. "They say that the witches will come here and remove us from our beds at night."

"Nonsense," said King Bartholomew.

"They can turn into crows," she replied. "We fear for you. There is a legend that when a man but judges another man, that man be visited by demons if that judgment be unjust."

Bartholomew sat down on the bench next to Eda. He looked at her compassionately. "Do you think that I am unjust?" he asked.

Eda was distraught and there was a tear in her eye. "Who can judge what is right, my lord? God sees all things, but the eyes of men are weak."

"Do not worry about me," said the King, and he put his hand on her arm. "I know that you are a kind woman. I am lucky to have you."

"It's the crows," she insisted. "The crows bring with them the dark magic of the otherworld."

King Bartholomew did not like to hear such talk. Hilda Gruden also worried about crows, and it was due to her fear of the unknown that poor Izaak Kelly was tried at all.

"The crows . . . they talk to the devil," she continued. "They tell him things with their gutter speech and they watch us and they wait for us to fall asleep."

"Crows are just noisome, odious birds," Bartholomew declared. "For every crow there are a thousand songbirds, Eda. That is because the Lord rejoices in song. Trouble not your good self with the dirty cackling of crows."

"I'm afraid to go into the potato field without a handful of salt," she admitted. "They watch me from the trees."

"I'll have Fritz look into that," Bartholomew replied. "I'll see to it that a scarecrow is put into the field, Eda."

Eda began to relax. "Pray, my lord, do not direct the scarecrow out to sea that it look out and mock the world. The devil is clever."

The King exhaled slowly. He softened to the goodness of his people. "I want to hear no more frightful tales of crows and devils though they be clever. You are a clever woman with a potato, Eda."

She smiled out of humility. And though she knew that other women were just as clever with potatoes, she felt the warmth of the King through his words.

The King left the kitchen. He threw on a brown jerkin and headed for the barn where he kept his hunting gear. Fritz the gardener was at the grindstone, sharpening his tools. Briefly he told him about the scarecrow and how it might be fashioned. Then the King wished him well and bolted out of the barn. Soon he was alone in the fields outside of his home and he felt rejuvenated. Too much thought makes a man sick, he often said to himself. The best way to clear the mind was with action, not greater and greater thought. He walked out to a little copse less than a mile from his home. As a child, this is where he liked to hide when he wanted to be alone with his thoughts. There he lay down his pack and set his mind right for hunting. There he waited and waited, until . . .

The hare nibbled nervously on a tender piece of grass near the old [33]rowa n tree that grew along the Silverburn just outside of Ballasalla. The hare wrinkled its nose and twitched thoughtfully before taking another piece of grass into its quickly chewing mouth. Suddenly one of its ears twitched in a spasm as if a new sound was entering close by. Just then the fox poked his head up to see if it was being watched. The fox sniffed a few times, hoping to catch a scent. Then it quickly jerked its head, first right then left, looking for signs of danger. Sensing that it was safe to emerge from the safety of the bush it brought forth a slowly probing paw and inched forward in a stealthy crouch. But then it stopped abruptly as a new scent now became known to it. Still crouched down, its belly touching the dense patches of grass, it became aware of something new. The giant hare that it had been stalking was suddenly forgotten as a new sensation, a sensation of fear, mounted. The fox's head darted back and

---

[33] *Rowan. One of the nine sacred woods burned by Druids in Beltane Fires. Thought to protect against evil spirits and misfortune.*

forth because it was still trying to place a peculiar scent that it had caught hold of.

King Bartholomew, cunningly disguising his scent, crouched down in a clump of heather and slowly removed an arrow from his quiver. He had been waiting for a chance to get a shot at one of the giant hare that lived in the glen, but now he was interested in bigger game as he spied the careful advancement of the fox.

To catch a fox on the Isle of Man is not an easy thing to do. To catch a fox on the Isle of Man is a special thing. There are many places for the fox to hide, but there is something else, something less easily defined that has given the fox such an esteemed honor for being caught. It is believed that the fox have been endowed with the supernaturalism of the flowing cross-currents of witchery and Druidism and Christianity and the creeping lore of ancient Paganism. And from this brew, the fox has sampled from every rodent and fowl and mammal and tree. Therefore it is considered good luck for that the King seek out the fox and capture it. Over the years the tradition has taken on a new meaning as the Kings have been more reluctant and the fox have become more clever. In truth, Bartholomew had not captured a fox in many years, which was all the same to him. Nevertheless, the tradition remained, and though it was no more practiced, remnants of it remained and reemerged in new traditions.

He saw that the fox had become alert. It was aware that something was amiss and that there was a new danger to consider. Bartholomew tried to remain perfectly still and not to even move a finger. He could see the fox, but as of yet, the fox did not see him. The fox looked around carefully and thoroughly. When his gaze turned in the direction of Bartholomew, it stopped. Now the fox looked more carefully, and it was Bartholomew's judgment that the fox saw him and knew who he was. The fox now narrowed its glassy eyes and looked directly into Bartholomew's eyes. For a moment there was an understanding, a mutual respect that Bartholomew had never experienced before. There was something unsettling about the way the fox looked at him and Bartholomew had the impression that the fox was clever in more ways than one. Then the fox bared his teeth fiercely, turned and ran away into the brush.

Bartholomew jumped up and dashed after the fox as fast as possible. He ducked into the brush where he saw the fox disappear. The path dropped sharply and went down along an enclosed tunnel of overhanging, arched trees and thick bracken. The intrepid Bartholomew fell headlong into the narrow fissure and tumbled to the bottom unceremoniously. Dazed and disoriented, he stood up and brushed off his clothes. The fox had stopped and was ahead looking back at him. Taking a deep breath, the king charged forward again after the cunning fox. It looked as if the pathway had been carved through the living flesh of the forest. It was dark inside the tunnel, but Bartholomew could see where he was going through a shimmering of rays of light that cut through the thick canopy above. Bartholomew didn't stop to wonder at the existence of such a place because he was trailing the fox and he could see the furry tail ahead as it disappeared around bends in the pathway. He ran as fast as possible but the fox was always just out of reach. After almost an hour of chasing, Bartholomew stopped to rest, for he was exhausted and covered with sweat. He sat down right in the middle of the path and allowed himself to lay back. Soon he was asleep. When he awoke it was dark. He must have slept for hours he realized angrily. Jumping up, he looked around.

Bartholomew saw a strange light ahead. He tried to focus his vision on the light, but it was blinding to look at and he had to avert his gaze. With the passing of the light the forest closed in around him and the denseness of the air and the denseness of the darkness weighed on his tired body. The only illumination came from the strange manifestation ahead. Even being a King he was frightened, but his curiosity was stronger than his apprehension and he crept closer.

The light floated above the treetops, suspended. It was now revealed to be a brightly glowing orb and it radiated an inner light that could not be contained. He was certain that no light such as this had ever before shone upon the Isle of Man. The intensity of the light changed as it began to shimmer and pulse like the beating of a heart. Then the orb descended to earth and floated just above the ground. By degrees, the intensity of the light diminished until Bartholomew could distinguish a shape. Slowly forming out of the shining miasma the form of a man stood on the ground within the radiance of the soft light that surrounded his body like the corona around the moon.

King Bartholomew stood in awe. It was a fiery angel. The angel wore flowing white robes and in his hand he carried a scepter made of wood. He was tall and stately.

"Why have I been banished from your island?" said the angel defiantly.

"I do not know you," Bartholomew replied timidly, for he was thunderstruck by the apparition and did not know what to do. "It was not I that sent you away. Tell me who you are, and tell me why you have summoned me here so that I can serve you."

The angel softened a bit. "No, as you say, it was not you that has banished me. But it was one of your brethren, one of your blessed saints."

"What is your name?" Bartholomew asked suspiciously.

"I have many names, and I am called many things. Is it not enough for you to see that I am an angel?"

"If you are banished from the Isle of Man, how do you come to be here?" asked Bartholomew with growing awareness.

"You are not on the Isle of Man," the angel replied cryptically. "I could not come to you, so I have brought you to me. To catch a king is not an easy thing to do, but I have caught you."

"And why do you come to me?" Bartholomew responded as he realized his position had suddenly shifted.

"You are the lord of Man," said the angel. "It is important that I pay tribute, for I do not wish to rewrite the word of God."

"Nor do I," Bartholomew answered.

"There is much that I could teach you, if you were to take heed of my words. Much that is, has never been written into language, and much that will be has never been spoken."

"My time on this earth is limited," said the King. "Our precious lives run like swift water to the sea, for the slow moving water is easily diverted into shallow pools and becomes rank."

The angel smiled. "Do not think that you are mortal," he said. "Your existence is as ephemeral as your words though they be spoken by the mouth of God. All is illusion. Even your birth is an illusion. When you understand the knowledge which I will teach you, you will see that your very existence is also but an illusion. Do you suffer loss? Do you suffer pain or hunger? These things that you suffer are trappings and they tie you to a mortal body, but I say to you that you are not mortal. Wicked men would confine you into a body and then bury you alive when that body was no longer useful."

"Dust to dust!" Bartholomew declared emphatically.

"Dust is for men of the world and peasants and travelers cloaks," said the angel calmly.

"Heaven on earth: Is that what you would sell me in exchange for my soul and for my fealty?" Bartholomew spat angrily. He now knew that he was in the presence of an angel demon.

"Heaven, yes," replied the angel calmly. Then the angel pointed at the King. "Heaven yes, but not heaven on earth, for heaven is not such a place. Heaven is not a destination. Alas, heaven is that which all the trappings of earth and earthly possessions disguises, and hides from you. If I were to teach you that heaven is in the present moment and that the present moment be eternal, this is what heaven on earth is. If I tempt you, I do so out of love for mankind. You were born simply to make a choice, Bartholomew. All else is illusion. All else is folly."

"You have been judged!" thundered the King. "You have been judged and you have fallen from grace. And now you would seek to gather more fallen flesh into your fold."

The fallen angel contemplated for a moment. "I have loved God even before the Incarnation. I will love Him until the end of time, for to know Him is to love."

"You are wrong," said Bartholomew. "You are trying to trick me. Tell me your purpose so that I may understand, for I do not understand your clues."

"Your entire life you have been given clues, but you have chosen not to see them and not to acknowledge them. Surely you must know that there is no good and there is no evil. There is no right or wrong. There is no death. There is only a choice, a simple choice to make. That is the entire meaning of your life."

King Bartholomew was becoming exasperated. "I cannot understand you!" he cried. "Speak clearly unless it is your intention to deceive me."

"The choice is between gnosis and ignorance, and it is a choice between being and becoming. The purpose of [34]*pistis* is *pistis*, but gnosis is the first step toward immortality."

"Take your mysticism and be gone!" shouted Bartholomew. "I have no need for one that would twist the words of God."

"You do not have to die to find God," said the angel. "God exists inside of you, and to know yourself is to know God. And if you should die, you will never find him. I offer you the knowledge to cast off the flesh so that you may continue. If you refuse this choice, you will die and your spirit will disperse into the ocean of being, and you will no longer exist."

"Are you one of the *Watchers*? Are you a fallen angel? Would you come again to my island to mate with the daughters of men? Would you come again to join to the flesh of woman? No, I would not let you bring this evil to my people. I have no need of your counsel. Be gone, worm!"

The angel pointed the scepter at Bartholomew as if to smite him down with it, but relented instead and lowered his hand. He knew that Bartholomew would not yield to the temptation and that he had failed. The angel was deeply disappointed, for he truly loved the world of men and hoped one day to lead them. He looked closely at Bartholomew and saw that his faith was strong. There was nothing further to be gained from him.

"Where will you turn when the gods have all been extinguished?" the angel said finally.

"The Isle of Man has been washed clean with blood. We have no more need of serpents and fallen angels. Patrick swept clean the filth from our island. You will find no welcome there. His judgment is the judgment of the Lord."

---

[34] *Pistis. Greek word that is translated into English as faith. Foundational belief from which we take action.*

Then King Bartholomew turned to leave and as he walked away he heard the final proclamation of the fallen angel. The words angered him, but he did not turn around.

"You may well find your way off of my island, Bartholomew . . . some day."

King Bartholomew stood alone in the murky darkness of the forest of the fallen angel. The light seemed to radiate from the very vegetation like some dismal combination of opposing [35]humors from a rank and decaying, but still living, body. A dankness of washed-out color, the color of gloom, attached to the trees like clinging lichen. The very ground he stood upon felt soft and soggy like a vast hidden mire surrounding a dead land. He started walking along the path but he could not remember which direction to go. Realizing that it probably didn't matter which direction he walked, he walked straight ahead. Now the trees crouched lower and lower as their spindly branches came close to his head and held in a most suffocating atmosphere like the atmosphere of death. The King walked and walked until he became tired and weak. Of course there was no way out of such a loathsome and detestable place, and he knew it. He stopped and sat down on a patch of dry ground. Then he heard a noise that sounded like walking. Turning, he saw a tall man approach from the gloom. Bartholomew knew that it was another angel, a second angel. This angel was not as tall as the first and there was no hint of angelic beauty in his face. The second angel had a peaceful countenance, the countenance of one who has accepted a great burden but is content because it be unavoidable. There was no smile on the angel's face, but Bartholomew saw in the expression of calmness, something beautiful. He knew that this angel was different.

"Are you a *Watcher*?" asked the King. He didn't know what to expect, or whether he would be injured. There was no way to avoid meeting with this angel, so he walked up to the angel confidently like one of the proud Kings of old.

"I am Allistera," answered the angel. "Yes, I am a *Watcher*."

"I am trapped in your forest," said Bartholomew.

---

[35] *Humors. One of the four fluids of the body in Medieval physiology, including blood, phlegm, choler, and black bile. The dominance of these humors was thought to control the character and health of the body.*

"Do not fear," said Allistera. "I will lead you out of the forest, and I will allow no harm to befall you. I am also trapped in this forest, for I am a sentinel and I must guard this place lest other men are lured here and become lost."

"You are fallen?" asked Bartholomew.

"Sometimes I like to walk here in the forest," Allistera answered. "What I miss most are the conversations with the Lord, for he liked to wander his garden and dip his toe into cool streams."

"You spoke with the Lord?"

Allistera did not answer directly. Instead, he simply said. "One is merely to exist in the presence of the Lord for one to be eclipsed by His glory."

"Why did you disobey, Allistera? Tell me why you have fallen," asked Bartholomew passionately.

"Some of the *Watchers* became lost in the darkness," Allistera began. "The great separation of light into darkness was begun. It was at this time that a choice was offered, a choice between obedience and of the knowledge of all things. Some of the angels chose to be with the Lord and to serve His will. Other angels chose to follow the will of their own. Pride it was, but what is pride that it should separate us from love? We saw the flesh of men, and we wanted it for ourselves. Yes, I was one of these angels . . . the fallen ones."

The King bowed. He felt compassion but not anger for this angel. Indeed, he felt sadness because he knew that the flesh was weak. "I bear no ill will against you," he said.

Allistera bowed slightly in deference to the King. "My punishment I bear because I must," he acknowledged. "But I would have it otherwise, if it were within my power to change."

"How long have you been here?" Bartholomew asked.

"I have been here for eternity," said the angel. "The only actions which happen are actions which God allows to happen in time. Existence is outside of time, but God allows some things to be ordered. The life that you call your own is imprinted in the mind of God. In my arrogance I sought to be apart from God, so now I am apart from God."

"Do you watch this forest now?" Bartholomew said. "And are there other *Watchers* that live here?"

"I exist only now and only for you," Allistera answered. "When you are free from this realm, I will no longer exist in the mind of God but will be exhaled like a poisonous vapor when you are gone."

The King was confused. "Are you dead?" he inquired.

"There is no death," Allistera replied calmly. "There is only separation. You are the closest I will ever come to God again, "Allistera lamented. "And that is why I love you. Go now and remember my words. Our greatest punishment does not come from the Lord. Our greatest punishment is the darkness of separation. This is the great illumination of which your great sages and philosophers so carefully speak, and though it be hidden in words and symbols it be not hidden. God exists in all things, and all things are part of God."

"And you, Allistera. Are you also a part of God?"

"God has left me," Allistera said sadly. "When God leaves us, we become stone. Now I am a stone."

Allistera led the King down the path, and soon they were standing at the place that would take the King back to his own world. The *Watcher* motioned with his hand.

"You are free to leave," he said.

"The other *Watcher*, the one that tried to trick me," said the King. "What will happen to him?"

"The fox is clever," Allistera answered. "But men are not foxes, and they are not so easily controlled. And while it may be that men may hunt the fox, beware that you do not become too proud in the hunt. For in truth I tell you, the fox is not so clever as the mind of God."

"You do not sound evil," said Bartholomew, "though you exist in an evil place."

Bartholomew turned to leave. He took one last look at the *Watcher*, and then he climbed up the path. At the top of the path he looked down once more into the forest, and where the angel Allistera had stood, now only a giant hare remained.

King Bartholomew walked alone in the darkness, but he knew that he was not alone. He knew that he was never alone. The Lord was everywhere at all times, and he knew that the darkness of the evening sky was not enough to hide him from the eyes of the Lord.

Allistera had fallen into darkness when he desired a life of flesh. How was he so much different than that of a lonely King with a terrible secret and a love that was impossible? And yet the King punished those around him with no more blame than that they were to believe in silly folklore and sweep dust from their door with charmed corn brooms. King Bartholomew stopped in the road. The way forward led him back home. The way foreword led him to the acknowledgment of a sin to which he had gladly accepted. He could hide his secret from the people around him, but he could not expect a greater mercy than that which was given to a harlot long ago and that she be stoned to death even as she wept.

Bartholomew shed a tear in the darkness. Because for all the love and trust that was bestowed upon him, though he be just to the limit of his wisdom, he was himself a fallen angel. And those around him, though their love be great, be damned by his weakness. That the King, the ruler of men should also suffer the torment of the flesh was a bitter testament to the power of temptation. The laws of men were made to be molded and formed to maintain the integrity and authority of a State. But the laws of God were made to be followed. The laws of men were written to be righteous, but the laws of God defined righteousness. The pride of the angels was the pride that men accept with accolades and praises and signs of honor. How much greater is the pride of the Lord when men sacrifice their will to a greater authority than their own will be fulfilled?

The King headed home. It was pitch dark and he could see the splendor of the starry firmament and know that the crystal sphere withheld the vault of heaven beyond the seventh sphere. Once he was safely on the path that would take him to his home he began to relax. He thought to himself that the majesty of the Lord must be infinite for that He should condemn them to perdition and yet they still love Him. Raising his head to heaven he thanked God for guiding him these many years and keeping him safe. It was true, his tiny island was alive with the spirit of God, and if one were only to look carefully at the beauty of His work, they should be convinced that it was good. Before he went into the castle he stopped at one of his gardens and pulled out a beautiful flower for Iona. Then he went in and completely forgot that he was supposed to have brought something home for dinner.

"You've been off hunting all day, and all you can come home with is a flower?" said Iona with playful mockery as she took the flower from his fingers.

Bartholomew blushed and smiled sheepishly, for what else could he do? He didn't want to tell her what he was really doing. Could he tell her about angels and foxes and hidden realms and not frighten her by the sound of his own folly? She had waited up for him when all the other servants had long since gone to bed. She had waited near the window so that she would know of his approach and feel relieved. That is the way it had been and that is how it would be.

"Some hunter you are," she said, but there was a knowing smile on her face and her words were tender. Her love for her King was so complete that she was happy inside his happiness.

"Let's go into the pantry and forage," Bartholomew replied with a smile. And he reached for Iona's hand.

The Punishment of Loki the Enchanter

"What are you afraid of, Iona?" the King asked.

"I am afraid of being tricked," she answered.

"By the devil?" the King asked again.

"No," she answered. "I am not afraid of the devil because he cannot deceive me. I am afraid of an enchanter."

"There are no enchanters here, Iona."

"There are enchanters everywhere," she replied with conviction.

The subterranean passages that exist beneath Castle Rushen are legendary as they are mythical. The stories are varied, but they all recount the existence of underground passages and dwellings buried far within the depths beneath the castle. In most of these legends the door that leads down into the passageway is locked, sealed in perpetuity; this is to assure that no more brave, but unable and unprepared men are lost within the catacombs. These legends are not kept secret, and in truth it is legends such as these that have helped keep the spirit of the Manx forever turned inward and onward, for the spirit of the Manx is in their stories. But on the Isle of Man, these small legends do more to support the character than that of the legends and writings of folklore tell.

This tale, as recounted by King Bartholomew's long-time servant, is rich in detail but must not be judged as a textural account. Instead, it must be understood and seen through the eyes of Iona, and taken with a grain of salt . . . knowing the propensity of Bartholomew to say more with his words than the words alone. Thus, it is not certain just what Bartholomew was trying to say or to whom he was even speaking to. And then there is also the possibility that Bartholomew was merely telling a story . . . nothing more.

The obvious embellishments to the character of Bartholomew we leave intact for purposes of textural accuracy and consistency, because it is believed that these embellishments, filtered as they are through such an innocent and simple source, do much to uncover the character of the real man behind the legend. The hagiographic imagery we also leave untouched, for it is not the intent here to breakdown and analyze the document for contextual reasons, but only to present it forthwith.

. . . All day long it had rained, it had rained the night before, and it was raining now. The dampness of the air was so thick and heavy and the sky so pale and grey that King Bartholomew didn't feel like leaving his castle at all. Instead, he decided to stay inside and find something to do.

Never before was there a more handsome or brave King on the Isle of Man, for his battle-scars were in his heart and not on his face. His handsomeness was met however with only indifference and aplomb by the King, for he was not a vain man and had no use for the praise of other men. He courted many fair maidens in his fiery youth, but some people said that he had a secret love, a secret relationship that was doomed as it was heartbreaking for the King to endure, for he could not take the young lady as his wife for fear of upsetting the class caste of those feeble days. And so the King lived a secret life, a life of such passion that it often spilled into the many endeavors to which he put his hand.

One such endeavor was his adventure into the secret catacombs isolated beneath his castle. So, finding no reason to brave the inclement weather, he decided to survey the deepest interior of his castle for he was not unaware of their legendary existence.

When Bartholomew was a child he wanted to find new places to hide and new places to play in his castle. He was allowed to play anywhere he wished, but there was one place he invariably avoided. That place was in the lowest regions of the castle, regions that went even further beneath the wine-cellars and casks and cold-storage rooms with which he was only too familiar. There was a little door hidden behind a large wine-rack that he knew of. He asked his father about it once and he told him to forget about the door and that it did not lead to anywhere. Now that Bartholomew was himself a King, those words came back to him again and they made him wonder. And now he was down in the wine-cellar, moving the large wine-rack to see for himself if the door was something he needed to worry about or if his father were merely trying to protect him.

By the time he had emptied the huge wine-rack of all the thousands of old bottles of vintage wine, he was sweating though it was uncommonly cool in the wine-room. When the rack was empty he pushed the heavy, dusty rack away from the wall. The door was arched, carved to fit the aperture to which it was fitted. It was made from rough-hewn timber and was faded and glassy from the thick coats of resin that was used to seal it. Bartholomew reached for the handle which he was already expecting would have to be forced, but found that the door was unlocked. His curiosity increased dramatically. With him he had brought a heavy woolen cloak and a torch. He donned his cloak, lit the torch, and then opened the door.

A gentle rush of stale, fetid air blew into his face like a weak exhalation from centuries of built up tension finally being released again. He thrust the torch into the opening. The narrow way went down. There was a long flight of steps carved into the stone channel out of which the passageway down had been hewn. The sides of the passage were irregular as if they had been chiseled away hastily. Bartholomew set his foot down on the first step; it was damp and a little slippery. The torch wavered in the unstable air. The King was not afraid however. He took one more breath of good air from his home, and then he started his descent into the underworld.

The stairway went straight down and was cut into a circular winding path that went around and around a central axis, and always down. He had to be careful lest he slip and take a fall, but there was nothing to keep him alert and he soon fell into a mindless, hazy swoon as he continued to descend. Hours passed this way until he finally came to the bottom, many leagues below Castle Rushen.

The way now branched off from the main tunnel and disappeared on either side and vanished into darkness. Bartholomew took the left path because he didn't want to become lost and if he took only left turns he would always know where he was.

The air was stagnant, but it was breathable. The passageway was narrow and looked sinister in the shifting glow from the torchlight. The King pressed onward to find where such a forgotten and forsaken path could lead. Several times he stumbled on the uneven floor, but he did not fall. After almost an hour, he was ready to turn back and concede that there was nothing down here. He stopped to rest his legs for a moment before heading back, and that is when he heard a noise, a faint cry. He lunged forward and just a little further down the corridor he saw something that shocked him out of his lethargy. On a raised platform, a dais carved from the moldering stone within, was a strange creature. The creature was chained to the dais by heavy chains that were driven deep into the stone. It was moving awkwardly and it was trying to speak. The King got closer until he realized that it was a man, or what had once been a man, for it was completely encased in a mane of wooly, matted hair from a hundred lifetimes of existence.

"Are you here to save me?" harkened the entreaty of a soft voice coming from the mass.

Bartholomew could not see the face and only a few hairs moved to indicate where the sound was coming from. "Who are you?" said the King.

"My name is Loki," the weak voice sounded.

"Why are you chained to this rock?" the King demanded to know. "Tell me, Loki, who did this to you?"

"This is my punishment," answered Loki. "I was an enchanter in life, but now I am nothing."

"Who did this to you?" Bartholomew asked again.

"Patrick," answered Loki strangely, as if Bartholomew should know.

"I know of no Patrick," Bartholomew said warily.

"The snake charmer banished me from the world, but he is no longer living. Is my punishment over?"

"Are you a snake?" the King asked decisively.

"I was once a man, in life. Now I have been banished from my own world and forced to remain in the netherworld of Patrick's punishment."

"Do you mean Patrick the Bishop, Loki?"

"The apostle of Kilpatrick," Loki said. "He bound me in chains until one day when I should be released by a just and powerful King."

"What King?" Bartholomew insisted. "Tell me which King it is for to release you from perdition."

"Perhaps you are that King," said Loki. "Tell me, does the world still exist?"

"The world exists in a state of grace," said Bartholomew.

"He said that a powerful King would come to me when my punishment was over and that the compassion of this King would be felt throughout his kingdom."

And so it was that on that day, King Bartholomew released Loki the Enchanter from his chains and unleashed a great evil back into the world of Man. The compassion King Bartholomew felt for all living things was natural to his heart, but the King was deceived by the great deceiver.

"I release you," declared King Bartholomew ceremoniously. And with the giant heft of his arm, he hewed the chains from the stone on which Loki was imprisoned.

In an instant the illusion conjured by Loki the Enchanter dissipated into a watery fog. King Bartholomew watched helplessly as the consequences of his actions slowly became known to him. The mist cleared and the scales fell away from the King's eyes as he beheld the true form of Loki the Enchanter. The Enchanter was young and virile. He had a sharp, Roman nose with a powerful jaw and deep black hair and his eyes were dark and mystifying as if his malice emanated from his eyes. He had the physical attributes of an athlete, but Bartholomew could not trust this illusion either, lest he turn into another creature more hideously endowed. The Enchanter winked, and then he was gone.

The King chased the Enchanter with renewed vengeance and would surely have put him back in chains, but he lost him in the long passageway back to the castle as the Enchanter filled the tunnel with visions of demons and slippery serpents and thick mist. In the distance Bartholomew could hear his terrible laugh and he remembered the sound forever more, for it was the terrible sound of his laugh that gave away his identity to the King.

Loki the Enchanter set off to terrorize the good people of Man. His evil was manifested in stages, with each subsequent stage becoming more evil and more violent. There were sightings of strange vapors and weird shifting winds and sheet lightning, followed by the disappearance of a sheep or a chicken. Schools of silvery, luminous fish washed up on shore and burst open. Wild animals jumped off cliffs into the sea. Barns were mysteriously set ablaze during the night and everywhere would be heard the strange laughter that came to be feared by all. At first it was just the loss of an animal or two which would alert the people that the sorcerer was in their midst, but slowly the transgressions took on a darker, more sinister tone and the people were frightened to leave their homes. In a small village just north of Peel several people died from poisoning, and when they discovered the source of the poison, it turned out that the soil in the village was putrid and malignant. Further investigation uncovered a mutilated corpse buried in the garden of one home. In another village, an old woman was found dead in her turnip patch and there was an expression of deathly fear on her face. The people were afraid to eat turnips after that until the turnips turned black and sprouted poisonous boils. Most of all the children were frightened at night and would not sleep in their own beds. Rumors spread that a hungry goblin was stealing children from their beds and chewing their faces off. More panic spread when the sleeping sickness struck a village near Cronk Dhoo. When a concerned Manxwoman went to the house of her dear aunt it was discovered that all the people in the village were frozen dead, their souls taken away in their sleep.

The King would always arrive too late to prevent the terrible events from happening. Once in Kirk Michael a strange waterspout was seen racing across the meadow, and once above the standing stones at Ballaharra, in the village of St. John's, a ghost was seen. Strange happenings were reported around ancient, prehistoric sites, and sometimes the carcass of a captured animal would be found, ritually killed and eaten. Other times the stones would be awash in blood but no carcasses would be found. A creeping, lingering sickness soon came to these ancient places and some of the trees died or petrified. The simple and innocent women outside of the larger villages reported spectral mists that would envelope them in thick clouds of vapor, and then they would suddenly become alive with child or become disoriented and fall into the sea. King Bartholomew knew that he had to do something. He needed help to fight such a foe as could transmogrify into torrid vapors and creatures of the air.

King Bartholomew humbled himself and acknowledged his limited wisdom to understand all the horrors and evils weighing on the world. He prayed for the intercession of Patrick, hoping that the saint would surely sympathize with his plight. His solemn pleas were heard and the intercession came after he finished morning prayers. And now Bartholomew went about the countryside with an aura surrounding his purpose and an aureole above his head, and there was a reverence, a sense of holiness about him. Those that saw him in those days knew, for his essence surrounded him like a halo of glory.

And now King Bartholomew chased Loki the Enchanter from one end of the island and back again. He chased him day and night, matching the Enchanter's shape-shifting, illusion spinning wizardry with an equal measure of wizardry of his own. Loki would fling a tornado at the King, and the King would turn it into a helpless puff of smoke. Loki would transform into a hawk, and the King would swiftly turn into a falcon. Loki would attempt to burn down a village, and the King would bring forth a tempest from the dust. The King was always one step behind the Enchanter, but he was getting closer.

Exhausted, the King returned home late one night to his castle. He was tired and weary and in need of rest. And so it was that the woman of his life was there to help him. It was she that tended to his needs and it was she that tended to his failing health and failing resolve and listened to him as he poured out his heart to her in the darkness. It was she that was always there to care for him when he was weak and in need of the nourishing effects of selfless love. The name of this woman is now lost to history, but surely such undying, unyielding love never existed before on the Isle of Man.

What the King did not know was that the Enchanter had followed him home to his castle. The King was weak and he was not able to perceive the danger he was bringing back home with him. The lady tended and comforted him during his long hours of darkness of mind and darkness of spirit, for in truth, it was he that had loosed such evil upon his land and it was he that must bear the crushing burden. In the King's darkest hour, the lady came to him during the night, and their embrace was discovered by the first rays of morning light that streamed in through his open window. He kissed the lady and was with her in all his heart and he was sad, unbearably sad for the strictness of protocol that prevented him from taking her as his wife. He kissed her on the head and left the room quietly, comforted in the knowledge that she would never be discovered or disgraced and that she would always be with him. But when the King closed the door behind him, something terrible and frightening happened.

A faint tapping at the door woke the lady from her sleep and she smiled as the King came back into the room. He began removing his clothes but would not look directly into her eyes.

"Are you sick?" the lady asked. She sat up and instinctively covered her nakedness from sheer modesty. "Is the hunt now over?"

The King smiled faintly and suppressed an urge to laugh. He said nothing but only continued to undress. His eyes were glazed over like the dead eyes of a crow. The lady looked at him with deep concern, for she feared that something terrible would happen soon.

"Would you like me to bring you some warm milk?" she uttered softly.

The King stood naked before her and held her with his gaze. Then he pulled the covers aside with a quick sweep of his hand and crawled into bed. The lady felt suddenly frightened as a cold revulsion spread through her body. Her mouth opened in a silent scream just as the King pressed his hungry lips to her quivering mouth.

Bartholomew went into the stable to retrieve his horse. The hour was still early and he tried to be quiet lest he wake his good servants, asleep in their bed. He patted his horse and gave her a few grains of wheat from his hand. Then he reflected for a moment on the terrible wrath that his arrogance had wrought, for he was so easily tricked by the Enchanter when his own pride was so malevolently praised with sweet words about his wisdom. He now knew that all wisdom is the wisdom of the Lord, and all pride is false pride, for in truth, the Lord alone can work wisdom through our weak bodies.

He strapped the saddle on and climbed up with the reins. Slowly he walked his horse out of the stable and onto the path. Saying a silent prayer to give him strength, he tried to see in his mind where the Enchanter was now hiding. In his mind all he could sense was the anger and ugliness of Loki. He could feel his endless lust for deceit and all things broken. Finally Bartholomew nudged his horse onto the path and with his heels brought his horse to a gallop. He turned onto the road leading out of Ballasalla and bolted down the road. But after a few moments he had such a visceral sense of revulsion that he stopped in the middle of the road and nearly fell off his mount. He knew something was terribly wrong. Whipping the reins around, he galloped as fast as possible back to his castle and hoped that he was not too late.

King Bartholomew burst into his sleeping chamber with his sword drawn, for he knew what he would find. Loki was struggling with the lady who fought to defend herself against the Enchanter. Bartholomew leveled his sword against the Enchanter and sliced the blade across his arm as he tried to disengage himself from the woman. In a moment, Loki the Enchanter had found his sword and engaged the King in a bloody battle that raged from wall to wall. King Bartholomew was brave and fearless as he fought and mounted staggering, lunging attacks. His arms were thick and strong as oak trees and his hair shone bright against the darkness of his foe. They fought a frightful battle and the Enchanter grew more furious.

But this time Bartholomew had the upper hand because he was a trained swordsman and the Enchanter was already injured. Now the King had his foe backed up against a wall, but just as he was about to deliver the final blow, the Enchanter transformed into a small bird and flew toward the open window to escape certain death. And this is when the lady helped seal the fate of the Enchanter, for just as the Enchanter was about to fly out the casement, she threw the heavy windowpane closed just in time. The Enchanter slammed into the leaded glass with such tremendous force that he was knocked insensible. The King quickly bound the small bird with strong wire and sealed him in a cage. Thus was Loki the Enchanter brought to justice by King Bartholomew and his mystery lady.

And so it was decreed by the King on the following day that such punishment as he saw fit, should befall the Enchanter. He held Loki the Enchanter, still in the form of a bird, between his strong hands and he fought bravely against the temptation to tear him to pieces. Instead, he decreed.

"I hereby banish you from the world of men to inhabit a world of stone until such time as Patrick releases you or the Lord set you free. With no eyes with which to see, and with no voice with which to speak, I condemn you to a private perdition."

Then the King nodded his ascent and the punishment of Loki the Enchanter was carried out. Several men brought forward two halves of a cleaved stone. Between the stones a small hole had been carved away. The King handed Loki the Enchanter to one of the men. The bird had been banded tightly with bands of metal; the eyes had been sewed closed, and the beak had been bound together with wire. The bird was placed inside the hole and the stones then were closed together and bound with a prayer that the King spoke softly to himself. Then the stones were removed to a lonely spot at Cronk Karran and planted in the ground where they await the coming of the Lord. It is sometimes said that from time to time curses can sometimes be faintly heard coming from the monolith, but that is just a legend. And so it shall ever more be called, "The Standing Stone of Loki." Such was the wisdom of King Bartholomew, King of Man.

Edward the Dreamchaser

The King sat in a well-padded chair near the open window and smoked. It was late, but only a single candle burned brightly on the nightstand. Iona tapped lightly on the door before entering.

"Are you alright?' she asked cautiously. Often she found him sitting alone in the darkness, and she was always reticent to ask him why.

"I feel another nightmare coming on," said the King. "I have no wish to fall asleep this night."

"Don't think about your dreams," Iona suggested. "Perhaps if you try not to think about them, you will not have them."

The King looked up and with tired eyes said: "Well then, perhaps I should pay someone to worry for me."

King Bartholomew was often haunted by strange, foreboding and peculiar dreams . . . nightmares, his entire life. No one could ever remember a King with such a penchant for such ominous dreams. Some people called them visions and they begged to hear all the King's dreams until they became much discussed by the good people of Man in the local taverns and pubs. Astrologers and men of learning were convinced that inside the dreams of the King were contained elements of secret and sometimes esoteric knowledge. Court pages were assigned to record the King's dreams on paper if he happened to mention one during breakfast. The King would smile whenever he had a dream to describe because he knew that it would keep them busy for hours. Sometimes it was even suggested that the King invented his own dreams for the purpose of entertaining those that chose to pay attention, but in truth, King Bartholomew had no reason to invent his dreams and he was always honest in such matters.

One morning during breakfast King Bartholomew was unusually late. The cooks had endeavored to keep everything warm, but unfortunately the bacon was overcooked and the coffee became bitter. When Bartholomew came down the stairs he had a curious smile on his face. Iona noticed it right away.

"Did you have an interesting dream?" she asked. "Or was it perhaps a nightmare?"

Still smiling, Bartholomew sat down at the table and poured himself a cup of coffee from the pot. His hair was uncombed as if the thought had completely slipped his mind, which was unusual for the handsome and meticulous King.

"You may want to wake Edward," he said with a knowing smile. "I think this one will interest him greatly."

Edward the Dreamchaser, as he was called, readied his pen and prepared to record the royal dream. His dream chasing abilities were renowned throughout all of royal society and he was sometimes sent for and escorted in carriages to country estates and bourgeois homes tucked away beneath towering tree lined avenues. But the services of a Dreamchaser are often fickle and he had allowed himself to become stagnant, comfortable and predictable in the King's retinue. In truth, he sometimes lamented that the King's dreams were more important than the substance of his own life. Alas, it is as it was and forever will be, until once again everything becomes new.

"It was the strangest thing," said Bartholomew. "I dreamed that I was sitting down for a meal just like I am now. Only, in my dream, I didn't know if it was breakfast, lunch, or dinner because the table at which I was sitting was prepared with all three meals together."

"That is very interesting," said Edward the Dreamchaser writing furiously and trying to follow the line of thought coming from the King. "But tell me now sire, was there more to this dream that just food?"

"Oh, much more," answered Bartholomew. "I am just getting started. At the table was every meal I have ever eaten."

"That is impossible!" Edward interrupted spiritedly.

"It is true," Bartholomew responded with conviction. "Even meals that I remember eating as a child and meals that I refused to eat as a child were there on this table."

"All this was on one table?" Edward asked in order to confirm the King's statement lest he ascribe to the dream more than was intended.

"It was a large table," Bartholomew responded. "Miles and miles of food filled this table, hundreds and thousands of miles of food in truth. It was everything I could ever ask for."

King Bartholomew helped himself to some eggs kept warm for him on a covered tray. Then he went for some bacon because he could never eat eggs without bacon. His toast was already buttered and sliced diagonally. The fruit he passed over, considering such colorful delicacies little more than decorations. He stuffed an entire piece of bacon in his mouth and washed it down with a sip of tepid coffee. This breakfast was not up to his expectations, but he was so excited about his dream that he thought he could let it pass. Then he continued to eat voraciously all the while watching Edward making notes and annotations to his text.

Edward looked up. "Did you eat any of it?" he said, preparing to write down the response. "Did you sample any of the food?"

"Well, yes I sampled some of it," Bartholomew responded. "And do you know what I discovered? Each meal and each particular dish corresponded with a particular memory. In a strange way, I was reliving my entire life through the associations I had made with food."

"This is very interesting," Edward had to agree. "Your memory of your life had become transformed into food. How charming, Bartholomew."

The King tried to dunk a corner of a piece of toast in egg-yoke, but the yoke was already too hard and his toast too dry. He dropped his toast and looked up.

"And some of the dishes were a real mystery to me until I tasted them, at which time the memory would come rushing back like a bitter aftertaste."

"An aftertaste you say? I see."

"Yes, but perhaps the word aftertaste does not quite describe the experience. Imagine this," he said. "There is one memory of a potato that I have . . ."

"A potato? Did you say a potato, sire?" said Edward, continuing to write furiously.

"Indeed. Now then, when I tasted this potato . . ."

"The potato in your dream, or the real potato, sire?' asked Edward cautiously but fearing more the possibility of getting the dream wrong.

"The real potato," Bartholomew answered curtly. "Now then, when I tasted this potato the first time, it was so hot that I burned my mouth. Well, when I burned my mouth I stood up so fast that I fell backward in my chair and banged my head on the floor until I saw stars. Now, every time I eat a potato, I see stars."

"I see," said Edward the Dreamchaser. "Is there more?"

"When I tasted the potato in my dream I did not see stars, Edward. Instead, I saw a beautiful woman I had once known."

"In your head, Bartholomew? You saw her in your mind, like the stars?"

"No, Edward. I saw her sitting at my table as if she too, were nothing more than a delicacy, a tender fruit for me to sample."

"Well now. What did she say, Bartholomew? Do you remember what she said?"

Bartholomew set down the pepper shaker he was peppering his eggs with and unconsciously reached for the salt even though he had already salted his eggs. Spreading some marmalade across his cold toast, he said.

"She said that she thought she was dreaming and that it was very strange for me to have followed her into her dream. But when I told her that I too, was dreaming, she demanded that I go away and leave her alone."

"Do you remember anything else? Do you remember what you were wearing? Do you know what time it was?"

"At one point, I reached the end of the table. There was one more dish there. But somehow I knew that this dish was different. Somehow I knew that this dish was to be my last meal, and were I to eat it . . ."

"You would die?" Edward said, finishing Bartholomew's thought.

"That is exactly right," said the King. "It is almost as if you were there."

"But tell me, Bartholomew, how did you know that you would die? How did you come to understand?"

"I knew because it was the one meal I always wanted to eat, but to this day I have never tasted it. I have never found anyone that can prepare it for me."

"What is it?" Edward said.

"It is called spaghetti," the King answered. "The dish is commonly hidden beneath a thick layer of sauce so that it is completely buried. Next to it was a piece of my favorite pie, Rhubarb. But now I can never eat this dish or I am afraid that I will die."

"Extraordinary," said Edward. "You have been given a rare vision. This is not only a vision of the future, no indeed. It is a vision of the past and how it can once again be lived into the future. You have been given a second chance, Bartholomew. Congratulations."

"I don't understand," said Bartholomew.

"There is a great feast prepared for you, Bartholomew. But first you must accept what has happened in the past. Great things await you."

"But of course I have to die first in order to receive these gifts. Perhaps I should save that for the future, Edward."

Just then, a servant came into the room carrying a tray. A silver cover prevented him from seeing what was on the tray, but his nose knew.

"I have brought you a special treat, sire," said the servant. Then she took the cover off the tray revealing a golden brown, Rhubarb pie. "I made this especially for you," she said with joy.

King Bartholomew looked at the pie and smiled. Then he looked at Edward and smiled again. The Dreamchaser held his pen ready in case there were more words that needed to be written. Bartholomew smiled again as the irony of the situation dawned on him.

"What should I do with this?" he said to the Dreamchaser.

"Slide that over here," said Edward the Dreamchaser. "You should better not even take a chance."

And then they both laughed heartily even as the servant girl left the room shaking her head in bewilderment.

The King's Terrible Dream of Infinity.

What could be so terrible about eternity? Why does everyone want it with their mind but fear it with their heart? Do not fear death if it be not eternal. And if there is no eternity and our life should suddenly cease . . . what then? Indeed, what then . . .?

The King retired to his chamber early. He had a slight headache and the soft tissue between his bones was sore and swollen. The King was feeling old this night, and as if his age had finally caught up with him after years of pursuit, he accepted his growing condition. So, lighting a lantern and stopping to ask Iona to bring him a cup of hot milk, he slowly treaded the empty stairs to his royal chamber.

He set the lantern on his nightstand and changed into his bedclothes. While he was slipping his feet into his wool slippers Iona came in with a tray. She smiled gently to her King, the kind of smile that only many years of familiarity can give, but it was a smile of tenderness as she could see that he was in pain.

"I thought you might like something sweet to help you sleep," she said. "So I have brought you hot chocolate."

"Is there to be a storm tonight, Iona?" asked the King. "I always feel sick before a storm. My mother used to tell me that sickness was caused by bad thoughts." The King smiled to himself as the memory came flashing back through time.

"You were a young boy and that was many years ago," said Iona with playful compassion. "What bad thoughts could occur to such a young boy?" and then she laughed.

The King took the cup from Iona. Then he sat on the edge of his bed but continued to look at Iona as another thought occurred to him.

"Why have you never married, Iona?" the King suddenly asked awkwardly as if the very idea of a life of her own had suddenly occurred to him, or that his own discomfort had only just now reminded him that there were other people in the world.

Iona was surprised by the suddenness of such a question from the King. The King was given to frequent stages of melancholy, and Iona was always there to listen to his raving. Iona knew that the King needed someone that would listen to him without judgment, and Iona never uttered a single bitter word in his presence. But she did not expect such a direct question, and never one directed at her. Iona blushed in the flickering light.

"I have wanted to serve you since you were very young," she said. "You were the most handsome man on the island . . . and I fell in love with . . ." Iona checked herself. "I love to hear your stories," she admitted. "If I were to marry, my lord, I should never hear your stories again."

The King had been looking down. He raised his eyes to look into the face of his faithful servant and they were moist with hidden tears. Looking at her now, the King realized that as Iona had aged, so had he. Alas, they had aged together.

"Thank you for the kindness you have shown me for these long years," said King Bartholomew suddenly and without modesty. "I don't know how many more stories I shall be allowed to tell you, but I am glad that you have listened to me."

"I shall draw you a hot bath in the morning," said Iona. "Tomorrow you will be feeling much better I predict." Then Iona left the room and Bartholomew watched her fade into the darkness of the hall and he wondered just for a moment where she would go.

The King sipped his chocolate and shuffled over to the window. Raising his astrolabe to the heavens hastily he was forced to put it down again as a large cloud passed overhead and sealed the heavens from the King's questioning gaze. And in a mood of uncertainty the King went to bed.

But as the King slept the clouded heavens and the endlessly spinning universe continued to revolve over a single point that was his tiny castle. The air became thick and damp as a creeping mist swept across the island. Sometime during the night the mist turned to a downy white fog, and it was during this time that the King slept a fitful sleep and was visited by such a terrible dream of infinity . . .

The King looked and looked and looked, but he could not find it. Where was it? Where could it have gone? The King turned over every stone, looked beneath every rock, and searched every inch of his kingdom until every inch of his kingdom was revealed, but he still could not find it. The King asked every person he had ever known but none could say. In his exasperation he had talked to every wise man, every sorcerer, every sage, witch, wizard, bishop and town crier, but none could tell him.

Finally the King sat down on a stone and began to lament. He lamented everything he had ever said, and he lamented everything he had ever done. He lamented his birth, and then a moment later, he lamented his death though he was not dead. He lamented everything he ever knew and he lamented everything there was left to be known, and still he lamented. Then he lamented everything he could not think to lament, and still he was not satisfied. Finding nothing else to do he turned and kicked the rock with all his strength.

The King started walking. He walked until he came to the end of his kingdom, and finding nothing better to do, he walked back to the place from where he began. Then he waited. Finding nothing better to do he started walking again. This time he walked back and forth until it was certain that he had walked over every single inch of his kingdom, but still he was not satisfied. Finally, having nothing better to do, he started walking in circles. He walked and walked and walked until he fainted from exhaustion. When he woke there was a small child staring at him and he waited to see what the child would do. The child waited. Finally, having nothing better to do the King asked the child why it was there.

"I'm waiting," said the child.

"What are you waiting for?" asked the King.

"I don't know," said the child. "That is why I am waiting."

"But you need to do something," said the King. "You can't just sit there and do nothing! Time is short. Do something."

"If you tell me what to do then I will do it," said the child. "But if you do not tell me what to do I will have to wait."

"Wait for me," said the King. And then he ran away as fast as he could.

This time the King was even more intent on finding what he was looking for. He could not remember what it was, it was important only to find it again. He retraced every step that he had ever stepped and every inch of land that he had ever searched in case he had missed it, but it could not be found. Finally the King had to accept the fact that what he was looking for was not in his kingdom any longer. But where could it have gone? It had escaped his kingdom.

Having nothing better to do the King decided to leave his kingdom. The King thought and thought but he could not remember how to get out of his own kingdom so large had it become. Finally he had to accept the fact that he was trapped. Finding nothing to kick, the King let out a terrible cry that penetrated every inch of his kingdom and every creature great or small feared for the King.

The King was tired and exhausted unto death and he decided to go back home and maybe then he could remember what he was looking for. After a single step the King stopped. He couldn't remember how to get home! His kingdom was all around him, but where was his home?

The first person the King came to was a simpleton. After asking the simpleton where his home was the King waited for a reply.

"You must retrace every step and undo every action to get back to your home," said the simpleton. "Your home has been buried beneath the weight of your life."

Surely the simpleton was much too simple to know anything for sure the King decided. Then he started walking again until he met a man on the road selling potatoes.

"You're going in the wrong direction," said the man scratching his beard. "Home is a tricky place to find you know. One moment it is all around you, and then the next moment it is gone."

"Gone?" asked the King.

"Every step that one makes takes one further and further from home until home is lost into infinity. Forget about it," said the man. "If you want my advice, never call a place your home." And with that said, the man offered the King a potato.

Every person the King met was a simpleton. The King wondered what had happened to his home. None of the people he met recognized him. They all had heard tales about a King that had ruled in ancient times, but that was long ago.

The King wandered and wandered for many years. His face became hardened by the wind and a long beard covered his once beautiful face. He was now worn *and walked with a slight limp as he bent his back to the wind. The birds landed on his arm and spoke to him in a language that he came to know. The King wandered and wandered until he forgot that he was once a King, and there came a day when he stopped along the road to take a rest.*

Squinting through his failing eyesight the King saw a child standing next to him. What kind of a world was this where children were abandoned in the road? The King looked long and hard at the boy. The boy smiled.

"Are you lost?" asked the King.

"I am waiting," answered the boy.

"For what?" said the King.

"I have been waiting for you," said the boy. "I have been waiting to take you home."

The King woke with a start. He was sweating profusely and his body was slick with perspiration. Throwing the covers off his body he set his feet on the cold floor and got out of bed. Then he went to the window and opened the shutter. A cold wind blew into his face.

The Story of the King

"Are all these stories really true?" Iona asked. She saw the distant look in his face, the glassiness of his eyes, and she wondered just where he had been and from where he had just returned.

"That all depends, Iona," said the King slowly. "It depends on who is writing them, and it also depends upon who is reading them. All stories are true in a way. I guess it depends on what it is that you think the story is."

She laughed: "Then how is anyone supposed to know what the story is? If it is different for everyone, how is that a story?"

"Alas, perhaps we only see ourselves in every story, Iona. Every story is a mirror."

Everything passes away into eternity and nothing that is old is ever new again. One never steps into one's own footsteps and the further one walks the further away one draws, for the destiny of us all is like smoke. Our good intentions are like smoke. Smoke . . . all is smoke. But all things must pass as all seasons submit and come to pass in measure, for the Lord is wise and the Lord's will be done.

The good King Bartholomew liked to sit at his window and stare out over his kingdom. His kingdom was not large and he had no inclination to make it larger; in truth, he loved it the way it was. Instead, his thoughts were directed elsewhere. The King liked to write fairytales. Yes, in those past days there were many fantastic stories told by passing minstrels and troubadours, and alehouses were often filled with hearty Manxmen anxious to hear all tales told. Folklore and fairytale was as much a part of the Isle of Man as was the very soil from which the saints lay moldering. Many fairytales told in those days were written for children and it was for the sake of the children that these stories be told. Traditions were traditional and were meant to be followed. King Bartholomew had another idea, a wonderful idea . . . he had an idea of his own. He would write fairytales for aged men and aged women, and it twas his desire to make them younger but for having heard his stories, even as his own heart had become younger so much the more he told them.

Sleep could come easy to the hard-working Manxman, for his day was filled with fishing nets and fishing boats, potatoes, herring, and toil; but sleep came not so easy to a king, for King Bartholomew worked even in his sleep when it should come though he often woke tired and sweating for his labor. And it was said that a light could always be seen at night in the King's window, burning into the long hours of the nighttime, and that sometimes he could be seen walking inside his room. Indeed, in those times as in these days, the labors of one could be calculated in pounds and inches and blood and sweat, while the labor of another man could only be calculated in dreams and promises and expectations even though his eyes be shut or he soak alternately in tubs of hot water.

The aged King lit a candle and picked up a newly sharpened quill pen, and in the dreamy half-light of dusk he began to write . . .

Once there was a man, a lonely man who only sat near his window and thought about being a King. In those days, for this happened many years from now, all men were considered kings, and though their kingdom be small, all that was due to their kingship was their own.

Now in those days, days far distant and yet to come, Finn McCool . . .

The King set down his pen and sighed. "No," he said. "This will not do at all. I must do something different, something that is different."

With that the King sat up and went to the window. His garden below him trembled silently in the gloaming and the memory of his mother came to him like a specter that waited for him to appear as if he too were a specter. Sometimes when he walked in the garden late at night he could almost hear the gentle sigh of her and he liked to imagine that her spirit still walked the serpentine paths looking for King Sigmus, for in this way she remained young in his mind and the memory of her death pallor diminished. He looked down now into that magical garden and his mind drifted away to other, strange vistas. He leaned against the window sash and his eyes glazed over.

When he turned away from the window it was dark inside his room but for the single candle burning at his writing desk. He went to his desk and sat down again. Then he took up his pen again and began to write.

*In a far away distant future time when men had no need of Kings and Queens;
when the mortal borders between countries no longer were recognized and
defended with blood and bone; when all evil and all evil intentions were
contained, for the work of the Lord was complete; in such a distant time as this
in an idyllic time lived an idyllic man. All men were their own King in this
idyllic time, but he did not call himself a King, instead he called himself John
and those who knew him called him John.*

*Crops grew in abundance and needed only to be harvested by those that were
intent on harvesting; the world overflowed with abundance, and livestock
roamed the earth unmolested until they too should be harvested for there was no
joy in killing; all joy was derived by eating. Men continued to work in guilds
because knowledge was vast and needed to be passed on by those that could make
use of it, and this knowledge was bartered because it was fair and because it was
good. In this way the world was built and the skills of all men were important
to some. Many skilled men were skilled at trading the skill of other men though
they themselves did not possess those skills, and in this way the world fell into
the hands of guilds of men with no other skill than to connect the needs of the
many with the skills of the few.*

*All magic was forgotten in this time for there were no mystical and ghostly
events that could not be explained and it was the purpose of luminous men to
explain all things. And so, many guilds were created by these brilliant men,
who joined together with no other skill than their fundamental brilliance, and
they were skilled at making decisions for other men to follow; and the people
were happy to do so because they were safe. One day a bitter frost came early
and many crops were destroyed. Brilliant men set to work to explain this new
phenomenon for this had never happened in anyone's memory before. The
brilliant men consulted history books to know if such a thing could be natural or
unnatural. In the end it was determined that such things were natural and that
there was nothing to fear and the people rejoiced and learned to preserve food for
such times of bitter need. In this way all fears were alleviated and the people
knew no fear. When a child would be killed by a wild animal the people knew
that these things were natural and their sorrows would be assuaged because the
brilliant men said it would be so.*

*At night the people would gather together to listen to these luminous men read
from books because there was no need for all men to learn to read. The luminous
men never read books from the past, but instead read books about the future and
how wonderful it would become. Like the men, the women also liked to hear
stories about the future and it was for them to help the men establish such a
world; all things were good and it was good to help in all things. Stories about
the past and the past ways of men were considered unsuitable and the people*

*scorned them, for the world was the way God intended it to be, the luminous
men said it was so . . .*

King Bartholomew looked up from his writing; the candle had gone out
and he had fallen asleep. "Who's there?" he called out into the darkness.
Then, rubbing his eyes he resigned himself to sleep. "It is late," he said.
"Tomorrow is another day," he continued. Then he shuffled across the
thick rug to his bed and slept the rest of the night.

He woke with the strong scent of tea in his nostrils. Iona was in the
room preparing his breakfast. She was his most trusted servant and his
affection for her had only grown fonder over the years. It was Iona that
would listen to the King as he told her wild stories long into the night
and speculated about how it would be, and he had nothing to prove to
her, for she was his friend and would never betray that trust. Iona knew
of the King's fondness for her and in her heart she was content to be near
him. Bartholomew watched her deft hands as she prepared the tea and
arranged a few pieces of fruit and a scone with blackberry jam on a plate.

"Oh," she exclaimed. "You're awake I see. Are you hungry this
morning sire? It is a lovely day and the birds are singing in the garden."

"I hear them Iona," Bartholomew answered. "Our hermit thrush has
found a new home I see."

"Yes, I heard him singing this morning," she said. "The garden is filled
with music, for sweet is the song of the Lord."

"Yes it is," he agreed with a smile. "And so is the fruit from your hand,
Iona."

Later that day King Bartholomew rode with one of his guards and a local
deemster, to a little hamlet along the Herring Road near the village of
Peel. An extraordinary story was being told by local fishermen of a
gigantic sea serpent prowling the icy waters, and some of the fishermen
refused to go back into the perilous waters until the serpent was
destroyed. The men were saying that the creature had returned.
Herring was the blood of the island, and were it not for the gigantic
shoals of the silver fish many would go hungry and lose their livelihood,
for to work on the Isle of Man was to work the sea.

At a small inn near the road King Bartholomew met with a few of the most outspoken fishermen, many of whom claimed to have seen the monster. Outside the inn hung a sign that read *Mac Killian's*, and below the sign was the carving of a giant herring, with the silver cup of Manannan mac Lir, in its mouth. The proprietor was a man named Jole Mac Killian, and before him his father and his father's father worked the inn, and in this way *Mac Killian's Inn* had faithfully served the kipper and ale that the people lived on as well as lamb shank and stewed potatoes as well as a chicken or two. The inn was also a place for the men to gather for a pint and an earful of gossip, for in truth the men were just as bad as the women when their tongues were loosened with strong drink. Many a Manxman wandered no farther than *Mac Killian's* when the winds blew bitter and the news of witchcraft was afoot.

When the King entered the inn the men rose to their feet as was the custom. Bartholomew acknowledged them and with a gesture commanded them to take their seats again. The deemster, a short, stocky man named Kormin, knew the proprietor well and the two of them exchanged words while Bartholomew stood in the doorway and waited. Soon Bartholomew and the deemster were seated at a large table in a corner while the guard waited outside. A large plate of herring and a mug of ale were brought for the King, and when he set down his mug again all the men began to speak excitedly. The deemster raised his hand to stop them. Then he pounded his fist on the table.

"The King can't hear all of you at the same time now you strange kettle of fish. You there," and he pointed at the brightest looking one of the bunch, "you tell us what you saw, and don't waste our time with useless blather."

The man looked clever, and he was. He looked right past the deemster to Bartholomew. Then he smiled knowingly. "I ain't bout to tell no fools tale," he said. "And you can tell whether I am wasting your time in all."

The King nodded his ascent. "Go on," he said. "Tell me what you saw. Take your time now and don't be afraid. I will listen."

"Out with my young sons I was," the man began slowly, gathering confidence. "Cause that's what good men do, you see. We pushed our way into the shoal before the sun was up and we went to casting the nets. The herring was making so much noise beneath the boat, for I can hear them you see . . ."

"And that's when you saw the monster?" the deemster interrupted impatiently.

The man merely snorted. "Huh . . . that's when I hanged the ole kipper out the boat to relieve myself, I did."

Laughter erupted. The King smiled, but said nothing. He loved the honesty of his people over whom he ruled.

"There is was," the man said suddenly. "Slipping through the water it was like a slippery eel. Near is my shirt, but nearer is my skin if I'm telling a lie. It was enormous as it was long and I but nearly fell out of the boat. Long and coiled like a snake, sections stuck out of the water like humps of scaly flesh. Passed right beneath me it did . . . but then it turned around, and that was when the fear took me."

The room erupted as men nodded their heads in agreement and added their voice to the clamor. They had waited for this moment.

"Avoid all evil," an old man shouted.

"Evil is as evil does!" another man shouted.

"It is the work of a wizard!" another man shouted.

Soon the voices came from all directions. Oaths were sworn, cries of vengeance, spitting and farting, shouting and cursing and vociferous voices were thrown into the mêlée. The King waited patiently, and he listened, because this was his best way to learn the truth, for the truth comes not from careful words but from panic.

"The herring will be lost forever!" thundered a screeching voice over the top of all other sounds.

King Bartholomew stood up at once and shouted. "The herring will not be lost, and that is true! I say so now." Then he raised his hand to be heard. "Wait," he said. "I want to hear more." Then, looking to the man once again he said. "Tell me what happened then."

"The serpent turned and then rose up out of the water. It had the head of a dragon with large green eyes. Then I saw the beast's terrifying serpent head. Rows of sharp teeth, I remember seeing rows of teeth. Never have I seen before a creature more terrible."

"And what did you do then?" Bartholomew asked patiently.

"Praise the fine day in the evening," is what I said, "and I turned my boat to shore and rowed like the devil caught my tail."

"Did anyone else see this creature?" the King asked.

The room erupted again as everyone began speaking at once. And for the remainder of the afternoon the King heard the tale told over and over. The Manx are very thorough, and when a man spoke of a thing, he made an account and sighted the experiences of fellow Manxmen as the only proof there was to learn. And the Manx had long memories woven closely together during long cold night's together and weathered storms. When the tale was told the sun was almost down and long shadows formed inside the crowded inn.

"Go back to your families," said the King. "Come back tomorrow, for I shall spend the night here at the inn. Tomorrow I will have an answer."

The King was shown to the best room at the inn, the better of the two it offered, but it was small and contained nothing more than a bed and a candle-stand next to a writing desk. Inns in those days were few for the Manx liked to stay at home and travelers from the England were rare. After talking to the deemster and bidding him goodnight the King retired to his room for he was very tired. He thought about the day's events and he didn't wonder that such a tale could emerge on such an island, for this was the island of the saints. But then he sighed; such an enchanted panacea of beliefs was part of the substance of the island. Were it not so, perhaps it should sink again into the misty sea and disappear. Lighting the small candle, the King took out a sheaf of parchment and began to write.

Fear no longer haunted the people in those days. Fear comes from the unknown, but in those days the illuminated men had learned many things and now there were many things that were known and few things that could not be explained even though they too remained unknown so that things that were unknown seemingly were known. Over a period of time the world became less and less frightening, but with this new feeling of security something else was lost.

When the work was done the people would return to their homes. They would enjoy their supper because they were in no fear of going hungry. When supper was over they would sit together around warm fires and talk about how wonderful their supper was. Then, they would look forward to the next day and how much work they would be able to do for lack of nothing. They would then think about all the fine suppers that were yet to be eaten. All this talking would make them very tired, and soon they would go to their warm beds and sleep until morning, for sated men and women sleep deeply.

One evening after another fine supper, John asked his wife if she had any dreams, because he had many dreams, all of them unfulfilled. His wife looked at him with a question in her eyes.

"We have no need of dreams," she answered with a warm smile. "What a silly thing to say," she said.

"I can imagine a better life," John replied.

"Where could that be?" she asked calmly.

"In my dreams," John answered. "I see it all in my dreams."

"But we have everything," she said with a note of concern growing in her voice.

"I'm just teasing you," said John, for now he felt guilty for making her anxious. Her life he regarded as more precious than his own. "Let's go to bed now for the night is short and tomorrow is another day."

But soon after going to bed, John lay with one eye open and waited for his wife to fall asleep. Soon she was sleeping. Then he slipped out of bed and sat down at his writing table. Lighting a special lamp that needed no fire he withdrew a sheet of parchment and began to write.

Long, long ago there lived a King. In this time there was only one King of the land and the people looked to the King for protection and for guidance. There was much fear throughout the land for evil roamed the world unchecked and those not nourished by the grace of the Lord were harvested by the devil. Even the King was to be feared because there were many evil Kings in other lands and much blood was spilled by those acting in the King's name. Wizards and witches, spirits and sea monsters prowled the coastal waters and the people were afraid. Powders and serums and vapor and flecks of dust could be enchanted and many people were entranced by substances and spoken words. But there was reason for hope.

Brave men walked the land and hunted evil that they may destroy it forever. Men of honor looked to heaven and cried for they were ashamed of their own weakness. In their shared virtue men banded together and fought of honor and justice.

In that time a sea serpent roamed the coastal waters and devoured fishermen and destroyed many vessels. The people lamented their fate and wondered if it was a sign . . .

Bartholomew put down his pen and rubbed his eyes. "I must get some sleep," he said to himself. He said his prayers that his actions be pleasing to the Lord. Then he blew out his candle and went to sleep.

The inn was full when the King emerged from his room. Men were sitting with cups of hot tea and pouches of tobacco. Bottles of rum were passed from hand to hand in silence. Smoke filled the room with a thick, blue cloud. Still dressed in his cloths from the previous day the King stood in the passageway and surveyed the crowd of people even before they took notice of his presence.

Large candelabras hung from the thick oaken beams that supported the steepled roof and dripped hot wax, giving the room a close, acidic odor that mixed with the smoke and burned the eyes of the weary fishermen who sat and scowled. Old nets and harpoons and oarlocks and talismans were mounted on the walls out of respect for the tradesmen who earned their living from the sea. Large fins and jawbones testified to those unfortunate men who had been bitten thus, for the inn was also a graveyard of fishing stories remembered by the perilous few that had survived. Death was the certain aspect of the sea, and the sea thus giveth death in its woe. Already the windows were flung open and dampness blew in like a creeping mist from the misty, foamy shores. A cat arched its back and crawled beneath a hutch filled with teacups and saucers that was pushed into a corner against the wall. The King took all this in presently before coming into the room unannounced. The chatter died down as the King began to speak.

"We've all heard the tale," he said. "Ours is a land of mist. Ours is a land of magic. Ours is a land of legend!"

"There's much between saying and doing," a man cried out.

"There's much lost between the hand and mouth!" shouted another man.

The men were getting unsettled. The King could see them squirming in their seats, for the men were accustomed to doing and then talking. The King knew what they wanted.

"We search for the monster if monster it be," he said with conviction.

The men cheered, for they were up for a fight if it be righteous. Pride comes from action as buttermilk comes from action; death comes from inaction as evil comes from rot. King Bartholomew knew his people well, but he also knew them to be impetuous and easy to provoke. He knew they were not cowards though cowards the better so.

"To the wharf," he said. "If there be a man with a sturdy boat let him come forth, for I am too old for a skiff. We will see what there is to see, and let us see if there are any amongst us with the stomach for a monster."

Down to the wharf they trampled together like a mob. Past old houses and shacks they paraded and women and children leaned out of dirty windows to catch a glimpse of the King. Old men stood in front of their shops with pipes in their mouth to see the procession. Along the cobbled, narrow street they went and the sound of their boots was like the sound from a great multitude. On the wharf was moored a small cog ship, a single mast square sailed vessel. A man dressed in red breeches and a grey waistcoat stood before her as the news of the procession preceded the arrival of the King. He stepped forth when the King was close.

"There's room for twelve men," he said with pride. "You may stand on the forecastle, if it be your purpose," he said to the King. "I am at your service, sire," he said with a nod.

Twelve men willing to hunt down the beast was not hard to find when even the King had the courage to join the fray. Pikes and swords and harpoons and lances and barbed weapons of every kind were brought to the ship for the fight, knives and scabbards and axes, saws, and hammers too, but the King stopped them.

"There's time for killing when the killing is due. Take back your weapons and allow your senses to clear as the sky clears after a storm."

"Tis madness to go out without a way to defend ourselves!" cried the captain of the cog. "We must have weapons, sire."

"Tis madness to tempt the devil with a feather," the King replied resolutely. "Now then, who is will to go with me?"

Before they sailed out of the harbor a young woman came rushing along the quay. She held a cross of rowan, and reaching up to the King begged him to take it along. The captain took hold of the cross and nailed it forthright to the mast. Then he gave the order to trim the sail. And that is how the King left on his voyage to discover the Serpent of [36]Glenmaye. Along with the King was the man who had spotted the serpent, who was called Godred, and the King had him direct the captain southward to those fateful waters.

The sea was calm and under a fair wind they returned to the deep water beyond the shoal. Vast ribbed arches of rock protruded away from the island like giant scales which would slice open a keel like a knife through a cold herring, and many ships had been lost because the fishing ground was rich and many men were willing to take the risk. But the captain would not draw any closer to the island for fear of running aground. King Bartholomew peered into the water and waited. Many hours passed and still there was no sign of the monster. The cog rode high in the water for she was empty, but the captain kept her trim to avoid any possible danger.

Slowly they drifted into a thick mist that rolled off the island, obscuring the sight of land from the men like cotton. The men began to get restless. Thicker and thicker it became until they too were enveloped in the icy vapor.

"I don't like this at all," the captain said. He then ordered the sailors to spill the wind.

Then all was quiet. The sound of screeching birds through the mist was the only sound as the puffin and diving petrels returned to their nests in the cliffs. Everyone was expecting something to happen. And then King

---

[36] *Glen Maye. Meaning Yellow Glen. This is named for the iron residue which is washed down the river from South Barrule and the surrounding hills turning the water yellow.*

Bartholomew saw something in the water. "Look," he said. "Look into the water!"

Everyone saw. Everyone saw a deep, shimmering iridescence off the bow. It was moving, alive, sliding beneath the ship.

"It's the monster!" men began to shout.

"No!" Bartholomew shouted. "Wait!"

"Tis but a school of fish," declared an old fisherman with a snort. "We are in good fishing ground and that is true. Above us only sky, below us is myriads upon myriads of herring. All of em, sliding and slipping and wiggling together until they glow like the very moon. They shine like silver in the light. We are on top of a living shoal."

Bartholomew looked at the man who had spotted the monster with a question in his glance, but he remained silent. Could this be what he had seen? The King made no judgment, he merely said to the captain. "It is time to go home now. Perhaps tomorrow . . ."

"This ain't what I saw," the man pleaded, for suddenly he was ashamed before the King. "What is wisdom to a wise man is folly if it be not guided in wisdom."

The King cocked his head and smiled. "Wise words Godred," he said with a grin. "I do not doubt your words good man, but the time is short and we have seen all that there is to see this day. We cannot raise a beast if that beast be not raised."

The captain needed no encouragement to turn around for in truth he was bored by expeditions of folly and tales unfounded. And he was not earning any money in such folly. This was but another tale to be told over tall glasses with old friends. The captain gave the order and the sail was unfurled and filled with a fair tailwind like a sigh. Suddenly a man cried out.

"Look! Look off the portside! Lord Almighty!"

A giant creature slowly reared its head out of the water. Like the head of an eel with a ridged protruding forehead the skin was textured and rough with the scaly body of a snake. Large lidless eyes the color of seaweed and glowing with faint iridescence of an insect peered forth and in its mouth were sharp piercing fangs. The men were drawn to those eyes and were spellbound. Higher the creature rose, revealing a large tapered neck as large around as the body of a man. The creature was long, coiled, protruding out of the water in sections that were like the body of a snake thirty feet in length. The men cried out in fear so bewildering became the presence of the creature. Falling from the creature's mouth were the shredded, half eaten bodies of many fish for they had disturbed the creature during its feeding.

"Full sail!" the captain roared with such force that the men were broken of the bewitching spell of the creature.

Safely back in port the King tried to calm the men. They gathered on the pier and talked amongst themselves about having narrowly survived, for they had not forgotten that it was the King that forbade them to bring arms.

"We are safe," said the King. "Our boat was not attacked and we are all alive to tell the story."

"No one is safe!" cried one of the sailors who had not spoken until now. "We can all sleep in our bed tonight, but tomorrow we could be devoured. No one is safe until the monster is dead."

In the end the King acquiesced. "We will do this thing you speak of," he said. "But not until tomorrow. Not until tomorrow when we have all had time to think clearly without ire and venom lest we act imprudently and someone is killed without cause."

The men saw the wisdom in this and everyone went home to their family. The King went back to the inn where he decided to spend the night once more. News passes quickly and soon the inn was filled with men, all wanting to hear the story from the King.

"A story half finished is a story half told," said the King.

Then he ordered his dinner before going to his room to rest, for he was tired and weary from standing all day in the boat. After his dinner was finished he was still weary, so he decided to stay in his room and possibly retire to sleep early. He pulled back the covers and prepared to undress, and then he remembered his story, still unfinished, spread out on the desk near the window. "Yes, a story half finished is a story half told," he said softly. After a moment, he sat down at his desk and prepared his pen. Then he started to write.

The people, fearful and uncertain, knowing not else to do, appealed to the King for protection. They begged and begged and pleaded, for they were truly frightened and their survival was at stake. Banners were flown, trumpets were blown, babies cried the people complied and old women groaned. The King paraded through the town beneath streamers of confetti and the people smiled for their prayers were answered. They were fortunate to have a brave King as their own, one of the bravest in all the land it was said. And so it was that the King waved to the people and calmed their fears and restored hope as he made his way to the wharf where a swift boat awaited to take him to the monster. A white dove was released into the air, signaling the peoples' freedom, when the King stepped onto the boat that whisked him away.

In those bygone days the life of a King was usually unpredictable, violent, and short. Wars, usurpations, palace intrigues, witchcraft, war-craft, and statecraft conspired to bring need of a steady supply of Kings, and they did their best to honor those obligations by supplying a steady genealogy of children from the many wives and concubines they owned. Magic was used by evil necromancers to thwart the effort of the King to live in peace, so many knights and wizards and scribes were dispatched throughout the land to counter the evil intentions of the enemy. Sometimes sea monsters and krakens were used by the enemy to stir woe and fear amongst the good people. For this purpose the good King John sailed into the teeth of the monster without fear, for he had the Lord on his side. With him he carried only his gleaming sword and a single lance made from the sacred wood of a rowan tree.

The monster uncoiled to its true length as the King approached. He was fully sixty feet by six with six rows of terrifying teeth. Such was the terror of the beast that no light could abide its evil and only an empty, black mass of nothingness defined its dimensions. The men on board were so frightened they abandoned ship, leaving the King to fight the monster alone.

And then the creature attacked. The King drew his sword and fought back the powerful jaws of the beast. The creature snapped and snapped its fangs and shredded the deck like kindling wood. But the King only fought harder. Driven to the stern, the King stood valiantly on the transom as the enormous creature heaved its tremendous body onto the deck, thrusting the bowsprit into the sea and raising the King high into the air as the ship began to founder.

The King stood tall and fearless with nothing but his lance and stared into the gaping yaw of the serpent. The sea boiled and churned with white spume and in this turbulence the King thrust his lance into the mouth of the creature forcefully.

The creature writhed and thrashed in the water until it at last succumbed to death and disappeared beneath the surface . . .

John set down his pen and rubbed his eyes. His wife slept soundly through the entire ordeal, never once suspecting the upheaval happening within his vivid and tumultuous imagination. John sat alone and smiled, for the triumph of his wonderful King was also the triumph of his very soul against the crippling burden of such a life of security and boredom. If only the moment could last forever, somehow be extended to encompass his entire life . . . ah, the glory it would be.

But he knew this dream could never be true, and he knew that in a few short hours he would be called upon again to attach himself to the comfortable yoke that was his own life and tied him to this Earth. But at least for a few more minutes he could breathe a different, more rarefied air where it was still possible to live. And so he sat until he knew it was time to make an end. He stood up and gathered the parchment together lovingly. Then he placed the contents inside of a small box and hid it beneath his bed, and with a sigh undressed and crawled into his own bed to sleep a few hours before the dawn.

King Bartholomew looked up and rubbed his eyes. The sun had set and it was almost completely dark inside of his room. A plate of cheese was there untouched where he had forgotten it. He had been working in the dark!

He stood up and walked to the window. Outside it was dark but for the faint glow of the oil lamps that burned for their light. The stars were already visible and the waxing moon was almost full. In the distance he could see a few stragglers on their way home and the sound of their voices was comforting to him. Here he was, a King, standing alone in the darkness inside of a small, unadorned room, but he had no misgivings for he was truly happy. The moon would continue to wax until it was full just as his life would continue to wax until it too was full. "Such is my life," he sighed. Then he closed the shutter and turned to his bed. But then he stopped. A thought still bothered him and he hesitated. At last he threw open the window, smiled furtively, and then crawled out into the darkness.

Outside the air was cool and he walked a few steps away before turning back. Faint light peeped out of his window for he had left the candle burning. "Just a short walk," he muttered. Then he disappeared into the darkness.

In the moonlight his figure was that of an ordinary man and those that would have seen him would only have thought him to be an intrepid Manxman walking in the night when only night-creatures prowled. In truth no one saw him, for at night the Manx sleep and dream about the herring. He took the path that led down to the wharf and soon he stood alone, looking out to sea with only the watery sounds of gurgling, splashing water in his ears and the salty sea-spray in his nostrils.

Against the starry night sky the dark silhouettes of masts and sailcloth and rigging filled his vision; across the wharf stood the old warehouses and alehouses overlooking the harbor. A few small vessels were moored in their berth. Barrels and crates were lined up to be loaded, and the smell of fish was overwhelming. Nets and coils of rope and pails of smelly, soapy water lined the wharf. Down the quay was an old shack, used as an office by the fishing captains to conduct business and record figures into account books. The wharf is where a Manxman breathed the sweet air of freedom, for the sea made all men equal, and it was said that the smell of the fish was the smell of a man's soul.

Bartholomew walked along the wharf, cold and slippery beneath his feet, and his mind turned with thoughts. His mind was never fully at ease near the sea. He preferred the fields and bracken and forested glens of the interior and seldom came down to the wharf. The sounds on the wharf were loud and course, but the sounds on the moor gave way to wispy creatures and whispering winds. One could know the trees, the yellow gorse, the meandering streams, but one could never know the sea, for the sea was truly mysterious.

"I truly invent my life by living," he thought to himself as he stared out into the bay. "And yet, by living my life is lived though the Lord waits patiently for me to act and knows my thoughts as they were his own. But to what end?"

This was the one thought that kept him from his bed. And even as he spoke to no one but through the lines of his pen, the Lord spoke with all men but with nagging visions and dreams and sleeplessness, for the way of the Lord was mysterious only to the heart of men. In this way, men truly were instruments of the Lord and our lives the parchment on which it was written, and in this way the will of the Lord is the will of man.

The King continued to stare forth as if expecting an answer from the sea, but the gentle reverberations of the tides like the florid thoughts of his soul, only swelled like tiny breaths exhaled. Deep as the sea are the depths of one's soul.

A scudding cloud passed over and covered the moon and in the sudden peering darkness the King thought he heard the sound of a footfall. "Ah," he thought fearlessly. "What man is frightened by the sounds of his own feet? Tis but the sound of my own useless shuffling." He turned at last and began to walk back along the quay. Halfway back he stopped and looked back again. Still he saw nothing. Finally he continued on his way and did not look back again.

When he got back to the inn, the innkeeper was waiting for him. The King saw him standing near the open window, and when he was near, the man smiled.

"I thought that you were ill," he said softly and with a knowing smile.

"I am well," the King answered. "I only stepped out for a breath of air."

"But you have forgotten your pipe," said the innkeeper.

"Why are you not asleep?" asked Bartholomew.

"It is not often one gets the privilege to serve the King," he replied. "I frequently sleep with one eye open, for such is my trade."

The King laughed and said quietly, "It is my trade to find a sea monster."

"Do not take it away from us," said the innkeeper. And when he spoke he looked at the King thoughtfully.

The light that came from his window was faint, but the King could clearly see the face of the innkeeper. He wore an expression of concern and in his eyes there was no lie.

"That is a strange thing to say," said Bartholomew. "Do you not want to see the creature destroyed?"

The innkeeper chuckled softly. Then he pulled out his pipe and struck a flame, at last puffing out a great cloud of smoke.

"I'm an innkeeper," he began. "Tales are a part of an innkeeper's trade. An inn without tales is an empty inn. A tale worth telling is a tale well told, and that is the truth. But when a tale comes to an end . . ."

"You would have me do nothing then?"

Blowing out another cloud of smoke silently the innkeeper said, "You have done much already, sire. I have heard many a tale, and I have told more than a few. A moment of haste can bring a lifetime of regret. This creature will do more harm if it dies than ever should it be allowed to live."

"You are wise," said Bartholomew. "I will consider your words carefully, but now I must get some sleep if I am to act as a King."

With a nod the innkeeper stood aside and waited for the King to crawl back through the open window. Before Bartholomew closed the window however he said to the innkeeper.

"I also trade in tales, Jole. Goodnight." Then he closed the window and blew out the candle.

The next morning when he woke he felt stiff and sore, for he was not used to sleeping in strange beds. Once again, the men were anxiously waiting for him to emerge. Today was the day they would take revenge upon the monster. With few words and little fanfare the King led them through the streets on their way to the wharf. This time however, the windows along the way remained closed and no one waved and no confetti streamed and no flowers were cast before them. Today no women stood with their babies and pointed at the King; today no sound of greeting or cheers was heard, but only the sound of a solitary raven perched on top a roof. The sky was overcast and dark clouds scudded across the bay.

The captain was waiting for them. "Step lively!" he shouted.

There were so many men willing to go aboard that they had to be turned away. Bartholomew stood by and watched patiently as the boat was loaded with weapons. This was to be a killing mission and the men were prepared for battle. And then the captain gave the order and they pulled away from the pier; no one looked back.

When they finally reached the battle ground the King was almost asleep as the steady rocking of the boat had lulled him into a strange torpor. The men had forgotten that he was on board as they watched the sea for signs of the serpent.

"Starboard!" shouted one of the seamen.

All eyes turned to the creature as a jolt went through the crew. The King was suddenly knocked out of the torpor to which he had succumbed. Even the captain stopped abruptly and stared at the creature.

It was floating above the water perhaps one hundred feet off the starboard side. In its mouth were the devoured remains of many fish. The King watched without passion and his expression was quizzical and reasoned, but the men were possessed, nearly jumping overboard to get to the creature. They were born into a living mythology full of danger and fear, living and dying in ignorance without respite, and they had no time for observation and prudence and the careful twittering of delicate details. The captain took charge, steering the boat directly at the creature, maneuvering them closer the better to attack.

"Present arms!" the captain shouted.

The men held forth an array of spears, lances, pikes, knives, and assorted instruments, anything that would kill, maim, mutilate, injure, or hurt. The moment drew near as the ship drifted closer and closer to the monster. The monster however, paid no attention to the ship as if it did not even exist, for in truth, the creature had never seen a ship before.

[37]The men stared at the creature in awe until suddenly a new leader came forth and captured their spirit in the whirlwind that was his presence. The leader of the men, whose name was Illiam, was the loudest and most brazen of the men for it was he that had the most scars from the sea, the most to lament, and the sea owed him his due. Many a man had lost a son at sea; he had lost two. He held a long spear in his tight, stubby fist, and his heart raced with the eagerness of blood. Illiam

---

[37] *This represents a battle of imagery. Illiam represents the old, folklore of Finn Mac Cool. King Bartholomew uses the imagery of Christ.*

was a leader of men. Though not a king, the men who worked the sea looked to their own for bravery, and it was in this way that men learned to follow as a herring learns to follow until all men are hurtling headlong together swimming and slithering with one mind.

"Steady now!" cried Illiam, ignoring the commands of the captain, for Illiam was the captain of killing. There was fire in his eyes, the same iridescence as those of the creature. He cocked his head to face the men and captured them with his blazing stare and held them so they could not look away. "Do you feel it, men? Do you feel your blood turning to ice? The creature hails from the Otherworld and will drag us down to perdition. Look at it," he commanded. "It feels your blood. It knows . . . it knows! We bring death, and we shall taste it."

The serpent floated on the watery surface and chewed, indifferent to the approaching ship. The enormous swell of fish to the reef had attracted it from far out to sea, for it was want to come any closer to the island.

Illiam was not a bad man. He was a man of faith and of fiery passions, but his passion was for the old ways and the old traditions handed down for generations on top of generations bound by blood and oaths. Such was his faith, and no new faith or wandering saint could persuade him to change, for he had become old and petrified in the old ways. The old ways were hard but they were true, and it was the old ways that made men strong and like a skeleton, held up their weary flesh. He watched the creature intently and then turned to the men again suddenly.

"Is this the ghost of St. John," thundered Illiam, "Or is this a dragon from hell's depths?"

Illiam transfixed them with his oration. "There's fire enough in my eyes and in my blood!" he shouted. "Let the monks' of [38]Winchomb burn bones and sticks and rubbish. We burn flesh this day!"

Spellbound by the power of his voice everyone watched the creature as the voice of Illiam bore into their brains like nails. And like a sorcerer he

---

[38] *On St. John's Eve, Midsummer's Eve for pagans, fires were lit to drive away dragons which were abroad poisoning springs and wells. On St. John's Eve boys collect bones and rubbish and burn them, and the smoke is said to drive away the dragon. This was compiled in sermons of the monk of Winchomb, Gloucestershire in the 13th century.*

worked the men and drew them to his side so that they would follow him without question.

[39]"Look to the great worm! The Sun Lizard! Basilisk! Behold, Jormungand, the Midgard Serpent divine beast of Ragnarok!"

But the King was watching Illiam with great apprehension and the King feared for all on board in the wake of such speechifying. He wore a plaid hunting tartan, hose, a green shirt and a silver waist plait. Tied to his belt he wore a well-wore sporran filled with knives, tobacco, cork, magic powders, and magical fishhooks. His strong hands were calloused and bloodless, his face cracked like aged vellum, his left ear had been torn asunder by a hook so that he always cocked his head to the right side the better to hear, and in truth it was his lacerated ear of which he was most proud. The King knew about men such as Illiam, men of old ways, men of dark caves and dark books and dark thoughts.

Suddenly the creature took notice of the slowly approaching ship full of ominous, writhing, threatening men bent on destruction and it quivered on the sea like a floating carcass. More ominous than an approaching storm was the approaching ship of Captain Erik. Closer and closer the ship drifted. The creature shifted in the water, and like the wake from a cleaving hull its body uncoiled in a paroxysm even as a paroxysm went through the men like that of a single beast. For it is in this way that men can be chained together and move together in terrible harmony. And in this way good men, like the monsters of old, become even more monstrous in their passion. The King could not abide such useless killing and in his great trembling he felt the trembling of the creature. And now the King saw not a creature in the water, but in his very boat, and the words of the innkeeper came back to him with purpose.

Mighty Leviathan it was, messenger of the Lord, mighty Leviathan, messenger of the deep. No, indeed some things should never be known, for it is the Lord that knows all things and we are but minnows in such a vast ocean. And to fathom the depths of our soul is to fathom the very depths of that which can never be known. This is the way the Lord intended his creatures to live, for the ocean of the soul is vast.

---

[39] *Illiam is evoking the serpents of yore: Basilisk, legendary reptile whose breath can be fatal; Ragnarok, Doom of the gods, the end of the cosmos in Norse mythology; Jormungand, Sea serpent so large it surrounds the Earth and grasps its own tail. When it lets go, the world will end.*

The time had come for killing, but before Illiam could give the order to attack, the King burst forth across the deck and jumped in front of the men defiantly. The youthful vitality of the King then surged and woke up his sleeping body and all timidity faded. His voice was powerful and resolute.

"No!" he thundered with the force of a hurricane. "Draw down!" he shouted. "Draw down I say! I forbid you to harm this creature."

The men stepped back in shock as the sight of the King jolted them out of their passion. Bartholomew stood before them like a giant and the sheer power of his will captivated them, for such is the power of a King to lead his people.

"This is not a monster," the King said with certainty and his voice was clear and true. "Come to your senses, men! Look!"

Like a man suddenly woken from sleep the men awoke from the madness that held them together in a unified connection and now they could see clearly through their own eyes as each man remembered his own mind. The King had restored their sanity. The spell had been broken in an instant, for such is the power of revelation that can come like a blow and leave one breathless and stunned. Suddenly the men saw the creature for what it was and the sound of the King gave them strength. The creature was large, the creature was awesome and mighty, but it was not a monster and but for the need for food would prowl the shores no more. And even as the King spoke, the creature slowly descended beneath the waves and disappeared. Moments later, further out to sea they saw the wake of the creature as it swam further and further away from the island.

"No!" shouted Illiam as if he had been thunderstruck. "No, no, no." His cries were like bitter lamentations. Even more strident he now became, cursing and running from side to side in front of the men in a panic. "No, damn yea do not let it get away! Damn yea!" And then his eyes beheld the King and his rage intensified even more. "You!" he shouted. "You let the monster get away, it is you . . . it is you that is evil." And then he raised his hand against the King and would have killed him in his terrible wrath but for the men. They surrounded Illiam and held fast his arm, even as the stricken man attempted to unleash his anger against the King.

"Be careful with him men," said King Bartholomew gently and with compassion, for he was sorry of the sickness that had come over the heartbroken man who had been delivered from his own vengeance. He would have more compassion for Illiam than would have been shown to the creature.

And so, not with a cry but with a whimper ended the war of the Sea Serpent of Glenmaye. Alas, if only I had acted earlier when I was told about this creature. Alas, if only I would have listened then. I pray that the sins of the father not be visited on the son, but such is our fate, such is the bitterness of fate. Perhaps if I had acted then things could have been different, but such is the heart of man that it should ache with regret for the folly of love.

Over the years many men reported seeing the creature, but as the years continued such sighting became rare. Occasionally someone would report seeing the monster, even to being attacked and narrowly escaping with their own life, but these stories always seemed to come out after long bouts of drinking in the surrounding pubs and alehouses. One man, a strange man with a missing ear, even claimed to have killed the beast with his own hands and rid the world forever, but his story was always laughed at until he tired of telling it. In a few years the legend of the Serpent of Glenmaye became myth.

The Good King Bartholomew, as he was later to be called, went back to his castle on the third day of the adventure. He was welcomed home like a hero and a great feast was held that day. Later that night when the King was alone he gathered together the sheaf's of parchment from his unfinished story. With a gentle sigh of acceptance he rolled them together and tied them with a string. Then he took out a box from beneath his bed. Inside were a few keepsakes, a candle, a flute, and a few paper flowers. He put the rolled up manuscript into the box and slid it beneath his bed, and then he too went to bed.

The Christmas Rose

"Yes, the bitterness of love lost can destroy the bravest man, the noblest knight, the humblest servant, even the greatest king. But how much more bitter it is to lose a child. Talk to that man about hope. Tell that man about fate. Tell that man about grace . . . for what can ever grow in such a garden of despair?"

"My heart is breaking," said Iona.

"I wept until the tears were frozen on my face," said the King. "It was the first snowfall of the year. A crisp layer of snow covered the ground all around me. But when I looked down Iona, I saw that a delicate and tender rose had pushed its way up out of the frozen ground and was turned to the sun. That is when I discovered hope."

Iona started to cry, but she said nothing and only listened.

"Like Cog, I too wanted to die. Like Cog, I too had thrown away my life and any expectation of mercy, for I had cursed the Lord that I should endure such sorrow. How does one expunge such shame? Yes Iona, someday I too will be a flower in God's garden . . . I would like to be a rose."

Although it was Christmas Eve and a bitter hoarfrost clung to the tender trees just outside the thinly glazed window, prompting little Sara Tillman to pull the covers all the way up to her nose, the aging man went about his business without the slightest hesitation or fear that he would be discovered. The house was dark, but in the early morning twinkling of the distant stars and the pale light cast by the sleepy moon, his eyes twinkled as the memory rushed back to his overwrought mind and calmness washed over him once more. His work did not require much time and he was almost finished before he saw the note left on the table for him. He picked it up and looked at it with a smile before putting it in his pocket and silently closing the door behind him braced himself for the long ride back to his home in the bitter air.

Through the dim light he rode past the sleeping men and women and children of his kingdom. Coming around a steep turn in the path overgrown with thick bracken and untended for years he came to the Crossag Bridge. He rode to the middle of the stone bridge that was built by restless monks' centuries ago. There he reined his horse and stood alone gazing into the slowly moving water below. It was a clear night and the sky was filled with stars. The water shimmered with the faint light from the firmament and it seemed to him like a reflection of something from a time long ago when he was a boy. The water reminded him of the present that was not his own, and the longer he looked the younger he became until the memory captured him. . .

The castle was alive with activity for Christmas was just around the corner. A very young boy with long blonde hair and bright blue eyes ran from room to room laughing and asking the servants for candies and treats because it was a time of great joy and of special things. The servants always found a way to sneak goodies for the boy because they liked him so much. They would press a sugar cookie into his small hand and say, "now you don't come back again Bartholomew," and they would smile because he always did.

One day the boy found a package hidden away in a remote closet. The package was wrapped in brilliant red wrapping paper and tied with a golden ribbon. The boy knew that he had found a present that was meant for him but he must not reveal his secret, and he must forget about the present. The boy however, could not forget about the present, and in truth, it was all he could think about and dream about. He knew that it could be anything, so to the boy the present became everything, and anything became possible but for his vivid imagination. These were anxious and exciting days in which his daydreams carried him away with all the possibilities contained within the bright wrapping. The imagination of a young boy is endless and has no boundaries, no edges, and no constraints to keep it from expanding. The imagination of a young boy is only to be tempered by his fearless innocence as he can climb the tallest towers without falling. Woe to the man that tells him to look down, for the dreams of children are sacred and bear fruit that shall not taste bittersweet.

Finally the day had come and the morning light of Christmas morning found the boy already awake and eager for the moment when he would be given the present.

"Would you like to come along with me on a little errand?" Bartholomew's father asked cryptically.

The boy certainly did and soon they were driving in their beautiful carriage away from the castle and across the Crossag Bridge. They came to a fork in the road and merged onto another road that was ruddy and in disrepair, curling and twisting this way and that, jostling the boy until he was increasingly curious for he had never before visited this part of the island. Here the houses were modest if not entirely small. On some of the houses could be seen patches on the roof where attempts had been made to repair the effects of age. It was still very early, but it was Christmas morning! Windows opened when the King rode by and greetings and silent waves from the sleepy children rubbing their eyes behind glass windows were exchanged.

"These are the good people of Man," said Bartholomew's father. "They are poor, but they love all that is their own."

And then the carriage stopped in front of the lowliest hovel of all, the home of an unfortunate woman who had recently lost her husband at sea.

"This will only take a minute," said the King to his young son.

Then the boy watched as his father removed from the back of the carriage a package. It was his present! The boy's heart sank. The King went into the house carrying the bright red package with the gold ribbon and a moment later returned empty handed. On the ride back to the castle the boy tried to remain cheerful though his heart was heavy. When they were almost home, Bartholomew's father turned to him and said.

"Everyone needs help my boy. Sometimes there is no one to help, and then we must trust in God. Remember Bartholomew, the world belongs to the Savior, and we should not be selfish with his gifts. All gifts great and small come from God."

And then they were home.

"We must return the carriage to the stable," said the King.

But when they went into the stable, the boy saw something that he did not expect . . . a pony. The pony was freshly combed and had a ribbon around his neck.

"Imagine that," said the King. "What do you think it says?"

The boy jumped out of the carriage to read the writing on the ribbon. It said, Bartholomew . . .

King Bartholomew looked up from the water. That was many years ago but it was a memory of his father that he would always cherish. He would return home in a great state of uncertainty as the vacillations in his mind left him feeling more and more melancholy.

The darkness became deeper and the heavens burned cobalt blue as he came around the last corner in the road that brought him to his place of birth. He walked his loyal horse the rest of the way so that even the soft footfalls of his silent companion would not wake the restful servants asleep in their beds. The gentle rocking motion of his favorite horse, his companion all these long years, was comforting and increasingly sad, and instead of his usual feeling of pure joy that this moment always brought, he felt like he was walking into the unknown and that this familiar road was no longer familiar. He now walked a lonely road with a single destination. Clop clop clop, the sound comforted him even as it led him away from his turning inner thoughts.

And then to Bartholomew's utter disbelief, it started to snow. At first it was just a few tiny flakes floating down from the heavens, but suddenly something changed, something was different and Bartholomew was caught off guard by a sudden shift in perspective. It was not unheard of for snow to fall in the isles, but it was very rare, and then when it did, it was not like this. Large snowflakes gently floated down to earth partially obscuring his vision and making him forget for a moment where he was going. And then he heard the sound of hoofed feet striking something hard as if he and his mount had suddenly merged onto a different path. Bartholomew looked down and saw that indeed he was riding along a different path, one that was cobbled with stone that glittered like gold by starlight. The path narrowed on both sides until he sat on his horse within a narrow fissure that led onward and upward like a gate into a great walled city. Ahead he could see peaks of towers and tall spires shooting up to pierce the night sky. Everywhere tiny lights gleamed and glittered as if a great festival were taking place within its walls, or like a prodigal son they had waited up all night for, to return.

Bartholomew sat motionless and looked on afraid that the slightest movement or gesture would cause the beautiful mirage to dissolve before his eyes. The snow continued to fall, covering his shoulders and riding cloak and causing him to shiver as it began to accumulate all around him. So fragile was the illusion that he was almost afraid to exhale. Bright pennants and banners caught the wind and hung from every turret and tower and Bartholomew tried to imagine such a King that could rule such a city. This was a magnificent city, a gossamer city balanced between life and death as between two possibilities of awareness. Then suddenly up ahead a white stag bounded out of the forest and crossed his path, and when Bartholomew looked up again to the city in the snow it was gone and his own home stood before him. He cupped his hands over his tired eyes and tried to believe that what he had seen was real, but now the stiffness had returned to his tired bones and the vision faded from his mind.

King Bartholomew slipped his robe on over his nightshirt and walked with the candle up to his bed chamber. With him he carried a cup of warm milk to remove the chill from his bones before committing himself to sleep. Clenched in his hand he carried a piece of carefully folded paper. He took a sip of milk before unfolding the paper. Then he sat on the edge of his bed and began to read . . .

Tears flooded his eyes as he bowed his head to the memory. "Yes, yes I do remember," he mused. "Sleep well sweet child," he said. "You are forgiven. You have made me cry again."

King Bartholomew stood up slowly and walked to the window. He opened the shutters and as he did a cold rush of air swept into the room. The air felt cold on his skin but he still felt warm from an inner emotion that he could not reconcile, an emotion that only grew stronger but for his many years to relinquish it.

"Why have I been blessed with such a capacity to feel pity?" he spoke into the evening sky. "The greater my capacity to feel, the greater is my pain. How can I endure such a gift, and must my heart burst?"

The stars did not answer and his lamentation disappeared into the starry night. He waited for an answer or even the gentle echo of his own bitter thoughts, but his mind had gone completely empty and he peered into the inky darkness like a lost soul in the wilderness.

"I can only live my life," he cried. "Can I give hope to the hopeless? Is it my gift to share their pain? I am just a man," he said.

Then he saw that there was a snowy owl perched on the balustrade just outside his window. He blinked, for the owl had not been there a moment ago. The owl was looking at him through black, penetrating eyes.

"I have nothing for you to eat," said Bartholomew. "I have only questions to offer this night."

The owl remained and its eyes became fixed on the eyes of the King who strangely, could not look away.

"Are you a messenger, or a message?" said Bartholomew.

The owl spread its wings, revealing a brilliant, white coat of feathers that emanated an intense radiance that struck the King like a creeping mist from the moors. Bartholomew fell into a deep rumination as his eyes like blazing meteors were captured in a vortex. Down, down, down he plunged into a muse that took him back through time to a time when he was young, a time before he was old enough for questions . . .

The Isle of Man is an island of rare beauty and stark diversity ranging from the steep cliffs and craggy windswept coastline to the tender meadows overflowing with wildflowers and bottle-flies, to thick forested glens surrounded by ancient rune-stones and Celtic monuments. Every legend, wives tale, mystery, superstition, and myth is taken seriously and is understood innately as if the essence of the island had slowly penetrated and transformed them, but their humble heritage is tempered in the strong arms of Christianity. The Manx have leaned to see the world differently, as if by breathing a different air they had gradually become part of the rich mythology of legend. All these things exist in harmony in the isles where the saints did sail.

Young Bartholomew looked elegant and sleek as he rode away on his fleet footed horse across the Crossag Bridge with his red scarf flapping in the wind. The Manxman said he was an impetuous prince, but a fine hunter; the Manxwomen mostly blushed when he turned his attention on their pretty faces, for the young prince was handsome. His hair, the color of chestnuts, was parted down the middle and hung about his shoulders carelessly until he would fling it back with a quick snap of his head. And his blue eyes shone brightly across his high cheekbones that held up a most delicate mouth forever tinged with a sly smile that revealed his propensity for adventure. Across the bridge he thundered as if all his errands always required all his energy. Such was the mind of the young Prince. But the people did not know everything about young Bartholomew, for today he was on a very special errand, and he would not have his meanderings gossiped about frivolously.

Reining his horse in front of a very modest house he politely knocked on the door and waited to be invited though no one would ever refuse the young Prince passage.

"How is little Omma?" he asked emphatically as he squeezed the hand of a middle aged woman standing in her doorway thoughtfully. He could see that she had been crying.

"My little Omma is weak, my lord. I have been praying for her on this fine Christmas Eve. She has been dreaming of having her own pony, my lord. Just imagine, I say's to her, such a fine young girl doing with a pony on the Isle of Man."

"Dreams of ponies are just as important as dreams of kingdoms, my lady," said Bartholomew politely. "Our dreams always want to take us to places we can never go and tread paths we can never follow. Many of our dreams are the dreams of others. Blessed are the dreams that belong to our dreams. May I see her?"

Omma lay with her eyes open. She smiled broadly when Bartholomew entered and would have tried to sit up had he not prevented her.

"Easy now young lady," he spoke tenderly. "Your mother tells me you will be better before you know it . . . and even that you said something about wanting your own bunny."

"My own pony," the young Omma spoke up. "My own pony silly."

"A pony is it?" Bartholomew repeated playfully as a smile formed on his face. "I'm not sure our little island is big enough for you and your own pony. Hum . . . you won't make him fly will you?"

They laughed and laughed until Bartholomew knew it was time to be serious. He took her little hand and said to her: "Tonight is Christmas Eve, Omma. Do you believe in angels?"

"Yes, because my mommy says that they are watching over me when I sleep."

"And they are," Bartholomew answered. "Would you like to know a secret?"

"Yes, I would," Omma answered joyfully. "Tell me," she begged.

"Angels love flowers," said Bartholomew with great difficulty. "Angels love roses in particular, and do you know why?"

Omma shook her head and watched Bartholomew intently.

"It is because there are no roses in heaven, Omma."

"Why are there no roses in heaven?"

"Because roses exist only for our sake," he told her. "And that is why the angels have to come all the way down to Earth just to smell them."

"That is sad," said Omma.

"Would you like to make a rose to give to the angels?" said Bartholomew. "I have brought some paper with me and I will show you how to make one out of paper."

When Bartholomew and Omma were finished making the rose he looked at her again and said: "Now you must leave it on the table tonight and when the angel comes to look at you, he will see it. They will all say in heaven that the rose that was made by Omma McIntosh was the finest rose ever."

"Will I see the angels when I get to heaven?" Omma said quietly.

Bartholomew knelt down on the floor near Omma and brought his lips next to her ear. "You are like a rose Omma," he said. But he could speak no more, so he kissed her on the forehead and left her room.

The Isle of Man is not a large island. Bartholomew rode like the wind and did not stop until he got to the edge of the island where he boarded a small ship. After talking with the captain for a few minutes, and having a Christmas toast of mulled wine, the captain handed him a small package and he handed the captain a small bag of coins. "Farewell," said Bartholomew, and then he mounted his horse and galloped away. Bartholomew kept the package next to his heart to keep it warm and the package warmed his heart in turn.

Omma McIntosh said her prayers with special joy because it was Christmas Eve and she knew that little Jesus was born on that day a very long time ago and that the angels still sang songs about it in heaven. She was very tired and felt sick even as her mother was telling her that she was getting better, but she was also excited because she knew that the angels would see her rose and it would be just as Prince Bartholomew said. Her mother always told her to be happy with all of the wonderful things that were given to them by Jesus, so Omma said an extra prayer to Jesus and thanked him for giving her such a wonderful mother. Then her mother brought them both a cup of hot cider to drink before bed, but before blowing out her candle, Omma's mother kissed her on the head and said:

"Sleep tight, little sugar plum, and don't let the man in the moon come."

"You're the man in the moon," answerer Omma, and they both laughed.

"I am the man in the moon," she said reaching for the door.

"Mommy?" said Omma. "Do you think the angels will like my rose?"

"Very much," she said softly as she closed the door.

Prince Bartholomew was woken by a servant in the middle of the night. He had left special instructions before going to bed.

"It's after two, "he said. "You asked me to wake you. "

"Thank you," said Bartholomew. "Merry Christmas Sorren, now go back to bed and sleep well. There is no need to wait up for me"

Before leaving the castle he said a prayer for it was now Christmas morning and he felt especially peaceful in the early hours before dawn. The morning air was brisk. Bartholomew wrapped a riding cloak around him and rode away quietly into the darkness. After crossing the Crossag Bridge he stopped in the middle of the road. Looking up to heaven he was overwhelmed by the beauty before him so often neglected and taken for granted. He knew that the stars always would be there, but it wasn't often that he remembered who put them there. He knew there were messages in the heavens, messages not unlike the one sent to the three wise men long ago on just such a night. But the messages were often so hard to find, and were it not for simple faith he should perish from the weight of these enigmas.

Outside the house he prepared himself to enter. With him he carried a small candle and flint. Bartholomew entered the house with such an intense feeling of joy that he nearly gave himself away. Moving quietly to the corner near the prayer lamp he unburdened himself of the parcel he concealed in his riding cloak. On the table was a small glass vessel out of which a single, paper rose reflected brightly in the faint candlelight. Carefully he reached out his hand and took the rose and put it in his riding cloak; then he busied himself with the package. He hesitated for a moment, said a silent prayer, and left the house unnoticed by either one of its inhabitants. When he was safely back in his castle, he removed the paper rose from his cloak and put it in a small box he kept hidden beneath his bed.

Omma opened her eyes to the first faint light of day. It was Christmas! She pushed back the covers and put her feet on the cold floor. The room was cold. Omma painfully rose from her bed and steadied herself. Then she shuffled out to the front room quietly so as not to wake her mother. Omma went straight to the corner table where she had left her rose, and beheld a miracle. She stood awed before her rose, for it was still there, but it was changed. It was alive! Protruding from the makeshift vase she and Bartholomew had used, was a rose, a real rose, and surrounding the rose was the thinnest, most brilliant halo of angel hair she had ever seen. The angels had breathed life into it! She no longer felt cold. Then she felt a gentle hand on her shoulder.

"Look mommy," she said. "The angels were here."

The second miracle was the expression on her mother's face as the tears streamed down her cheeks from pure joy. "There is something else on the table for you," she said tenderly. "What do you think it is, Omma?"

Omma looked again, and then she saw them. On the table was the finest pair of black riding gloves she had ever seen, and when she picked them up she felt as light as a feather.

King Bartholomew returned from his vision as the wind whipped through his white hair and across his once beautifully chiseled face and blinked several times to make sure he was awake. His once bright blue eyes now had become pale as if something that once was had faded and they were fixed upon something that was to be. Slowly he closed the shutters, but he remained standing at the window. He felt calm, the stillness that comes after a violent storm or the tranquility of a sleeping baby. The owl was gone. He had traveled back through time to a day when everything was possible, a time when everything made sense to his young, agile mind.

There was a presence in the room; he felt it as surely as one feels the fast approaching storm being pushed by the scudding clouds. He knew that this storm was different; he knew that it was the spirit of Christmas, and it was not in his room, but in his heart.

"There is much misery in the world, that is true," he said to himself. "I cannot change the world or alter the plan of our Lord. Perhaps the pain I accept is truly taken from the world and the world be free from such pain as I can bear. If that is so, I accept it willingly, for why should my heart be immune to pain?"

Bartholomew was exhausted. His years were multiplied even as his bones were tired and brittle. It was getting harder and harder for him to continue his long tradition and someday soon he would have to stop as his age would spare him no longer. He took one last glimpse of his kingdom. Across his kingdom they would be asleep, except for the quickly darting hands of those with secret gifts to bear. He smiled because he knew that everything was as it would be. Then he walked to his bed and took off his robe. He laid his robe across the end of the bed, pulled back the covers, and then turned to blow out the candle on the nightstand. Suddenly he stopped. He took up his robe, and from the pocket he removed a crumpled, paper rose. He looked at the rose and smiled. Then he carefully inserted it into a small vase that he kept on his nightstand. Lastly, he said a prayer and remembered how the birth of a small child had given meaning to his lonely life. Then he went to sleep.

The next morning a soft knock on the door went unanswered. Iona slowly opened the door and came in with a tray of steaming hot coffee and a blueberry tart. It was Christmas morning!

Iona was King Bartholomew's oldest and dearest servant. She had been with him for so many years that she scarcely needed to address him as King anymore, and when she did it was always to make herself feel better. Iona knew Bartholomew's faults, but she also knew his generosity and his humble benevolence toward all his servants as if in some small way he were serving them. Bartholomew was a King, but he was also a man. Though his once blonde hair had now turned white and his strong hands withered and weak, he was strong in ways that only years of joy and suffering can temper against the creeping sickness of despair. Life had taught him to sing when others wept, and it was to his great strength that they turned in times of need. She was young when he was young, and together they had grown old together.

"Good morning, sire," she said. "It is Christmas morning, wake up and see the snow."

Bartholomew lay facing the window. He slept the sleep of the righteous, the sleep of compassion, the sleep of forgiveness, and he would not be woken. Iona smiled to herself as her King liked to tease her in the morning with his stubbornness.

Iona went to the nightstand to set down the tray. On his nightstand protruding from a small vase, emerged a beautiful flower, a single red rose. Iona smiled warmly.

"Look sleepy," she said. "The angels were here."

The Blood of the King

As the passing of all things can never be foretold, would that we could pass with dignity and that our passing should please the Lord even as a passing storm brings stillness, for no storm can last for eternity. By the grace of God our life is our own, and by the grace of God we are chosen. And would it be greater to live again then never to have lived at all?

After the unexpected death of King Bartholomew the island was thriving with rumors and speculation, nervousness and apprehension, for the King had left no heir and the island was left without a King. There was no one living that could remember a time when there was no King. In truth, that had never been such a time. Some people thought that when news of Bartholomew's death reached the Continent there would be dangerous uncertainty and the possibility of war or an armed invasion was inevitable as eager families eyed with satisfaction the good Isle of Man. But presently, it was still a time to grieve, for the King was much loved by all the people of Man and his passing was the passing of a righteous King.

Deemsters from the local parishes met to discuss the law and protocols for such an odd occurrence. It was agreed that all vestiges of the King's blood were to be traced and classified. It was important only that his blood be preserved, for to break the bloodline was considered an evil and dangerous endeavor and one not to be taken lightly. The blood of the King was the blood of the island, and all the goodness and wisdom and judgment of Bartholomew were thought to be manifestations of his bloodline; the people would have it no other way and their superstitious minds were atwitter with portentous visions of doom if the bloodline were to fail. It was even suggested that all women with whom Bartholomew had ever had any contact with be questioned and their children examined, but cooler heads prevailed and it was decided to postpone such measures until every other possibility had been exhausted.

In the beautiful garden of Bartholomew, designed and built by King Sigmus, Bishop Jacob sat on a stone bench near the center grotto and spoke passionately about his dear friend King Bartholomew. It was tea-time and he and his companion crunched on delicate confections and drank the delicious tea, Bartholomew's special blend. The Bishop set his cup down and wiped his humbled mouth. He spoke with respect, but with obvious sadness . . .

"Yes, as you well know, Bartholomew was very precious to me. Ah, the times we spent together in this noble garden are a thing I will never forget. His mind traveled far and wide and though I tried to tame him, his mind could not be contained by even the beauty of such a charming island."

Bishop Jacob's guest was an elderly man; his hair, shot through with streaks of white, was thin and long. He looked rather dignified but his smile revealed his youthful good humor from a man that has tasted love and found it satisfying. He raised an eyebrow curiously.

"He died unhappily then?"

"No, no, not at all," Jacob reiterated happily as competing memories filled his relenting mind. "I do believe that he found peace at last in acceptance to his ultimate fate. And it was to fate that he at last spoke a final word into the endless heavens."

"Such a terrible fate it was to die on Christmas Eve." the man replied. "He loved the holidays. I shall always remember him fondly at Christmas."

"As will I," Jacob replied.

With the formalities exchanged politely, Bishop Jacob began to make his point. He leaned back in his chair and tightened his cassock around his neck for he felt a chill.

"I had a conversation with Bartholomew many years ago. It consisted of the scenario to which we are now endeavoring to bring to a suitable end."

The man listened quietly and did not interrupt Bishop Jacob though he had no idea for the reason for such careful parsing of words.

"We sat in this very spot. I remember feeling apprehensive because I was already familiar with his propensity for stubbornness . . .

'The people are beginning to ask questions,' I said."

"I'm happy to hear that," answered Bartholomew with a smile, for he knew that Jacob was merely prodding him.

"They wonder that such a handsome King should choose to live alone."

"I do not live alone, Jacob," Bartholomew replied. "I have servants, as you know only too well."

"Bartholomew . . . as a friend . . . I think you know what I am trying to say. The people expect a Queen. Only you can give that to them. They also want to know that an heir will be produced."

"So, you are still trying to marry me away Jacob?" Bartholomew folded his hands on his lap, a sign of his resoluteness. "You know that I am already in love."

"With a servant girl, Bartholomew? You know that such a union can never be sanctioned. Have you lost your respect for tradition?"

"Would you have me marry a whore then, Jacob? Is my blood so important?"

"No, Bartholomew, I would not have you marry a whore. You know as well as do I that the bloodline is a symbol, a symbol likely to be worth fighting for. But you must marry for love, for to marry without love is blasphemy and a sacrilege to God."

"Yes, it is as you say, my friend. I will not marry without love, but my heart is already given away."

"You are a King, Bartholomew. It is imperative that you give your heart to another."

"I will never do that," Bartholomew responded quickly.

"You must!"

"I will not!" the King thundered . . .

"So that was the end of it then?" asked the man, trying to anticipate the direction of the conversation.

Bishop Jacob laughed. "No sir, not at all. That was the beginning," he said. "Bartholomew's mind was unwavering when it was bent to a task or a principal."

"Yes, not unlike his father," the patient man replied.

"Some people say," Jacob reflected thoughtfully, "that a king in a time of peace is an ineffective king. I do not believe that will be the legacy of Bartholomew."

"He will be remembered as a good king," the man replied.

"Much of the duty of a king involves letters and contracts and figures of numbers, some of them quite large I have heard. Yes, I have heard Bartholomew say that a man of strong character and a sharp mind for numbers would do well as king."

"A man of numbers?" the man repeated incredulously.

"Yes, of course," Jacob said. "There comes a time when all men want to pass something on to the next generation. Ah . . . do you believe this or do you not?"

"Are you referring to children?" Jacob.

"No, I wasn't speaking about children, Patrick. I was referring to something less tangible than children, for children are built from more than blood, are they not?"

Patrick Beauchamp smiled broadly. He knew what was coming.

"One passes along the legacy of a life well lived, that is true. But what is this legacy, Patrick? What should the legacy of a man consist of if not the thoughts in his head and the temperament of his judgment?"

"My blood is not royal, Bishop Jacob. I'm certain that Bartholomew mentioned to you that I am the son of his wife's father, not his own father."

"Yes he did, Patrick. The blood in your veins however, was the same blood that flowed through the veins of Queen Kathryn, and it was King

Sigmus and the Lady Kathryn that together produced a son in
Bartholomew. Your blood is royal, Patrick, for the same blood that made
Bartholomew royal also flows in your veins. But I thought you believed
that blood was not important, and so it isn't. The legacy of a man can be
measured by those that come after he has passed, for the memory of a
man is a measure of the memory about the man. A legacy is the lasting
impression of the life lived, and when that memory dies, the man dies
with the memory."

"What exactly are you trying to say, Jacob?"

"You are the King now, Patrick. Bartholomew decreed that upon his
death, if you or any member of your lineage should survive him that
they were to be declared reigning sovereign King of Man. When you
die, the honor will turn to your first-born male child. It is done, and now
the linage is saved. Shall the people have a King, Patrick?"

Patrick remained silent and pensive as the words of Jacob registered
fully in his aging mind. "I am no King," he said quietly. "Call me what
you may, but that I may bleed blue blood does not make me a King. I
am old, Jacob. You know that I am much older than Bartholomew. How
am I to rule a kingdom at such an age?"

Bishop Jacob rose from his chair. "Come with me," he said with a smile.
"I want to show you something."

They went into the castle through the garden doors, passing between
two thick hedges of crafted yew forming a living cornice of sinewy
vegetation. Through the large vestibule they passed across the formal
drawing room where paintings of passed Kings, forlorn and silent,
locked in oil, looked down unhappily from dusty wooden frames, until
at last they came to the staircase leading up to the King's chamber. On
the wall were once-brilliant tapestries and coats of arms awash in red
velvet and bleeding historical significance that was almost completely
lost and forgotten. Another long hallway lined with dented and
creaking, rusting armor led to a large oaken door. Bishop Jacob stopped
at the door and turned to his guest.

"This is Bartholomew's chamber," he said without comment. Then he
opened the door and went in, motioning for Patrick to follow.

The King's room had been kept the same way it was kept when he left this earth. His bed sheets had been changed and some dishes had also been removed, but besides an occasional dusting, everything was exactly as he left it Christmas Eve when he went to bed.

Patrick looked around and smiled, for many of the objects he saw were familiar to him, having once been described by Bartholomew in his occasional letters. The room was filled with personal objects, precious gifts, and memories, the accumulated detritus of an entire lifetime now abandoned. Bishop Jacob stood in the doorway as the ambience of the personal space of Bartholomew washed over him like a warm breath, a sigh not yet acknowledged. The experience brought a tear to Patrick's eye as he remembered his long-time friend.

And then Patrick noticed something out of place yet vaguely familiar. On a small shelf near the window casement was a small drum alongside some very old and crude musical instruments. Patrick walked to the shelf and looked at the drum. He knew that it was something he should know, but the memory was too distant, too far buried beneath a lifetime of competing memories. At last he picked up the drum and held it in his hands.

"Do you know what that is?" asked the soft voice of Jacob from behind.

"No," Patrick answered slowly. "But I feel like I should remember."

"It was a present," said Jacob.

"Why should Bartholomew save such a simple and worthless object," said Patrick, tapping the old and decaying skin with his fingers. But even as he spoke he could feel the hair on his neck tingle.

"It was given to Bartholomew by you," Jacob said knowingly. "When Bartholomew was just a young prince. Do you not remember?"

And then the memory came back to Patrick and he remembered the occasion. It was during a period of great loss. Patrick had come to the island to wait for his sister, the Lady Kathryn's death. His eyes suddenly filled with tears and he had to put the drum down and hold the table, but he did not turn to face Bishop Jacob for he was ashamed of his tears. And then he felt the presence of a strong hand on his shoulder.

"Memories are not always private, Patrick. Bartholomew was alone, but memories are sometimes shared, are they not?"

Patrick said nothing, but his heart was flooded with emotion.

"After all these years it seems that the drum you gave to Bartholomew is still in tune, for it beats in your heart."

"I loved her so very much," cried Patrick into the empty room. "It happened too fast," he lamented. "It happened too fast for me to do anything to save her."

"You saved her son," Jacob said compassionately.

"What are you talking about?" said Patrick. And then he turned to face Jacob. "How do you know this?"

"He was also a very close friend of mine," said Jacob. "He told me once that it was you that taught him how to dream."

"I think that you give me more credit than I deserve," said Patrick.

"I thought that you would say that," Jacob answered gently. Then he went into the room and in front of Bartholomew's bed he got down on his hands and knees and retrieved a box from beneath the bed. Pulling it out carefully, he said. "His servant Iona showed this to me. Perhaps you can tell me what it means."

Patrick watched as Bishop Jacob brought out a long box and carried it up to the bed. Then he opened the latch and raised the lid. Inside were dozens of carefully folded paper flowers carefully preserved. They were all identical, copied from the same form and folded with patient love. Jacob took the one off the top and handed it to Patrick.

"Do you know what this is?" he asked.

Later that night as Patrick slept in one of the guest bedrooms of the castle he woke during the night and could not get back to sleep again. He went to the window and threw open the shutters. A heavy and thick wind came in from across the sea, blowing through his thin white hair. A lingering thought continued to come to the surface. So, he really did help influence his nephew after all. His sister would be proud of how the young Prince had grown up. What she had set in motion had now concluded a complete revolution and he stood now in admiration of the young nephew that had turned a tragedy into such a beautiful sacrament of devotion. Such was life and such were the vicissitudes of an imagination set free by the power of love. The thought made him smile. Now truly awake, he decided to go down into the pantry for a glass of milk.

In the darkness he struggled to find his way without making too much noise, for he had no intention of waking the servants. When he was pouring a glass of milk he heard the light treading of feet on the floor and soon a woman came into the pantry carrying a lighted candle. It was King Bartholomew's oldest servant, Iona.

"Is everything all right Mr. Beauchamp?" she asked politely.

"Please, Iona. Call me Patrick. I couldn't sleep and I thought that a glass of milk would calm my nerves. I am sorry if I have woken you."

"Bartholomew used to come to the pantry at night," she said smiling as the memory came back to her. "He had much difficulty sleeping and would roam the halls at night lost in his thoughts."

"Was he very lonely?" Patrick asked with growing sadness.

Iona smiled and a gleam shone in her eye. Patrick saw it and felt ashamed, for he now knew that Iona and Bartholomew lived a life together, a life of shared grief and shared happiness. Bishop Jacob had all but said so.

"Forgive me, Iona," he said. "Bartholomew must have loved you very much indeed. I can see it all now."

"He was always worried about your happiness," said Iona. "He said to me that one day you would come back to the island riding a giraffe, just like you promised."

Patrick suddenly took hold of Iona's hand and brought it to his lips. Then he kissed it tenderly. "Thank you, Iona," he said. "I have not ridden a giraffe in many years now." Then he grew somber.

Iona waited for Patrick to speak again, for she could see that his mind was now in a faraway place and she waited for him to return. A moment later Patrick did return, but now his expression was changed and his face was positively radiant. He took hold of Iona by her strong shoulders.

"Iona," he said. "I have returned. I have come back to the island again, and I am going to be King."

"Welcome home," she answered. "Bartholomew always said that you would return."

"And you will stay," Patrick cried with excitement. "Tell me that you will stay. You will stay as my servant if that is your wish."

"Your servant?" she replied with a wry smile though her days of coquettishness were long past. "I think that I am too old to be your servant."

Patrick laughed heartily at his own naivety. "No, Iona," he replied still laughing. "You are no servant. I am much too old to have a servant. It is I that will be a servant. I will be your servant and you can teach me to ride giraffes again."

And so the reign of King Patrick lasted for many more years and he served his people well. Music was once more heard throughout the castle as Patrick returned to his love. He brought his sons and they too came to the island of enchantment and loved it as their own. Iona, now no longer a servant, lived for many years by herself in Bartholomew's old bedroom and she could sometimes be seen in the moonlight, dancing by herself in front of the open shutters that looked out over her wonderful garden, the garden built by King Sigmus and given to her by King Patrick.

Epilogue

King Sigmus looked up from his writing desk and smiled. Happy with his work he put his pen down and stretched. His pipe hung down from between his clenched teeth, and with a few quick puffs he brought it back to life. Blowing out a great stream of blue smoke, he took the pipe from his mouth and stared out the window; the same window from which he stared out while waiting for carts, laden with supplies for his garden, to come up the road to his castle. That was so many years ago, and the memory filled him with warmth but no longer brought tears to his eyes. He still felt her presence in the garden and each new season renewed her spirit in his heart. In truth, the many hours spent with Kathryn were more magical than any other memory in his life. He rolled up the only just finished parchment and tied it with a string.

After taking another puff from his pipe the King began to reflect. Did the story of Cog have to be so tragic? And was there no other way but for that his beautiful wife should die? "Ah, such is the life of all men," he thought.

And Sylvan, what about Sylvan? Could not Bartholomew even manage to sustain the one friend that was so dear to him? Yes, even Sylvan had to be cast away in the end.

Sigmus smiled when he remembered Hagen the Woodchopper. "Ah, how I loved writing about Hagen," he mused. "All men should have a mentor as wise as Hagen, and but for all his faults, his heart remained true."

When he thought about "The Christmas Rose," his heart fluttered a bit and a tear formed in his eye. It all came rushing back to him like a fond memory, but he had to check his own growing emotion. "Ah," he thought. "Such is the life of a sentimental King for that even such a memory that was built upon smoke should make him cry. But, I have done no harm," he thought rightfully. "No, I will not apologize for that wonderful memory."

But then he thought about something else and his lamentations quickly turned to mirth. It was Iona he thought about now. He smiled, but in truth he was uneasy. Yes, he had given Iona away to Bartholomew, but he hoped that she would forgive him for what he had done. Yes, he had given her away, but never in his own heart. "Stories," he said out loud. "All life is stories." But perhaps Iona deserved something better, he mused.

Finally he grew very pensive and his heart nearly broke. In the midst of all this was the one image of his beautiful son that he would take to his own grave . . . the image of his perished son. His mind reeled, but in a few moments he was able to control it.

"Ah, the only thing I have left of my son is the memory of a memory, but I have not the strength to carry it further. It is time to let the poor child rest, for I have given him all that I have to give."

He looked up to heaven and said a silent prayer. "Forgive me Bartholomew," he said. "Forgive me Bartholomew, for I have lived the life that was intended for you. Forgive me my son."

Emotions are God's gift to men, but they are paid with a bitter price. Only, pity the man that is unmoved by emotion, for his heart is truly forsaken.

"Yes," he thought, "I could have done many things differently. But such is life. Alas, perhaps memories were meant to taste bittersweet, but one cannot subsist on such memories for they often make us sick."

But now he only breathed a sigh of relief because he knew that the story was finished and that he had done as he wished. He smiled because he knew that Kathryn would be proud of the wonderful life he had given to her beloved son, and had he lived, the King knew that his life would have been every bit as wonderful. Yes, in truth Bartholomew had lived in Kathryn's heart long before that dreadful day of his birth; he had lived in both their hearts. By the grace of God, Sigmus had brought him to life.

The King stood up and walked across the room. A small table set against the wall held a bucket with a bottle of chilled wine, for the King knew that today was a special day. He took the bottle and smiled again as he read the vintage of such a wonderful day when he and the Lady Kathryn were married so long ago now. This bottle he had been saving for just such a special day.

Alone with his tender thoughts he tried to compose, in his head, a suitable toast for his beloved wife on such a fine day. In his head he searched for words that could only be said from his heart. The effort proved to be beyond his ability. There are words that come from the mind, and there are words that come from the heart. Words that come from the mind are spoken with our mouth; words that come from the heart are spoken through our hands. When the mind turns weak from words the heart grows strong from deeds. But when the heart grows weary through deeds, it is only love that can make us strong again.

And then unexpectedly he felt the familiar arms of Iona around his chest as she embraced him and held him tight. She had come into the room when she saw him standing alone and she wanted to be near him. He felt the warmth, the softness, the gentleness of her touch and a rush of warmth spread throughout his body like the calm after a gentle rain. She giggled playfully. Turning around, he kissed her tenderly.

"Where have you been Iona?" he asked affectionately.
Iona smiled. Then she looked down and saw the parchment in his hands. She looked up quickly and a flash of remorse shone in her eyes.

"I'm sorry if I have bothered you," she said.

"Don't be sorry," the King answered. "Oh, no Iona, do not be sorry for me. Today is not a day to be melancholy, Iona. Today is a day to be happy."

"You have finished another story?" she asked eagerly.

"I am finished," he replied resolutely, and that said, he let out a gentle sigh.

But Iona was so happy that she could not hold her secret any longer and the King's final resolution was lost on her. She smiled happily. "Oh Sigmus, I have a surprise for you. Patrick is here."

His demeanor changed noticeably. "My brother Patrick, did you say my brother Patrick was here?"

"Yes," she answered cheerfully. "He is waiting for you."

"I have not seen him in . . . it has been over twenty five years now, Iona.

He left after . . ."

"I know," Iona said tenderly. "But he is here now, Sigmus."

"Do you know what he did for me Iona? I thought I would never see him again. After what happened to Kathryn his heart was broken. No, I never expected to see him again."

"Yes Sigmus, I know what he did for you."

Then the King hugged her tightly and smiled, for he was truly happy. "Ah, the old rascal has made me very happy. I told you he would come back again, Iona, I told you."